The Book of the Sleuth

Anthologies compiled by Alan K. Russell include:

The Book of the Sleuth

The Book of the Dead

H. Rider Haggard: The Classic Adventures

Jules Verne: Collected Novels

Science Fiction Classics by Edgar Rice Burroughs

The Rivals of Sherlock Holmes 2

Science Fiction by the Rivals of H. G. Wells

Classic Science Fiction: Jules Verne

The Best of Jules Verne

The Collector's Book of Science Fiction by H. G. Wells

Rivals of Sherlock Holmes

The Original Illustrated Sherlock Holmes

The Book of the Sleuth
Fourteen Classic Tales of Mystery & Suspense

Edited by
Alan K. Russell

NEW ORCHARD EDITIONS
Poole · New York · Sydney

First published 1986 by
New Orchard Editions Ltd
Robert Rogers House
New Orchard
Poole, Dorset BH15 1LU

ISBN 1 85079 034 5

Copyright © 1986 New Orchard Editions

Printed in Great Britain by
The Bath Press, Avon

CONTENTS

The Book of the Sleuth

1
J. J. BELL

A Thread of Scarlet

2
The Little More

A THREAD OF SCARLET

IN broad daylight the smoke-room of the Old Rainbow Inn, which in those days, twenty years ago, harboured an over-night guest only once in a while, looked a bare and shabby apartment; but on this black February night, when a bitter wind raged and sleet came in dense blatters against the leaded panes of the window, it offered, with its yellow lamplight and ruddy fire, a snug enough refuge.

Yet while its relative snugness might, and did, encourage customers to sit till the last lawful moment, the weather, violent since nightfall, had deterred a number of Mr. Flett's regular callers from seeking their usual refreshment within its dingy walls, and at twenty minutes before closing time there were but three persons in the room. They sat at a table between the window and the hearth, with tankards before them. The tankards were empty; had been empty for some little time, for a reason which shall shortly be made apparent.

For the moment let us make the acquaintance of the three customers, all respectable, middle-aged tradesmen from the village of Lower Ashley, well known to one another, though on the present occasion, which was certainly an abnormal one, they used the formal "Mister."

They were Migsworth, a lanky, clean-shaven man, who fancied himself a bit superior intellectually; Smith, a stumpy person, genial and indiscreet, with a heavy, drooping, ruddy moustache, which gave him a somewhat foolish look; and Butters, bulky of body and grizzly bearded, normally sociable to a moderate degree, but to-night strangely inert and self-absorbed, his occasional glances at the others being those of a half-dazed intelligence.

The door was open, and Migsworth and Smith were intent on a little scene being enacted in the passage between Mr. Flett, the landlord, and a tall, spare man of dire and sodden aspect, whose limbs yet bore him steadily enough.

11

"No, Mr. Breen," the landlord was saying in tones of finality, "I can't serve ye, and my advice to ye is to go home, and to your bed."

"Haven't I told ye, man, ye'll get the money in the mornin' ?"

"Quite so! But that's not my point, Mr. Breen. I've got a licence to lose. In other words——"

"Come on ; gimme a bottle o'whisky."

"No ! Ye've had enough—moren'n enough, though not in my place. Not another drop do ye get from me. Good night !"

"Damn ye !"

The man called Breen turned abruptly and went down the passage. The landlord watched him go ; then, as the outer door slammed, came into the smoke-room, wiping his perspiring face. He was a stoutly-built man, not timid, as a rule.

"Quite right, Mr. Flett," said Migsworth. "He'd surely had more'n enough."

"Queer, though, how steady he walks," remarked Smith. "Don't he, Mr. Butters ?"

"Who ?" Butters blinked. "Oh, Breen ! I'm sick o' Breen. Never out o' my shop, spyin' and pokin' around, and tryin' to get somethin' for nothin'. Was there to-night when I was closin' up. Had to turn him out." So saying, Butters relapsed into himself, huddling in his chair.

" 'Tis not his head, nor yet his legs, that takes it all," the landlord said. "I never see anything like him. To tell the truth, gentlemen, I'm afeared—not of, but for him. Trade's rotten bad, the Lord knows, but I'd sooner be without Mr. Breen's custom. He's been hard at it for a solid month now, and he's gettin' worse every blessed day ! Can't think when, or where, he earns the money. Never heard o' an odd-job man with so much o' the ready. Maybe he buys nothin' but whisky." The speaker pulled himself up. "But you was ringin', gentlemen ?"

"We was, Mr. Flett." Migsworth included the three tankards in a graceful wave. "Same again, if you please."

As Mr. Flett proceeded to collect the tankards, Butters, as one waking up, laid a hand on his muttering : "No more for me. Must be gettin' home."

"Tut, Mr. Butters," said Migsworth ; "ye need another.

We all need another, after what we've gone through this day. Take his tankard, Mr. Flett. And, mind ye, Mr. Flett, I don't wonder at Breen goin' it hard after all he's gone through—losin' his only friend. Both shiftless chaps; still——"

"True, true, Mr. Migsworth. Only I prefer to see a man drownin' his sorrows in moderation," said the landlord, and went out with the tankards.

. . . . .

Migsworth laid down his pipe and gave a heavy sigh. "Ah, what a day ! Longest and strangest I've ever known !"

"But not," said Smith, with a sagacious wag of the head, "not so long as last night must ha' been to Jacob Forge."

A groan came from Butters. "Last night—oh, my soul !"

The others glanced at him.

"Aye, Butters," said Smith, kindly, "it must ha' been bad for you, too, you havin' been on the jury. Always wondered why ye didn't get out o' that job. I believe ye could—but, then, maybe ye couldn't. Well, well !" With an attempt at cheerfulness : "And yet here's the three o'us, sittin' round this table for close on three hours, chattin' about 'most everything but the thing we're thinkin' on."

"Well, as two single men and a widower without off-spring," observed Migsworth, " 'twouldn't be natural to sit alone in our houses, dumb, and thinkin' o' Jacob Forge, our neighbour—that was. I, for one, couldn't do it."

"Oh, oh !" cried Smith, in a sudden burst of emotion, "to think that, at eight o'clock o' this blessed—I mean cursed —mornin', Jacob Forge was hanged by—by the neck until he——"

Butters made a fluttering gesture of what might have been protest, and Migsworth said :

"Hush, Mr. Smith ! No need for to go into the painful details. Forge has paid the penalty o' his crime, havin' been found guilty by a jury o' good men and true, includin' our worthy neighbour here, William Butters, who——"

Butters sat up. "I must be gettin' home. 'Tis on my mind that I left the keys o' my safe on the counter, and didn't lock up anything proper. Was too upset." He made to rise, but Migsworth interposed.

"Don't you worry, Mr. Butters. Your safe's all right.

And as for Jacob Forge, his awful end was no fault o' yours. He had a fair trial and full justice. We can pity him, though none o' us ever liked him—not that I'd ever ha' dreamed o' him bein' a murd——"

Butters threw out a shaking hand. "Don't be sayin' the word! 'Tis too dreadful! Jacob was a strange man, and yet . . ." His hand fell. "Still—still, we've got to remember that the jury gave him guilty because o' the evidence."

"That's it!" cried Smith. "Because o' the evidence! And yet, this mornin', when I see the black flag goin' up—they did hoist it slow!—I says to myself——"

"Was you there?" Migsworth exclaimed.

"Aye, walked every step o' them long eight miles! I saw ye, Mr. Migsworth, all muffled up. 'Twas a bitter mornin', though. Was muffled up myself. And you, Mr. Butters—I thought I saw ye too."

The shaggy head of Butters went lower. "I went to pray," he whispered; "to pray that the black flag might—not go up. Oh, my soul!"

"Now that was a strange thing to do," said Migsworth, and just then the landlord entered with the tankards. "We're talkin' o' the melancholy episode of this mornin', Mr. Flett."

"Ah, yes, yes. Very shockin', to be sure; very shockin'," Mr. Flett replied, picking up the coins put down by Migsworth. "Thank 'ee, sir. I understood from his remarks that Mr. Breen had been there likewise."

"What? Him!" ejaculated Smith, while Migsworth said: "Oh, how could he? His only friend bein' hanged!"

"He was talkin'," the landlord proceeded, "o' puttin' a knife in the judge and poisoning' the jury."

"That's awful!" said Smith. "Breen must be goin' stark crazy."

"When a man takes to 'Scotch,'" Migsworth sagely remarked, "he's done."

"Beggin' your pardon," observed Smith with another attempt at humour, "but judgin' from Mister Breen's case, he's never done!"

The landlord laughed, but most discreetly. "Oh, very good, Mr. Smith, very good!"

Butters lifted his head and shuddered. "What if Breen is right?"

"Right?" cried the others.

"What—what's to happen to the judge and jury, if we was all wrong?"

The landlord spoke. "What's all this, Mr. Butters?"

Butters relapsed without responding.

"Nerves, Mr. Flett," said Migsworth confidentially, "just nerves."

"I see, I see, Mr. Migsworth; and I can well understand it. Fact is, I'm a bit that way myself at the moment."

"How so, Mr. Flett?" Smith was thirsty and, raising his tankard, nodded to Migsworth. "Good health!"

"Cheerio!" replied Migsworth. "Sorry! I shouldn't ha' said that."

"I've got a notion," said Mr. Flett, "a preminotion, if ye understand what I mean, gentlemen, that our unfortunate friend, Mr. Breen, will come back to-night, and I don't half like it."

"You shall have our support, Mr. Flett," said Migsworth, "our moral support in refusin' him refreshment."

"Thank 'ee, sir, thank 'ee! I'm bound to refuse him. There's my conscience to be considered——"

"And your licence," said Smith. "Besides, he has, most likely, got no money."

"True, Mr. Smith," said the landlord, and went out.

Smith gave Butters' arm a friendly shake. "Wake up, old man! This is real good beer—comfort ye and make ye sleep sound."

Said Butters, as one suddenly awakened: "I saw Breen there this mornin'. Our mufflin's was nothin' to his. But I spied his face—oh, my God, shall I ever forget his face when the flag was goin' up?"

"What was it like?" Smith eagerly asked.

"Hush, Mr. Smith," said Migsworth reprovingly. "It was suppused with grief, no doubt."

"It was like," faltered Butters, "a soul in torments."

"Ah, well," said Migsworth, setting down his tankard, "he seems to ha' got some decent feelin's after all—though I have doubted it when seein' him sittin' in yonder corner, night after night, drinkin' on his own. Shows how careful we should be in judgin' our neighbours."

"True, true," assented Smith, and took a long pull. "Maybe there was more real friendship between him and Jacob Forge than we thought. They was both such terrible unsociable chaps. Hullo! That was a horn! Sounds as if a car was goin' to stop here.'' He got up, went to the window, and peered into the sleety mirk. "My goodness! I don't envy any man his car on a night like this! Black as hell; sleet drivin' well-nigh level! Ugh!'' He shivered. "Glad I haven't far to——'' He sprang backwards.

The window flared with a throbbing flash of lightning, which was swiftly followed by a frightful thunder-crash.

With a wild cry, Butters leapt up and sank back, shaking.

"Bit unexpected at this season,'' Migsworth remarked; first to recover from the scare. "Why, Mr. Butters, y'ere lookin' sickish! No danger, ye know.''

With emotion Butters said : "Oh, there's somethin' wrong in the world this night—some awful thing is abroad! I'm feared to take the road now.''

"Come, come, this won't do at all!'' said Smith, returning to the table. "Take a good swig o' your beer. Give ye comfort. Ye should never ha' gone to the hangin' this mornin'.''

Said Butters, still shaking : "I tell ye—in yon flash I saw Jacob Forge, and he was hung—hung on a—a thread o' scarlet!''

Migsworth and Smith started and exchanged uneasy glances.

Migsworth cleared his throat. "Tut, tut!'' he said, and again, "Tut, tut!''

Said Butters, in a low, frantic voice : "Nothin' but a thread o' scarlet—and he was dead, and starin', and his head all sideways—but he was sort o' smilin' to himself, as if——''

"Smilin'!'' exclaimed Smith, horrified.

"Hush!'' said Migsworth as the door opened.

.   .   .   .

A stranger came in, followed by the landlord, and began to remove his wet wraps.

"Oh, this will do,'' he said impatiently. "Have a bedroom fired for me, and another for my man. But first let me have a double 'Scotch,' some boiling water, sugar, and lemon.'' He threw his things on a chair, went over to the fire, and stood there, chafing his hands.

"Very good, sir,'' said the landlord, going out.

There was a pause, during which Migsworth and Smith

glanced at the stranger and at each other. Butters, chin on chest, took no notice.

Suddenly from the night came a scream of wind and a rattling on the window. Smith leapt, Migsworth started, but Butters paid no attention.

"Only hail. The thunder's brought it down." Migsworth addressed the remark to the stranger's back.

Said Butters dreamily : "Hung by a thread o' scarlet and smilin'—smilin' the smile"—his voice almost failed—"o' an innocent man."

"Oh, my !" said Smith softly, looking at the stranger's back.

Migsworth leaned over and patted Butters on the shoulder. "Don't you worry about it, old man," he said soothingly, and winked at Smith. "I'm beginnin' to think he must ha' been loadin' up before he came along to the 'Rainbow.'" He cleared his throat and addressed the stranger. "Terrible night, sir."

The stranger turned. "Horrible ! I trust," he said with dry courtesy, "I am not intruding here. Only room with a fire going."

"Not at all, sir," Migsworth replied in his best manner. " 'Tis a public room, sir, and if 'twas private ye'd be welcome on such a night."

"Much obliged, I'm sure." The stranger's manner seemed to thaw with his hands. He took a chair at the hearth, yawned, produced a silver case and selected a cigarette, watched the while with furtive interest by Migsworth and Smith. "There's a village about here, isn't there ?" he inquired as he dropped the match into the fire.

"Two, sir," answered Migsworth. "Lower Ashley and Upper Ashley. This inn is midway betwext them."

"I see ! If you reside here, perhaps you can tell me whether the population includes a tall man who is stone-deaf—possibly dumb also ?"

"Oh, dear, no, sir," replied Migsworth.

"But," put in Smith hopefully, "we've got a paralytic, sir."

"H'm ! This man was apparently bound for one or other of the Ashleys—at least, we encountered him not far from this inn—and he gave my chauffeur and myself the shock of our lives."

"How was that, sir ?" Migsworth asked respectfully.

Here Mr. Flett entered with a tray, which he set on a small table at the new customer's elbow.

"Thanks," said the stranger, and proceeded to mix his toddy. "Well, in the midst of a blizzard, our lamps showed him walking in the middle of the road. We kept sounding the horn, a pretty powerful one, and the wind was on his back, but he took no notice. We slowed, and my man was going to risk the ditch, when the fellow stepped aside, and we carried on. Next moment he was back in the middle of the road." The speaker paused and took a cautious sip of the steaming mixture.

The landlord, who had moved to the door, halted there, listening for the rest of the story.

.   .   .   .   .

"It was the nearest thing !" the stranger resumed. "Of course, we braked hard, but I swear the bonnet touched him, when the car stopped with a jerk that I really thought had finished her. And the fellow walked on, without so much as turning his head."

"My gracious !" cried Migsworth. "Did anyone ever hear the like ? What did you do, sir ?"

"Shouted to him to stop, but again he paid no attention. I think he must have left the road soon after, for when we got going once more—the car had suffered, you understand ; that's why I'm here—there was no further sign of him. But" —grimly—"I'd like very much to meet him again."

"Sounds like a loony, sir," said Migsworth. "And ye never saw his face ?"

"Nothing but his back." The stranger sipped his toddy. "A tall man, as I've said, in a long, black tarpaulin coat and soft felt hat."

"Plenty o' tarpaulins and soft felts—old ones—hereabouts," observed Smith, seizing the chance of getting in a word.

"He had a heavy muffler coming above his coat collar, as though to shield the back of his head from the blast. I noted it in the lamplight—a scarlet muffler."

At the utterance of the last two words Smith started as though knifed, while Migsworth screeched, "A what ?"

"A scarlet muffler !" shouted the landlord, clutching the edge of the door, and Butters moved as one in a doze.

The stranger stared. "Yes, a scarlet muffler. Odd taste, no doubt. Still . . . But, I say, what's the matter with your friend ?" His gaze was on Butters.

Said Butters hazily : "Hung on a thread o' scarlet, he was, and smilin'——"

"Kindly excuse him, sir," said Migsworth. "Unknown to us he has got rather too much."

"Smilin' the smile of an——"

"Come, come, old man !" Migsworth murmured anxiously.

As though hearing him not, Butters turned slowly to the stranger and extended a quivering forefinger. " 'Twas a ghost ye saw this night," he mumbled ; "the ghost o' Jacob Forge, who was hung for murder this mornin' in Lakeford Jail. And he was hung on a thread o' that same scarlet muffler—God rest his soul !"

Having said this, Mr. Butters relapsed into his inert condition.

The stranger addressed Migsworth. "This is rather beyond me," he said. "Incidentally, I should say that your friend is suffering, not from any over-indulgence, but from some severe mental and nervous strain."

Smith managed to anticipate Migsworth.

" 'Tis like enough ye're right, sir. William Butters is a sober man, and as honest as any grocer could be, in these hard times. Has had his difficulties, he has, but he's come through them. But he should never ha' gone to see the black flag hoisted this mornin'. Ye see, sir, he had the ill-luck to be one o' the jury that sent Jacob Forge, our neighbour —though not our friend—to the gallows, and he don't seem to get over the idea. To-night he had started sayin' to himself : 'What if me and the judge was wrong ?' "

The stranger nodded sympathetically. "And this Jacob Forge—and the scarlet muffler ?"

"Why, sir——" began Smith.

"In the winter-time," Migsworth firmly interposed, "Jacob Forge always wore the scarlet muffler—he was known by it, there being nothin' like it in the neighbourhood. And on a dark winter's night, on the high road, he murdered an old farmer comin' home from market wi' a bag o' money— near four hundred pound. Beat in the old man's head wi' a hammer, so he did !"

"I knew that money-bag," said Smith. "Seen it often in my shop. Made o' blue canvas——"

"Same here," said the landlord. "Farmer Jukes never passed my door."

"And," hastened Smith, "they found the hammer hid in Forge's tool-shed, wi' blood and a grey hair or so on it. And they found three cheques belongin' to the farmer there also. But the bag o' notes and cash they never found; Forge must ha' hid it too safe, or destroyed it. And 'twas proved that Forge was needin' money at the time. We all was, for that matter. Of course, at the trial he denied everything; swore he was sleepin' in his bed when it happened."

.　　　　.　　　　.　　　　.　　　　.

The speaker paused for refreshment, and Migsworth took up the tale.

"But, sir, it was the scarlet muffler that did for him in the end. He must ha' hid it, or burned it, for 'twas never found. He declared he had lost it; thought he had dropped it in one o' the village shops, but couldn't say which——"

"But in the farmer's nails," Smith interposed, wiping his moustache, "they found a thread o' it! So 'tis true enough, sir, that Jacob Forge was hung on a thread o' scarlet!"

The landlord, with an apologetic cough, took a step forward.

"It should be told, sir, that, even after he was condemned, Forge always believed—or pretended to believe—that somethin' would happen to save him. But"—a headshake—"the black flag went up, sure enough, at eight o'clock this mornin'. I didn't know Forge—he never was in the 'Rainbow'—but I allow it has been a sorrowful day."

Out in the passage a clock heavily and solemnly struck ten.

"Bound to cast a gloom over the place," the stranger remarked. "Was this Jacob Forge married?"

Migsworth, on the alert, replied: "No, sir. He had no friends, exceptin' a man called Breen—a solitudinarian like himself, who has, unfortunately, been tryin' to drown his grief ever since, as Mr. Flett there will confirm."

"Too true, sir, though I ha' done my best to check it." Mr. Flett took out his watch. "Well, gentlemen, I'm real sorry, but the law must be obeyed."

Migsworth sighed and emptied his tankard.

"Your clock's fast, Mr. Flett," said Smith, who had already drained his. "Considerin' the day it has been, and considerin' the night it is—hark to that blast!—Mr. Migs-worth and me ought to have just one more. We'll take it standin', if ye like."

The landlord held up the stout and ancient silver watch. "Correct time's here, gentlemen; very sorry indeed."

They rose reluctantly, and Migsworth was about to arouse Butters, now in a sort of lethargy, when the stranger spoke.

"Perhaps you gentlemen will give me your company, as my guests, a little longer." Their smiles were sufficient acceptance. "Right! Two pints, landlord."

"Very good, sir. But if ye'll excuse me, I'll lock up first," said Mr. Flett, and retired.

"Be seated, gentlemen."

" 'Tis too kind," murmured Smith, while Migsworth, in his best manner, declared that he was deeply obliged.

"Not at all," said the stranger politely. "But what about your friend? He's looking worse than ever."

"Best not disturb him, sir. Mr. Smith and me will see him home in due season. He should never ha' been on the jury."

Lighting a fresh cigarette, the stranger asked: "What do you gentlemen think about your friend's ghost theory?"

"Well, sir," answered Migsworth, "I don't believe in ghosts as a general rule——"

"Nor me—ever!" said Smith.

"But, nevertheless, I'd swear there's not a livin' man within twenty miles o' the Ashleys would wear a scarlet muffler."

"Hadn't thought o' that," remarked Smith. Then, abruptly, he put up his hand. "I say, there's somebody comin' in! Listen!"

From the passage came the sounds of altercation, and presently the landlord's voice was heard, saying: "No, no; I can't have it. After ten, you know!"

"Oh, Lord," muttered Migsworth, "if it isn't Breen come back!"

"Breen?" said the stranger quickly. "The friend of the murd—the dead man?"

"Yes, sir, and I'm afraid it means trouble for Mr. Flett. Of course, Mr. Flett can't serve him now."

The noise came nearer, Breen was cursing; the landlord protesting and imploring.

"Oh, damn it all, he's comin' in," exclaimed Smith. "Hope he won't be unpleasant, sir."

"Now, Mr. Breen," they heard the landlord say, "don't ye be so unfair. Surely ye wouldn't like me to lose my licence ! 'Tis after hours, and if anybody saw ye comin' into the 'Rainbow' . . . Oh, damme, why didn't I lock the door on the stroke ?"

"Lemme pass !" stormed a hoarse voice. "Gimme a bottle o' whisky. Got the money. Hear that ? I've got the money, curse ye ! Ye hear ? All right, then, fetch the whisky !"

"Stop, Mr. Breen, stop, for God's sake !"

The sound of a struggle, then :

"Well, well, if I let ye in for just a minute, will ye promise not to—oh, dear, dear !"

The door flew in. Breen, followed by the dismayed and dishevelled Mr. Flett, entered. He wore a long tarpaulin coat, buttoned to the chin, and streaming wet. He was hatless. His face was chalky, his eyes glazed and staring. He walked in a stiff mechanical fashion to a chair in the corner farthest from the company—his usual place.

The stranger drew in his breath. "Good God, what a case !" he muttered, and beckoned to the landlord, who had halted helplessly near the door.

The landlord came on tiptoe.

"Whatever it may cost you," whispered the stranger, "not a drop !"

"Oh, never, sir ! But—but is he—is he drunk ?"

"Past drunk ! He's on the verge of a— But never mind that now. Go back to the door. Wait there ! Be ready !"

Like a dreadful image, Breen for a while sat motionless in the corner. Then in a toneless voice he spoke.

"Poison for the daft jury, and a bottle o' whisky for me."

The stranger, gripping the arms of his chair, leaned forward, watchful. Smith was gaping stupidly behind his foolish moustache. Butters, though not apparently interested, seemed to be coming out of his lethargy.

Migsworth cleared his throat, and behind his hand addressed the stranger. "What about givin' him some strong coffee, sir ?"

With some impatience the stranger made a sign for silence.

It was very still in the room, but outside the wind screamed again and a great gust of hail bombarded the window.

"Bottle o' whisky!" said Breen.

Now Butters seemed to realize his presence, for he sat up slowly and gazed in his direction.

A flare of lightning—a crackle of thunder. All the occupants of the smoke-room, save Butters and Breen, started violently. Then with a sob the wind died, and there was complete silence till:

"Bottle o' whisky!" said Breen. Presently his expression changed slightly, as though another idea had stirred in his clogged intelligence. "Money! Ye want the money!" Like an automaton he stood up. The two lowest buttons of the tarpaulin were missing, and drawing aside and upwards the skirt, he got at a pocket. His actions were slow, but not uncertain, the actions of a man under hypnotic rather than ordinary alcoholic influence—so, at least, it appeared.

Breen withdrew his fist, and for a moment or two stood rigid. Suddenly:

"Money!" He flung a handful of coins on the floor. "Money! . . . Whisky!"

No one stirred.

Breen's gaze never shifted, but he stood as one listening intently. At last:

"Not enough money, eh?" Once more his hand went under the tarpaulin.

This time he fetched forth a large object.

"Bottle o' whisky! Money! . . . Take it!"

At the landlord's feet the blue canvas bag fell with a crash.

And, recoiling a step in sheer horror, as from a viper, the landlord cried:

"Oh, my good God, the farmer's money-bag!"

Smith, clutching Migsworth's arm, made inarticulate sounds and pointed at the bag. Butters, eyes starting, rose heavily to his feet and stood swaying and clutching the back of his chair, while his lips moved speechlessly.

Breen was speaking again, but his voice had changed. It wavered.

"Bottle o' . . ." A pause. "Bottle of whi . . ." A longer pause. "Black flag—black flag—black . . ." His mouth began to open and shut like that of a gasping fish.

The stranger, rising softly, signalled to the landlord.

Abruptly the gasping action ceased, the mouth remaining wide. Breen took two mechanical steps forward.

The stranger and the landlord stole nearer.

Breen rose on his toes.

"Look out!" snapped the stranger—none too soon—at the landlord.

Something seemed to give and Breen pitched forward, to be caught by ready arms.

"Quick! Into the chair!" said the stranger. "Now off with his coat!"

He proceeded to undo the buttons, and threw it open —exposing a scarlet muffler drawn across the breast.

"Why, it's the man I nearly—well, I'm——"

The landlord, with a gurgling noise, staggered backwards and, while Migsworth's hands went to his face, from Smith came the words, in a high falsetto:

"Oh, oh, oh—the farmer's money-bag—and the scarlet muffler too!"

"Quiet!" commanded the stranger and, dropping on his knees, laid his ear to Breen's chest.

After a while he lifted a grave countenance and rose, shaking his head.

In the silence Migsworth uncovered his face. "So Butters' idea was right, after all," he said in a soft, awed voice, and turned to the man he had named, saying: " 'Tis a terrible thing for you, Butters, but not a soul could blame ye, and— and here's my hand."

Butters neither heard nor saw the kindly offer. For a moment or two he stood rigid, his countenance congested; then, of a sudden, he reeled forward three paces and stopped, one hand to his head, the other pointing shakily, accusingly, down at the still figure with the scarlet muffler.

"Breen, ye blasted thief," he croaked, "ye've been burglin' my safe!"

Now all was still, even Nature. Then slowly, on tiptoe, with fearful countenances, Migsworth, Smith and the land-lord, drew away from Butters.

Only the stranger held his ground and at last spoke: "You double-murderer!"

THE LITTLE MORE

WHEN Mr. Godfrey Longman was detained in the City after seven o'clock, which happened fairly often, or when his house was shut up for a period, he would take a taxi across London and dine in the Planet grill-room. As a place of residence the Planet Hotel is pretty exclusive ; Mr. Longman sometimes put up there ; but to dine in its grill-room one need only have decent garments, with a pound or two in the pockets.

Mr. Godfrey Longman was in his fifties, a man of medium stature, rather bulkily built, grey-haired, with a smooth, well-featured, healthy-looking countenance which, though usually good-humoured and alert, could assume a peculiarly dull and wooden expression. He had a wife, but unfortunately the poor lady was now in a "home," having, some ten years ago, developed the most absurd delusions respecting, of all things, her husband's commercial integrity.

Gourmet rather than gourmand, Mr. Longman had, this warm September evening, made a chaste, if somewhat costly, repast. He was no wine-bibber ; a modest pint of fine Hock, or delicate Moselle, was his usual dinner drink ; to-night he had enjoyed a pint of "The Doctor" (Orange Seal, 1921) ; but he invariably finished with a cognac of 1865, which he sipped very leisurely, before lighting, not a lordly Corona, but a cigarette of the ordinary sort—twenty for a shilling—which he took, not from a gold case, but from the original carton. He was not, however, the first man to have indulged in the most expensive viands and vintages, and to have smoked the cheapest cigarettes. Whether such an idiosyncrasy tells anything about a man's character is a question that may be left to the psychologists ;

25

but it will be shown immediately that Mr. Godfrey Longman had other peculiarities.

He was in the act of lighting his first cigarette, having
laid the carton on the cloth, when a tall, lean man, dark-
haired, with a short, thick moustache emphasizing the
pallor of his face, rose from a table near by, deliberately
approached ; then halted, bowed slightly, and gravely
said :

"Good evening, Mr. Davidson."

Mr. Longman blew out the match, laid it on the plate,
and raised a dull glance to the intruder's face.

"Good evening, sir," he said ; "but have you not
made a mistake ? My name is Longman—Mr. Godfrey
Longman."

"Then good evening—Mr. Longman." The lean man
drew out the chair on Mr. Longman's right hand and
seated himself.

"You will excuse me," said Mr. Longman, exhaling,
"but I do not seem to have the pleasure of your——"

"I am not quite sure that it will be a pleasure, Mr.
Longman, but my name is Harrison Yates. But pardon
me just a moment." Mr. Yates half-turned and beckoned
to a waiter, who had arrived at his lately vacated place
with something on a plate. The man came over, and Mr.
Yates said pleasantly : "Waiter, this gentleman kindly
insists on paying my bill."

Mr. Longman, stolid of countenance, made no remark,
and the waiter, who knew him as a frequent customer,
laid the plate and folded slip at his left hand, bowed, and
retired.

"Thank you so much, Mr. Davidson," murmured Mr.
Yates, "and may I take one of your cigarettes ?" He
helped himself from the carton.

The involuntary host seemed to consider before he
said : "May I ask why you persist in calling me 'Davidson,'
when I have told you my name is 'Longman' ?"

"Because I am more interested in Mr. Davidson than
in Mr. Longman. Mr. Longman is merely a successful
and highly respected foreign merchant in the City ; but—"

the speaker lowered his voice, which had never been high—"Mr. Davidson is the most successful dealer in the country—in stolen jewels."

Mr. Longman stiffened slightly, but certainly did not start. He flicked the ash of his cigarette into the exact centre of the plate, and regarded the other with eyes that had become shrewd.

"Well?" he said at last.

It would seem that Mr. Yates had underestimated his man, for he said rather too quickly: "It's all right, you know. I'm not from the Yard, or——"

"Yes, you are!" came the quiet interruption; "the prison yard." Mr. Longman examined his guest and added: "About six weeks ago, I should say."

Mr. Yates shrugged, grinning weakly. "You know us, Mr.—Longman!" he said.

"I don't know *you*! Hadn't you better explain!"

"That is what I am anxious to do—but I should like a drink, if you please. Believe me, my impudence has cost an awful effort."

Mr. Longman picked up the slip of paper from the plate on his left and cast his eye over the pencilled figures. "You seem already to have done yourself pretty well—at my expense," he remarked good-humouredly.

"It has cost me several pretty expensive dinners here before I got the luck of this evening. Either you were joined by somebody, or——"

"Never mind that. Why did you choose this method of meeting me?"

"It seemed the most casual one. I didn't fancy you would approve of my coming to your office or house, and I don't believe in correspondence."

"Quite right! Well, control your thirst till I've settled with the waiter, and we shall make a move to the smoke-room. In fact, you might find your way there now."

"Righto!" said Mr. Yates—then hesitated, with a sharp look.

"Don't be silly," said his host amiably. "Do you think I'm going to bring in the police, or fly the country,

because you have called me 'Davidson'?" In the same
instant his expression hardened. "But mark me, Mr.
Yates, I won't stand for anything in the blackmail line.
Be sure of that. I have means of dealing with the person
who tries it."

"It isn't my line," replied the other. "I don't need to
tell you that I do want something out of you, but I'm not
a blood-sucker. I didn't become what I am to-day
deliberately. It has always been a case of impulse—
impulse, Mr. Longman—and when you have heard my
story——"

"Well, well; I'll hear it in the smoke-room presently.
Off you go."

Left to himself, Mr. Longman ordered coffee and
settled his score and that of the uninvited guest. He wanted
a few minutes for thought. He was not deeply perturbed
by the encounter; such a thing had happened to him
before now, though not in precisely similar circumstances,
nor with a person entirely unknown; and he did not
doubt that he could, by a judicious combination of firmness
and apparent generosity, manage Mr. Harrison Yates—
or whatever the man's real name might be—who, despite
his show of temerity, had not revealed a strong character—
as he had managed others in the past. Yet it was annoying
that the encounter should have chanced so unseasonably,
just when he had arranged finally to withdraw from the
perilous trade, his fortune being assured, his chief clients
in gaol, and likely to remain there for the next five years
or so. He guessed that Mr. Yates must have learned of
'Mr. Davidson's' identity from some fellow-prisoner, though
such a betrayal—malicious or otherwise—had never before
been his experience; for he had always made it worth
the while of his clients, whether in durance or at liberty,
to preserve the secret. There *is* an honour among thieves.

That his guess was correct he learned, a few minutes
later, in the smoke-room.

"Yes," said Yates with a sigh, setting down the big
goblet of whisky-and-soda; "Danbury told me about you,
after I had sworn to keep the truth to myself——"

"But Danbury is dead."

"He died shortly after telling me—pneumonia, I believe. He was feeling ill when he told me. He had taken a fancy to me, not long after I got there—we worked at neighbouring benches, and managed to pass a few words occasionally ; we became friends, if you can imagine that possible in such a place. Our sentences would expire about the same time, and we planned to come together outside, and go—straight."

"Really !" Mr. Longman's tone was dry, yet not unkind. He was planning to go straight himself.

"It wouldn't have been so very difficult," proceeded Yates, "for Danbury, at any rate, with that thousand pounds to start on. You *had* promised to give him a thousand when he came out, hadn't you, Mr. Dav—Mr. Longman ?"

"Well, yes, as a matter of fact, I had," Longman assented. "He had served me pretty well in the past. Go on."

"I fancy you see what I'm driving at." Yates took a drink, and regarded his companion anxiously. "It seemed to me that having promised the thousand—earmarked it, as they say—you would not grudge it. In other words, since poor Danbury is gone and has no use for it, I'm— I'm asking you for it for myself. That's all—except that the man who's asking you does want to make good, Mr. Longman—he really does—and now he's at his last pound-note."

"H'm !" Mr. Longman lighted a cigarette. "I dare say your request might be made to appear almost reasonable," he said slowly ; "but, at the same time, I would point out that, unlike Danbury, you have never, in any way, served me."

"That's true, but—" Yates's tone was becoming desperate—"I'd be willing to serve you, if I possibly could, in the future. God knows, I'd try—in any lawful way, I mean."

There was a pause. He stared at the goblet, averted his gaze, let it return, and—drank.

"Tell me this," said his host, frowning at the goblet ;

"what would you do, supposing I refused to give you one penny ?"

The guest let out a small gasp. "Do ? Nothing ! What could I do ?"

"You might, to begin with, utter threats."

Yates wagged his head. "Believe me, Mr. Longman, I'm not that sort. Your help is my last hope, and if you don't give it—well, then, I'm finished."

"What do you mean by 'finished' ?"

"I'll go down and down till I get out." Yates pointed to the goblet. "That's my only friend at present, but it's too costly a friend. If I had work, I'd forget it. As I've said, I'm at my last pound."

Mr. Longman thought rapidly. Yates was not in himself dangerous—Mr. Longman could easily believe that he was "not that sort"—but there was a danger in this failing of his. In the past Mr. Longman had refused to have dealings with men who drank spirits ; his best clients had been abstainers. He did not want to have dealings with Yates—yet dare he refuse ? Suppose he gave Yates twenty pounds, or even fifty, and bade him clear out—would that be the end of it ? He could hardly hope so. He did not fear Yates as a blackmailer or a deliberate betrayer, but he did fear him as a babbler in his cups, and he could not afford to risk that—not yet awhile, anyway. Six months hence it would be different ; then the last of the stolen "stuff" would be out of his hands, the last of his old tracks covered. Meanwhile his safety depended, more or less, on Yates's sobriety. Assuming that Yates had given his pledge to abstain, what was most likely to urge him to keep it ? Not want, surely ; certainly not despair. But with enough to live on and keep a decent appearance in his search for employment, plus the prospect of a further sum of money, conditional on his abstention for six months, the chances were that, having something of the gentleman in him, he would hold to his promise. Thus reasoned Mr. Longman, telling himself that in this case cheese-paring methods would be vain, and that generosity was the only way ; and at last he said, quietly :

"Look here, Yates; suppose I gave you help, what about that—h'm—friend—eh ?"

"Help me, and I'll take the pledge, and—and, by God, I'll keep it !"

" 'Sh ! You're inclined to raise your voice. Don't take any more of that whisky." Mr. Longman inhaled and exhaled several times before he spoke again. "Listen very carefully ! It is perfectly true that by Danbury's death I have saved a thousand pounds. But I'm not sorry to have saved it. I'm going out of the business, and, as I've always kept faith with my clients, I've got to remember that I shall have calls on me, sooner or later, from men who, like yourself, have been—h'm—unlucky. Still, in exchange for your written promise—which, by the way, will be a sort of security to me—I'll give you—five hundred. Five hundred, that is, in two equal portions—the first as soon as I can manage it, the second six months hence. What do you say ?"

Yates, checking a sob, thrust out his hand.

"Man, for heaven's sake control yourself and pay attention," said Mr. Longman. "Hear my point of view now. You couldn't have blown in at a more awkward moment. I'm leaving for Scotland to-night, to take a much-needed holiday—to wander around, alone, for four weeks and adjust my ideas. I am not disposed to give you a cheque, or to postpone my departure till after the banks are open to-morrow. My luggage is already in the cloak-room at Euston. Couldn't you contrive somehow to carry on for a month ?" He wanted to make quite certain of the urgency of the other's need.

"A month !" echoed Yates in sheer dismay. "Believe me, I've tried and tried to get work before I came to this."

"What was your work before you were—unlucky ?"

"Bank."

"Poor chap ! Well, well, you've caught me in a soft humour to-night. Maybe it's because I'm almost done with the big adventure of twenty years—yes, I've been in it all that time, Yates—and am going to spend the next thirty days in gazing at the mountains—or the mist—Lord

knows I don't care which, or what, so long as it's not
humanity. No! don't look at that whisky-and-soda.
Listen! I'll find you the money to-night, my friend, though
I'd sooner rest here till train-time."

"God bless you!"

"None of that, please. It'll be a sort of thank-offering—
or sin-offering, if you like. Once upon a time I had a
Bible, and read it. However, I mustn't begin to ramble.
To get the money, I'll have to go to my house, which is
out beyond Enfield. I keep a certain reserve at my house—
you may imagine why! On the whole, it is your lucky
evening, Yates. To-morrow I should have been gone
North." Mr. Longman glanced at his watch. "We'd
better be moving."

A page-boy came up.

"Wanted at the phone, Mr. Longman."

"Confound it—but I'll be back in a minute," said the
host. "I'll take you with me to the house, and then, when
we've done our business, I can go straight to Euston."

Alone, Yates stared at the remaining inch or so of his
whisky-and-soda. He was feeling weak physically. For
the space of a slow minute he kept saying "No" to himself.
Then he signed to the waiter.

"Double whisky—plain—quick!"

The waiter was quick. Yates, having paid him, added
a very little water to the spirit, drank it off—and placed
the glass on a neighbouring table.

Mr. Longman was rather tardy in returning, but Yates
did not worry. A sense of well-being now pervaded body
and mind. Five hundred pounds—a very decent bit of
money, even in instalments. He had never really expected
to get the thousand. He would start a little business somewhere, abjure drink, and make no more blunders. The
cursed impulse that had started all the trouble in the
bank—perhaps it would never have been had he not taken
an extra glass of whisky. God! he remembered it so well—
that day when he was worried to madness by the stock-
brokers and— Oh, damn that extra glass! Somewhere,
long ago, he had read a poem containing the line "The

little more, and how much it is !" But let him forget the past. He was going dead straight from now. No more crookedness. And no more whisky—after to-night ! He reached out for the goblet, and emptied it.

A minute later his benefactor touched him on the shoulder.

"Dreaming—eh ? My friend, you're surely going to sign the pledge to-night ! But come now. We haven't too much time."

It seemed a very long drive, and in its course Yates's whole being suffered a reaction. Towards the end of it he could have done with another drink. His companion, fortunately, seemed equally disinclined for conversation. During the latter part of the journey Mr. Longman was watching the landmarks and giving the driver instructions.

At last the cab stopped.

"I'm going to dismiss it. We can phone for another," said Mr. Longman, and got out.

There was a full moon. Yates found himself standing in front of an old-fashioned iron gate closed to an avenue which wound through grounds apparently of considerable extent.

Blinking about him, he remarked, a trifle thickly : "Pretty lonely here, Mr. David—Mr. Longman."

"You could fire a gun here, with the chances of your nearest neighbours taking no notice." So saying, Mr. Longman opened the gate with a small key attached, along with others, to a chain. "My house is closed for a month," he remarked. "The servants went on holiday yesterday. Go in."

Following his guest, he relocked the gate.

"Come along, Yates ! Wake up ! You seem to be getting drowsy. That whisky-and-soda was unwise."

"It's the sultriness," Yates replied, pulling himself up. Somehow he resented the other's remark.

They trod an avenue that must have been nearly two hundreds yards long, and came to a large square house, whose architecture suggested a century ago. The lower part had an oddly blank look, which was explained by the fact that there were no windows at less than seven feet from the ground. A steep flight of steps led up to the door.

With another small key on the chain the owner opened the ponderous, unglazed door. Stepping inside, he took an electric torch from a table and moved the button, saying :

"I get my light from a private installation, and it's off at present. We'll have to manage with that oil-lamp." He took it from the table and gave it a shake. "Not much oil. Not like my man to forget. However, it must serve. Hold the torch, please."

He closed the door and proceeded to light the lamp. That done, he said : "Come along," and led the way towards the rear of the house, then into a short passage ending at a door.

"My predecessor here," he observed, fitting the key, "was a very wealthy recluse and collector of antiques in gold and silver. He had the place adapted accordingly, which was why I bought it. His stuff is now mostly in the British Museum, and mine has had some narrow escapes from being in Scotland Yard. Well, I'll be glad to get rid of what's left of it, which is a good deal. And yet I don't know. Odd how one gets attached to precious stones. Maybe there are some that I'll never be able to part with." He laughed and pushed open the door. "Go in, Yates."

He followed, and pushed the door shut. It closed with a soft thud.

The long panelled room had three tall, narrow windows, which were now covered with steel shutters. The furniture was shrouded in dust-sheets.

"Heavens, it's beastly close already," said Mr. Longman. "Those shutters do fit ! I'd open one of them, and the window, but my man has the key. However, it wouldn't be worth while."

At the end of the room, near the fire-place, he drew the sheet from a writing-table and set the lamp on it.

"Now give me the torch, Yates, and I'll get the money, and then you'll sign your promise."

Yates handed over the torch. He seemed to have nothing to say. His mouth was dry, his eyes felt hot, with a vague ache, as if grit had got in behind them. That last glass, he told himself, must have been bad whisky. Other men have said the same. Always the quality, never the quantity.

Torch in hand, Mr. Longman moved away towards the far end of the room. After a moment or two, Yates began to follow.

Mr. Longman halted abruptly and wheeled about. "Kindly go back to where you were," he said rather sternly, "and stay there !"

Yates returned to the writing-table. He resented the other's tone, resented it bitterly. After all, what had Longman—or Davidson—to kick at? He was saving half of the money that he had promised to Danbury. Two-fifty down wasn't so very great, after all. In fact, it was very little—too little.

"Come, come, Mr. Longman, make it the thousand—down !" That was what he was going to say, but, some-how, did not say. The atmosphere was, indeed, horribly close. His whole body was fevered. He was hot to the finger-tips. If only——

Mr. Longman was fitting another key from his chain into an ordinary-looking door.

Yates sat on a corner of the table, his arid eyes staring. His burning hand, straying over the mahogany, fell on something cold.

Mr. Longman dragged open the door and took out the key.

Yates, who had seen strong-rooms in his day, was peering into the shadows of one now. A strong-room ! Precious stones and money there, in plenty. Without a doubt, thousands in money, ready for Longman's instant flight, if ever he dreamed of the truth being whispered. But, of course, he, Yates, would never think of betraying Longman ! He wasn't that sort. Still, five hundred wasn't enough, not nearly enough. And he no longer liked Longman. The man was a bigger criminal, by far, than himself, and he had been most offensive, really most offensive. . . .

Mr. Longman had opened a large steel box. "I find I can let you have it in tens and fives, which, I fancy, you will prefer," he called pleasantly. "What did you say?"

"Nothing," answered Yates, who had been muttering the words "two thousand." He got off the desk. The cold thing was in his hand. He advanced three steps.

"Stop! Go back to the table!" cried Mr. Longman.

Yates stopped, but he did not go back. He was more resentful than ever. Longman's tone and manner were unpardonable! His fingers tightened on the thing, no longer so cold—a solid, oblong block of glass, a paper-weight, very heavy.

"Damn you!" said Mr. Longman, in the voice of one suddenly fearful for the safety of a great treasure. "I warn you, I've got a revolver here."

"Mr. Davidson, I must have five thousand pounds!" Yates meant to say that, but he didn't—couldn't. He seemed to be all torrid blood. And now, after the other's most offensive remark of all, he felt justly entitled to some precious stones as well.

"Go back!" commanded Mr. Longman, still groping. "Go back, you—scoundrel!"

The crowning insult. Yates threw up his arm, grunted, and flung the block.

The whisky did not affect his aim, if aim there was; but the whisky assuredly gave the impulse that sent the block on its way—to Mr. Longman's right temple.

The sound of the impact was plainly audible, sickening, and was followed by a loud gasp from the stricken man, who reeled backward, then forward, and grasped the inner handle of the door. As he struggled to pull himself up by it his weight dragged it to, and it shut with a gentle click.

For a long time Yates stood gaping at it. Then he staggered up the room and, after foolishly striving to open it, beat upon the painted steel.

Of a sudden he realized his own situation. He must be gone without delay—though, in all probability, it would be a month before anything could be discovered.

He was sober enough now, physical discomfort lost in mental misery and terror. A murderer !

Unevenly he crossed to the door by which they had entered. As he reached it, the lamp gave a flicker. He gripped the handle and made to turn it. It refused to move, being, in fact, immovable and having no connection with the lock. And the key of the lock was on Longman's chain—in the strong-room !

Yates did not cry out—then. He leaned against the steel-lined door, no longer fevered, but sweating coldness.

Again the lamp flickered. His eyes watched it in horror and hopelessness.

In a little while darkness ; afterwards—What ?

3
WILLIAM WILKIE COLLINS
The Biter Bit

THE BITER BIT

[Extracted from the Correspondence of the London Police]

FROM CHIEF INSPECTOR THEAKSTONE, OF THE DETECTIVE
POLICE, TO SERGEANT BULMER OF THE SAME FORCE

LONDON, *4th July*, 18—.

SERGEANT BULMER,—This is to inform you that you
are wanted to assist in looking up a case of importance,
which will require all the attention of an experienced member of the force. The matter of the robbery on which
you are now engaged, you will please to shift over to the
young man who brings you this letter. You will tell him
all the circumstances of the case, just as they stand; you will
put him up to the progress you have made (if any) towards detecting the person or persons by whom the money
has been stolen; and you will leave him to make the best
he can of the matter now in your hands. He is to have
the whole responsibility of the case, and the whole credit of
his success, if he brings it to a proper issue.

So much for the orders that I am desired to communicate to you.

A word in your ear, next, about this new man who is
to take your place. His name is Matthew Sharpin; and he
is to have the chance given him of dashing into our office
at a jump—supposing he turns out strong enough to take
it. You will naturally ask me how he comes by this privilege. I can only tell you that he has some uncommonly
strong interest to back him in certain high quarters which
you and I had better not mention except under our breaths.
He has been a lawyer's clerk; and he is wonderfully conceited in his opinion of himself, as well as mean and under-
hand to look at. According to his own account, he leaves
his old trade, and joins ours, of his own free will and
preference. You will no more believe that than I do. My
notion is, that he has managed to ferret out some private

information in connection with the affairs of one of his master's clients, which makes him rather an awkward customer to keep in the office for the future, and which, at the same time, gives him hold enough over his employer to make it dangerous to drive him into a corner by turning him away. I think the giving him this unheard-of chance among us, is, in plain words, pretty much like giving him hush-money to keep him quiet. However that may be, Mr. Matthew Sharpin is to have the case now in your hands; and if he succeeds with it, he pokes his ugly nose into our office, as sure as fate. I put you up to this, Sergeant, so that you may not stand in your own light by giving the new man any cause to complain of you at headquarters, and remain yours,

FRANCIS THEAKSTONE.

FROM MR. MATTHEW SHARPIN TO CHIEF INSPECTOR
THEAKSTONE

LONDON, *July 5th*, 18—.

DEAR SIR,—Having now been favoured with the necessary instructions from Sergeant Bulmer, I beg to remind you of certain directions which I have received, relating to the report of my future proceedings which I am to prepare for examination at headquarters.

The object of my writing, and of your examining what I have written, before you send it in to the higher authorities, is, I am informed, to give me, as an untried hand, the benefit of your advice, in case I want it (which I venture to think I shall not) at any stage of my proceedings. As the extraordinary circumstances of the case on which I am now engaged, make it impossible for me to absent myself from the place where the robbery was committed, until I have made some progress towards discovering the thief, I am necessarily precluded from consulting you personally. Hence the necessity of writing down the various details, which might, perhaps, be better communicated by word of mouth. This, if I am not mistaken, is the position in which we are now placed. I state my own impressions on the subject, in writing, in order that we may clearly understand each other at the outset; and have the honour to remain, your obedient servant,

MATTHEW SHARPIN.

FROM CHIEF INSPECTOR THEAKSTONE TO MR. MATTHEW
SHARPIN

LONDON, *5th July*, 18—.

SIR,—You have begun by wasting time, ink, and paper.
We both of us perfectly well knew the position we stood
in towards each other, when I sent you with my letter to
Sergeant Bulmer. There was not the least need to repeat
it in writing. Be so good as to employ your pen, in future,
on the business actually in hand.

You have now three separate matters on which to write
to me. First, You have to draw up a statement of your instructions received from Sergeant Bulmer, in order to show
us that nothing has escaped your memory, and that you are
thoroughly acquainted with all the circumstances of the case
which has been entrusted to you. Secondly, You are to
inform me what it is you propose to do. Thirdly, You are
to report every inch of your progress (if you make any)
from day to day, and, if need be, from hour to hour as
well. This is *your* duty. As to what *my* duty may be,
when I want you to remind me of it, I will write and tell
you so. In the meantime, I remain, yours,

FRANCIS THEAKSTONE.

FROM MR. MATTHEW SHARPIN TO CHIEF INSPECTOR
THEAKSTONE

LONDON, *6th July*, 18—.

SIR,—You are rather an elderly person, and, as such,
naturally inclined to be a little jealous of men like me, who
are in the prime of their lives and their faculties. Under
these circumstances, it is my duty to be considerate towards
you, and not to bear too hardly on your small failings. I
decline, therefore, altogether, to take offence at the tone
of your letter; I give you the full benefit of the natural
generosity of my nature; I sponge the very existence of
your surly communication out of my memory—in short,
Chief Inspector Theakstone, I forgive you, and proceed to
business.

My first duty is to draw up a full statement of the instructions I have received from Sergeant Bulmer. Here they
are at your service, according to my version of them.

At number 13, Rutherford Street, Soho, there is a stationer's shop. It is kept by one Mr. Yatman. He is a
married man, but has no family. Besides Mr. and Mrs.
Yatman, the other inmates in the house are a young single
man named Jay, who lodges in the front room on the second
floor—a shopman, who sleeps in one of the attics,—and a
servant-of-all-work, whose bed is in the back-kitchen. Once
a week a charwoman comes for a few hours in the morning
only, to help this servant. These are all the persons who,
on ordinary occasions, have means of access to the interior
of the house, placed, as a matter of course, at their disposal.

Mr. Yatman has been in business for many years, carrying
on his affairs prosperously enough to realise a handsome in-
dependence for a person in his position. Unfortunately for
himself, he endeavoured to increase the amount of his
property by speculating. He ventured boldly in his investments, luck went against him, and rather less than two
years ago he found himself a poor man again. All that was
saved out of the wreck of his property was the sum of two
hundred pounds.

Although Mr. Yatman did his best to meet his altered
circumstances, by giving up many of the luxuries and com-
forts to which he and his wife had been accustomed, he
found it impossible to retrench so far as to allow of putting
by any money from the income produced by his shop. The
business has been declining of late years—the cheap advertising stationers having done it injury with the public. Consequently, up to the last week the only surplus property
possessed by Mr. Yatman consisted of the two hundred
pounds which had been recovered from the wreck of his fortune. This sum was placed as a deposit in a joint-stock
bank of the highest possible character.

Eight days ago, Mr. Yatman and his lodger, Mr. Jay, held
a conversation on the subject of the commercial difficulties
which are hampering trade in all directions at the present
time. Mr. Jay (who lives by supplying the newspapers
with short paragraphs relating to accidents, offences, and
brief records of remarkable occurrences in general—who is,
in short, what they call a penny-a-liner) told his landlord
that he had been in the city that day, and had heard un-
favourable rumours on the subject of the joint-stock banks.
The rumours to which he alluded had already reached the

ears of Mr. Yatman from other quarters; and the confirmation of them by his lodger had such an effect on his mind —predisposed as it was to alarm by the experience of his former losses—that he resolved to go at once to the bank and withdraw his deposit.

It was then getting on towards the end of the afternoon; and he arrived just in time to receive his money before the bank closed.

He received the deposit in bank-notes of the following amounts;—one fifty-pound note, three twenty-pound notes, six ten-pound notes, and six five-pound notes. His object in drawing the money in this form was to have it ready to lay out immediately in trifling loans, on good security, among the small tradespeople of his district, some of whom are sorely pressed for the very means of existence at the present time. Investments of this kind seemed to Mr. Yatman to be the most safe and the most profitable on which he could now venture.

He brought the money back in an envelope placed in his breast-pocket; and asked his shopman, on getting home, to look for a small flat tin cash-box, which had not been used for years, and which, as Mr. Yatman remembered it, was exactly of the right size to hold the bank-notes. For some time the cash-box was searched for in vain. Mr. Yatman called to his wife to know if she had any idea where it was. The question was overheard by the servant-of-all-work, who was taking up the tea-tray at the time, and by Mr. Jay, who was coming down stairs on his way out to the theatre. Ultimately the cash-box was found by the shopman. Mr. Yatman placed the bank-notes in it, secured them by a padlock, and put the box in his coat-pocket. It stuck out of the coat pocket a very little, but enough to be seen. Mr. Yatman remained at home, up stairs, all the evening. No visitors called. At eleven o'clock he went to bed, and put the cash-box along with his clothes, on a chair by the bedside.

When he and his wife woke the next morning, the box was gone. Payment of the notes was immediately stopped at the bank of England; but no news of the money has been heard of since that time.

So far, the circumstances of the case are perfectly clear. They point unmistakably to the conclusion that the robbery must have been committed by some person living in the house. Suspicion falls, therefore, upon the servant-of-all-work, upon the shopman, and upon Mr. Jay. The two first knew that the cash-box was being inquired for by their master, but did not know what it was he wanted to put into it. They would assume, of course that it was money. They both had opportunities (the servant, when she took away the tea—and the shopman, when he came, after shutting up, to give the keys of the till to his master) of seeing the cash-box in Mr. Yatman's pocket, and of inferring naturally, from its position there, that he intended to take it into his bedroom with him at night.

Mr. Jay, on the other hand, had been told, during the afternoon's conversation on the subject of joint-stock banks, that his landlord had a deposit of two hundred pounds in one of them. He also knew that Mr. Yatman left him with the intention of drawing that money out; and he heard the inquiry for the cash-box, afterwards, when he was coming down stairs. He must, therefore, have inferred that the money was in the house, and that the cash-box was the receptacle intended to contain it. That he could have had any idea, however, of the place in which Mr. Yatman intended to keep it for the night, is impossible, seeing that he went out before the box was found, and did not return till his landlord was in bed. Consequently, if he committed the robbery, he must have gone into the bedroom purely on speculation.

Speaking of the bedroom reminds me of the necessity of noticing the situation of it in the house, and the means that exist of gaining easy access to it at any hour of the night.

The room in question is the back-room on the first-floor. In consequence of Mrs. Yatman's constitutional nervousness on the subject of fire (which makes her apprehend being burnt alive in her room, in case of accident, by the hampering of the lock if the key is turned in it) her husband has never been accustomed to lock the bedroom door. Both he and his wife are, by their own admission, heavy sleepers. Consequently the risk to be run by any evil-disposed persons wishing to plunder the bedroom, was of the most trifling kind. They could enter the room by merely turning the handle of the door; and if they moved with ordinary caution, there was no fear of their waking the sleepers inside. This fact is of importance. It strengthens our conviction that the money must have been taken by one of the inmates of the house, because it tends to show that the robbery, in this case, might have been committed by persons not possessed of the superior vigilance and cunning of the experienced thief.

Such are the circumstances, as they were related to Sergeant Bulmer, when he was first called in to discover the guilty parties, and, if possible, to recover the lost bank-notes. The strictest inquiry which he could institute, failed of producing the smallest fragment of evidence against any of the persons on whom suspicion naturally fell. Their language and behaviour, on being informed of the robbery, was perfectly consistent with the language and behaviour of innocent people. Sergeant Bulmer felt from the first that this was a case for private inquiry and secret observation. He began by recommending Mr. and Mrs. Yatman to affect a feeling of perfect confidence in the innocence of the persons living under their roof; and he then opened the campaign by employing himself in following the goings and comings and in discovering the friends, the habits, and the secrets of the maid-of-all-work.

Three days and nights of exertion on his own part, and on that of others who were competent to assist his investigations, were enough to satisfy him that there was no sound cause for suspicion against the girl.

He next practised the same precaution in relation to the shopman. There was more difficulty and uncertainty in privately clearing up this person's character without his knowledge, but the obstacles were at last smoothed away with tolerable success; and though there is not the same amount of certainty, in this case, which there was in that of the girl, there is still fair reason for supposing that the shopman has had nothing to do with the robbery of the cash-box.

As a necessary consequence of these proceedings, the range of suspicion now becomes limited to the lodger, Mr. Jay.

When I presented your letter of introduction to Sergeant Bulmer, he had already made some inquiries on the subject of this young man. The result, so far, has not been at all favourable. Mr. Jay's habits are irregular; he frequents public houses, and seems to be familiarly acquainted with a great many dissolute characters; he is in debt to most of the tradespeople whom he employs; he has not paid his rent to Mr. Yatman for the last month; yesterday evening he came home excited by liquor, and last week he was seen talking to a prize-fighter. In short, though Mr. Jay does call himself a journalist, in virtue of his penny-a-line contributions to the newspapers, he is a young man of low tastes, vulgar manners, and bad habits. Nothing has yet been discovered in relation to him, which redounds to his credit in the smallest degree.

I have now reported, down to the very last details, all the particulars communicated to me by Sergeant Bulmer. I believe you will not find an omission anywhere; and I think you will admit, though you are prejudiced against me, that a clearer statement of facts was never laid before you than the statement I have now made. My next duty is to tell you what I propose to do, now that the case is confided to my hands.

In the first place, it is clearly my business to take up the case at the point where Sergeant Bulmer has left it. On his authority, I am justified in assuming that I have no need to trouble myself about the maid-of-all-work and the shopman. Their characters are now to be considered as cleared up. What remains to be privately investigated is the question of the guilt or innocence of Mr. Jay. Before we give up the notes for lost, we must make sure, if we can, that he knows nothing about them.

This is the plan that I have adopted, with the full approval of Mr. and Mrs. Yatman, for discovering whether Mr. Jay is or is not the person who has stolen the cash-box:

I propose, to-day, to present myself at the house in the character of a young man who is looking for lodgings. The back room on the second-floor will be shown to me as the room to let; and I shall establish myself there to-night, as a person from the country who has come to London to look for a situation in a respectable shop or office.

By this means I shall be living next to the room occupied by Mr. Jay. The partition between us is mere lath and plaster. I shall make a small hole in it, near the cornice, though which I can see what Mr. Jay does in his room, and hear every word that is said when any friend happens to call on him. Whenever he is at home, I shall be at my post of observation. Whenever he goes out, I shall be after him. By employing these means of watching him, I believe I may look forward to the discovery of his secret—if he knows anything about the lost bank-notes—as to a dead certainty.

What you may think of my plan of observation I cannot undertake to say. It appears to me to unite the invaluable merits of boldness and simplicity. Fortified by this conviction, I close the present communication with feelings of the most sanguine description in regard to the future, and remain your obedient servant,

MATTHEW SHARPIN.

FROM THE SAME TO THE SAME

7th July.

SIR,—As you have not honoured me with any answer to my last communication, I assume that, in spite of your prejudices against me, it has produced the favourable impression on your mind which I ventured to anticipate. Gratified beyond measure by the token of approval which your eloquent silence conveys to me, I proceed to report the progress that has been made in the course of the last twenty-four hours.

I am now comfortably established next door to Mr. Jay; and I am delighted to say that I have two holes in the partition, instead of one. My natural sense of humour has led me into the pardonable extravagance of giving them appropriate names. One I call my peep-hole, and the other my pipe-hole. The name of the first explains itself; the name of the second refers to a small tin pipe, or tube, inserted in the hole, and twisted so that the mouth of it comes close to my ear, while I am standing at my post of observation. Thus, while I am looking at Mr. Jay through my peep-hole, I can hear every word that may be spoken in his room through my pipe-hole.

Perfect candour—a virtue which I have possessed from my childhood—compels me to acknowledge, before I go any further, that the ingenious notion of adding a pipe-hole to my proposed peep-hole originated with Mrs. Yatman. This lady—a most intelligent and accomplished person,

simple, and yet distinguished, in her manners—has entered
into all my little plans with an enthusiasm and intelligence
which I cannot too highly praise. Mr. Yatman is so cast
down by his loss, that he is quite incapable of affording
me any assistance. Mrs. Yatman, who is evidently most
tenderly attached to him, feels her husband's sad condition
of mind even more acutely than she feels the loss of the
money; and is mainly stimulated to exertion by her desire
to assist in raising him from the miserable state of prostration into which he has now fallen.

"The money, Mr. Sharpin," she said to me yesterday
evening, with tears in her eyes, "the money may be re-
gained by rigid economy and strict attention to business.
It is my husband's wretched state of mind that makes me so
anxious for the discovery of the thief. I may be wrong,
but I felt hopeful of success as soon as you entered the
house; and I believe, if the wretch who has robbed us is to
be found, you are the man to discover him." I accept this
gratifying compliment in the spirit in which it was offered
—firmly believing that I shall be found, sooner or later, to
have thoroughly deserved it.

Let me now return to business; that is to say, to my peep-
hole and my pipe-hole.

I have enjoyed some hours of calm observation of Mr.
Jay. Though rarely at home, as I understand from Mrs.
Yatman, on ordinary occasions, he has been in-doors the
whole of this day. That is suspicious, to begin with. I
have to report, further that he rose at a late hour this morning (always a bad sign in a young man), and that he lost
a great deal of time, after he was up, in yawning and complaining to himself of headache. Like other debauched characters, he ate little or nothing for breakfast. His next proceeding was to smoke a pipe—a dirty clay pipe, which a
gentleman would have been ashamed to put between his
lips. When he had done smoking, he took out pen, ink, and
paper, and sat down to write with a groan—whether of
remorse for having taken the bank-notes, or of disgust at
the task before him, I am unable to say. After writing a
few lines (too far away from my peep-hole to give me a
chance of reading over his shoulder), he leaned back in his
chair, and amused himself by humming the tunes of certain
popular songs. Whether these do, or do not, represent secret

signals by which he communicates with his accomplices remains to be seen. After he had amused himself for some time by humming, he got up and began to walk about the room, occasionally stopping to add a sentence to the paper on his desk. Before long, he went to a locked cupboard and opened it. I strained my eyes eagerly, in expectation of making a discovery. I saw him take something carefully out of the cupboard—he turned round—and it was only a pint bottle of brandy! Having drunk some of the liquor, this extremely indolent reprobate lay down on his bed again, and in five minutes was fast asleep.

After hearing him snoring for at least two hours, I was recalled to my peep-hole by a knock at his door. He jumped up and opened it with suspicious activity.

A very small boy, with a very dirty face, walked in, said, " Please, sir, they're waiting for you," sat down on a chair, with his legs a long way from the ground, and instantly fell asleep! Mr. Jay swore an oath, tied a wet towel round his head, and going back to his paper, began to cover it with writing as fast as his fingers could move the pen. Occasionally getting up to dip the towel in water and tie it on again, he continued at this employment for nearly three hours; then folded up the leaves of writing, woke the boy, and gave them to him, with this remarkable expression:— " Now, then, young sleepy-head, quick—march! If you see the governor, tell him to have the money ready when I call for it." The boy grinned, and disappeared. I was sorely tempted to follow " sleepy-head," but, on reflection, considered it safest still to keep my eye on the proceedings of Mr. Jay.

In half an hour's time, he put on his hat and walked out. Of course, I put on my hat and walked out also. As I went down stairs, I passed Mrs. Yatman going up. The lady has been kind enough to undertake, by previous arrangement between us, to search Mr. Jay's room, while he is out of the way, and while I am necessarily engaged in the pleasing duty of following him wherever he goes. On the occasion to which I now refer, he walked straight to the nearest tavern, and ordered a couple of mutton chops for his dinner. I placed myself in the next box to him, and ordered a couple of mutton chops for my dinner. Before I had been in the room a minute, a young man of highly suspicious manners and appearance, sitting at a table opposite, took his glass of porter in his hand and joined Mr. Jay. I pretended to be reading the newspaper, and listened, as in duty bound, with all my might.

" Jack has been here inquiring after you," says the young man.

" Did he leave any message? " asks Mr. Jay.

" Yes," says the other. " He told me, if I met with you, to say that he wished very particularly to see you to-night; and that he would give you a look in, at Rutherford Street, at seven o'clock."

" All right," says Mr. Jay. " I'll get back in time to see him."

Upon this, the suspicious-looking young man finished his porter, and saying that he was rather in a hurry, took leave of his friend (perhaps I should not be wrong if I said his accomplice) and left the room.

At twenty-five minutes and a half past six—in these serious cases it is important to be particular about time—Mr. Jay finished his chops and paid his bill. At twenty-six minutes and three-quarters I finished my chops and paid mine. In ten minutes more I was inside the house in Rutherford Street, and was received by Mrs. Yatman in the passage. That charming woman's face exhibited an expression of melancholy and disappointment which it quite grieved me to see.

" I am afraid, Ma'am," says I, " that you have not hit on any little criminating discovery in the lodger's room? "

She shook her head and sighed. It was a soft, languid, fluttering sigh;—and, upon my life, it quite upset me. For the moment I forgot business, and burned with envy of Mr. Yatman.

" Don't despair, Ma'am," I said, with an insinuating mildness which seemed to touch her. " I have heard a mysterious conversation—I know of a guilty appointment—and I expect great things from my Peep-hole and my Pipe-hole to-night. Pray, don't be alarmed, but I think we are on the brink of a discovery."

Here my enthusiastic devotion to business got the better of my tender feelings. I looked—winked—nodded—left her.

When I got back to my observatory, I found Mr. Jay

digesting his mutton chops in an arm-chair, with his pipe in his mouth. On his table were two tumblers, a jug of water, and the pint bottle of brandy. It was then close upon seven o'clock. As the hour struck, the person described as " Jack " walked in.

He looked agitated—I am happy to say he looked violently agitated. The cheerful glow of anticipated success diffused itself (to use a strong expression) all over me, from head to foot. With breathless interest I looked through my Peephole, and saw the visitor—the " Jack " of this delightful case—sit down, facing me, at the opposite side of the table to Mr. Jay. Making allowance for the difference in expression which their countenances just now happened to exhibit, these two abandoned villains were so much alike in other respects as to lead at once to the conclusion that they were brothers. Jack was the cleaner man and the better dressed of the two. I admit that, at the outset. It is, perhaps, one of my failings to push justice and impartiality to their utmost limits. I am no Pharisee; and where Vice has its redeeming point, I say, let Vice have its due—yes, yes, by all manner of means, let Vice have its due.

" What's the matter now, Jack? " says Mr. Jay.

" Can't you see it in my face? " says Jack. " My dear fellow, delays are dangerous. Let us have done with suspense, and risk it the day after to-morrow."

" So soon as that? " cried Mr. Jay, looking very much astonished. " Well, I'm ready, if you are. But, I say, Jack, is Somebody Else ready too? Are you quite sure of that? "

He smiled as he spoke—a frightful smile—and laid a very strong emphasis on those two words, " Somebody Else." There is evidently a third ruffian, a nameless desperado, concerned in the business.

" Meet us to-morrow," says Jack, " and judge for yourself. Be in the Regent's Park at eleven in the morning, and look out for us at the turning that leads to the Avenue Road."

" I'll be there," says Mr. Jay. " Have a drop of brandy and water? What are you getting up for? You're not going already? "

" Yes, I am," says Jack. " The fact is, I'm so excited and agitated that I can't sit still anywhere for five minutes together. Ridiculous as it may appear to you, I'm in a perpetual state of nervous flutter. I can't, for the life of me, help fearing that we shall be found out. I fancy that every man who looks twice at me in the street is a spy——"

At those words, I thought my legs would have given way under me. Nothing but strength of mind kept me at my Peep-hole—nothing else, I give you my word of honour.

"Stuff and nonsense!" cried Mr. Jay, with all the effrontery of a veteran in crime. "We have kept the secret up to this time, and we will manage cleverly to the end. Have a drop of brandy and water, and you will feel as certain about it as I do."

Jack steadily refused the brandy and water, and steadily persisted in taking his leave.

"I must try if I can't walk it off," he said. "Remember to-morrow morning—eleven o'clock, Avenue Road side of the Regent's Park."

With those words he went out. His hardened relative laughed desperately, and resumed the dirty clay pipe.

I sat down on the side of my bed, actually quivering with excitement.

It is clear to me that no attempt has yet been made to change the stolen bank-notes; and I may add that Sergeant Bulmer was of that opinion also, when he left the case in my hands. What is the natural conclusion to draw from the conversation which I have just set down? Evidently, that the confederates meet to-morrow to take their respective shares in the stolen money, and to decide on the safest means of getting the notes changed the day after. Mr. Jay is, beyond a doubt, the leading criminal in this business, and he will probably run the chief risk—that of changing the fifty-pound note. I shall, therefore, still make it my business to follow him—attending at the Regent's Park to-morrow, and doing my best to hear what is said there. If another appointment is made for the day after, I shall, of course, go to it. In the meantime, I shall want the immediate assistance of two competent persons (supposing the rascals separate after their meeting) to follow the two minor criminals. It is only fair to add, that, if the rogues all retire together, I shall probably keep my subordinates in reserve. Being naturally ambitious, I desire, if possible, to have the whole credit of discovering this robbery to myself.

8th July.

I have to acknowledge, with thanks, the speedy arrival of my two subordinates—men of very average abilities, I am afraid; but, fortunately, I shall always be on the spot to direct them.

My first business this morning was, necessarily, to prevent mistakes by accounting to Mr. and Mrs. Yatman for the presence of two strangers on the scene. Mr. Yatman (between ourselves, a poor feeble man) only shook his head and groaned. Mrs. Yatman (that superior woman) favoured me with a charming look of intelligence.

" Oh, Mr. Sharpin! " she said, " I am so sorry to see those two men! Your sending for their assistance looks as if you were beginning to be doubtful of success."

I privately winked at her (she is very good in allowing me to do so without taking offence), and told her, in my facetious way, that she laboured under a slight mistake.

" It is because I am sure of success, Ma'am, that I send for them. I am determined to recover the money, not for my own sake only, but for Mr. Yatman's sake—and for yours."

I laid a considerable amount of stress on those last three words. She said, " Oh, Mr. Sharpin! " again—and blushed of a heavenly red—and looked down at her work. I could go to the world's end with that woman, if Mr. Yatman would only die.

I sent off the two subordinates to wait, until I wanted them, at the Avenue Road gate of the Regent's Park. Half an hour afterwards I was following in the same direction myself, at the heels of Mr. Jay.

The two confederates were punctual to the appointed time, I blush to record it, but it is nevertheless necessary to state, that the third rogue—the nameless desperado of my report, or if you prefer it, the mysterious " Somebody Else " of the conversation between the two brothers—is a woman! and, what is worse, a young woman! and what is more lamentable still, a nice-looking woman! I have long resisted a growing conviction, that, wherever there is mischief in this world, an individual of the fair sex is inevitably certain to be mixed up in it. After the experience of this morning, I can struggle against that sad conclusion no longer.

—I give up the sex—excepting Mrs. Yatman, I give up the sex.

The man named " Jack " offered the woman his arm. Mr. Jay placed himself on the other side of her. The three then walked away slowly among the trees. I followed them at a respectful distance. My two subordinates, at a respectful distance also, followed me.

It was, I deeply regret to say, impossible to get near enough to them to overhear their conversation, without running too great a risk of being discovered. I could only infer from their gestures and actions that they were all three talking with extraordinary earnestness on some subject which deeply interested them. After having been engaged in this way a full quarter of an hour, they suddenly turned round to retrace their steps. My presence of mind did not forsake me in this emergency. I signed to the two subordinates to walk on carelessly and pass them, while I myself slipped dexterously behind a tree. As they came by me, I heard " Jack " address these words to Mr. Jay:—

" Let us say half-past ten to-morrow morning. And mind you come in a cab. We had better not risk taking one in this neighbourhood."

Mr. Jay made some brief reply, which I could not overhear. They walked back to the place at which they had met, shaking hands there with an audacious cordiality which it quite sickened me to see. They then separated. I followed Mr. Jay. My subordinates paid the same delicate attention to the other two.

Instead of taking me back to Rutherford Street, Mr. Jay led me to the Strand. He stopped at a dingy, disreputable-looking house, which, according to the inscription over the door, was a newspaper office, but which, in my judgment, had all the external appearance of a place devoted to the reception of stolen goods.

After remaining inside for a few minutes, he came out, whistling with his finger and thumb in his waistcoat pocket. A less discreet man than myself would have arrested him on the spot. I remembered the necessity of catching the two confederates, and the importance of not interfering with the appointment that had been made for the next morning. Such coolness as this, under trying circumstances, is rarely to be found, I should imagine, in a young beginner, whose reputation as a detective policeman is still to make.

From the house of suspicious appearance, Mr. Jay betook himself to a cigar-divan, and read the magazines over a cheroot. I sat at a table near him, and read the magazines likewise over a cheroot. From the divan he strolled to the tavern and had his chops. I strolled to the tavern and had my chops. When he had done, he went back to his lodging. When I had done, I went back to mine. He was overcome with drowsiness early in the evening and went to bed. As soon as I heard him snoring, I was overcome with drowsiness, and went to bed also.

Early in the morning my two subordinates came to make their report.

They had seen the man named " Jack " leave the woman near the gate of an apparently respectable villa-residence, not far from the Regent's Park. Left to himself, he took a turning to the right, which led to a sort of suburban street, principally inhabited by shopkeepers. He stopped at the private door of one of the houses, and let himself in with his own key—looking about him as he opened the door, and staring suspiciously at my men as they lounged along on the opposite side of the way. These were all the particulars which the subordinates had to communicate. I kept them in my room to attend on me, if needful, and mounted to my Peep-hole to have a look at Mr. Jay.

He was occupied in dressing himself, and was taking extraordinary pains to destroy all traces of the natural slovenliness of his appearance. This was precisely what I expected. A vagabond like Mr. Jay knows the importance of giving himself a respectable look when he is going to run the risk of changing a stolen bank-note. At five minutes past ten o'clock, he had given the last brush to his shabby hat and the last scouring with bread-crumb to his dirty gloves. At ten minutes past ten he was in the street, on his way to the nearest cab-stand, and I and my subordinates were close on his heels.

He took a cab, and we took a cab. I had not overheard them appoint a place of meeting, when following them in the Park on the previous day; but I soon found that we were proceeding in the old direction of the Avenue Road gate.

The cab in which Mr. Jay was riding turned into the

Park slowly. We stopped outside, to avoid exciting suspicion. I got out to follow the cab on foot. Just as I did so, I saw it stop, and detected the two confederates approaching it from among the trees. They got in, and the cab was turned about directly. I ran back to my own cab, and told the driver to let them pass him, and then to follow as before.

The man obeyed my directions, but so clumsily as to excite their suspicions. We had been driving after them about three minutes (returning along the road by which we had advanced) when I looked out of the window to see how far they might be ahead of us. As I did this, I saw two hats popped out of the windows of their cab, and two faces looking back at me. I sank into my place in a cold sweat;—the expression is coarse, but no other form of words can describe my condition at that trying moment.

" We are found out! " I said faintly to my two subordinates. They stared at me in astonishment. My feelings changed instantly from the depth of despair to the height of indignation.

" It is the cabman's fault. Get out, one of you," I said, with dignity—" get out and punch his head."

Instead of following my directions (I should wish this act of disobedience to be reported at head-quarters) they both looked out of the window. Before I could pull them back, they both sat down again. Before I could express my just indignation, they both grinned, and said to me, " Please to look out, sir! "

I did look out. The thieves' cab had stopped.

Where?

At a church door!!!

What effect this discovery might have had upon the ordinary run of men, I don't know. Being of a strong religious turn myself, it filled me with horror. I have often read of the unprincipled cunning of criminal persons; but I never before heard of three thieves attempting to double on their pursuers by entering a church! The sacrilegious audacity of that proceeding is, I should think, unparalleled in the annals of crime.

I checked my grinning subordinates by a frown. It was easy to see what was passing in their superficial minds. If I had not been able to look below the surface, I might, on observing two nicely-dressed men and one nicely-dressed woman enter a church before eleven in the morning on a week day, have come to the same hasty conclusion at which my inferiors had evidently arrived. As it was, appearances had no power to impose on *me*. I got out, and, followed by one of my men, entered the church. The other man I sent round to watch the vestry door. You may catch a weasel asleep—but not your humble servant, Matthew Sharpin!

We stole up the gallery stairs, diverged to the organ loft and peered through the curtains in front. There they were all three, sitting in a pew below—yes, incredible as it may appear, sitting in a pew below!

Before I could determine what to do, a clergyman made his appearance in full canonicals, from the vestry door, followed by a clerk. My brain whirled, and my eyesight grew dim. Dark remembrances of robberies committed in vestries floated through my mind. I trembled for the excellent man in full canonicals—I even trembled for the clerk.

The clergyman placed himself inside the altar rails. The three desperadoes approached him. He opened his book, and began to read. What?—you will ask.

I answer, without the slightest hesitation, the first lines of the Marriage Service.

My subordinate had the audacity to look at me, and then to stuff his pocket-handkerchief into his mouth. I scorned to pay any attention to him. After I had discovered that the man " Jack " was the bridegroom, and that the man Jay acted the part of father, and gave away the bride, I left the church, followed by my man, and joined the other subordinate outside the vestry door. Some people in my position would now have felt rather crestfallen, and would have begun to think that they had made a very foolish mistake. Not the faintest misgiving of any kind troubled me. I did not feel in the slightest degree depreciated in my own estimation. And even now, after a lapse of three hours, my mind remains, I am happy to say, in the same calm and hopeful condition.

As soon as I and my subordinates were assembled together outside the church, I intimated my intention of still following the other cab, in spite of what had occurred. My reason for deciding on this course will appear presently. The two

subordinates were astonished at my resolution. One of
them had the impertinence to say to me:—

" If you please, sir, who is it that we are after? A man
who has stolen money, or a man who has stolen a wife? "

The other low person encouraged him by laughing. Both
have deserved an official reprimand; and both, I sincerely
trust, will be sure to get it.

When the marriage ceremony was over, the three got into
their cab; and once more our vehicle (neatly hidden round
the corner of the church, so that they could not suspect it
to be near them) started to follow theirs.

We traced them to the terminus of the South-Western
Railway. The newly-married couple took tickets for Richmond—paying their fare with a half-sovereign, and so
depriving me of the pleasure of arresting them, which I
should certainly have done, if they had offered a bank-note.
They parted from Mr. Jay, saying, " Remember the address,
—14 Babylon Terrace. You dine with us to-morrow week."
Mr. Jay accepted the invitation, and added, jocosely, that he
was going home at once to get off his clean clothes, and to
be comfortable and dirty again for the rest of the day. I
have to report that I saw him home safely, and that he is
comfortable and dirty again (to use his own disgraceful
language) at the present moment.

Here the affair rests, having by this time reached what
I may call its first stage.

I know very well what persons of hasty judgment will
be inclined to say of my proceedings thus far. They will
assert that I have been deceiving myself all through, in the
most absurd way; they will declare that the suspicious conversations which I have reported, referred solely to the
difficulties and dangers of successfully carrying out a runaway match; and they will appeal to the scene in the church,
as offering undeniable proof of the correctness of their
assertions. So let it be. I dispute nothing up to this point.
But I ask a question, out of the depths of my own sagacity
as a man of the world, which the bitterest of my enemies
will not, I think, find it particularly easy to answer.

Granted the fact of the marriage, what proof does it
afford me of the innocence of the three persons concerned
in that clandestine transaction? It gives me none. On
the contrary, it strengthens my suspicions against Mr. Jay

and his confederates, because it suggests a distinct motive for their stealing the money. A gentleman who is going to spend his honeymoon at Richmond wants money; and a gentleman who is in debt to all his tradespeople wants money. Is this an unjustifiable imputation of bad motives? In the name of outraged morality, I deny it. These men have combined together, and have stolen a woman. Why should they not combine together, and steal a cash-box? I take my stand on the logic of rigid virtue; and I defy all the sophistry of vice to move me an inch out of my position.

Speaking of virtue, I may add that I have put this view of the case to Mr. and Mrs. Yatman. That accomplished and charming woman found it difficult, at first, to follow the close chain of my reasoning. I am free to confess that she shook her head, and shed tears, and joined her husband in premature lamentation over the loss of the two hundred pounds. But a little careful explanation on my part, and a little attentive listening on hers, ultimately changed her opinion. She now agrees with me, that there is nothing in this unexpected circumstance of the clandestine marriage which absolutely tends to divert suspicion from Mr. Jay, or Mr. " Jack," or the runaway lady. " Audacious hussy " was the term my fair friend used in speaking of her, but let that pass. It is more to the purpose to record that Mrs. Yatman has not lost confidence in me and that Mr. Yatman promises to follow her example, and do his best to look hopefully for future results.

I have now, in the new turn that circumstances have taken, to wait advice from your office. I pause for fresh orders with all the composure of a man who has got two strings to his bow. When I traced the three confederates from the church door to the railway terminus, I had two motives for doing so. First, I followed them as a matter of official business, believing them still to have been guilty of the robbery. Secondly, I followed them as a matter of private speculation, with a view of discovering the place of refuge to which the runaway couple intended to retreat, and of making my information a marketable commodity to offer to the young lady's family and friends. Thus, whatever happens, I may congratulate myself beforehand on not having wasted my time. If the office approves of my conduct, I have my plan ready for further proceedings. If the office blames me, I shall take myself off, with my marketable information, to the genteel villa-residence in the neighbourhood of the Regent's Park. Any way, the affair puts money into my pocket, and does credit to my penetration as an uncommonly sharp man.

I have only one word more to add, and it is this:—If any individual ventures to assert that Mr. Jay and his confederates are innocent of all share in the stealing of the cash-box, I, in return, defy that individual—though he may even be Chief Inspector Theakstone himself—to tell me who has committed the robbery at Rutherford Street, Soho.

I have the honour to be,
Your very obedient servant,
MATTHEW SHARPIN.

FROM CHIEF INSPECTOR THEAKSTONE TO SERGEANT BULMER

Birmingham, *July 9th.*

SERGEANT BULMER,—That empty-headed puppy, Mr. Matthew Sharpin, has made a mess of the case at Rutherford Street, exactly as I expected he would. Business keeps me in this town; so I write to you to set the matter straight. I enclose, with this, the pages of feeble scribble-scrabble which the creature, Sharpin, calls a report. Look them over; and when you have made your way through all the gabble, I think you will agree with me that the conceited booby has looked for the thief in every direction but the right one. You can lay your hand on the guilty person in five minutes, now. Settle the case at once; forward your report to me at this place; and tell Mr. Sharpin that he is suspended till further notice.

Yours,
FRANCIS THEAKSTONE.

FROM SERGEANT BULMER TO CHIEF INSPECTOR THEAKSTONE

London, *July 10th.*

INSPECTOR THEAKSTONE,—Your letter and enclosure came safe to hand. Wise men, they say, may always learn something, even from a fool. By the time I had got through Sharpin's maundering report of his own folly, I saw my way clear enough to the end of the Rutherford

Street case, just as you thought I should. In half an hour's time I was at the house. The first person I saw there was Mr. Sharpin himself.

" Have you come to help me? " says he.

" Not exactly," says I. " I've come to tell you that you are suspended till further notice."

" Very good," says he, not taken down, by so much as a single peg, in his own estimation. " I thought you would be jealous of me. It's very natural; and I don't blame you. Walk in, pray, and make yourself at home. I'm off to do a little detective business on my own account, in the neighbourhood of the Regent's Park. Ta-ta, sergeant, ta-ta! "

With those words he took himself out of the way—which was exactly what I wanted him to do.

As soon as the maid-servant had shut the door, I told her to inform her master that I wanted to say a word to him in private. She showed me into the parlour behind the shop; and there was Mr. Yatman, all alone, reading the newspaper.

" About this matter of the robbery, sir," says I.

He cut me short, peevishly enough—being naturally a poor, weak, womanish sort of man. " Yes, yes, I know," says he. " You have come to tell me that your wonderfully clever man, who has bored holes in my second-floor partition, has made a mistake, and is off the scent of the scoundrel who has stolen my money."

" Yes, sir," says I. " That *is* one of the things I came to tell you. But I have got something else to say, besides that."

" Can you tell me who the thief is? " says he, more pettish than ever.

" Yes, sir," says I, " I think I can."

He put down the newspaper, and began to look rather anxious and frightened.

" Not my shopman? " says he. " I hope, for the man's own sake, it's not my shopman."

" Guess again, sir," says I.

" That idle slut, the maid? " says he.

" She is idle, sir," says I, " and she is also a slut; my first inquiries about her proved as much as that. But she's not the thief."

" Then in the name of heaven, who is? " says he.

" Will you please to prepare yourself for a very dis-
agreeable surprise, sir? " says I. " And in case you lose
your temper, will you excuse my remarking that I am the
stronger man of the two, and that, if you allow yourself
to lay hands on me, I may unintentionally hurt you, in
pure self-defence? "

He turned as pale as ashes, and pushed his chair two
or three feet away from me.

" You have asked me to tell you, sir, who has taken
your money," I went on. " If you insist on my giving you
an answer——"

" I do insist," he said faintly. " Who has taken it? "

" Your wife has taken it," I said very quietly, and very
positively at the same time.

He jumped out of the chair as if I had put a knife into
him, and struck his fist on the table, so heavily that the wood
cracked again.

" Steady, sir," says I. " Flying into a passion won't help
you to the truth."

" It's a lie! " says he, with another smack of his fist on
the table—" a base, vile, infamous lie! How dare you——"

He stopped, and fell back into the chair again, looked
about him in a bewildered way, and ended by bursting out
crying.

" When your better sense comes back to you, sir," says
I, " I am sure you will be gentleman enough to make an
apology for the language you have just used. In the meantime, please to listen, if you can, to a word of explanation.
Mr. Sharpin has sent in a report to our inspector, of the
most irregular and ridiculous kind; setting down, not only
all his own foolish doings and sayings, but the doings and
sayings of Mrs. Yatman as well. In most cases, such a
document would have been fit for the waste-paper basket;
but, in this particular case, it so happens that Mr. Sharpin's
budget of nonsense leads to a certain conclusion, which the
simpleton of a writer has been quite innocent of suspecting
from the beginning to the end. Of that conclusion I am
so sure, that I will forfeit my place, if it does not turn
out that Mrs. Yatman has been practising upon the folly
and conceit of this young man, and that she has tried to
shield herself from discovery by purposely encouraging him
to suspect the wrong persons. I tell you that confidently;

and I will even go further. I will undertake to give a
decided opinion as to why Mrs. Yatman took the money,
and what she has done with it, or with a part of it. Nobody
can look at that lady, sir, without being struck by the great
taste and beauty of her dress——"

As I said those last words, the poor man seemed to find his
powers of speech again. He cut me short directly, as
haughtily as if he had been a duke instead of a stationer.

"Try some other means of justifying your vile calumny
against my wife," says he. "Her milliner's bill for the
past year, is on my file of receipted accounts at this
moment."

"Excuse me, sir," says I, "but that proves nothing.
Milliners, I must tell you, have a certain rascally custom
which comes within the daily experience of our office. A
married lady who wishes it, can keep two accounts at her
dressmaker's; one is the account which her husband sees
and pays; the other is the private account, which contains
all the extravagant items, and which the wife pays secretly,
by instalments, whenever she can. According to our usual
experience, these instalments are mostly squeezed out of the
housekeeping money. In your case, I suspect no instalments
have been paid; proceedings have been threatened; Mrs.
Yatman, knowing your altered circumstances, has felt herself driven into a corner; and she has paid her private account
out of your cash-box."

"I won't believe it," says he. "Every word you speak
is an abominable insult to me and to my wife."

"Are you man enough, sir," says I, taking him up short,
in order to save time and words, "to get that receipted
bill you spoke of just now off the file, and come with
me at once to the milliner's shop where Mrs. Yatman
deals?"

He turned red in the face at that, got the bill directly,
and put on his hat. I took out of my pocket-book the
list containing the numbers of the lost notes, and we left
the house together immediately.

Arrived at the milliner's (one of the expensive West-end
houses, as I expected), I asked for a private interview, on
important business, with the mistress of the concern. It
was not the first time that she and I had met over the same
delicate investigation. The moment she set eyes on me, she

sent for her husband. I mentioned who Mr. Yatman was, and what we wanted.

" This is strictly private? " inquires her husband. I nodded my head.

" And confidential? " says the wife. I nodded again.

" Do you see any objection, dear, to obliging the sergeant with a sight of the books? " says the husband.

" None in the world, love, if you approve of it," says the wife.

All this while poor Mr. Yatman sat looking the picture of astonishment and distress, quite out of place at our polite conference. The books were brought—and one minute's look at the pages in which Mrs. Yatman's name figured was enough, and more than enough, to prove the truth of every word I had spoken.

There, in one book, was the husband's account, which Mr. Yatman had settled. And there, in the other, was the private account, crossed off also; the date of settlement being the very day after the loss of the cash-box. This said private account amounted to the sum of a hundred and seventy-five pounds, odd shillings; and it extended over a period of three years. Not a single instalment had been paid on it. Under the last line was an entry to this effect: " Written to for the third time, June 23rd." I pointed to it, and asked the milliner if that meant " last June." Yes, it did mean last June; and she now deeply regretted to say that it had been accompanied by a threat of legal proceedings.

" I thought you gave good customers more than three years credit? " says I.

The milliner looks at Mr. Yatman, and whispers to me— " Not when a lady's husband gets into difficulties."

She pointed to the account as she spoke. The entries after the time when Mr. Yatman's circumstances became involved were just as extravagant, for a person in his wife's situation, as the entries for the year before that period. If the lady had economised in other things, she had certainly not economised in the matter of dress.

There was nothing left now but to examine the cash-book, for form's sake. The money had been paid in notes, the amounts and numbers of which exactly tallied with the figures set down in my list.

After that, I thought it best to get Mr. Yatman out of the house immediately. He was in such a pitiable condition, that I called a cab and accompanied him home in it. At first he cried and raved like a child: but I soon quieted him —and I must add, to his credit, that he made me a most handsome apology for his language, as the cab drew up at his house door. In return, I tried to give him some advice about how to set matters right, for the future, with his wife. He paid very little attention to me, and went upstairs muttering to himself about a separation. Whether Mrs. Yatman will come cleverly out of the scrape or not, seems doubtful. I should say, myself, that she will go into screeching hysterics, and so frighten the poor man into forgiving her. But this is no business of ours. So far as we are concerned, the case is now at an end; and the present report may come to a conclusion along with it.

I remain, accordingly, yours to command,

THOMAS BULMER.

P.S.—I have to add, that, on leaving Rutherford Street, I met Mr. Matthew Sharpin coming to pack up his things.

" Only think! " says he, rubbing his hands in great spirits, " I've been to the genteel villa-residence; and the moment I mentioned my business, they kicked me out directly. There were two witnesses of the assault; and it's worth a hundred pounds to me, if it's worth a farthing."

" I wish you joy of your luck," says I.

" Thank you," says he. " When may I pay you the same compliment on finding the thief? "

"Whenever you like," says I, " for the thief is found."

" Just what I expected," says he. " I've done all the work; and now you cut in, and claim all the credit—Mr. Jay of course? "

" No," says I.

" Who is it then? " says he.

" Ask Mrs. Yatman," says I. " She's waiting to tell you."

" All right! I'd much rather hear it from that charming woman than from you," says he, and goes into the house in a mighty hurry.

What do you think of that, Inspector Theakstone? Would you like to stand in Mr. Sharpin's shoes? I shouldn't, I can promise you!

FROM CHIEF INSPECTOR THEAKSTONE TO

MR. MATTHEW SHARPIN

July 12th.

SIR,—Sergeant Bulmer has already told you to consider
yourself suspended until further notice. I have now
authority to add, that your services as a member of the
Detective Police are positively declined. You will please
to take this letter as notifying officially your dismissal from
the force.

I may inform you, privately, that your rejection is not
intended to cast any reflections on your character. It
merely implies that you are not quite sharp enough for our
purpose. If we *are* to have a new recruit among us, we
should infinitely prefer Mrs. Yatman.

> Your obedient servant,
> FRANCIS THEAKSTONE.

NOTE ON THE PRECEDING CORRESPONDENCE, ADDED BY MR. THEAKSTONE

The Inspector is not in a position to append any explanations of importance to the last of the letters. It has been
discovered that Mr. Matthew Sharpin left the house in
Rutherford Street five minutes after his interview outside
of it with Sergeant Bulmer—his manner expressing the
liveliest emotions of terror and astonishment, and his left
cheek displaying a bright patch of red, which might have
been the result of a slap on the face from a female hand.
He was also heard, by the shopman at Rutherford Street,
to use a very shocking expression in reference to Mrs. Yatman; and was seen to clench his fist vindictively, as he ran
round the corner of the street. Nothing more has been
heard of him; and it is conjectured that he has left London
with the intention of offering his valuable services to the
provincial police.

On the interesting domestic subject of Mr. and Mrs.
Yatman still less is known. It has, however, been positively
ascertained that the medical attendant of the family was
sent for in a great hurry, on the day when Mr. Yatman
returned from the milliner's shop. The neighbouring
chemist received, soon afterwards, a prescription of a sooth-

ing nature to make up for Mrs. Yatman. The day after, Mr. Yatman purchased some smelling-salts at the shop, and afterwards appeared at the circulating library to ask for a novel, descriptive of high life, that would amuse an invalid lady. It has been inferred from these circumstances, that he has not thought it desirable to carry out his threat of separating himself from his wife—at least in the present (presumed) condition of that lady's sensitive nervous system.

4
SIR ARTHUR CONAN DOYLE
The Adventure of the Speckled Band
5
The Adventures of Priory School

THE ADVENTURE OF THE SPECKLED BAND

IN glancing over my notes of the seventy odd cases in which I have during the last eight years studied the methods of my friend Sherlock Holmes, I find many tragic, some comic, a large number merely strange, but none commonplace; for, working as he did rather for the love of his art than for the acquirement of wealth, he refused to associate himself with any investigation which did not tend towards the unusual, and even the fantastic. Of all these varied cases, however, I cannot recall any which presented more singular features than that which was associated with the well-known Surrey family of the Roylotts of Stoke Moran. The events in question occurred in the early days of my association with Holmes, when we were sharing rooms as bachelors, in Baker-street. It is possible that I might have placed them upon record before, but a promise of secrecy was made at the time, from which I have only been freed during the last month by the untimely death of the lady to whom the pledge was given. It is perhaps as well that the facts should now come to light, for I have reasons to know there are widespread rumours as to the death of Dr. Grimesby Roylott which tend to make the matter even more terrible than the truth.

It was early in April, in the year '83, that I woke one morning to find Sherlock Holmes standing, fully dressed, by the side of my bed. He was a late riser as a rule, and, as the clock on the mantelpiece showed me that it was only a quarter past seven, I blinked up at him in some surprise, and perhaps just a little resentment, for I was myself regular in my habits.

"Very sorry to knock you up, Watson," said he, "but it's the common lot this morning. Mrs. Hudson has been knocked up, she retorted upon me, and I on you."

"What is it, then? A fire?"

"No, a client. It seems that a young lady has arrived in a considerable state of excitement, who insists upon seeing me. She is waiting now in the sitting-room. Now, when young ladies wander about the Metropolis at this hour of the morning, and knock sleepy people up out of their beds, I presume that it is something very pressing which they have to communicate. Should it prove to be an interesting case, you would, I am sure, wish to follow it from the outset. I thought at any rate that I should call you, and give you the chance."

" My dear fellow, I would not miss it for anything."

I had no keener pleasure than in following Holmes in his professional investigations, and in admiring the rapid deductions, as swift as intuitions, and yet always founded on a logical basis, with which he unravelled the problems which were submitted to him. I rapidly threw on my clothes, and was ready in a few minutes to accompany my friend down to the sitting-room. A lady dressed in black and heavily veiled, who had been sitting in the window, rose as we entered.

" Good morning, madam," said Holmes cheerily. " My name is Sherlock Holmes. This is my intimate friend and associate, Dr. Watson, before whom you can speak as freely as before myself. Ha, I am glad to see that Mrs. Hudson has had the good sense to light the fire. Pray draw up to it, and I shall order you a cup of hot coffee, for I observe that you are shivering."

" It is not cold which makes me shiver," said the woman in a low voice, changing her seat as requested.

" What then? "

" It is fear, Mr. Holmes. It is terror." She raised her veil as she spoke, and we could see that she was indeed in a pitiable state of agitation, her face all drawn and grey, with restless, frightened eyes, like those of some hunted animal. Her features and figure were those of a woman of thirty, but her hair was shot with premature grey, and her expression was weary and haggard. Sherlock Holmes ran her over with one of his quick, all-comprehensive glances.

" You must not fear," said he soothingly, bending forward and patting her forearm. " We shall soon set matters right, I have no doubt. You have come in by train this morning, I see."

" You know me, then? "

" No, but I observe the second half of a return ticket in

the palm of your left glove. You must have started early, and yet you had a good drive in a dog-cart, along heavy roads, before you reached the station."

The lady gave a violent start, and stared in bewilderment at my companion.

"There is no mystery, my dear madam," said he, smiling. "The left arm of your jacket is spattered with mud in no less than seven places. The marks are perfectly fresh. There is no vehicle save a dog-cart which throws up mud in that way, and then only when you sit on the left-hand side of the driver."

"Whatever your reasons may be, you are perfectly correct," said she. "I started from home before six, reached Leatherhead at twenty past, and came in by the first train to Waterloo. Sir, I can stand this strain no longer, I shall go mad if it continues. I have no one to turn to—none, save only one, who cares for me, and he, poor fellow, can be of little aid. I have heard of you, Mr. Holmes; I have heard of you from Mrs. Farintosh, whom you helped in the hour of her sore need. It was from her that I had your address. Oh, sir, do you not think you could help me too, and at least throw a little light through the dense darkness which surrounds me? At present it is out of my power to reward you for your services, but in a month or two I shall be married, with the control of my own income, and then at least you shall not find me ungrateful."

Holmes turned to his desk, and unlocking it, drew out a small case-book which he consulted.

"Farintosh," said he. "Ah, yes, I recall the case; it was concerned with an opal tiara. I think it was before your time, Watson. I can only say, madam, that I shall be happy to devote the same care to your case as I did to that of your friend. As to reward, my profession is its reward; but you are at liberty to defray whatever expenses I may be put to, at the time which suits you best. And now I beg that you will lay before us everything that may help us in forming an opinion upon the matter."

"Alas!" replied our visitor. "The very horror of my situation lies in the fact that my fears are so vague, and my suspicions depend so entirely upon small points, which might seem trivial to another, that even he to whom of all others I have a right to look for help and advice looks upon all that I tell him about it as the fancies of a nervous woman. He does not say so, but I can read it from his soothing answers and averted eyes. But I have heard, Mr. Holmes, that you can see deeply into the manifold wickedness of the human heart. You may advise me how to walk amid the dangers which encompass me."

" I am all attention, madam."

" My name is Helen Stoner, and I am living with my stepfather, who is the last survivor of one of the oldest Saxon families in England, the Roylotts of Stoke Moran, on the western border of Surrey."

Holmes nodded his head. " The name is familiar to me," said he.

" The family was at one time among the richest in England, and the estate extended over the borders into Berkshire in the north, and Hampshire in the west. In the last century, however, four successive heirs were of a dissolute and wasteful disposition, and the family ruin was eventually completed by a gambler, in the days of the Regency. Nothing was left save a few acres of ground and the two-hundred-year-old house, which is itself crushed under a heavy mortgage. The last squire dragged out his existence there, living the horrible life of an aristocratic pauper; but his only son, my stepfather, seeing that he must adapt himself to the new conditions, obtained an advance from a relative, which enabled him to take a medical degree, and went out to Calcutta, where, by his professional skill and his force of character, he established a large practice. In a fit of anger, however, caused by some robberies which had been perpetrated in the house, he beat his native butler to death, and narrowly escaped a capital sentence. As it was, he suffered a long term of imprisonment, and afterwards returned to England a morose and disappointed man.

" When Dr. Roylott was in India he married my mother, Mrs. Stoner, the young widow of Major-General Stoner, of the Bengal Artillery. My sister Julia and I were twins, and we were only two years old at the time of my mother's re-marriage. She had a considerable sum of money, not less than a thousand a year, and this she bequeathed to Dr. Roylott entirely whilst we resided with him, with a provision that a certain annual sum should be allowed to each of us in the event of our marriage. Shortly after our return to England my mother died—she was killed eight years ago in a railway accident near Crewe. Dr. Roylott then abandoned his attempts to establish himself in practice in London, and took us to live with him in the ancestral house at Stoke Moran. The money which my mother had left was enough for all our wants, and there seemed no obstacle to our happiness.

" But a terrible change came over our stepfather about this time. Instead of making friends and exchanging visits with our neighbours, who had at first been overjoyed to see a Roylott of Stoke Moran back in the old family seat, he shut himself up in his house, and seldom came out save to indulge in ferocious quarrels with whoever might cross his path. Violence of temper approaching to mania has been hereditary in the men of the family, and in my stepfather's case it had, I believe, been intensified by his long residence in the tropics. A series of disgraceful brawls took place, two of which ended in the police-court, until at last he became the terror of the village, and the folks would fly at his approach, for he is a man of immense strength, and absolutely uncontrollable in his anger.

" Last week he hurled the local blacksmith over a parapet into a stream, and it was only by paying over all the money that I could gather together that I was able to avert another public exposure. He had no friends at all save the wandering gipsies, and he would give these vagabonds leave to encamp upon the few acres of bramble-covered land which represent the family estate, and would accept in return the hospitality of their tents, wandering away with them sometimes for weeks on end. He has a passion also for Indian animals, which are sent over to him by a correspondent, and he has at this moment a cheetah and a baboon, which wander freely over his grounds, and are feared by the villagers almost as much as their master.

" You can imagine from what I say that my poor sister Julia and I had no great pleasure in our lives. No servant would stay with us, and for a long time we did all the work of the house. She was but thirty at the time of her death, and yet her hair had already begun to whiten, even as mine has."

" Your sister is dead, then? "

" She died just two years ago, and it is of her death that I wish to speak to you. You can understand that, living the

life which I have described, we were little likely to see anyone of our own age and position. We had, however, an
aunt, my mother's maiden sister, Miss Honoria Westphail,
who lives near Harrow, and we were occasionally allowed
to pay short visits at this lady's house. Julia went there at
Christmas two years ago, and met there a half-pay Major of
Marines, to whom she became engaged. My stepfather
learned of the engagement when my sister returned, and
offered no objection to the marriage; but within a fortnight
of the day which had been fixed for the wedding, the terrible
event occurred which has deprived me of my only companion."

Sherlock Holmes had been leaning back in his chair with
his eyes closed, and his head sunk in a cushion, but he half
opened his lids now, and glanced across at his visitor.

" Pray be precise as to details," said he.

" It is easy for me to be so, for every event of that dreadful
time is seared into my memory. The manor house is, as I
have already said, very old, and only one wing is now inhabited. The bedrooms in this wing are on the ground floor,
the sitting-rooms being in the central block of the buildings.
Of these bedrooms, the first is Dr. Roylott's, the second my
sister's, and the third my own. There is no communication
between them, but they all open out into the same corridor.
Do I make myself plain? "

" Perfectly so."

" The windows of the three rooms open out upon the lawn.
The fatal night Dr. Roylott had gone to his room early,
though we knew that he had not retired to rest, for my sister
was troubled by the smell of the strong Indian cigars which
it was his custom to smoke. She left her room, therefore,
and came into mine, where she sat for some time, chatting
about her approaching wedding. At eleven o'clock she rose
to leave me, but she paused at the door and looked back.

" ' Tell me, Helen,' said she, ' have you ever heard anyone
whistle in the dead of the night? '

" ' Never,' said I.

" ' I suppose that you could not possibly whistle yourself
in your sleep? '

" ' Certainly not. But why? '

" ' Because during the last few nights I have always, about
three in the morning, heard a low clear whistle. I am a light

sleeper, and it has awakened me. I cannot tell where it came from—perhaps from the next room, perhaps from the lawn. I thought that I would just ask you whether you had heard it.'

" ' No, I have not. It must be those wretched gipsies in the plantation.'

" ' Very likely. And yet if it were on the lawn I wonder that you did not hear it also.'

" ' Ah, but I sleep more heavily than you.'

" ' Well, it is of no great consequence at any rate,' she smiled back at me, closed my door, and a few moments later I heard her key turn in the lock."

" Indeed," said Holmes. " Was it your custom always to lock yourselves in at night? "

" Always."

" And why? "

" I think that I mentioned to you that the Doctor kept a cheetah and a baboon. We had no feeling of security unless our doors were locked."

" Quite so. Pray proceed with your statement."

" I could not sleep that night. A vague feeling of impending misfortune impressed me. My sister and I, you will recollect, were twins, and you know how subtle are the links which bind two souls which are so closely allied. It was a wild night. The wind was howling outside, and the rain was beating and splashing against the windows. Suddenly, amidst all the hubbub of the gale, there burst forth the wild scream of a terrified woman. I knew that it was my sister's voice. I sprang from my bed, wrapped a shawl round me, and rushed into the corridor. As I opened my door I seemed to hear a low whistle, such as my sister described, and a few moments later a clanging sound, as if a mass of metal had fallen. As I ran down the passage my sister's door was unlocked, and revolved slowly upon its hinges. I stared at it horror-stricken, not knowing what was about to issue from it. By the light of the corridor lamp I saw my sister appear at the opening, her face blanched with terror, her hands groping for help, her whole figure swaying to and fro like that of a drunkard. I ran to her and threw my arms round her, but at that moment her knees seemed to give way and she fell to the ground. She writhed as one who is in terrible pain, and her limbs were dreadfully convulsed. At first I thought that she had not recognised me, but as I bent over her she suddenly shrieked out in a voice which I shall never forget, 'O, my God! Helen! It was the band! The speckled band!' There was something else which she would fain have said, and she stabbed with her finger into the air in the direction of the Doctor's room, but a fresh convulsion seized her and choked her words. I rushed out, calling loudly for my stepfather, and I met him hastening from his room in his dressing-gown. When he reached my sister's side she was unconscious, and though he poured brandy down her throat, and sent for medical aid from the village, all efforts were in vain, for she slowly sank and died without having recovered her consciousness. Such was the dreadful end of my beloved sister."

"One moment," said Holmes; "are you sure about this whistle and metallic sound? Could you swear to it?"

"That was what the county coroner asked me at the inquiry. It is my strong impression that I heard it, and yet among the crash of the gale, and the creaking of an old house, I may possibly have been deceived."

"Was your sister dressed?"

"No, she was in her nightdress. In her right hand was found the charred stump of a match, and in her left a match-box."

"Showing that she had struck a light and looked about her when the alarm took place. That is important. And what conclusions did the coroner come to?"

"He investigated the case with great care, for Dr. Roylott's conduct had long been notorious in the county, but he was unable to find any satisfactory cause of death. My evidence showed that the door had been fastened upon the inner side, and the windows were blocked by old-fashioned shutters with broad iron bars, which were secured every night. The walls were carefully sounded, and were shown to be quite solid all round, and the flooring was also thoroughly examined, with the same result. The chimney is wide, but is barred up by four large staples. It is certain, therefore, that my sister was quite alone when she met her end. Besides, there were no marks of any violence upon her."

"How about poison?"

"The doctors examined her for it, but without success."

"What do you think that this unfortunate lady died of, then?"

"It is my belief that she died of pure fear and nervous shock, though what it was which frightened her I cannot imagine."

"Were there gipsies in the plantation at the time?"

"Yes, there are nearly always some there."

"Ah, and what did you gather from this allusion to a band—a speckled band?"

"Sometimes I have thought that it was merely the wild talk of delirium, sometimes that it may have referred to some band of people, perhaps to these very gipsies in the plantation. I do not know whether the spotted handkerchiefs which so many of them wear over their heads might have suggested the strange adjective which she used."

Holmes shook his head like a man who is far from being satisfied.

"These are very deep waters," said he; "pray go on with your narrative."

"Two years have passed since then, and my life has been until lately lonelier than ever. A month ago, however, a dear friend, whom I have known for many years, has done me the honour to ask my hand in marriage. His name is Armitage—Percy Armitage—the second son of Mr. Armitage, of Crane Water, near Reading. My stepfather has offered no opposition to the match, and we are to be married in the course of the spring. Two days ago some repairs were started in the west wing of the building, and my bedroom wall has been pierced, so that I have had to move into the chamber in which my sister died, and to sleep in the very bed in which she slept. Imagine, then, my thrill of terror when last night, as I lay awake, thinking over her terrible fate, I suddenly heard in the silence of the night the low whistle which had been the herald of her own death. I sprang up and lit the lamp, but nothing was to be seen in the room. I was too shaken to go to bed again, however, so I dressed, and as soon as it was daylight I slipped down, got a dog-cart at the Crown Inn, which is opposite, and drove to Leatherhead, from whence I have come on this morning, with the one object of seeing you and asking your advice."

"You have done wisely," said my friend. "But have you told me all?"

" Yes, all."

" Miss Roylott, you have not. You are screening your stepfather."

" Why, what do you mean? "

For answer Holmes pushed back the frill of black lace which fringed the hand that lay upon our visitor's knee. Five little livid spots, the marks of four fingers and a thumb, were printed upon the white wrist.

" You have been cruelly used," said Holmes.

The lady coloured deeply, and covered over her injured wrist. " He is a hard man," she said, " and perhaps he hardly knows his own strength."

There was a long silence, during which Holmes leaned his chin upon his hands and stared into the crackling fire.

" This is very deep business," he said at last. " There are a thousand details which I should desire to know before I decide upon our course of action. Yet we have not a moment to lose. If we were to come to Stoke Moran to-day, would it be possible for us to see over these rooms without the knowledge of your stepfather? "

" As it happens, he spoke of coming into town to-day upon some most important business. It is probable that he will be away all day, and that there would be nothing to disturb you. We have a housekeeper now, but she is old and foolish, and I could easily get her out of the way."

" Excellent. You are not averse to this trip, Watson? "

" By no means."

" Then we shall both come. What are you going to do yourself? "

" I have one or two things which I would wish to do now that I am in town. But I shall return by the twelve o'clock train, so as to be there in time for your coming."

" And you may expect us early in the afternoon. I have myself some small business matters to attend to. Will you not wait and breakfast? "

" No, I must go. My heart is lightened already since I have confided my trouble to you. I shall look forward to seeing you again this afternoon." She dropped her thick black veil over her face, and glided from the room.

" And what do you think of it all, Watson? " asked Sherlock Holmes, leaning back in his chair.

" It seems to me to be a most dark and sinister business."

" Dark enough and sinister enough."

" Yet if the lady is correct in saying that the flooring and walls are sound, and that the door, window, and chimney are impassable, then her sister must have been undoubtedly alone when she met her mysterious end."

" What becomes, then, of these nocturnal whistles, and what of the very peculiar words of the dying woman? "

" I cannot think."

" When you combine the ideas of whistles at night, the presence of a band of gipsies who are on intimate terms with this old doctor, the fact that we have every reason to believe that the doctor has an interest in preventing his step-daughter's marriage, the dying allusion to a band, and finally, the fact that Miss Helen Stoner heard a metallic clang, which might have been caused by one of those metal bars which secured the shutters falling back into their place, I think there is good ground to think that the mystery may be cleared along those lines."

" But what, then, did the gipsies do? "

" I cannot imagine."

" I see many objections to any such a theory."

" And so do I. It is precisely for that reason that we are going to Stoke Moran this day. I want to see whether the objections are fatal, or if they may be explained away. But what, in the name of the devil! "

The ejaculation had been drawn from my companion by the fact that our door had been suddenly dashed open, and that a huge man framed himself in the aperture. His costume was a peculiar mixture of the professional and of the agricultural, having a black top hat, a long frock-coat, and a pair of high gaiters, with a hunting-crop swinging in his hand. So tall was he that his hat actually brushed the cross-bar of the doorway, and his breadth seemed to span it across from side to side. A large face, seared with a thousand wrinkles, burned yellow with the sun, and marked with every evil passion, was turned from one to the other of us, while his deep-set, bile-shot eyes, and the high thin fleshless nose, gave him somewhat the resemblance to a fierce old bird of prey.

" Which of you is Holmes? " asked this apparition.

" My name, sir, but you have the advantage of me," said my companion quietly.

" I am Dr. Grimesby Roylott, of Stoke Moran."

" Indeed, Doctor," said Holmes blandly. " Pray take a seat."

" I will do nothing of the kind. My stepdaughter has been here. I have traced her. What has she been saying to you? "

" It is a little cold for the time of the year," said Holmes.

" What has she been saying to you? " screamed the old man furiously.

" But I have heard that the crocuses promise well," continued my companion imperturbably.

" Ha! You put me off, do you? " said our new visitor, taking a step forward, and shaking his hunting-crop. " I know you, you scoundrel! I have heard of you before. You are Holmes the meddler."

My friend smiled.

" Holmes the busybody! "

His smile broadened.

" Holmes the Scotland-yard Jack-in-office."

Holmes chuckled heartily. " Your conversation is most entertaining," said he. " When you go out close the door, for there is a decided draught."

" I will go when I have had my say. Don't you dare to meddle with my affairs. I know that Miss Stoner has been here—I traced her! I am a dangerous man to fall foul of! See here." He stepped swiftly forward, seized the poker, and bent it into a curve with his huge brown hands.

" See that you keep yourself out of my grip," he snarled, and hurling the twisted poker into the fireplace, he strode out of the room.

" He seems a very amiable person," said Holmes, laughing. " I am not quite so bulky, but if he had remained I might have shown him that my grip was not much more feeble than his own." As he spoke he picked up the steel poker, and with a sudden effort straightened it out again.

" Fancy his having the insolence to confound me with the official detective force! This incident gives zest to our investigation, however, and I only trust that our little friend will not suffer from her imprudence in allowing this brute to trace her. And now, Watson, we shall order breakfast, and afterwards I shall walk down to Doctors' Commons, where I hope to get some data which may help us in this matter."

It was nearly one o'clock when Sherlock Holmes returned from his excursion. He held in his hand a sheet of blue paper, scrawled over with notes and figures.

"I have seen the will of the deceased wife," said he. "To determine its exact meaning I have been obliged to work out the present prices of the investments with which it is concerned. Th total income, which at the time of the wife's death was little short of £1,100, is now through the fall in agricultural prices not more than £750. Each daughter can claim an income of £250, in case of marriage. It is evident, therefore, that if both girls had married this beauty would have had a mere pittance, while even one of them would cripple him to a serious extent. My morning's work has not been wasted, since it has proved that he has the very strongest motives for standing in the way of anything of the sort. And now, Watson, this is too serious for dawdling, especially as the old man is aware that we are interesting ourselves in his affairs, so if you are ready we shall call a cab and drive to Waterloo. I should be very much obliged if you would slip your revolver into your pocket. An Eley's No. 2 is an excellent argument with gentlemen who can twist steel pokers into knots. That and a tooth-brush are, I think, all that we need."

At Waterloo we were fortunate in catching a train for Leatherhead, where we hired a trap at the station inn, and drove for four or five miles through the lovely Surrey lanes. It was a perfect day, with a bright sun and a few fleecy clouds in the heavens. The trees and wayside hedges were just throwing out their first green shoots, and the air was full of the pleasant smell of the moist earth. To me at least there was a strange contrast between the sweet promise of the spring and this sinister quest upon which we were engaged. My companion sat in front of the trap, his arms folded, his hat pulled down over his eyes, and his chin sunk upon his breast, buried in the deepest thought. Suddenly, however, he started, tapped me on the shoulder, and pointed over the meadows.

"Look there!" said he.

A heavily-timbered park stretched up in a gentle slope, thickening into a grove at the highest point. From amidst the branches there jutted out the grey gables and high roof-tree of a very old mansion.

" Stoke Moran? " said he.

" Yes, sir, that be the house of Dr. Grimesby Roylott,"
remarked the driver.

" There is some building going on there," said Holmes;
" that is where we are going."

" There's the village," said the driver, pointing to a cluster
of roofs some distance to the left; " but if you want to get
to the house, you'll find it shorter to go over this stile, and
so by the foot-path over the fields. There it is, where the
lady is walking."

" And the lady, I fancy, is Miss Stoner," observed Holmes,
shading his eyes. " Yes, I think we had better do as you
suggest."

We got off, paid our fare, and the trap rattled back on its
way to Leatherhead.

" I thought it as well," said Holmes, as we climbed the
stile, " that this fellow should think we had come here as
architects, or on some definite business. It may stop his
gossip. Good afternoon, Miss Stoner. You see that we have
been as good as our word."

Our client of the morning had hurried forward to meet
us with a face which spoke her joy. " I have been waiting so
eagerly for you," she cried, shaking hands with us warmly.
" All has turned out splendidly. Dr. Roylott has gone to
town, and it is unlikely that he will be back before evening."

" We have had the pleasure of making the Doctor's acquaintance," said Holmes, and in a few words he sketched
out what had occurred. Miss Stoner turned white to the
lips as she listened.

" Good heavens! " she cried, " he has followed me, then."

" So it appears."

" He is so cunning that I never know when I am safe
from him. What will he say when he returns? "

" He must guard himself, for he may find that there is
someone more cunning than himself upon his track. You
must lock yourself from him to-night. If he is violent, we
shall take you away to your aunt's at Harrow. Now, we
must make the best use of our time, so kindly take us at once
to the rooms which we are to examine."

The building was of grey, lichen-blotched stone, with a
high central portion, and two curving wings, like the claws
of a crab, thrown out on each side. In one of these wings

the windows were broken, and blocked with wooden boards, while the roof was partly caved in, a picture of ruin. The central portion was in little better repair, but the right-hand block was comparatively modern, and the blinds in the windows, with the blue smoke curling up from the chimneys, showed that this was where the family resided. Some scaffolding had been erected against the end wall, and the stonework had been broken into, but there were no signs of any workmen at the moment of our visit. Holmes walked slowly up and down the ill-trimmed lawn, and examined with deep attention the outsides of the windows.

" This, I take it, belongs to the room in which you used to sleep, the centre one to your sister's, and the one next to the main building to Dr. Roylott's chamber? "

" Exactly so. But I am now sleeping in the middle one."

" Pending the alterations, as I understand. By the way, there does not seem to be any very pressing need for repairs at that end wall."

" There were none. I believe that it was an excuse to move me from my room."

" Ah! that is suggestive. Now, on the other side of this narrow wing runs the corridor from which these three rooms open. There are windows in it, of course? "

" Yes, but very small ones. Too narrow for anyone to pass through."

" As you both locked your doors at night your rooms were unapproachable from that side. Now, would you have the kindness to go into your room, and to bar your shutters."

Miss Stoner did so, and Holmes, after a careful examination through the open window, endeavoured in every way to force the shutter open, but without success. There was no slit through which a knife could be passed to raise the bar. Then with his lens he tested the hinges, but they were of solid iron, built firmly into the massive masonry. " Hum! " said he, scratching his chin in some perplexity, " my theory certainly presents some difficulty. No one could pass these shutters if they were bolted. Well, we shall see if the inside throws any light upon the matter."

A small side-door led into the whitewashed corridor from which the three bedrooms opened. Holmes refused to examine the third chamber, so we passed at once to the second, that in which Miss Stoner was now sleeping, and in which her sister had met her fate. It was a homely little room, with a low ceiling and a gaping fire-place, after the fashion of old country houses. A brown chest of drawers stood in one corner, a narrow white-counterpaned bed in another, and a dressing-table on the left-hand side of the window. These articles, with two small wickerwork chairs, made up all the furniture in the room, save for a square of Wilton carpet in the centre. The boards round and the panelling of the walls were brown, worm-eaten oak, so old and discoloured that it may have dated from the original building of the house. Holmes drew one of the chairs into a corner and sat silent, while his eyes travelled round and round and up and down, taking in every detail of the apartment.

" Where does that bell communicate with? " he asked at last, pointing to a thick bell-rope which hung down beside the bed, the tassel actually lying upon the pillow.

" It goes to the housekeeper's room."

" It looks newer than the other things? "

" Yes, it was only put there a couple of years ago."

" Your sister asked for it, I suppose? "

" No, I never heard of her using it. We used always to get what we wanted for ourselves."

" Indeed, it seemed unnecessary to put so nice a bell-pull there. You will excuse me for a few minutes while I satisfy myself as to this floor." He threw himself down upon his face with his lens in his hand, and crawled swiftly backwards and forwards, examining minutely the cracks between the boards. Then he did the same with the woodwork with which the chamber was panelled. Finally he walked over to the bed and spent some time in staring at it, and in running his eye up and down the wall. Finally he took the bell-rope in his hand and gave it a brisk tug.

" Why, it's a dummy," said he.

" Won't it ring? "

" No, it is not even attached to a wire. This is very interesting. You can see now that it is fastened to a hook just above where the little opening of the ventilator is."

" How very absurd! I never noticed that before."

" Very strange! " muttered Holmes, pulling at the rope. " There are one or two very singular points about this room.

For example, what a fool a builder must be to open a ventilator in another room, when, with the same trouble, he might have communicated with the outside air! "

" That is also quite modern," said the lady.

" Done about the same time as the bell-rope," remarked Holmes.

" Yes, there were several little changes carried out about that time."

" They seem to have been of a most interesting character —dummy bell-ropes, and ventilators which do not ventilate. With your permission, Miss Stoner, we shall now carry our researches into the inner apartment."

Dr. Grimesby Roylott's chamber was larger than that of his stepdaughter, but was as plainly furnished. A camp bed, a small wooden shelf full of books, mostly of a technical character, an arm-chair beside the bed, a plain wooden chair against the wall, a round table, and a large iron safe were the principal things which met the eye. Holmes walked slowly round and examined each and all of them with the keenest interest.

" What's in here? " he asked, tapping the safe.

" My stepfather's business papers."

" Oh! you have seen inside, then! "

" Only once, some years ago. I remember that it was full of papers."

" There isn't a cat in it, for example? "

" No. What a strange idea! "

" Well, look at this! " He took up a small saucer of milk which stood on the top of it.

" No; we don't keep a cat. But there is a cheetah and a baboon."

" Ah, yes, of course! Well, a cheetah is just a big cat, and yet a saucer of milk does not go very far in satisfying its wants, I dare say. There is one point which I should wish to determine." He squatted down in front of the wooden chair, and examined the seat of it with the greatest attention.

" Thank you. That is quite settled," said he, rising and putting his lens in his pocket. " Hullo! here is something interesting! "

The object which had caught his eye was a small dog lash hung on one corner of the bed. The lash, however, was curled upon itself, and tied so as to make a loop of whip-cord.

" What do you make of that, Watson? "

" It's a common enough lash. But I don't know why it should be tied."

" That is not quite so common, is it? Ah, me! it's a wicked world, and when a clever man turns his brain to crime it is the worst of all. I think that I have seen enough now, Miss Stoner, and, with your permission, we shall walk out upon the lawn."

I had never seen my friend's face so grim, or his brow so dark, as it was when we turned from the scene of this investigation. We had walked several times up and down the lawn, neither Miss Stoner nor myself liking to break in upon his thoughts before he roused himself from his reverie.

" It is very essential, Miss Stoner," said he, " that you should absolutely follow my advice in every respect."

" I shall most certainly do so."

" The matter is too serious for any hesitation. Your life may depend upon your compliance."

" I assure you that I am in your hands."

" In the first place, both my friend and I must spend the night in your room."

Both Miss Stoner and I gazed at him in astonishment.

" Yes, it must be so. Let me explain. I believe that that is the village inn over there? "

" Yes, that is the ' Crown.' "

" Very good. Your windows would be visible from there? "

" Certainly."

" You must confine yourself to your room, on pretence of a headache, when your stepfather comes back. Then when you hear him retire for the night, you must open the shutters of your window, undo the hasp, put your lamp there as a signal to us, and then withdraw with everything which you are likely to want into the room which you used to occupy. I have no doubt that, in spite of the repairs, you could manage there for one night."

" Oh, yes, easily."

" The rest you will leave in our hands."

" But what will you do? "

" We shall spend the night in your room, and we shall investigate the cause of this noise which has disturbed you."

" I believe, Mr. Holmes, that you have already made up your mind," said Miss Stoner, laying her hand upon my companion's sleeve.

" Perhaps I have."

" Then for pity's sake tell me what was the cause of my sister's death."

" I should prefer to have clearer proofs before I speak."

" You can at least tell me whether my own thought is correct, and if she died from some sudden fright."

" No, I do not think so. I think that there was probably some more tangible cause. And now, Miss Stoner, we must leave you, for if Dr. Roylott returned and saw us, our journey would be in vain. Good-bye, and be brave, for if you will do what I have told you, you may rest assured that we shall soon drive away the dangers that threaten you."

Sherlock Holmes and I had no difficulty in engaging a bedroom and sitting-room at the Crown Inn. They were on the upper floor, and from our window we could command a view of the avenue gate, and of the inhabited wing of Stoke Moran Manor House. At dusk we saw Dr. Grimesby Roylott drive past, his huge form looming up beside the little figure of the lad who drove him. The boy had some slight difficulty in undoing the heavy iron gates, and we heard the hoarse roar of the Doctor's voice, and saw the fury with which he shook his clenched fists at him. The trap drove on, and a few minutes later we saw a sudden light spring up among the trees as the lamp was lit in one of the sitting-rooms.

" Do you know, Watson," said Holmes, as we sat together in the gathering darkness, " I have really some scruples as to taking you to-night. There is a distinct element of danger."

" Can I be of assistance? "

" Your presence might be invaluable."

" Then I shall certainly come."

" It is very kind of you."

" You speak of danger. You have evidently seen more in these rooms than was visible to me."

" No, but I fancy that I may have deduced a little more. I imagine that you saw all that I did."

" I saw nothing remarkable save the bell-rope, and what purpose that could answer I confess is more than I can imagine."

" You saw the ventilator, too? "

" Yes, but I do not think that it is such a very unusual thing to have a small opening between two rooms. It was so small that a rat could hardly pass through."

" I knew that we should find a ventilator before ever we came to Stoke Moran."

" My dear Holmes! "

" Oh, yes, I did. You remember in her statement she said that her sister could smell Dr. Roylott's cigar. Now, of course that suggests at once that there must be a communication between the two rooms. It could only be a small one, or it would have been remarked upon at the coroner's inquiry. I deduced a ventilator."

" But what harm can there be in that? "

" Well, there is at least a curious coincidence of dates. A ventilator is made, a cord is hung, and a lady who sleeps in the bed dies. Does not that strike you? "

" I cannot as yet see any connection."

" Did you observe anything very peculiar about that bed? "

" No."

" It was clamped to the floor. Did you ever see a bed fastened like that before? "

" I cannot say that I have."

" The lady could not move her bed. It must always be in the same relative position to the ventilator and to the rope—for so we may call it, since it was clearly never meant for a bell-pull."

" Holmes," I cried, " I seem to see dimly what you are hitting at. We are only just in time to prevent some subtle and horrible crime."

" Subtle enough and horrible enough. When a doctor does go wrong he is the first of criminals. He has nerve and he has knowledge. Palmer and Pritchard were among the heads of their profession. This man strikes even deeper, but I think, Watson, that we shall be able to strike deeper still. But we shall have horrors enough before the night is over: for goodness' sake let us have a quiet pipe, and turn our minds for a few hours to something more cheerful."

About nine o'clock the light among the trees was extinguished, and all was dark in the direction of the Manor House. Two hours passed slowly away, and then, suddenly, just at the stroke of eleven, a single bright light shone out right in front of us.

"That is our signal," said Holmes, springing to his feet; "it comes from the middle window."

As we passed out he exchanged a few words with the landlord, explaining that we were going on a late visit to an acquaintance, and that it was possible that we might spend the night there. A moment later we were out on the dark road, a chill wind blowing in our faces, and one yellow light twinkling in front of us through the gloom to guide us on our sombre errand.

There was little difficulty in entering the grounds, for unrepaired breaches gaped in the old park wall. Making our way among the trees, we reached the lawn, crossed it, and were about to enter through the window, when out from a clump of laurel bushes there darted what seemed to be a hideous and distorted child, who threw itself on the grass with writhing limbs, and then ran swiftly across the lawn into the darkness.

"My God!" I whispered, "did you see it?"

Holmes was for the moment as startled as I. His hand closed like a vice upon my wrist in his agitation. Then he broke into a low laugh, and put his lips to my ear.

"It is a nice household," he murmured, "that is the baboon."

I had forgotten the strange pets which the Doctor affected. There was a cheetah, too; perhaps we might find it upon our shoulders at any moment. I confess that I felt easier in my mind when, after following Holmes' example and slipping off my shoes, I found myself inside the bedroom. My companion noiselessly closed the shutters, moved the lamp on to the table, and cast his eyes round the room. All was as we had seen it in the day-time. Then creeping up to me and making a trumpet of his hand, he whispered into my ear again so gently that it was all that I could do to distinguish the words:

" The least sound would be fatal to our plans."

I nodded to show that I had heard.

" We must sit without a light. He would see it through the ventilator."

I nodded again.

" Do not go to sleep; your very life may depend upon it. Have your pistol ready in case we should need it. I will sit on the side of the bed, and you in that chair."

I took out my revolver and laid it on the corner of the table.

Holmes had brought up a long thin cane, and this he placed upon the bed beside him. By it he laid the box of matches and the stump of a candle. Then he turned down the lamp and we were left in darkness.

How shall I ever forget that dreadful vigil? I could not hear a sound, not even the drawing of a breath, and yet I knew that my companion sat open-eyed, within a few feet of me, in the same state of nervous tension in which I was myself. The shutters cut off the least ray of light, and we waited in absolute darkness. From outside came the occasional cry of a night-bird, and once at our very window a long drawn, cat-like whine, which told us that the cheetah was indeed at liberty. Far away we could hear the deep tones of the parish clock, which boomed out every quarter of an hour. How long they seemed, those quarters! Twelve o'clock, and one, and two, and three, and still we sat waiting silently for whatever might befall.

Suddenly there was the momentary gleam of a light up in the direction of the ventilator, which vanished immediately, but was succeeded by a strong smell of burning oil and heated metal. Some one in the next room had lit a dark lantern. I heard a gentle sound of movement, and then all was silent once more, though the smell grew stronger. For half an hour I sat with straining ears. Then suddenly another sound became audible—a very gentle, soothing sound, like that of a small jet of steam escaping continually from a kettle. The instant that we heard it, Holmes sprang from the bed, struck a match, and lashed furiously with his cane at the bell-pull.

" You see it, Watson? " he yelled. " You see it? "

But I saw nothing. At the moment when Holmes struck the light I heard a low, clear whistle, but the sudden glare flashing into my weary eyes made it impossible for me to tell what it was at which my friend lashed so savagely. I could, however, see that his face was deadly pale, and filled with horror and loathing.

He had ceased to strike, and was gazing up at the ventilator, when suddenly there broke from the silence of the night the most horrible cry to which I have ever listened. It swelled up louder and louder, a hoarse yell of pain and fear and anger all mingled in the one dreadful shriek. They say that away down in the village, and even in the distant parsonage, that cry raised the sleepers from their beds. It struck cold to our hearts, and I stood gazing at Holmes, and he at me, until the last echoes of it had died away into the silence from which it rose.

" What can it mean? " I gasped.

" It means that it is all over," Holmes answered. " And perhaps, after all, it is for the best. Take your pistol, and we shall enter Dr. Roylott's room."

With a grave face he lit the lamp, and led the way down the corridor. Twice he struck at the chamber door without any reply from within. Then he turned the handle and entered, I at his heels, with the cocked pistol in my hand.

It was a singular sight which met our eyes. On the table stood a dark lantern with the shutter half open, throwing a brilliant beam of light upon the iron safe, the door of which was ajar. Beside this table, on the wooden chair, sat Dr. Grimesby Roylott, clad in a long grey dressing-gown, his bare ankles protruding beneath, and his feet thrust into red heelless Turkish slippers. Across his lap lay the short stock with the long lash which we had noticed during the day. His chin was cocked upwards, and his eyes were fixed in a dreadful rigid stare at the corner of the ceiling. Round his brow he had a peculiar yellow band, with brownish speckles, which seemed to be bound tightly round his head. As we entered he made neither sound nor motion.

" The band! the speckled band! " whispered Holmes.

I took a step forward. In an instant his strange headgear began to move, and there reared itself from among his hair the squat diamond-shaped head and puffed neck of a loathsome serpent.

" It was a swamp adder! " cried Holmes—" the deadliest snake in India. He has died within ten seconds of being bitten. Violence does, in truth, recoil upon the violent, and the schemer falls into the pit which he digs for another. Let us thrust this creature back into its den, and we can then remove Miss Stoner to some place of shelter, and let the county police know what has happened."

As he spoke he drew the dog whip swiftly from the dead man's lap, and throwing the noose round the reptile's neck, he drew it from its horrid perch, and, carrying it at arm's length, threw it into the iron safe, which he closed upon it.

Such are the true facts of the death of Dr. Grimesby Roylott, of Stoke Moran. It is not necessary that I should prolong a narrative which has already run to too great a length, by telling how we broke the sad news to the terrified girl, how we conveyed her by the morning train to the care of her good aunt at Harrow, of how the slow process of official inquiry came to the conclusion that the Doctor met his fate while indiscreetly playing with a dangerous pet. The little which I had yet to learn of the case was told me by Sherlock Holmes as we travelled back next day.

"I had," said he, "come to an entirely erroneous conclusion, which shows, my dear Watson, how dangerous it always is to reason from insufficient data. The presence of the gipsies, and the use of the word 'band,' which was used by the poor girl, no doubt, to explain the appearance which she had caught a horrid glimpse of by the light of her match, were sufficient to put me upon an entirely wrong scent. I can only claim the merit that I instantly reconsidered my position when, however, it became clear to me that whatever danger threatened an occupant of the room could not come either from the window or the door. My attention was speedily drawn, as I have already remarked to you, to this ventilator, and to the bell-rope which hung down to the bed. The discovery that this was a dummy, and that the bed was clamped to the floor, instantly gave rise to the suspicion that the rope was there as a bridge for something passing through the hole, and coming to the bed. The idea of a snake instantly occurred to me, and when I coupled it with my knowledge that the Doctor was furnished with a supply of creatures from India, I felt that I was probably on the right track. The idea of using a form of poison which could not possibly be discovered by any chemical test was just such a one as would occur to a clever and ruthless man who had had an Eastern training. The rapidity with which such a poison would take effect would also, from his point of view, be an advantage. It would be a sharp-eyed coroner indeed who could distinguish the two little dark punctures which would show where the poison fangs had done their work. Then I thought of the whistle. Of course, he must recall the snake before the morning light revealed it to the victim. He had trained it, probably by the use of the milk which we saw, to return to him when summoned. He would put it through the ventilator at the hour that he thought best, with the certainty that it would crawl down the rope, and land on the bed. It might or might not bite the occupant, perhaps she might escape every night for a week, but sooner or later she must fall a victim.

" I had come to these conclusions before ever I had entered his room. An inspection of his chair showed me that he had been in the habit of standing on it, which, of course, would be necessary in order that he should reach the ventilator. The sight of the safe, the saucer of milk, and the loop of whipcord were enough to finally dispel any doubts which may have remained. The metallic clang heard by Miss Stoner was obviously caused by her father hastily closing the door of his safe upon its terrible occupant. Having once made up my mind, you know the steps which I took in order to put the matter to the proof. I heard the creature hiss, as I have no doubt that you did also, and I instantly lit the light and attacked it."

" With the result of driving it through the ventilator."

" And also with the result of causing it to turn upon its master at the other side. Some of the blows of my cane came home, and roused its snakish temper, so that it flew upon the first person it saw. In this way I am no doubt indirectly responsible for Dr. Grimesby Roylott's death, and I cannot say that it is likely to weigh very heavily upon my conscience."

THE ADVENTURE OF THE PRIORY SCHOOL

WE have had some dramatic entrances and exits upon our small stage at Baker Street, but I cannot recollect anything more sudden and startling than the first appearance of Dr. Thorneycroft Huxtable, M.A., Ph.D., etc. His card, which seemed too small to carry the weight of his academic distinctions, preceded him by a few seconds, and then he entered himself—so large, so pompous, and so dignified that he was the very embodiment of self-possession and solidity. And yet his first action when the door had closed behind him was to stagger against the table, whence he slipped down upon the floor, and there was that majestic figure prostrate and insensible upon our bearskin hearthrug.

We had sprung to our feet, and for a few moments we stared in silent amazement at this ponderous piece of wreckage, which told of some sudden and fatal storm far out on the ocean of life. Then Holmes hurried with a cushion for his head, and I with brandy for his lips. The heavy white face was seamed with lines of trouble, the hanging pouches under the closed eyes were leaden in colour, the loose mouth dropped dolorously at the corners, the rolling chins were unshaven. Collar and shirt bore the grime of a long journey, and the hair bristled unkempt from the well-shaped head. It was a sorely stricken man who lay before us.

" What is it, Watson ? " asked Holmes.

" Absolute exhaustion—possibly mere hunger and fatigue," said I, with my finger on the thready pulse, where the stream of life trickled thin and small.

" Return ticket from Mackleton, in the North of England," said Holmes, drawing it from the watch-pocket. " It is not twelve o'clock yet. He has certainly been an early starter."

The puckered eyelids had begun to quiver, and now a pair of vacant grey eyes looked up at us. An instant later the man had scrambled on to his feet, his face crimson with shame.

" Forgive this weakness, Mr. Holmes ; I have been a little overwrought. Thank you, if I might have a glass of milk and a biscuit I have no doubt that I should be better. I came personally, Mr. Holmes, in order to ensure that you would return with me. I feared that no telegram would convince you of the absolute urgency of the case."

" When you are quite restored——"

" I am quite well again. I cannot imagine how I came to be so weak. I wish you, Mr. Holmes, to come to Mackleton with me by the next train."

My friend shook his head.

" My colleague, Dr. Watson, could tell you that we are very busy at present. I am retained in this case of the Ferrers Documents, and the Abergavenny murder is coming up for trial. Only a very important issue could call me from London at present."

" Important ! " Our visitor threw up his hands. " Have you heard nothing of the abduction of the only son of the Duke of Holdernesse ? "

" What ! the late Cabinet Minister ? "

" Exactly. We had tried to keep it out of the papers, but there was some rumour in the *Globe* last night. I thought it might have reached your ears."

Holmes shot out his long, thin arm and picked out Volume " H " in his encyclopædia of reference.

" ' Holdernesse, sixth Duke, K.G., P.C.'—half the alphabet ! ' Baron Beverley, Earl of Carston '—dear me, what a list ! ' Lord-Lieutenant of Hallamshire since 1900. Married Edith, daughter of Sir Charles Appledore, 1888. Heir and only child, Lord Saltire. Owns about two hundred and fifty thousand acres. Minerals in Lancashire and Wales. Address : Carlton House Terrace ; Holdernesse Hall, Hallamshire ; Carston Castle, Bangor, Wales. Lord of the Admiralty, 1872 ; Chief Secretary of State for——' Well, well, this man is certainly one of the greatest subjects of the Crown ! "

" The greatest and perhaps the wealthiest. I am aware, Mr. Holmes, that you take a very high line in professional matters, and that you are prepared to work for the work's sake. I may tell you, however, that his Grace has already intimated that a cheque for five thousand pounds will be handed over to the person who can tell him where his son is, and another thousand to him who can name the man, or men, who have taken him."

" It is a princely offer," said Holmes. " Watson, I think that we shall accompany Dr. Huxtable back to the North of England. And now, Dr. Huxtable, when you have consumed that milk you will kindly tell me what has happened, when it happened, how it happened, and, finally, what Dr. Thorneycroft Huxtable, of the Priory School, near Mackleton, has to do with the matter, and why he comes three days after an event—the state of your chin gives the date—to ask for my humble services."

Our visitor had consumed his milk and biscuits. The light had come back to his eyes and the colour to his cheeks as he set himself with great vigour and lucidity to explain the situation.

" I must inform you, gentleman, that the Priory is a preparatory school, of which I am the founder and principal. *Huxtable's Sidelights on Horace* may possibly recall my name to your memories. The Priory is, without exception, the best and most select preparatory school in England. Lord Leverstoke, the Earl of Blackwater, Sir Cathcart Soames— they all have entrusted their sons to me. But I felt that my school had reached its zenith when, three weeks ago, the Duke of Holdernesse sent Mr. James Wilder, his secretary, with the intimation that young Lord Saltire, ten years old, his only son and heir, was about to be committed to my charge. Little did I think that this would be the prelude to the most crushing misfortune of my life.

" On May 1 the boy arrived, that being the beginning of the summer term. He was a charming youth, and he soon fell into our ways. I may tell you—I trust that I am not indiscreet ; half-confidences are absurd in such a case— that he was not entirely happy at home. It is an open secret that the duke's married life had not been a peaceful one, and the matter had ended in a separation by mutual consent, the duchess taking up her residence in the South of France. This had occurred very shortly before, and the boy's sympathies are known to have been strongly with his mother. He moped after her departure from Holdernesse Hall, and it was for this reason that the duke desired to send him to my establishment. In a fortnight the boy was quite at home with us, and was apparently absolutely happy.

" He was last seen on the night of May 13—that is, the night of last Monday. His room was on the second floor, and was approached through another larger room in which two boys were sleeping. These boys saw and heard nothing, so that it is certain that young Saltire did not pass out that way. His window was open, and there is a stout ivy plant leading to the ground. We could trace no footmarks below, but it is sure that this is the only possible exit.

" His absence was discovered at seven o'clock on Tuesday morning. His bed had been slept in. He had dressed himself fully before going off in his usual school suit of black Eton jacket and dark grey trousers. There were no signs that any one had entered the room, and it is quite certain that anything in the nature of cries or a struggle would have been heard, since Caunter, the elder boy in the inner room, is a very light sleeper.

" When Lord Saltire's disappearance was discovered I at once called a roll of the whole establishment—boys, masters, and servants. It was then that we ascertained that Lord Saltire had not been alone in his flight. Heidegger, the German master, was missing. His room was on the second floor, at the farther end of the building, facing the same way as Lord Saltire's. His bed had also been slept in ; but he had apparently gone away partly dressed, since his shirt and socks were lying on the floor. He had undoubtedly let himself down by the ivy, for we could see the marks of his feet where he had landed on the lawn. His bicycle was kept in a small shed beside this lawn, and it also was gone.

" He had been with me for two years, and came with the best references ; but he was a silent, morose man, not very popular either with masters or boys. No trace could be found of the fugitives, and now on Thursday morning we are as ignorant as we were on Tuesday. Inquiry was, of course, made at once at Holdernesse Hall. It is only a few miles away, and we imagined that in some sudden attack of homesickness he had gone back to his father ; but nothing had been heard of him. The duke is greatly agitated—and as to me, you have seen yourselves the state of nervous prostration to which the suspense and the responsibility have reduced me. Mr. Holmes, if ever you put forward your full powers, I implore you to do so now, for never in your life could you have a case which is more worthy of them."

Sherlock Holmes had listened with the utmost intentness to the statement of the unhappy schoolmaster. His drawn brows and the deep furrow between them showed that he needed no exhortation to concentrate all his attention upon a problem which, apart from the tremendous interests involved, must appeal so directly to his love of the complex and the unusual. He now drew out his notebook and jotted down one or two memoranda.

" You have been very remiss in not coming to me sooner," said he severely. " You start me on my investigation with a very serious handicap. It is inconceivable, for example, that this ivy and this lawn would have yielded nothing to an expert observer."

" I am not to blame, Mr. Holmes. His Grace was extremely desirous to avoid all public scandal. He was afraid of his family unhappiness being dragged before the world. He has a deep horror of anything of the kind."

" But there has been some official investigation ? "

" Yes, sir, and it has proved most disappointing. An apparent clue was at once obtained, since a boy and a young man were reported to have been seen leaving a neighbouring station by an early train. Only last night we had news that the couple had been hunted down in Liverpool, and they prove to have no connection whatever with the matter in hand. Then it was that in my despair and disappointment, after a sleepless night, I came straight to you by the early train."

" I suppose the local investigation was relaxed while this false clue was being followed up ? "

" It was entirely dropped."

" So that three days have been wasted. The affair has been most deplorably handled."

" I feel it, and admit it."

" And yet the problem should be capable of ultimate solution. I shall be very happy to look into it. Have you been able to trace any connection between the missing boy and this German master ? "

" None at all."

" Was he in the master's class ? "

" No ; he never exchanged a word with him, so far as I know."

"That is certainly very singular. Had the boy a bicycle ? "

" No."

" Was any other bicycle missing ? "

" No."

" Is that certain ? "

" Quite."

" Well, now, you do not mean to seriously suggest that this German rode off upon a bicycle in the dead of the night bearing the boy in his arms ? "

" Certainly not."

" Then what is the theory in your mind ? "

" The bicycle may have been a blind. It may have been hidden somewhere, and the pair gone off on foot."

" Quite so ; but it seems rather an absurd blind, does it not ? Were there other bicycles in this shed ? "

" Several."

" Would he not have hidden *a couple* had he desired to give the idea that they had gone off upon them ? "

" I suppose he would."

" Of course he would. The blind theory won't do. But the incident is an admirable starting-point for an investigation. After all, a bicycle is not an easy thing to conceal or to destroy. One other question. Did any one call to see the boy on the day before he disappeared ? "

" No."

" Did he get any letters ? "

" Yes ; one letter."

" From whom ? "

" From his father."

" Do you open the boys' letters ? "

" No."

" How do you know it was from the father ? "

" The coat of arms was on the envelope, and it was addressed in the duke's peculiar stiff hand. Besides, the duke remembers having written."

" When had he a letter before that ? "

" Not for several days."

" Had he ever one from France ? "

" No ; never."

" You see the point of my questions, of course. Either the boy was carried off by force or he went of his own free will. In the latter case you would expect that some prompting from outside would be needed to make so young a lad do such a thing. If he has had no visitors, that prompting must have come in letters. Hence I try to find out who were his correspondents."

" I fear I cannot help you much. His only correspondent, so far as I know, was his own father."

" Who wrote to him on the very day of his disappearance. Were the relations between father and son very friendly ? "

" His Grace is never very friendly with any one. He is completely immersed in large public questions, and is rather inaccessible to all ordinary emotions. But he was always kind to the boy in his own way."

" But the sympathies of the latter were with the mother ? "

" Yes."

" Did he say so ? "

" No."

" The duke, then ? "

" Good heavens, no ! "

" Then how could you know ? "

" I have had some confidential talk with Mr. James Wilder, his Grace's secretary. It was he who gave me the information about Lord Saltire's feelings."

" I see. By the way, that last letter of the duke's— was it found in the boy's room after he was gone ? "

" No ; he had taken it with him. I think, Mr. Holmes, it is time that we were leaving for Euston."

" I will order a four-wheeler. In a quarter of an hour we shall be at your service. If you are telegraphing home, Mr. Huxtable, it would be well to allow the people in your neighbourhood to imagine that the inquiry is still going on in Liverpool, or wherever else that red herring led your pack. In the meantime I will do a little quiet work at your own doors, and perhaps the scent is not so cold but that two old hounds like Watson and myself may get a sniff of it."

That evening found us in the cold, bracing atmosphere of the Peak country, in which Dr. Huxtable's famous school is situated. It was already dark when we reached it. A card was lying on the hall table, and the butler whispered something to his master, who turned to us with agitation in every heavy feature.

" The duke is here," said he. " The duke and Mr.

Wilder are in the study. Come, gentlemen, and I will introduce you."

I was, of course, familiar with the pictures of the famous statesman, but the man himself was very different from his representation. He was a tall and stately person, scrupulously dressed, with a drawn, thin face, and a nose which was grotesquely curved and long. His complexion was of a dead pallor, which was more startling by contrast with a long, dwindling beard of vivid red, which flowed down over his white waistcoat, with his watch-chain gleaming through its fringe. Such was the stately presence who looked stonily at us from the centre of Dr. Huxtable's hearthrug. Beside him stood a very young man, whom I understood to be Wilder, the private secretary. He was small, nervous, alert, with intelligent, light blue eyes and mobile features. It was he who at once, in an incisive and positive tone, opened the conversation.

" I called this morning, Dr. Huxtable, too late to prevent you from starting for London. I learned that your object was to invite Mr. Sherlock Holmes to undertake the conduct of this case. His Grace is surprised, Dr. Huxtable, that you should have taken such a step without consulting him."

" When I learned the police had failed——"

" His Grace is by no means convinced that the police have failed."

" But surely, Mr. Wilder——"

" You are well aware, Dr. Huxtable, that his Grace is particularly anxious to avoid all public scandal. He prefers to take as few people as possible into his confidence."

" The matter can be easily remedied," said the browbeaten doctor. " Mr. Sherlock Holmes can return to London by the morning train."

" Hardly that, doctor, hardly that," said Holmes, in his blandest voice. " This northern air is invigorating and pleasant, so I propose to spend a few days upon your moors, and to occupy my mind as best I may. Whether I have the shelter of your roof or of the village inn is, of course, for you to decide."

I could see that the unfortunate doctor was in the last stage of indecision, from which he was rescued by the deep, sonorous voice of the red-bearded duke, which boomed out like a dinner-gong.

" I agree with Mr. Wilder, Dr. Huxley, that you would have done wisely to consult me. But since Mr. Holmes has already been taken into your confidence, it would indeed be absurd that we should not avail ourselves of his services. Far from going to the inn, Mr. Holmes, I should be pleased if you would come and stay with me at Holdernesse Hall."

" I thank your Grace. For the purposes of my investigation I think that it would be wiser for me to remain at the scene of the mystery."

" Just as you like, Mr. Holmes. Any information which Mr. Wilder or I can give you is, of course, at your disposal."

" It will probably be necessary for me to see you at the Hall," said Holmes. " I would only ask you now, sir, whether you have formed any explanation in your own mind as to the mysterious disappearance of your son ? "

" No, sir, I have not."

" Excuse me if I allude to that which is painful to you, but I have no alternative. Do you think that the duchess had anything to do with the matter ? "

The great minister showed perceptible hesitation.

" I do not think so," he said at last.

" The other most obvious explanation is that the child had been kidnapped for the purpose of levying ransom. You have not had any demand of the sort ? "

" No, sir."

" One more question, your Grace. I understand that you wrote to your son upon the day when this incident occurred."

" No ; I wrote upon the day before."

" Exactly. But he received it on that day ? "

" Yes."

" Was there anything in your letter which might have unbalanced him or induced him to take such a step ? "

" No, sir, certainly not."

" Did you post that letter yourself ? "

The nobleman's reply was interrupted by his secretary, who broke in with some heat.

" His Grace is not in the habit of posting letters himself," said he. " This letter was laid with others upon the study table, and I myself put them in the post-bag."

" You are sure this one was among them ? "

" Yes ; I observed it."

" How many letters did your Grace write that day ? "

" Twenty or thirty.   I have a large correspondence.   But surely this is somewhat irrelevant ? "

" Not entirely," said Holmes.

" For my own part," the duke continued, " I have advised the police to turn their attention to the South of France.   I have already said that I do not believe that the duchess would encourage so monstrous an action, but the lad had the most wrong-headed opinions, and it is possible that he may have fled to her, aided and abetted by this German.   I think, Dr. Huxtable, that we will now return to the Hall."

I could see that there were other questions which Holmes would have wished to put ; but the nobleman's abrupt manner showed that the interview was at an end.   It was evident that to his intensely aristocratic nature this discussion of his intimate family affairs with a stranger was most abhorrent, and that he feared lest every fresh question would throw a fiercer light into the discreetly shadowed corners of his ducal history.

When the nobleman and his secretary had left, my friend flung himself at once with characteristic eagerness into the investigation.

The boy's chamber was carefully examined, and yielded nothing save the absolute conviction that it was only through the window that he could have escaped.   The German master's room and effects gave no further clue.   In his case a trailer of ivy had given way under his weight, and we saw by the light of a lantern the mark on the lawn where his heels had come down.   That one dent in the short green grass was the only material witness left of this inexplicable nocturnal flight.

Sherlock Holmes left the house alone, and only returned after eleven.   He had obtained a large ordnance map of the neighbourhood, and this he brought into my room, where he laid it out on the bed, and, having balanced the lamp in the middle of it, he began to smoke over it, and occasionally to point out objects of interest with the reeking amber of his pipe.

" This case grows upon me, Watson," said he.   " There are decidedly some points of interest in connection with it. In this early stage I want you to realise these geographical features, which may have a good deal to do with our investigation.

" Look at this map. This dark square is the Priory School. I'll put a pin in it. Now, this line is the main road. You see that it runs east and west past the school, and you see also there is no side road for a mile either way. If these two folk passed away by road it was *this* road."

" Exactly."

" By a singular and happy chance we are able to some extent to check what passed along this road during the night in question. At this point, where my pipe is now resting, a country constable was on duty from twelve to six. It is, as you perceive, the first cross road on the east side. This man declares that he was not absent from his post for an instant, and he is positive that neither boy nor man could have gone that way unseen. I have spoken with this policeman to-night, and he appears to me to be a perfectly reliable person. That blocks this end. We have now to deal with the other. There is an inn here, the ' Red Bull,' the landlady of which was ill. She had sent to Mackleton for a doctor, but he did not arrive until morning, being absent at another case. The people at the inn were alert all night, awaiting his coming, and one or other of them seems to have continually had an eye upon the road. They declare that no one passed. If their evidence is good, then we are fortunate enough to be able to block the west, and also to be able to say that the fugitives did *not* use the road at all."

" But the bicycle ? " I objected.

" Quite so. We will come to the bicycle presently. To continue our reasoning : if these people did not go by the road, they must have traversed the country to the north of the house or to the south of the house. That is certain. Let us weigh the one against the other. On the south of the house is, as you perceive, a large district of arable land, cut up into small fields, with stone walls between them. There, I admit that a bicycle is impossible. We can dismiss the idea. We turn to the country on the north. Here there lies a grove of trees, marked as the ' Ragged Shaw,' and on the farther side stretches a great rolling moor, Lower Gill Moor, extending for ten miles, and sloping gradually upwards. Here, at one side of this wilderness, is Holdernesse Hall, ten miles by road, but only six across the moor.

It is a peculiarly desolate plain. A few moor farmers have small holdings, where they rear sheep and cattle. Except these, the plover and the curlew are the only inhabitants until you come to the Chesterfield high road. There is a church there, you see, a few cottages, and an inn. Beyond that the hills become precipitous. Surely it is here to the north that our quest must lie."

" But the bicycle ? " I persisted.

" Well, well ! " said Holmes impatiently. " A good cyclist does not need a high road. The moor is intersected with paths, and the moon was at the full. Halloa ! What is this ? "

There was an agitated knock at the door, and an instant afterwards Dr. Huxtable was in the room. In his hand he held a blue cricket-cap, with a white chevron on the peak.

" At last we have a clue ! " he cried. " Thank Heaven, at last we are on the dear boy's track ! It is his cap."

" Where was it found ? "

" In the van of the gipsies who camped on the moor. They left on Tuesday. To-day the police traced them down and examined their caravan. This was found."

" How do they account for it ? "

" They shuffled and lied—said that they found it on the moor on Tuesday morning. They know where he is, the rascals ! Thank goodness, they are all safe under lock and key. Either the fear of the law or the duke's purse will certainly get out of them all that they know."

" So far, so good," said Holmes, when the doctor had at last left the room. " It at least bears out the theory that it is on the side of the Lower Gill Moor that we must hope for results. The police have really done nothing locally, save the arrest of these gipsies. Look here, Watson ! There is a watercourse across the moor. You see it marked here in the map. In some parts it widens into a morass. This is particularly so in the region between Holdernesse Hall and the school. It is vain to look elsewhere for tracks in this dry weather ; but at *that* point there is certainly a chance of some record being left. I will call you early to-morrow morning, and you and I will try if we can throw some light upon the mystery."

The day was just breaking when I woke to find the long,

thin form of Holmes by my bedside. He was fully dressed, and had apparently already been out.

" I have done the lawn and the bicycle shed," said he. " I have also had a ramble through the Ragged Shaw. Now, Watson, there is cocoa ready in the next room. I must beg you to hurry, for we have a great day before us."

His eyes shone, and his cheek was flushed with the exhilaration of the master workman who sees his work lies ready before him. A very different Holmes, this active, alert man, from the introspective and pallid dreamer of Baker Street. I felt, as I looked upon that supple figure, alive with nervous energy, that it was indeed a strenuous day that awaited us.

And yet it opened in the blackest disappointment. With high hopes we struck across the peaty, russet moor, intersected with a thousand sheep-paths, until we came to the broad, light-green belt which marked the morass between us and Holdernesse. Certainly, if the lad had gone homewards, he must have passed this, and he would not pass it without leaving his trace. But no sign of him or the German could be seen. With a darkening face my friend strode along the margin, eagerly observant of every muddy stain upon the mossy surface. Sheep-marks there were in profusion, and at one place, some miles down, cows had left their tracks. Nothing more.

" Check number one," said Holmes, looking gloomily over the rolling expanse of the moor. " There is another morass down yonder, and a narrow neck between. Halloa ! halloa ! halloa ! What have we here ? "

We had come on a small black ribbon of pathway. In the middle of it, clearly marked on the sodden soil, was the track of a bicycle.

" Hurrah ! " I cried. " We have it."

But Holmes was shaking his head, and his face was puzzled and expectant rather than joyous.

" A bicycle certainly, but not *the* bicycle," said he. " I am familiar with forty-two different impressions left by tyres. This, as you perceive, is a Dunlop, with a patch upon the outer cover. Heidegger's tyres were Palmers, leaving longitudinal stripes. Aveling, the mathematical master, was sure upon the point. Therefore it is not Heidegger's track."

" The boy's, then ? "

" Possibly, if we could prove a bicycle to have been in his possession. But this we have utterly failed to do. This track, as you perceive, was made by a rider who was going from the direction of the school."

" Or towards it ? "

" No, no, my dear Watson. The more deeply sunk impression is, of course, the hind wheel, upon which the weight rests. You perceive several places where it has passed across and obliterated the more shallow mark of the front one. It was undoubtedly heading away from the school. It may or may not be connected with our inquiry, but we will follow it backwards before we go any farther."

We did so, and at the end of a few hundred yards lost the tracks as we emerged from the boggy portion of the moor. Following the path backwards, we picked out another spot, where a spring trickled across it. Here, once again, was the mark of the bicycle, though nearly obliterated by the hoofs of cows. After that there was no sign, but the path ran right on into Ragged Shaw, the wood which backed on to the school. From this wood the cycle must have emerged. Holmes sat down on a boulder and rested his chin in his hands. I had smoked two cigarettes before he moved.

" Well, well," said he at last. " It is, of course, possible that a cunning man might change the tyre of his bicycle in order to leave unfamiliar tracks. A criminal who was capable of such a thought is a man whom I should be proud to do business with. We will leave this question undecided and hark back to our morass again, for we have left a good deal unexplored."

We continued our systematic survey of the edge of the sodden portion of the moor, and soon our perseverance was gloriously rewarded.

Right across the lower part of the bog lay a miry path. Holmes gave a cry of delight as he approached it. An impression like a fine bundle of telegraph wires ran down the centre of it. It was the Palmer tyre.

" Here is Herr Heidegger, sure enough ! " cried Holmes exultantly. " My reasoning seems to have been pretty sound, Watson."

" I congratulate you."

" But we have a long way still to go. Kindly walk clear

of the path. Now let us follow the trail. I fear that it will not lead very far."

We found, however, as we advanced, that this portion of the moor is intersected with soft patches, and, though we frequently lost sight of the track, we always succeeded in picking it up once more.

" Do you observe," said Holmes, " that the rider is now undoubtedly forcing the pace ? There can be no doubt of it. Look at this impression, where you get both tyres clear. The one is as deep as the other. That can only mean that the rider is throwing his weight on to the handle-bar as a man does when he is sprinting. By Jove ! he has had a fall."

There was a broad, irregular smudge covering some yards of the track. Then there were a few footmarks, and the tyre reappeared once more.

" A side-slip," I suggested.

Holmes held up a crumpled branch of flowering gorse. To my horror I perceived that the yellow blossoms were all dabbled with crimson. On the path, too, and among the heather were dark stains of clotted blood.

" Bad ! " said Holmes. " Bad ! Stand clear, Watson ! Not an unnecessary footstep ! What do I read here ? He fell wounded, he stood up, he remounted, he proceeded. But there is no other track. Cattle on this side path. He was surely not gored by a bull ? Impossible ! But I see no traces of anyone else. We must push on, Watson. Surely, with stains as well as the track to guide us, he cannot escape us now."

Our search was not a very long one. The tracks of the tyre began to curve fantastically upon the wet and shining path. Suddenly, as I looked ahead, the gleam of metal caught my eye from amid the thick gorse bushes. Out of them we dragged a bicycle. Palmer-tyred, one pedal bent, and the whole front of it horribly smeared and slobbered with blood. On the other side of the bushes a shoe was projecting. We ran round, and there lay the unfortunate rider. He was a tall man, full bearded, with spectacles, one glass of which had been knocked out. The cause of his death was a frightful blow upon the head, which had crushed in part of his skull. That he could have gone on after receiving such an injury said much for the vitality and courage of the man. He wore shoes, but no socks, and his open coat disclosed a night-shirt beneath it. It was undoubtedly the German master.

Holmes turned the body over reverently, and examined it with great attention. He then sat in deep thought for a time, and I could see by his ruffled brow that this grim discovery had not, in his opinion, advanced us much in our inquiry.

" It is a little difficult to know what to do, Watson," said he, at last. " My own inclinations are to push this inquiry on, for we have already lost so much time that we cannot afford to waste another hour. On the other hand, we are bound to inform the police of this discovery, and to see that this poor fellow's body is looked after."

" I could take a note back."

" But I need your company and assistance. Wait a bit ! There is a fellow cutting peat up yonder. Bring him over here, and he will guide the police."

I brought the peasant across, and Holmes dispatched the frightened man with a note to Dr. Huxtable.

" Now, Watson," said he, " we have picked up two clues this morning. One is the bicycle with the Palmer tyre, and we see what that has led to. The other is the bicycle with the patched Dunlop. Before we start to investigate that, let us try to realise what we *do* know, so as to make the most of it, and to separate the essential from the accidental.

" First of all, I wish to impress upon you that the boy certainly left of his own free will. He got down from his window and he went off, either alone or with someone. That is sure."

I assented.

" Well, now, let us turn to this unfortunate German master. The boy was fully dressed when he fled. Therefore he foresaw what he would do. But the German went without his socks. He certainly acted on very short notice."

" Undoubtedly."

" Why did he go ? Because, from his bedroom window, he saw the flight of the boy. Because he wished to overtake him and bring him back. He seized his bicycle, pursued the lad, and in pursuing him met his death."

" So it would seem."

" Now I come to the critical part of my argument. The

natural action of a man in pursuing a little boy would be to run after him. He would know that he could overtake him. But the German does not do so. He turns to his bicycle. I am told that he was an excellent cyclist. He would not do this if he did not see that the boy had some swift means of escape."

" The other bicycle."

" Let us continue our reconstruction. He meets his death five miles from the school—not by a bullet, mark you, which even a lad might conceivably discharge, but by a savage blow dealt by a vigorous arm. The lad, then, *had* a companion in his flight. And the flight was a swift one, since it took five miles before an expert cyclist could overtake them. Yet we survey the ground round the scene of the tragedy. What do we find? A few cattle tracks, nothing more. I took a wide sweep round, and there is no path within fifty yards. Another cyclist could have had nothing to do with the actual murder. Nor were there any human footmarks."

" Holmes," I cried, " this is impossible."

" Admirable ! " he said. " A most illuminating remark. It *is* impossible as I state it, and therefore I must in some respect have stated it wrong. Yet you saw for yourself. Can you suggest any fallacy ? "

" He could not have fractured his skull in a fall ? "

" In a morass, Watson ? "

" I am at my wits' end."

" Tut, tut ; we have solved some worse problems. At least we have plenty of material, if we can only use it. Come, then, and, having exhausted the Palmer, let us see what the Dunlop with the patched cover has to offer us."

We picked up the track and followed it onwards for some distance ; but soon the moor rose into a long, heather-tufted curve, and we left the watercourse behind us. No further help from tracks could be hoped for. At the spot where we saw the last of the Dunlop tyre it might equally have led to Holdernesse Hall, the stately towers of which rose some miles to our left, or to a low, grey village which lay in front of us, and marked the position of the Chesterfield high road.

As we approached the forbidding and squalid inn, with the sign of a game-cock above the door, Holmes gave a sudden groan and clutched me by the shoulder to save himself from falling. He had had one of those violent strains of the ankle which leave a man helpless. With difficulty he limped up to the door, where a squat, dark, elderly man was smoking a black clay pipe.

" How are you, Mr. Reuben Hayes ? " said Holmes.

" Who are you, and how do you get my name so pat ? " the countryman answered, with a suspicious flash of a pair of cunning eyes.

" Well, it's printed on the board above your head. It's easy to see a man who is master of his own house. I suppose you haven't such a thing as a carriage in your stables ? "

" No ; I have not."

" I can hardly put my foot to the ground."

" Don't put it to the ground."

" But I can't walk."

" Well, then, hop."

Mr. Reuben Hayes's manner was far from gracious, but Holmes took it with admirable good humour.

" Look here, my man," said he. " This is really rather an awkward fix for me. I don't mind how I get on."

" Neither do I," said the morose landlord.

" The matter is very important. I would offer you a sovereign for the use of a bicycle."

The landlord pricked up his ears.

" Where do you want to go ? "

" To Holdernesse Hall."

" Pals of the dook, I suppose ? " said the landlord, surveying our mud-stained garments with ironical eyes.

Holmes laughed good-naturedly.

" He'll be glad to see us, anyhow."

" Why ? "

" Because we bring him news of his lost son."

The landlord gave a very visible start.

" What, you're on his track ? "

" He has been heard of in Liverpool. They expect to get him every hour."

Again a swift change passed over the heavy, unshaven face. His manner was suddenly genial.

" I've less reason to wish the dook well than most men," said he, " for I was his head coachman once, and cruel bad he treated me. It was him that sacked me without a character on the word of a lying corn-chandler. But I'm glad to hear that the young lord was heard of in Liverpool, and I'll help you to take the news to the Hall."

"Thank you," said Holmes. "We'll have some food first. Then you can bring round the bicycle."

"I haven't got a bicycle."

Holmes held up a sovereign.

"I tell you, man, that I haven't got one. I'll let you have two horses as far as the Hall."

"Well, well," said Holmes, "we'll talk about it when we've had something to eat."

When we were left alone in the stone-flagged kitchen it was astonishing how rapidly that sprained ankle recovered. It was nearly nightfall, and we had eaten nothing since early morning, so that we spent some time over our meal. Holmes was lost in thought, and once or twice he walked over to the window and stared earnestly out. It opened on to a squalid courtyard. In the far corner was a smithy, where a grimy lad was at work. On the other side were the stables. Holmes had sat down again after one of these excursions, when he suddenly sprang out of his chair with a loud exclamation.

"By Heaven, Watson, I believe that I've got it !" he cried. "Yes, yes, it must be so. Watson, do you remember seeing any cow-tracks to-day ? "

"Yes, several."

"Where ? "

"Well, everywhere. They were at the morass, and again on the path, and again near where poor Heidegger met his death."

"Exactly. Well, now, Watson, how many cows did you see on the moor ? "

"I don't remember seeing any."

"Strange, Watson, that we should see tracks all along our line, but never a cow on the whole moor ; very strange, Watson, eh ? "

"Yes, it is strange."

"Now, Watson, make an effort ; throw your mind back ! Can you see those tracks upon the path ? "

"Yes, I can."

"Can you recall that the tracks were sometimes like that, Watson "—he arranged a number of breadcrumbs in this

fashion—: : : : :—" and sometimes like this "—: •
: • : • : •—" and occasionally like this "—. • . . . •—
" Can you remember that ? "

" No, I cannot."

" But I can. I could swear to it. However, we will go back at our leisure and verify it. What a blind beetle I have been not to draw my conclusion ! "

" And what is your conclusion ? "

" Only that it is a remarkable cow which walks, canters, and gallops. By George, Watson, it was no brain of a country publican that thought out such a blind as that ! The coast seems to be clear, save for that lad in the smithy. Let us slip out and see what we can see."

There were two rough-haired, unkempt horses in the tumble-down stable. Holmes raised the hind leg of one of them and laughed aloud.

" Old shoes, but newly shod—old shoes, but new nails. This case deserves to be a classic. Let us go across to the smithy."

The lad continued his work without regarding us. I saw Holmes's eye darting to right and left among the litter of iron and wood which was scattered about the floor. Suddenly, however, we heard a step behind us, and there was the landlord, his heavy eyebrows drawn down over his savage eyes, his swarthy features convulsed with passion.

He held a short metal-headed stick in his hand, and he advanced in so menacing a fashion that I was right glad to feel the revolver in my pocket.

" You infernal spies ! " the man cried. " What are you doing there ? "

" Why, Mr. Reuben Hayes," said Holmes coolly, " one might think that you were afraid of our finding something out."

The man mastered himself with a violent effort, and his grim mouth loosened into a false laugh, which was more menacing than his frown.

" You're welcome to all you can find out in my smithy," said he. " But look here, mister, I don't care for folk poking about my place without my leave, so the sooner you pay your score and get out of this the better I shall be pleased."

" All right, Mr. Hayes—no harm meant," said Holmes. " We have been having a look at your horses ; but I think I'll walk after all. It's not far, I believe."

" Not more than two miles to the Hall gates. That's the road to the left." He watched us with sullen eyes until we had left his premises.

We did not go very far along the road, for Holmes stopped the instant that the curve hid us from the landlord's view.

" We were warm, as the children say, at that inn," said he. " I seem to grow colder every step that I take away from it. No, no ; I can't possibly leave it."

" I am convinced," said I, " that this Reuben Hayes knows all about it. A more self-evident villain I never saw."

" Oh ! he impressed you in that way, did he ? There are the horses, there is the smithy. Yes, it is an interesting place, this ' Fighting Cock.' I think we shall have another look at it in an unobtrusive way."

A long, sloping hillside, dotted with grey limestone boulders, stretched behind us. We had turned off the road, and were making our way up the hill, when, looking in the direction of Holdernesse Hall, I saw a cyclist coming swiftly along.

" Get down, Watson ! " cried Holmes, with a heavy hand upon my shoulder. We had hardly sunk from view when the man flew past us on the road. Amid a rolling cloud of dust I caught a glimpse of a pale, agitated face—a face with horror in every lineament, the mouth open, the eyes staring wildly in front. It was like some strange caricature of the dapper James Wilder whom we had seen the night before.

" The duke's secretary ! " cried Holmes. " Come, Watson, let us see what he does."

We scrambled from rock to rock until in a few moments we had made our way to a point from which we could see the front door of the inn. Wilder's bicycle was leaning against the wall beside it. No one was moving about the house, nor could we catch a glimpse of any faces at the windows. Slowly the twilight crept down as the sun sank behind the high towers of Holdernesse Hall. Then in the gloom we saw the two side-lamps of a trap light up in the stable-yard of the inn, and shortly afterwards heard the rattle of hoofs, as it wheeled out into the road and tore off at a furious pace in the direction of Chesterfield.

" What do you make of that, Watson ? " Holmes whispered.

" It looks like a flight."

" A single man in a dog-cart, so far as I could see. Well, it certainly was not Mr. James Wilder, for there he is at the door."

A red square of light had sprung out of the darkness. In the middle of it was the black figure of the secretary, his head advanced, peering out into the night. It was evident that he was expecting someone. Then at last there were steps in the road, a second figure was visible for an instant against the light, the door shut, and all was black once more. Five minutes later a lamp was lit in a room upon the first floor.

" It seems to be a curious class of custom that is done by the ' Fighting Cock,' " said Holmes.

" The bar is on the other side."

" Quite so. These are what one may call the private guests. Now, what in the world is Mr. James Wilder doing in that den at this hour of night, and who is the companion who comes to meet him there ? Come, Watson, we must really take a risk and try to investigate this a little more closely."

Together we stole down to the road and crept across to the door of the inn. The bicycle still leaned against the wall. Holmes struck a match and held it to the back wheel, and I heard him chuckle as the light fell upon a patched Dunlop tyre. Up above us was the lighted window.

" I must have a peep through that, Watson. If you bend your back and support yourself upon the wall, I think that I can manage."

An instant later his feet were on my shoulders. But he was hardly up before he was down again.

" Come, my friend," said he, " our day's work has been quite long enough. I think that we have gathered all that we can. It's a long walk to the school, and the sooner we get started the better."

He hardly opened his lips during that weary trudge across the moor, nor would he enter the school when he reached it, but went on to Mackleton Station, whence he could send some telegrams. Late at night I heard him consoling Dr. Huxtable, prostrated by the tragedy of his master's death, and later still he entered my room as alert and vigorous as he had been when he started in the morning. " All goes well, my friend," said he. " I promise that before to-morrow evening we shall have reached the solution of the mystery."

At eleven o'clock next morning my friend and I were walking up the famous yew avenue of Holdernesse Hall. We were ushered through the magnificent Elizabethan doorway and into his Grace's study. There we found Mr. James Wilder, demure and courtly, but with some trace of that wild terror of the night before still lurking in his furtive eyes and in his twitching features.

" You have come to see his Grace ? I am sorry ; but the fact is that the duke is far from well. He has been very much upset by the tragic news. We received a telegram from Dr. Huxtable yesterday afternoon, which told us of your discovery."

" I must see the duke, Mr. Wilder."

" But he is in his room."

" Then I must go to his room."

" I believe he is in his bed."

" I will see him there."

Holmes's cold and inexorable manner showed the secretary that it was useless to argue with him.

" Very good, Mr. Holmes ; I will tell him that you are here."

After half an hour's delay the great nobleman appeared. His face was more cadaverous than ever, his shoulders had rounded, and he seemed to me to be an altogether older man than he had been the morning before. He greeted us with a stately courtesy, and seated himself at his desk, his red beard streaming down on to the table.

" Well, Mr. Holmes ? " said he.

But my friend's eyes were fixed upon the secretary, who stood by his master's chair.

" I think, your Grace, that I could speak more freely in Mr. Wilder's absence."

The man turned a shade paler and cast a malignant glance at Holmes.

" If your Grace wishes——"

" Yes, yes ; you had better go. Now, Mr. Holmes, what have you to say ? "

My friend waited until the door had closed behind the retreating secretary.

" The fact is, your Grace," said he, " that my colleague, Dr. Watson, and myself had an assurance from Dr. Huxtable that a reward had been offered in this case.   I should like to have this confirmed from your own lips."

" Certainly, Mr. Holmes."

" It amounted, if I am correctly informed, to five thousand pounds to anyone who will tell you where your son is ? "

" Exactly."

" And another thousand to the man who will name the person or persons who keep him in custody ? "

" Exactly."

" Under the latter heading is included, no doubt, not only those who may have taken him away, but also those who conspire to keep him in his present position ? "

" Yes, yes," cried the duke impatiently.   " If you do your work well, Mr. Sherlock Holmes, you will have no reason to complain of niggardly treatment."

My friend rubbed his thin hands together with an appearance of avidity which was a surprise to me, who knew his frugal tastes.

" I fancy that I see your Grace's cheque-book upon the table," said he.   " I should be glad if you would make me out a cheque for six thousand pounds.   It would be as well, perhaps, for you to cross it.   The Capital and Counties Bank, Oxford Street branch, are my agents."

His Grace sat very stern and upright in his chair, and looked stonily at my friend.

" Is this a joke, Mr. Holmes ?   It is hardly a subject for pleasantry."

" Not at all, your Grace.   I was never more earnest in my life."

" What do you mean, then ? "

" I mean that I have earned the reward.   I know where your son is, and I know some, at least, of those who are holding him."

The duke's beard had turned more aggressively red than ever against his ghastly white face.

" Where is he ? " he gasped.

" He is, or was last night, at the Fighting Cock Inn, about two miles from your park gate."

The duke fell back in his chair.

" And whom do you accuse ? "

Sherlock Holmes's answer was an astounding one. He stepped swiftly forward and touched the duke upon the shoulder.

" I accuse *you*," said he. " And now, your Grace, I'll trouble you for that cheque."

Never shall I forget the duke's appearance as he sprang up and clawed with his hand like one who is sinking into an abyss. Then, with an extraordinary effort of aristocratic self-command, he sat down and sank his face in his hands. It was some minutes before he spoke.

" How much do you know ? " he asked at last, without raising his head.

" I saw you together last night."

" Does anyone else besides your friend know ? "

" I have spoken to no one."

The duke took a pen in his quivering fingers and opened his cheque-book.

" I shall be as good as my word, Mr. Holmes. I am about to write your cheque, however unwelcome the information which you have gained may be to me. When the offer was first made I little thought the turn which events would take. But you and your friend are men of discretion, Mr. Holmes ? "

" I hardly understand your Grace."

" I must put it plainly, Mr. Holmes. If only you two know of the incident, there is no reason why it should go any farther. I think twelve thousand pounds is the sum that I owe you, is it not ? "

But Holmes smiled, and shook his head.

" I fear, your Grace, that matters can hardly be arranged so easily. There is the death of this schoolmaster to be accounted for."

" But James knew nothing of that. You cannot hold him responsible for that. It was the work of this brutal ruffian whom he had the misfortune to employ."

" I must take the view, your Grace, that when a man embarks upon a crime he is morally guilty of any other crime which may spring from it."

" Morally, Mr. Holmes. No doubt you are right. But surely not in the eyes of the law. A man cannot be condemned for a murder at which he was not present, and which he loathes and abhors as much as you do. The instant that he heard of it he made a complete confession to me, so filled was he with horror and remorse. He lost not an hour in breaking entirely with the murderer. Oh, Mr. Holmes, you must save him—you must save him ! I tell you that you must save him ! " The duke had dropped the last attempt at self-command, and was pacing the room with a convulsed face and with his clenched hands raving in the air. At last he mastered himself and sat down once more at his desk. " I appreciate your conduct in coming here before you spoke to anyone else," said he. " At least we may take counsel how far we can minimise this hideous scandal."

" Exactly," said Holmes. " I think, your Grace, that this can only be done by absolute and complete frankness between us. I am disposed to help your Grace to the best of my ability ; but in order to do so I must understand to the last detail how the matter stands. I realise that your words applied to Mr. James Wilder, and that he is not the murderer."

" No ; the murderer has escaped."

Sherlock Holmes smiled demurely.

" Your Grace can hardly have heard of any small reputation which I possess, or you would not imagine that it is so easy to escape me. Mr. Reuben Hayes was arrested at Chesterfield on my information at eleven o'clock last night. I had a telegram from the head of the local police before I left the school this morning."

The duke leaned back in his chair and stared with amazement at my friend.

" You seem to have powers that are hardly human," said he. " So Reuben Hayes is taken ? I am right glad to hear it, if it will not react upon the fate of James."

" Your secretary ? "

" No, sir ; my son."

It was Holmes's turn to look astonished.

" I confess that this is entirely new to me, your Grace. I must beg of you to be more explicit."

" I will conceal nothing from you. I agree with you that complete frankness, however painful it may be to me, is the best policy in this desperate situation to which James's folly and jealousy have reduced us. When I was a young man,

Mr. Holmes, I loved with such a love as comes only once in a lifetime.   I offered the lady marriage, but she refused it on the grounds that such a match might mar my career. Had she lived I would certainly never have married anyone else.   She died, and left this one child, whom for her sake I have cherished and cared for.   I could not acknowledge the paternity to the world ; but I gave him the best of educations, and since he came to manhood I have kept him near my person.   He surprised my secret, and has presumed ever since upon the claim which he has upon me and upon his power of provoking a scandal, which would be abhorrent to me.   His presence had something to do with the unhappy issue of my marriage.   Above all, he hated my young legitimate heir from the first with a persistent hatred.   You may well ask me why, under these circumstances, I still kept James under my roof.   I answer that it was because I could see his mother's face in his, and that for her dear sake there was no end to my long-suffering.   All her pretty ways, too—there was not one of them which he could not suggest and bring back to my memory.   I *could* not send him away. But I feared so lest he should do Arthur—that is, Lord Saltire—a mischief that I dispatched him for safety to Dr. Huxtable's school.

" James came into contact with this fellow Hayes because the man was a tenant of mine, and James acted as agent. The fellow was a rascal from the beginning ; but in some extraordinary way James became intimate with him.   He had always a taste for low company.   When James determined to kidnap Lord Saltire it was of this man's service that he availed himself.   You remember that I wrote to Arthur upon that last day.   Well, James opened the letter and inserted a note asking Arthur to meet him in a little wood called the Ragged Shaw which is near to the school. He used the duchess's name, and in that way got the boy to come.   That evening James cycled over—I am telling you what he has himself confessed to me—and he told Arthur, whom he met in the wood, that his mother longed to see him, that she was awaiting him on the moor, and that if he would come back into the wood at midnight he would find a man with a horse, who would take him to her.   Poor Arthur fell into the trap.   He came to the appointment, and found this fellow Hayes with a led pony.   Arthur mounted, and they set off together. It appears—though this James only heard yesterday—that they were pursued, that Hayes struck the pursuer with his stick, and that the man died of his injuries. Hayes brought Arthur to his public-house, the 'Fighting Cock,' where he was confined in an upper room, under the care of Mrs. Hayes, who is a kindly woman, but entirely under the control of her brutal husband.

"Well, Mr. Holmes, that was the state of affairs when I first saw you two days ago. I had no more idea of the truth than you. You will ask me what was James's motive in doing such a deed. I answer that there was a great deal which was unreasoning and fanatical in the hatred which he bore my heir. In his view he should himself have been heir of all my estates, and he deeply resented those social laws which made it impossible. At the same time, he had a definite motive also. He was eager that I should break the entail, and he was of opinion that it lay in my power to do so. He intended to make a bargain with me—to restore Arthur if I would break the entail, and so make it possible for the estate to be left to him by will. He knew well that I should never willingly invoke the aid of the police against him. I say that he would have proposed such a bargain to me, but he did not actually do so, for events moved too quickly for him, and he had not time to put his plans into practice.

"What brought all his wicked scheme to wreck was your discovery of this man Heidegger's dead body. James was seized with horror at the news. It came to us yesterday as we sat together in this study. Dr. Huxtable had sent a telegram. James was so overwhelmed with grief and agitation that my suspicions, which had never been entirely absent, rose instantly to a certainty, and I taxed him with the deed. He made a complete voluntary confession. Then he implored me to keep his secret for three days longer, so as to give his wretched accomplice a chance of saving his guilty life. I yielded—as I have always yielded—to his prayers, and instantly James hurried off to the 'Fighting Cock' to warn Hayes and give him the means of flight. I could not go there by daylight without provoking comment, but as soon as night fell I hurried off to see my dear Arthur. I found him safe and well, but horrified beyond expression by the dreadful deed he had witnessed. In deference to my promise, and much against my will, I consented to leave him there for three days under the charge of Mrs. Hayes, since it was evident that it was impossible to inform the police where he was without telling them also who was the murderer, and I could not see how that murderer could be punished without ruin to my unfortunate James. You asked for frankness, Mr. Holmes, and I have taken you at your word, for I have now told you everything without an attempt at circumlocution or concealment. Do you in your turn be as frank with me."

" I will," said Holmes. " In the first place, your Grace, I am bound to tell you that you have placed yourself in a most serious position in the eyes of the law. You have condoned a felony, and you have aided the escape of a murderer ; for I cannot doubt that any money which was taken by James Wilder to aid his accomplice in his flight came from your Grace's purse."

The duke bowed his assent.

" This is indeed a most serious matter. Even more culpable, in my opinion, your Grace, is your attitude towards your younger son. You leave him in this den for three days."

" Under solemn promises——"

" What are promises to such people as these ? You have no guarantee that he will not be spirited away again. To humour your guilty elder son you have exposed your innocent younger son to imminent and unnecessary danger. It was a most unjustifiable action."

The proud lord of Holdernesse was not accustomed to be so rated in his own ducal hall. The blood flushed into his high forehead, but his conscience held him dumb.

" I will help you, but on one condition only. It is that you ring for the footman and let me give such orders as I like."

Without a word the duke pressed the electric button. A servant entered.

" You will be glad to hear," said Holmes, " that your young master is found. It is the duke's desire that the carriage shall go at once to the Fighting Cock Inn to bring Lord Saltire home."

" Now," said Holmes, when the rejoicing lackey had disappeared, " having secured the future we can afford to be more lenient with the past.   I am not in an official position, and there is no reason, so long as the ends of justice are served, why I should disclose all that I know.   As to Hayes I say nothing.   The gallows awaits him, and I would do nothing to save him from it.   What he will divulge I cannot tell, but I have no doubt that your Grace could make him understand that it is to his interest to be silent.   From the police point of view he will have kidnapped the boy for purpose of ransom.   If they do not themselves find it out, I see no reason why I should prompt them to take a broader view. I would warn your Grace, however, that the continued presence of Mr. James Wilder in your household can only lead to misfortune."

" I understand that, Mr. Holmes, and it is already settled that he shall leave me for ever and go to seek his fortune in Australia."

" In that case, your Grace, since you have yourself stated that any unhappiness in your married life was caused by his presence, I would suggest that you make such amends as you can to the duchess, and that you try to resume those relations which have been so unhappily interrupted."

" That also I have arranged, Mr. Holmes.   I wrote to the duchess this morning."

" In that case," said Holmes, rising, " I think that my friend and I can congratulate ourselves upon several most happy results from our little visit to the North.   There is one other small point upon which I desire some light.   This fellow Hayes had shod his horses with shoes which counterfeited the tracks of cows.   Was it from Mr. Wilder that he learned so extraordinary a device ? "

The duke stood in thought for a moment, with a look of intense surprise on his face.   Then he opened a door and showed us into a large room furnished as a museum.   He led the way to a glass case in a corner, and pointed to the inscription.

" These shoes," it ran, " were dug up in the moat of Holdernesse Hall.   They are for the use of horses ; but they are shaped below with a cloven foot of iron, so as to throw pursuers off the track.   They are supposed to have belonged to some of the marauding Barons of Holdernesse in the Middle Ages."

Holmes opened the case, and, moistening his finger, he

passed it along the shoe. A thin film of recent mud was left upon his skin.

"Thank you," said he, as he replaced the glass. "It is the second most interesting object that I have seen in the North."

"And the first?"

Holmes folded up his cheque, and placed it carefully in his notebook. "I am a poor man," said he, as he patted it affectionately, and thrust it into the depths of his inner pocket.

THE PURPLE DEATH

AROUND the big round table in the upper room of the Café de l'Univers the Crimes Club was holding its usual monthly meeting. All of the ten members, each of a different profession and each expert in his own walk of life, were present.

The *café noir* and liqueurs had been set, and the door locked, for no one was allowed at their secret deliberations, and no new member was admitted until death created a vacancy.

The secretary, the stout Madame Léontine van Hecke, suddenly addressed her companions in French, saying:

" Gentlemen, M. Dubosq wishes to consult you. I ask your attention, if you please."

Lucien Dubosq, smart in his dinner-jacket and wearing the coveted red rosette of the Legion of Honour in his lapel, rose, and after apologising for troubling the club, explained a problem which the English and French detective service had both failed to solve.

He said that in the interests of justice a very strange and mysterious affair was being hushed up by both Scotland Yard and the French police, a mystery upon which no light could be thrown, therefore he would briefly place the facts before the members for discussion, decision, and action.

On September 22nd, at four o'clock in the afternoon, two well-dressed men, one dark, half-bald and clean-shaven, about fifty-five years of age, and the other, a younger man in his early thirties, with fair, well-brushed hair and of a somewhat effeminate type, strolled along the beach road leading from the cinema to the fish market in the old town of Hastings, where the brown-sailed fishing smacks were lying ready to go out. There were still many London trippers about, and at a beach stall the two men bought some bananas, and, throwing themselves upon the shingle, ate them and smoked cigarettes. They conversed in low tones, evidently holding a consultation, the younger man differing from his companion.

Presently the younger man, having grown calm, drew his wallet from his pocket and, taking out something, handed it to his friend, who examined it. Then the other clapped his knee in satisfaction and returned it to his friend, who carefully replaced it in his pocket-book. Both laughed heartily, then rose, and walking back to the town, entered the Bodega, where a young, fair-haired girl of twenty-two awaited them, and they had a drink together. The girl was extremely well-dressed and had shingled hair. She wore a dark kid glove on her left hand, which apparently had some deformity.

All this was witnessed by Henry Hayes, an employee of the Hastings Corporation, whose duty was surveillance upon the beach fronting the old town, with its broken sea-wall and fishing harbour. He had noticed the rather unusual movements of the two well-dressed men, for such men did not usually eat bananas upon the beach. For that reason he noted their clothes. The elder man wore in his dark knotted cravat a beautiful cornflower-blue sapphire pin which had attracted Hayes as being very pretty.

When the men had entered the Bodega just as it had opened for its evening trade, Hayes relaxed his surveillance, for he had little to do, the trippers being orderly at that end of the town, which was the reverse to that stretch of beach between the Queen's Hotel and Hastings Pier.

That was the last seen of the two visitors to Hastings alive.

Thirty-four hours later, at three o'clock in the morning, the cross-Channel mail steamer, *Isle of Thanet*, when half-way between Dover and Calais, sounded her siren against a big sailing boat not showing the regulation lights. There was half a gale blowing, and the sails being set, she came straight across the bows of the *Isle of Thanet*, much to the anger of Captain Evans, who sounded his siren again and was compelled to alter his course sharply, avoiding a collision only by a few yards.

In the darkness he saw that it was a fishing smack, but there was no light nor any sign of life aboard. He drew up at risk of trouble at Calais Maritime over his delay, and so manœuvred his steamer as to follow the derelict.

Coming up alongside of her, he took up his megaphone and shouted to her skipper, first in French, then in Spanish, English, and Italian. But the fishing smack, tossing upon the heaving waters, made no sign.

"Ahoy, there !" he shouted. "Where the devil are you going ?" But again there was no response.

Realising that such a vessel adrift in the Channel without lights was a great danger to shipping, he at once sent off a boat's crew to board her, and stood by awaiting his men's report. The boat's crew had a difficult time in getting aboard in such a sea, but they managed to scramble up while Captain Evans turned on his searchlight to watch.

Most of the passengers were below because of the heavy gale blowing. Presently the second officer, named Richard Hardwick, who had gone with the party, came up and, waving his arms just as a heavy sea struck the smack, yelled to the Captain :

"There's something wrong here, sir ! We'll sail her into Calais and see you there."

"What's wrong ?" inquired Evans deeply through his megaphone.

"We can't tell yet, sir," was his officer's reply. Then Captain Evans waved farewell and continued on his course, knowing that he would delay the Paris mail by half an hour or even more.

Meanwhile Hardwick, the officer of the *Isle of Thanet*, had ordered the lights to be relit, the sails altered, and a course set for Calais, he having the flashing harbour light to steer by.

"Funny, ain't it, sir !" remarked Williams, the man at the helm, obeying Hardwick's orders as they followed in the wake of the brilliantly-lit cross-Channel steamer. "Can you make it out ?"

"No, I can't, Williams," was the officer's reply. "Keep her a point more westward." And then as the steersman altered the smack's course, another big sea struck her and she rose proudly from the trough. The night was not over-dark, but the moon was obscured by swift drifting clouds as it so often is in the Channel. Ever and anon, the stormy clouds parted and the moon shone in a long silver streak upon the wind-swept waters.

"The fellow for'ard looks like a gentleman," Williams remarked, just as another of his fellow-sailors passed along, a ghostly figure in the half light. " 'E's been done in, no doubt. I wonder 'ow ?"

"Who knows ? There will be an inquiry into the derelict

when we get into Calais," replied Hardwick. " The man's dead and we can't bring him to life. The only thing is to leave everything as it was—as I have given strict orders— and let the police solve the mystery of to-night's affair. It's beyond me, I admit, and—well—it gets on one's nerves. It is all so uncanny—three of them ! "

" Yes, sir, I agree. But where is the crew ? They've disappeared. They'll know something of 'em in Hastings, no doubt."

" Of course they will. But, as you say—where is the crew ? Three dead men aboard—and nobody else ! "

The fishing boat marked " CH. 38 " upon her sails, which had sailed the Channel for fifteen years, and was well known to every fisherman between the North Foreland and Port-land Bill, rose and fell, labouring heavily in the gale, the angry seas breaking over her every now and then, while the mail boat quickly out-distanced her in making for Calais harbour.

Two or three times the *Isle of Thanet* signalled dot-and-dash lights to the derelict, giving orders as to what Hardwick should do when entering the port.

Meanwhile Hardwick, who had spent his life on the Channel ferry, had all he could do to keep the brown-sailed old boat upon her course. The trawl was up—recently up, for fish, seaweed, and débris from it lay scattered about the swimming deck. But who had hauled it ? Certainly not the three men now aboard. The fishing crew had apparently suddenly disappeared, leaving the vessel to drift without lights, a serious menace to shipping. Indeed, as showing the strict watch kept upon the Channel waters, two tramp steamers, which had passed it an hour before, had reported it to the wireless station at Niton, in the Isle of Wight, as a dangerous derelict. This notice to mariners had, in turn, been transmitted to the Admiralty, who, a quarter of an hour later, had sent out a C.Q. message—which is the code-signal asking everyone to listen as all ships were warned of their danger.

Through the stormy waters the battered old fishing smack laboured on for a further two hours, until at last they were under the green and red lights which marked the entrance to Calais harbour, and a dexterous turn of the wheel from Williams brought her into calm water where, after much manœuvering, the boat was at last brought into the fishing port and tied up to the quay.

At once two French police agents, in hooded cloaks, boarded her, the Prefect of Police having already been notified by Captain Evans on the arrival of the *Isle of Thanet*. Evans and a plain-clothes policeman accompanied them.

" Well, Hardwick, what's wrong here ? " asked the Captain in his sharp, brusque way.

" I can't tell, sir. But you can see for yourself," was his officer's reply.

Examination of the dirty, dismal little vessel showed an amazing state of things.

In the bows lay the body of a fair-haired young man in a cheap tweed suit. He lay curled up, his features distorted, his eyes bulging, and his countenance a curious bright purple ; while down below in the small cabin lit by a single swinging oil lamp there were the remains of a rough supper upon the table, and dregs of red wine in enamelled cups. Lying on the floor were two other men, dead from no apparent cause. None of the trio were seafaring men, but the faces of all three were horribly distorted, their hands open instead of being clenched, and their faces bright purple. Yet there was no trace of the crew of four or five which such a vessel would carry.

In the cabin were signs of a violent quarrel. Some broken plates lay upon the floor, but they might have been swept off the table by the pitching of the boat when the trawl was down.

The police began a thorough search of the dead men's clothing, finding absolutely nothing to serve as a clue. But their investigations proved that the young man who was found in the bows of the boat was not a man at all, but a girl of about twenty-two or three with fair, close-cropped hair !

The curious discovery was at once reported by telephone to the Chief of Police of Calais, who, with his chief inspector, a well-known detective named Dufour, arrived on board. The bodies of all three were searched. The elder man, who was half-bald, wore in his cravat a cornflower sapphire pin set with four diamonds, and had in his pocket the return half of a first-class ticket from London Bridge to Hastings. The inside pocket of his jacket had been torn almost out, and his face had been bruised on the left jaw either through somebody striking him with their fist, or, perhaps, in falling.

The girl attired as a man seemed a lady. Upon her arm was a solid gold slave-bangle worth at least fifty pounds, while around her neck, beneath her man's shirt, she wore a thin gold chain from which was suspended a circle of emerald-green stone which was afterwards identified as chrysoprase. In her trousers pocket was a twenty-franc gold piece, evidently a souvenir. But upon her was no mark of violence except a slight discoloration of the thumb-nail on the right hand. The glove, on being removed from the left hand, showed it to be withered and looking almost like the hand of a skeleton, the thin skin upon the bones being white as marble.

The third man appeared to be aged about thirty. He wore sea-boots like his two companions, but upon his dead countenance was a look of inexpressible horror, as though he had faced some terrible shock at the moment of his death. His clothes were well-made, and upon him was found two pounds in Treasury notes and fifty francs in French bank notes. The palm of his open right hand was cut and had bled.

Beyond that all was mystery. Where was the crew of the fishing boat " CH. 38 " ?

The French police at once became active and telephoned a brief report of the discovery to Scotland Yard, and they, in turn, telephoned to the Hastings police asking them to at once make inquiry as to the owner of the " CH. 38," and what had become of the missing crew.

Soon a strange state of affairs became revealed. The boat belonged to a fishing company which had its headquarters at Grimsby and owned boats sailing from Brixham, Yarmouth and elsewhere. The skipper's name was Ben Benham, a man recently from Grimsby, as were the three hands. The original crew of the vessel had been transferred to Grimsby, Benham and his men taking their place. They had only been out on four previous trips, but what had happened to them that night was a complete mystery.

The Hastings police, assisted by two expert officers from Scotland Yard, made every inquiry, but all fruitless. The Calais police had done the same, and inquiries had been made at all the ports of the Pas-de-Calais, but without avail.

Thus the problem put before the club by Monsieur Dubosq was an extremely complex one. Who were the two men and the girl dressed as a man? Why were they on board the fishing boat? Where were the crew? What was the motive of their journey? What had occurred during the fatal voyage?

"Have photographs of the dead persons been taken?" asked Maurice Jacquinot.

"Yes. I have the photographs here," replied the Chef de la Sûreté. And he handed round three unmounted photographs which had been taken of the dead persons in the position in which they were found.

Each member gazed at them in turn as they were passed round the table. But the member most interested was the elderly, white-bearded Dr. Henri Plaud. He examined and re-examined them very minutely through his large round spectacles, and pursing his lips slightly, passed them to the podgy Baron d'Antenac, who sat at his right hand.

A discussion followed lasting over two hours, in which Gustave Delcros, Gordon Latimer, and the pretty dark-haired Parisienne, Fernande Buysse, took part. The latter, who had been so successful in the case of "The Golden Grasshopper," was eager and enthusiastic. She suggested that the members of the club should unite at once and make independent inquiries.

This course was adopted, and it was decided that the direction of the investigation should be left in the hands of the white-bearded Doctor Plaud, while Gordon Latimer, spruce and active, being English, should go to Hastings at once, accompanied by Mademoiselle Fernande and the young journalist Maurice Jacquinot.

The judicial inquiry held by the French authorities at Calais revealed nothing, so it was decided that the affair should be kept out of the newspapers in order not to alarm anyone who held secret knowledge of what had happened. The bodies of the unknown victims were duly buried, and the case left in the hands of the Crimes Club.

On the 20th December, Gordon Latimer and Fernande Buysse, who, with others, had been pursuing active inquiries in Hastings, Folkestone, Calais, London, Paris, and elsewhere for nearly three months, were sitting together in a low-pitched, underground room where dancing and drinking were being indulged in, a den in Greek Street, Soho, which was one of the most disreputable spots in London's underworld. Gordon had gone there alone and had stood drinks to two or three girls of the usual type which haunt such places. Then he had pretended to " pick up " Fernande, the smart young French girl with whom he was now seated, and who had in the past few weeks become a nightly habituée there.

They were drinking Russian tea, and as she raised her glass, she whispered in French :

" That's the girl—in the cinnamon frock, with reddish hair ! "

The girl she indicated was about twenty-five, rather refined, delicate-looking and well-dressed. By her free manner, her painted lips, and her careless laughter it was plain that she was one of similar type to the other girls who frequented the place, some of them of the worst character. The fair-haired young man she was dancing with at the moment was known as " Jimmy the Painter," and was, indeed, one of the several cat burglars who, from time to time, arouse great alarm among London householders.

Latimer looked at the girl, and asked :

" Are you quite sure ? "

" I'm never sure of anything," laughed the chic French girl. " Only from what she's let out, I feel sure she knows something about the stuff. Shall I ask her across to sit with us ? "

" No. I'll come here alone to-morrow night," he said, and they sat drinking their tea, smoking cigarettes, and afterwards danced together.

Molly was the name by which the girl whom Fernande had pointed out was known. Such girls have no surnames. They change them too often when the police are following them. She laughed across to Fernande with whom she had become acquainted, and then glanced inquisitively at her companion, as though summing him up, perhaps, as a pigeon to be plucked—which was exactly what Latimer desired.

By their combined efforts, the five members of the Crimes Club had, in a way, been successful. They had discovered Henry Hayes, the employee of the Hastings Corporation, who had identified the photographs of the two men and the

girl found upon the fishing boat as the pair whom he had
seen eating bananas on the beach and afterwards meeting
the girl in the Bodega.   That was all.   How they came to be
on board the boat, or how or for what reason the girl had
been transformed into a man, was an absolute enigma.

Old Dr. Plaud, as director of the investigations, had, by
his unerring instinct, transferred his sphere of inquiry to
London, and there Latimer and Fernande, with the astute
journalist, Jacquinot, and M. Delcros had gone to work in a
careful, methodical and scientific manner, always keeping
in mind that whenever a great crime is committed, there is
always a woman in the case.

But what was the crime ?   What had happened in mid-
Channel on that fateful September night ?   The foreigner
can always learn more in London's cosmopolitan underworld than the Englishman, as every London detective will
tell you.   The cosmopolitan criminal looks upon every
Englishman as a " nark," or policeman's " nose " or in-
former.   Hence the foreign detective in London always has
an easier task if he knows the haunts of crooks and becomes
a habitué.

This is what Plaud had pointed out, and his suggestion
had been at once adopted.

Indeed, the sprightly Fernande and her dancing had
become quite a feature of that den known to the West End
criminal as " Old Jacob's."   To that cellar, or series of
cellars, with their boarded, white-painted walls, with crude
Futuristic designs upon them, many visitors to London were
enticed to spend a " merry evening," and left there minus
their wallet, or doped and taken to some den even more foul.
The police knew " Old Jacob's " well, and Jacob himself,
once a solicitor but now a wily old criminal who had spent
some years in Dartmoor for appropriating his clients' money,
always took ample precautions, and when raided, the place
was found to belong to somebody else who was duly fined,
and " Old Jacob " next day removed to another underground den.

At " The Yard " it was always declared that at " Jacob's "
there congregated the most dangerous crowd of criminals in
London.

All efforts of Plaud and his companions had failed to
establish the identity of the two strangers who had arrived on

that September evening in Hastings, who had met the girl and given her a glass of wine, and who later had been discovered dead upon the derelict in mid-Channel.

The Crimes Club had held three meetings in Paris at which progress had been reported and the matter had been discussed, but it seemed after three months that the whole organisation of experts was up against a blank wall. On the other hand, it was argued that the crew of four men of the fishing boat could not have all disappeared—unless they had been drowned, which was not likely. Besides, the ship's lights had been deliberately extinguished, which gave colour to the theory that the three had been murdered and the boat abandoned. In addition, one of the small boats was missing, though it had not been sighted. It might have escaped to either the French or English coast in the darkness.

The clue which the shrewd young French lady journalist was following—the public being in ignorance of the highly sensational discovery—was only a slender one. In the course of the long investigations in which Jacquinot had been most active, it was found that a person somewhat resembling the man who wore the sapphire in his cravat, was known in the dregs of the London underworld as an expert thief named Orlando Martin, who had a dozen or so *aliases*. He had never been in trouble apparently, neither had his companion, for the finger-prints of the dead hands taken by the Calais police did not correspond with any of the hundreds of thousands of records filed at Scotland Yard.

In such circumstances, with failure after failure to record, and with Dr. Plaud openly pessimistic as regards finding any solution to the mystery, Gordon Latimer, dressed in a dinner-jacket, lounged into " Jacob's " on the following night, and was soon in conversation with the neat-ankled girl, Molly. They sat together, drank coffee and cointreau, and watched the dancing, he pretending to live in Cornwall, and up from Truro on a holiday. He told her that he was a motor dealer, and having unexpectedly sold half a dozen cars he had determined to take a holiday in London.

The girl soon saw that he was an easy victim to her charms. Indeed, he promised to meet her and take her out to lunch next day, which he did. For the following three days he was mostly in her company and constantly spending money upon her, but at night they always danced at " Old Jacob's," where twice they met Fernande alone, and she joined them.

One evening, in consequence of a telegram he had received from Paris regarding yet another discovery, Gordon resolved to make a bold endeavour to learn something, for if what Fernande suspected were true, then Molly might be able to supply the key to the enigma.

They left " Jacob's " at three o'clock in the morning, and he had offered to see her in a taxi as far as her flat at Baron's Court, out by West Kensington.

While in the taxi he suddenly took her hand, and said :

" Molly, you are dense. Haven't you recognised me ? "

" Recognised you ? " she cried, starting suddenly. " What do you mean ? "

" You take me for a mug. You don't recognise Bert Davies—Sugar's friend ! "

" Bert Davies ! " gasped the girl. " Are you really Bert—his best pal ? "

" I am. I came out of the Scrubbs a month ago and went over to Paris to find Maisie. But I can't find Sugar anywhere. Where is he ? I know he was deeply in love with you. He told me so lots of times. I hope he isn't doing time ? "

The shrewd girl, whose wits were sharpened by the criminal life she led, was silent for a few moments. Teddy Candy, known in the London underworld by the sobriquet of " Sugar," and with whom she was in love, had often spoken of his intimate friend, an expert blackmailer named Bertie Davies who was in prison owing to a little slip he had made.

" You aren't a nark, are you ? " asked the girl cautiously.

" Certainly not. Maisie knows me. So does Dick Dale. Sugar used to wear a blue sapphire tie-pin that he pinched from a young Italian prince one night, didn't he ? "

" Dick is doing time—shot at a copper in Kingsland and got it in the neck from the Recorder."

" I'm sorry. Dickie's one of the best. Recollect the Humber Street affair—a nasty business—but Dickie helped Teddy, didn't he ? "

" Yes. It was a narrow shave for all of us. I don't like guns. But we got nearly two thousand apiece."

"But what about Sugar? Where can I find him?" asked her good-looking companion.

"I don't know—and that's a fact," she replied, with a regretful air. "I haven't seen him or heard of him since September."

"Perhaps he's doing time?"

"Oh, no. He's disappeared."

"How?"

"I don't know," the girl replied. "He and Tony Donald had a big thing on hand—a bit of bank business, he told me. One day in September he left me after lunching at the Trocadero, and I haven't seen him since. Tony's missing, too!"

"Was Sugar ever about with a big, thick-set man with a beard, a rough, rather deep-voiced, unkempt fellow, who looked like a sailor?"

"The man who came up from Hastings, you mean—eh? Sugar told me he was one of us, and they were doing business together."

"Is that all he told you?" asked Latimer.

"What are you so inquisitive for, young man?" asked the girl pertly. "What business is it of yours—eh? I took you for a mug, but you certainly aren't one," she laughed. The cab had stopped outside her door, and seeing this, she said: "Come in and have a drink before you go back."

Latimer, delighted with the information he had obtained, accepted the girl's invitation and ascended to the third floor, to a little three-roomed flat cosily furnished, where he sat down and took the whisky and soda she poured out for him.

Ten minutes later she went below and paid the taxi driver, telling him that her friend was remaining, but the actual fact was that Gordon Latimer was at that moment lying senseless upon the floor heavily drugged.

"You're a nark, you damned swine!" she cried on returning, kicking his inanimate body savagely. "And you'll be sorry for your inquisitiveness. You are no friend of Sugar's or of Ben Benham's either!"

She went to the telephone and rang up somebody named Joe, urging him to come at once.

Half an hour later an ill-dressed, ill-conditioned man of forty with a sinister, criminal face arrived, and to him she told the story.

The man knit his heavy brows and was silent for a few moments. Then he said :

" If he really knows something about Sugar he might possibly help us. Don't do anything rash. It may be better for us if he is alive, than if he died. We'll let him recover and loosen his tongue," added the ex-convict. " There's certain to be somebody with him, and he may have been watched here. So there's no time to lose. Give him the stuff that brings them round," he urged.

She passed into an adjoining room, and returned with a small phial bottle from which she poured about twenty drops into water, and held it to his lips. Unconsciously he drank it, and ten minutes later he was again fully conscious, and amazed at finding himself face to face with the stranger.

" Well, sonny ? " asked the sinister man who had served many years of penal servitude, " what's all this you know about Sugar ? If you can tell me where he is you'll get out of this alive. But if you don't, well, you'll be found dead by the police to-morrow," he said fiercely, drawing a revolver and holding it close to his brow. " Now, let's talk business. What do you know about Sugar ? "

Gordon Latimer, realising that he was in a tight corner, decided that the best course was to tell the truth.

" I only know that he is dead."

" Dead ! " cried the girl hysterically. " How do you know that ? "

" Before I answer I want to ask a question. Is Ben Benham alive ? "

" Certainly," was Molly's reply.

" Then I may tell you that Sugar is dead, and here is his photograph taken by the French police," said Latimer boldly, taking the three pictures from his pocket-book.

On sight of the first the girl Molly shrieked, and almost fainted.

" Yes, it is Sugar—poor, dear Sugar ! Dead, and he loved me ! Do forgive me—forgive us—and tell us all that you know. What happened to Sugar and to Tony Donald ? "

" They are both dead—and this girl too—dressed as a man." And he showed them the other pictures.

" Gwen ! " gasped Molly. " It's Gwen ! She's dead also ! Tell us what happened. Where were they found ? "

Both stood open-mouthed and aghast as Latimer described the finding of the bodies on the derelict ship.

" How did your little French friend find out that we knew these people ? " asked the old criminal whose name was Joe Hawker, an expert forger.

" If I tell you I shall expect you to tell me all that you know regarding the affair," said Latimer.

" That's agreed," replied Molly.   " We have a lot to tell you—more curious than you can possibly imagine.   How did she suspect that I knew anything ? "

For a few seconds Latimer reflected, then he decided that straightforwardness was best.

" The fact is, Miss Molly," he said, " Professor Plaud, the French medico-legist, on seeing the photographs, at once suspected, from the position and appearance of the bodies, the fact of the palms being outstretched and the purple colour of the countenances, that death was due to an almost unknown but very subtle and deadly narcotic poison called enconine.   From only one person in London, whose name is known to the Professor, can the poison be obtained in secret, and a very high price is charged for it.   That fact led us to search the underworld of London thoroughly for persons who had purchased it.   There were six of them known to us, but our inquiries were narrowed down to yourself.   You bought the poison for your friend Candy, and you kept some for yourself.   It was that which you gave me in my drink just now.   You can't deny it ! "

The girl stood aghast at the allegation, unable to utter a word.

" I do not seek to harm you," he at once assured her. " I only want to solve the mystery.   We have ascertained the truth up to a certain point—that you obtained the drug which cost Candy, Donald, and the girl Gwen, their lives."

" But what happened to them ? " the girl asked breathlessly.   " They wouldn't all commit suicide."

" Before I tell you I want to know the nature of the bank business in which Candy and Donald were ' interested.' "

" Well—you, no doubt, saw in the papers last August how the strong-room of Carron's, the big private bank in the City, had been blown open after the night watchman had been gassed, and how nearly a quarter of a million had been carried away in a blue motor-car."

" Yes, I remember," Latimer answered.

" Well, Sugar and Tony did the trick, while Gwen gassed the watchman. They hid the money in a house down by the sea at Pevensey Bay, but one day they were all three missing as well as old Ben Benham, and we've had no word of any of them till now you've shown us that they're dead."

" What actually occurred becomes quite plain," Latimer replied. " Candy and your other two friends no doubt feared the police and were anxious to get the loot in secret across the Channel, where the securities could be disposed of. They arranged with the skipper Benham, whom they had found to be a clever smuggler, to take them and their treasure over to France on that night. They went on board after dark and steered a course presumably to fish as usual, when Benham, who had evidently stolen the drug from Candy without his knowledge, offered all three a drink, which they took with fatal results. He then seized the money and securities, paid the crew well for their silence, lowered a boat, and having extinguished the vessel's lights, they rowed forward to the French coast, where he and the crew, whom he had sworn to silence and to remain in France, separated. Three hours later the vessel was sighted by the cross-Channel steamer, and the bodies discovered in the position in which you see them."

" Then Benham killed them ! " cried the girl hysterically. " We'll kill him ! "

" There is no necessity," was Latimer's reply. " This afternoon I received a telegram from the Paris police to the effect that a man much resembling the skipper Benham, though he had shaved off his grey beard and moustache, was discovered at a small hotel in Rouen. When the police went to arrest him, however, he shot himself. In the room nearly seventeen thousands pounds in cash and nearly the whole of the securities were found."

"**B**UT why is it crooked?" asked Maurice Jacquinot. He held in his hand, closely scrutinising it, a French copper coin of one sou, worn almost smooth by many years of handling, but still bearing quite legibly the head of Napoleon III. It was a thin little coin, a French halfpenny, not quite round, for a little piece had been broken off on one side deliberately and not by wear and tear. Yet its crookedness, three heavy dents across it, as though to disfigure the face of the head of the last Empire, was most apparent. In addition it was bent hollow and had a hole pierced in it. Some heavy mechanical force must have been used to treat the humble coin in that manner.

Such was the view of the secret assembly seated around the club table on that warm August night.

The *haut monde* was at the little seaside *trous*, including such places as Deauville, Dinard and Granville, and Paris was given over to the cheap, gaping tourist from all corners of the earth. Though the capital was *en campagne*, yet the so-called *attractions* and *galas* still flourished for the benefit of the foreigner, without whom Montmartre could not exist.

"An enigma! A complete enigma!" declared the Baron d'Antenac, placing his monocle in his eye. To strangers he looked an empty-headed man of means, prone to an exotic life of indulgence and over-eating, yet his real nature was exactly the contrary. No keener student of the psychology of crime was there in all France. When faced with a mystery he never rested until he, with other members of the club, had arrived at its solution.

The mystery surrounding the discovery of that bent and worn French halfpenny, which Jacquinot held in his fingers, was one which seemed beyond solution. The Brussels police, as well as Scotland Yard, had endeavoured to probe the curious affair, but without the least result. The Big Four in London and Monsieur Mommaert, chief of the

Brussels Sûreté, with his excellent staff had made every effort before the matter was, as a last resource, referred to the Crimes Club for their opinion and assistance.

On that breathless evening with the noise of the Paris traffic and the incessant hooting of motor horns coming in through the open window, the affair had been briefly outlined by Professor Ernest Lemelletier, Dubosq being absent on vacation. His vacation was, as a matter of fact, a flying visit to Cairo after a certain pseudo-Baron who had murdered his lady secretary in Bordeaux. The Professor, lean and shrunken in his well-brushed black clothes, with the red rosette in his lapel, had recounted to the eight persons seated around the table the actual facts regarding that crooked sou as far as the police had been able to ascertain them.

It seemed that six months before, just after twelve o'clock on a very foggy February night in London, a young man-about-town, Gilbert Rothwell, only son of Sir Gilbert Dargate Rothwell, Baronet, of Broadstone Manor, Buckinghamshire, was passing along Howland Street, which runs between Cleveland Street and Tottenham Court Road, on his way home to his rooms in Ryder Street, when, in the dense fog, he collided with an elderly, well-dressed man who had a young girl on his arm. He apologised, whereupon the girl began to pour forth upon her companion a torrent of abuse. Her voice was refined, and she was apparently a lady. Her companion uttered some words in a foreign language and disengaged his arm from hers, whereupon the girl gave vent to a loud scream, swayed forward, and fell to the pavement while the man, who was short and stout, left her hurriedly and disappeared in the fog.

Next moment a passer-by came up from the gloom. He was a working-man of whom young Rothwell sought assistance. The pair tried to lift the fallen girl, but she was inert and silent, apparently having fainted. The working-man, whose name was Fawcett, hurried to the corner of Tottenham Court Road, where he eventually found a constable, and subsequently the girl was conveyed to the Middlesex Hospital in the police ambulance, where, in the light, it was discovered that she was dead. She was well-dressed in a dead-black evening-gown with half-sleeves, beneath a rich fur coat, and wore two valuable rings, but when undressed, it was found that tied around her well-moulded left arm above the elbow and hidden by her sleeve was a thin silken cord, which passed through a hole in a bent copper coin—the crooked French sou—the coin which Maurice Jacquinot at that moment held in his hand.

The two young surgeons and the two nurses at once saw that there had been foul play, and told the police constable so, while young Rothwell, to his surprise and chagrin, instantly found himself the central figure in a mysterious tragedy of the London streets.

The autopsy held on the following day revealed that the unknown girl had been killed in a very unusual manner, for in the nape of the neck, just visible because her hair was shingled, was a puncture so light as to be almost imperceptible. Examination of the tiny wound showed that a long, thin instrument, possibly a long pin, had been driven into the neck to the spinal cord, thus causing almost instant death.

The affair was a complete mystery. The girl's clothing was of the finest quality, but identification was impossible because there was nothing upon her to serve as a clue as to who she was. She carried no handbag—not even a handkerchief, while the laundry marks had been cut out of her linen, a fact which seemed to establish that the murder had been committed as the result of some deep plot. The only thing found was slipped in the wide fur cuff of her rich heavy coat, a tram-ticket which showed that its bearer had, five days before, travelled by electric tram from the Bourse, in Brussels, up the steep hill to the Porte Louise.

At the inquest, which, in the interest of justice, was so arranged that the reporters missed it, Gilbert Rothwell deposed to meeting the dead girl and her companion suddenly in the fog, and described the man as far as the distortions of a London fog at night with the unreal glow of the street lamps would allow. He was broad-faced, high-browed, with narrow-set eyes, and wearing round glasses. He had a dark beard, but no moustache—evidently a foreigner. That was how he described him. To the police he made an even more minute statement concerning the stranger's voice, the contour of his face, as far as he was able to discern, and gave every information possible. The result was that descriptions of the alleged murderer and his victim were circulated by every channel possible, and also broadcast by wireless, a reward of £500 being offered for any information which would lead to the arrest of the man.

Every clue proved to be false. Weeks and months went by. Because of the ticket of the Tramways Bruxellois found in the girl's coat-cuff Monsieur Mommaert, chief of the Brussels police, made every effort to discover whether the girl had been staying at any of the many Brussels hotels. All that had been established was that a girl, much resembling the victim, had been staying at the Hôtel du Trône, an unpretentious little place in the Rue Royale, at the time the tram-ticket had been purchased. She had registered in the name of Mary Beeton, and had as companion a girl somewhat older than herself, named Edith Ray. They had occupied a double room, and were travelling under the auspices of a second-class tourist agency. Their tour was a cheap one by Harwich to the Hook of Holland, Rotterdam, Antwerp, six days in Brussels, up the Meuse to Namur and Dinant, back to Brussels, and returning via Antwerp to Harwich and London. Both the proprietor and concierge of the hotel remembered them quite distinctly, because at about ten o'clock one night an Englishman had called and asked for Miss Beeton. She refused to see him, and insisting, he became so infuriated that at last she came down and went out for a walk with him, talking very excitedly as they left the hotel.

The description of the man did not, however, tally in the least with that of the man whom Gilbert Rothwell had seen in Howland Street. He was a tall, white-bearded old man, whereas the man suspected was a dark, extremely well-dressed foreigner. That the murderer was possessed of some surgical knowledge was shown by the manner in which the attack had been made, the doctors having demonstrated to the police with what consummate ease a person can be killed almost instantly by that means, and with no more formidable weapon than a lady's hat-pin. The swiftness and unerring manner in which the fatal blow had been struck astounded the investigators, who were baffled from the very outset.

Fortunately, the face of the murderer had been seen, and young Gilbert Rothwell declared that he would be able to recognise him again anywhere.

Time had passed, yet no girl answering the description was reported missing in England or in Belgium. At the inquest a verdict of " wilful murder " was returned, and then the enigma of the crooked sou had already been added by the police to the long list of London's unsolved mysteries.

For that reason the famous medico-legist, Professor Lemelletier, had placed the details briefly before the members of that exclusive little circle, the Crimes Club, and for an hour it had been discussed.

" And now, I presume, ladies and gentlemen, you would like to confer with the only person who saw the murderer's face—young Mr. Gilbert Rothwell," said the grey-haired expert in criminology. He rose, and unlocking the door, admitted a smartly-dressed young Englishman, clean-shaven, with well-brushed hair. He bowed on entering, and the Professor, welcoming him, drew a chair to the round table for him.

In reply to a question from Jean Tessier, he gave a minute description of the tragic encounter in the fog, while the pretty Fernande Buysse regarded the new-comer approvingly.

" When I accidentally brushed up against her she turned upon me wildly, and then abused her companion," Rothwell said. " I just apologised, and her companion merely uttered a few foreign words. ' Come,' she said, ' let us go on. We shall be late ! ' Then next second she uttered a sharp cry, and as he unloosened her arm, she collapsed upon the pavement, while in an instant the man vanished from sight."

" Did you actually see his arm uplifted, ready to strike ? " asked the Baron, much interested in the curious story.

" I noticed that he raised his arm, but I saw no blow struck. The shriek was a cry of pain, and she put her hand to the back of her head as she staggered. She tried to articulate some words. They seemed like ' Father ! Father ! ' but I am not quite certain what they were. I was too startled at the suddenness of it all."

" Was the man a foreigner ? " asked Gordon Latimer.

" I think so, but am not quite positive," was Rothwell's reply. " He was short, and rather stout. In the uncertain light thrown by the street lamp, through the fog, I took him to be a southerner, perhaps a Spaniard, on account of his dark beard and his quick, piercing eyes behind the big round spectacles."

"He might have been a doctor," remarked the *chic* little Fernande.

"And there is not the slightest clue to the identity of either the victim or the culprit?" remarked the stout, plethoric Baron, resting his elbows upon the table and looking across at the sole witness of the tragedy.

"Not the slightest. Superintendent Bawdon told me at Scotland Yard three days ago that, without knowledge of who the dead girl was, no motive could be assigned for the perpetration of the crime. It is a complete mystery."

"And the clue to the mysterious affair lies in this," declared Jacquinot, holding up the crooked French halfpenny. "What can it denote? Perhaps the unfortunate girl regarded it as a talisman, or, perhaps, she kept it to remind her of some lost or dead friend. At any rate, she treasured it. That she was not a common person is proved by her well-manicured hands; the perfume she used was one of the most exclusive and expensive; her clothes, even her lingerie, had, no doubt, been made in Paris at an expensive establishment, yet all the tabs bearing the name of the makers had been carefully cut out."

"Cut out purposely by those who plotted her death, Superintendent Bawdon thinks," remarked Rothwell. "It is evident that the murderer took every precaution to conceal his victim's identity, and yet, at the same time, he was audacious enough to strike down the girl in my presence."

"It seems incredible that he should have done so and been able to withdraw whatever weapon he used without you noticing his action," remarked Doctor Plaud, who had not hitherto spoken.

"I agree. But I was so taken aback by the girl's violent abuse that my interest was centred in her. And perhaps the more so because she was extremely good-looking," he admitted.

The entire absence of any clue as to the dead girl's identity rendered the mystery utterly inscrutable. But, as Professor Lemelletier pointed out, the club had successfully investigated several affairs in which clues had been wanting, hence there was no reason why they should not all combine in an endeavour to solve the latest problem. After a long discussion, in which the tragedy was thoroughly debated, it was resolved to assist the young Englishman in his determination to investigate further the brutal murder of the unknown girl.

So, without the least suspicion of a clue, the club began the investigation of one of the most remarkable mysteries of our modern London.

A few days later the ex-minister, Delcros, together with Jacquinot, Dr. Plaud and Mademoiselle Fernande, formulated a plan. It was the latter who suggested it. She would first go to Brussels and see Monsieur Mommaert, the Chief of Police. This she did. The clothing of the dead girl had been sent from Scotland Yard to Brussels for an expected identification, which was not realised, and Mademoiselle was allowed to examine the various garments at the Prefecture of Police. It was a pathetic little pile of delicate lingerie, soiled by the many police officials and others that had handled it. It lay upon the table in the cold, bare room. The black charmeuse evening-gown, the rich fur coat, and the smart patent shoes taken from a box by a detective, were placed on one side of the table, while on the other was the murdered girl's underclothing.

Fernande, who was alone with the detective, slowly examined every article. The man pointed out where the laundry marks and maker's tabs had been cut away, saying :

" They were evidently obliterated prior to the crime. Mademoiselle was, no doubt, in ignorance that precautions had been taken to destroy any clue to her identity."

" No doubt," remarked Fernande, as though speaking to herself as she held each piece of lingerie in her hand, spread it upon the table, and minutely examined it.

As she spread out a pretty camisole in ibis Siamese crêpe with ochre lace, she knit her brows thoughtfully. Several times she examined it, and then stood for a few moments pondering. Of the detective she requested the loan of a tape measure, and he went at once to obtain one. Again she spread the expensive little garment out upon the table and closely examined it, especially the position where the maker's name had been.

On obtaining the tape-measure she lost no time in carefully taking the measurements, and noting them upon a scrap of paper. A sweet odour greeted her nostrils as she did so, that of one of the most expensive and exclusive of all the Parisian perfumes.

Suddenly a thought occurred to her. The introduction from the club to Monsieur Mommaert had instantly opened the doors of the police department to her, therefore why should she not take advantage of it and request the loan of the dainty article of underwear for a few days?

With this end she again sought the Director of Police, who at once granted her request on condition that it should be returned.

That night, without making inquiry at the Hôtel du Trône, she eagerly travelled by the *rapide* back to Paris, and next morning, with the camisole in her little dispatch-case, called at the Maison Boulaye, in the Place Vendôme, that very expensive *couturière*, and asked to see Monsieur Neuville, its director.

Fernande Buysse was an expert in women's clothes, earning her living, as she did, by writing about fashions, and she had recognised the dead girl's camisole as one of M. Neuville's models of nine months before.

She explained her errand, and showed it to him, together with the measurements she had taken. The brown-bearded, elegant designer examined it critically, and, leaving her, went to his bureau where records were kept by the clerks.

On his return, he asked her to call on the morrow when a complete search would have been made for the name of the customer whose measurements coincided with those of the garment.

That night she called at Jacquinot's apartment, in the Rue du Bac, and explained what she had done, which at once aroused his interest. He was one of the keenest members of the club, for he was ever active and untiringly on the look-out for crime stories for *Le Journal*.

They sat together in the journalist's cosy room, she smoking the cigarette he had given her, while they discussed the difficult problem. They were old friends and fellow-workers, for she frequently contributed fashion articles to *Le Journal*, and he had long ago found her to be a very charming little companion, whose tastes were greatly in common with his own, and how in their criminal investigations she was not only astute but daring to a degree.

The hot summer's day was ending, and the red glow of

sunset fell into the room as they chatted. Fernande looked very charming in her light summer gown and a black, close-fitting hat to match. She knew most of the fashionable *couturières* in Paris, hence she could always dress both well and cheaply.

" I am afraid you will have some difficulty in determining the woman for whom the camisole was made," Maurice remarked at last. " Yours is a worthy effort, without a doubt, and I wish you all success, Fernande. Let us go out to Armenonville and dine. We can afterwards have a stroll in the Bois. It will be cool. Besides, I have promised to meet Dupuis of the *Petit Parisien* there."

And so they went forth together to spend the evening. Later, when they returned to the Grand Café, they came across Gordon Latimer. The trio sat together in a corner and, over their coffee, further discussed the affair of the Crooked Sou.

" The mystery interests me very much," Latimer said. " If our inquiries lead us to London, I'll be ready to go there at any moment."

Next day Fernande called upon Monsieur Neuville.

" You are faced with considerable difficulties, Mademoi-selle," declared the great dress designer. " Exactly the same design, the same material and the same exact measure-ments have been supplied to seven different customers. Since last December we have ceased to make that design."

" May I have their names and addresses ? " asked the lady journalist eagerly.

In a few minutes the list was handed to her. There were seven names, but only five addresses. The other two customers had been staying at Paris hotels, one at the Ritz and the other at the Chatham. The first name was that of the Baronne de Fontaneilles, of the Château Thiaville, in the Vosges, who was well known in Paris society, and being middle-aged, was certainly not the victim of the tragedy in Howland Street. Neither was the second person to whom a similar garment had been supplied, Mademoiselle Yvonne Vierzy, the lady artist, living at Barbizon. There were three others whose addresses were given, and the two who had been temporarily in Paris were evidently Americans, their respective names being Stevens and Marsden.

Fernande went back to her own apartment *au troisième* in

the Rue Chardin, and there wrote to the three other ladies, Madame Darboux living in Blois ; the Vicomtesse Helya de Marolles, at the Château de Vèreux, in the Alpes-Maritimes, and Mademoiselle Lavisse, living in Provins, explaining the reason of her search, and enclosing stamped envelopes for replies.

She was about to put on her hat and go out to post them when a sudden thought occurred to her. In writing she was acting most injudiciously. It might alarm the assassin. She would see each of the ladies personally, even though it must entail long journeys across France. So she tore up the three letters, and, taking a small suit-case, she left the Gare de L'est that afternoon for the quaint old town of Provins, where she arrived about six o'clock. An hour later she had an interview with Mademoiselle Lavisse, who lived in a large house near the church of St. Ayoul, and found that instead of being a young girl, she was a wealthy, middle-aged maiden lady. Fernande briefly explained the object of her call, and then apologising, left and returned to the Hôtel de la Boule d'Or where she spent the night.

It took her all the following day to reach the old town of Blois, it being a cross-country journey, but she was determined upon making a thorough investigation, and at last, after spending the night in the capital of the Loir-et-Cher, with its narrow streets and flights of steps, she found the house of Madame Darboux in the Avenue Victor Hugo, close to the old Castle. Madame, she learnt, was the wife of the Prefect, therefore it was useless to call. So she left Blois for Cannes, where next day she took a taxi up the valley beyond Mandelieu to the fine old Château de Vèreux. At the hotel she had learned that the Vicomtesse Helya de Marolles was quite young and was English, and further that neither she nor her husband had been seen at the Château for nine months or more.

Fernande drove beneath the great grim walls of the old fortress of François I, and then returning to Cannes, at once telegraphed to Professor Lemelletier requesting him to ask young Mr. Rothwell to meet her at the Hôtel du Parc at once.

Two days later the smart young Englishman arrived, full of expectancy, and when they were alone, Mademoiselle told him of her discovery that the Vicomtesse was English, that her husband was much older than herself, and that they were supposed to be abroad.

" But the girl did not wear a wedding ring," Rothwell remarked.

" No. But does not the report of the autopsy say that there was a distinct mark upon her finger, as though a wedding ring had been worn ? If the marks on her clothing had been removed, why not the ring ? "

Together they took a taxi that afternoon out to the Château, and entering the spacious courtyard, rang a great, clanging bell.

Of the liveried man-servant who appeared Fernande inquired for Madame la Vicomtesse, to which he replied :

" Madame, with Monsieur, is absent abroad. She will not return until next Friday."

" Then she is returning ? " asked Fernande eagerly.

" Certainly, Mademoiselle."

Fernande and the young Englishman exchanged glances. She thought quickly. Then, with a winning smile, she asked the man-servant :

" When did you last hear from her ? "

" Oh, I think it was about last December. She wrote to me from New York, giving me several orders. But I heard from Monsieur Le Vicomte only about six weeks ago. He wrote from the Turf Club in Cairo."

Mademoiselle put further questions to him, but could obtain no more information. Therefore they re-entered the taxi and returned to Cannes.

" I wonder if we are on the scent ? " asked Rothwell reflectively as they drove along.

" I have every hope that we are. The Vicomtesse is young ; she has not been seen for months. Only you can establish her identity—but how ? "

" Certainly not by seeing her," said Rothwell. And they both lapsed into thoughtful silence.

On their return to Cannes, Mademoiselle did not relinquish her activity, but with the young Englishman accompanying her she called at Bellots', the fashionable photographers in the Rue d'Antibes, where she asked the young lady who received her whether they had of late taken a photograph of the Vicomtesse de Marolles.

" The Vicomtesse, who is a great friend of mine, told me

that you have taken a portrait of her. The fact is, I want some cabinets taken in the same style," Fernande added, making a blind shot, for she felt that the châtelaine of Vèreux would certainly be photographed by that highly-fashionable establishment.

" I think we took a portrait about a year ago," replied the girl. " If you will take a seat I will see," and she conducted the pair to a waiting-room, where they sat impatiently for nearly a quarter of an hour.

At last the girl reappeared, saying :

" Yes. We did take a portrait, and fortunately I have a print of it."

And she exhibited to them the picture of a refined young woman in an elegant evening-gown.

Rothwell's face fell, as he remarked :

" No, it is not her ! The Vicomtesse is much older."

Then the pair, with excuses, rapidly withdrew.

All their efforts had been in vain. The only course now was to return to Paris and acknowledge themselves beaten.

Instead of doing so, however, Fernande, accompanied by Rothwell, travelled by way of Dijon and Bâle, back to Brussels, where they put up at the small Hôtel du Trône, and from the proprietor obtained as much information as they could concerning the girl Mary Beeton, who so closely resembled the victim, and her friend Edith Ray. Nothing was known of either except that they had gone sight-seeing each day and often went out in the evening. The frail, white-bearded old Englishman who had called for Miss Beeton had given his name as Mr. Thomas, and it was apparent that she had been greatly annoyed by his call. It was known that a second man called on the following day, but he was seen by a porter who had since been dismissed and could not be found.

All was therefore shadowy and unsatisfactory. Indeed, it was not entirely established whether the dead girl was actually Miss Beeton. The only evidence that the dead girl had been in the Belgian capital was upon the assumption of that tram-ticket.

They returned once again to Paris, where they reported their failure to Professor Lemelletier, who simply shrugged his shoulders and counselled patience.

Another week passed. Several members of the club were

in favour of giving the mystery up as beyond solution. But
still undaunted, Fernande determined to make yet a last
attempt, and with that object she again called upon the
dress designer, Neuville, to report the failure of her inquiries.

" It may be that the garment in question was made for
one or other of the American ladies who were visitors to
Paris," he said. " They paid cash, so we merely delivered
the goods to them at their hotels. In that case you will, as
I feared, Mademoiselle, experience considerable difficulty."

" Well," said Fernande, unrolling the dead girl's camisole
from a sheet of tissue paper. " I have been wondering
whether this might perhaps be identified by the work-room
hand who made it."

" Possibly," said the head of the famous dress-making
house. " Only four hands have been employed in making
those special designs. I will see, if you will leave it with me
till to-morrow. They will then have an opportunity to
identify it. Had the tab with the number remained, then
we could have traced it in a few minutes."

Next day, when the lady fashion writer was ushered into
Monsieur Neuville's room, he had with him one of his
workwomen, a thin-faced young Frenchwoman, who had
the camisole in her hand :

" I made this myself, Mademoiselle. I made an error in
this seam, and corrected it. See ! " And she pointed to a
seam at the side. " I recognised it as my work. It was
made for Madame Darboux of Blois, wife of the Prefect."

" Is she young ? " asked Fernande.

" I regret I do not know," the woman replied. " It was
an order by post. She sent a self-measurement form."

The wife of the Prefect ! Fernande had been in Blois,
but had not called at the house in the Avenue Victor Hugo.
She thanked the great designer of frocks and quickly sought
young Rothwell. Together that night they left for Blois,
and next day Fernande rang the bell of the large old-
fashioned residence standing back from the Avenue in a
pretty garden ablaze with flowers.

The iron gates were unlatched by an unseen hand, as
they so often are in France, and walking up to the house,
they found a middle-aged woman waiting at the door.

On inquiring for Madame Darboux, the woman replied
that Monsieur le Prefect lived there no longer. He had

resigned his position some months before, and the house was up for sale, she, the wife of the butler, being left in charge.

After some conversation, during which they learnt that the ex-Prefect had been there as recently as six weeks before, Fernande explained that, while in Deauville the previous season, she had made the acquaintance of a Madame Darboux, who said her husband was Prefect, but she had doubted her. She wished, for her own curiosity, to make sure.

" If Mademoiselle will enter there is a photograph of Madame in the petit-salon—also one of Monsieur," the woman said politely.

Scarce daring to breathe in their excitement, Fernande and her companion followed the woman.

The instant Rothwell's eye fell upon the large, framed photograph, he exclaimed :

" That's her ! And that's the man ! Yes, I'm certain ! "

The caretaker, somewhat surprised at Rothwell's ejaculations, remarked :

" Madame is English, and quite young. I do not understand English, I regret."

" You are an old servant of Monsieur le Prefect. Have you ever seen this coin ? " asked Mademoiselle Fernande, producing the crooked sou from her handbag.

The woman opened her eyes as though startled and took the worn French halfpenny in her hand, examining it closely.

" Why, yes ! " she replied. " I have seen this very often. Madame always wore it on her arm as her mascot. She once told me that her only brother, who fought with the English at Hill 60, was struck by a German bullet, and this coin deflected the bullet and saved his life. That is why it is bent and broken."

" And Madame ? " asked the girl. " Where is she ? "

" Ah ! I have no idea," was the reply, " except I believe she is in England with Monsieur."

Further than that they could obtain no other information. But they pursued other inquiries regarding the Prefect, and during the next few hours learnt of his sudden resignation and decision to sell his fine house and its contents. About two years before he had married a smart young English girl, apparently of very good family, who had been on a visit at the château in the vicinity, where he had met her. But his reputation was that of a man of many amours, and it was believed that they did not get on very well together. That was all that was known in Blois.

Next day Rothwell and Mademoiselle called at the Prefecture and there saw Monsieur Gaschard, his successor, and from him they learnt that the retired official had written only a few days before, from an address at Putney, in London. This address, which he gave to the pair, proved to be in a block of flats overlooking the River Thames, near Putney Bridge.

Without delay the pair of investigators once more returned to Paris, where a special meeting of the club was convened, and at the famous round table in the Café de l'Univers, the result of their inquiries was reported.

Professor Lemelletier was unanimously requested to go to London with Gordon Latimer, Maurice Jacquinot, Fernande and the witness Rothwell.

Forty-eight hours later, Maurice Jacquinot, accompanied by young Rothwell, and followed by a detective-inspector, left their companions at the foot of Putney Bridge, on the Surrey side, and walked to a great block of flats facing the river. It was seven o'clock in the evening, and still light. Of the hall-porter, Rothwell made inquiry as to who lived in the flat indicated by the Prefect at Blois, and was told that it was a French gentleman named Deprez, who had taken the flat furnished, but had gone away somewhere in the country, where he was about to be married. He would not be back for a month. The porter did not have his address, but said that a tailor named Evans, who lived in the High Street, near Putney Station, had been making him a suit, and that he might know.

" Going to be married again ! " remarked Maurice with a grin as they thanked the porter and hurried towards the tailor's shop, which was only five minutes away. Arrived there, they quickly ascertained that a new suit of clothes had, on the previous night, been sent to Monsieur Deprez, at the Queen's Hotel at Leeds.

Within two hours the party were on their way from King's Cross, and duly arrived early in the morning. From the hall-porter at Leeds, Latimer, who took a room at the hotel, learnt that the French gentleman was to be married to the daughter of a wealthy manufacturer on the following day at St. Peter's Church, in Kirkgate. But an unpleasant surprise awaited the bridegroom when on his return to the hotel half an hour later, he was confronted by Gilbert Rothwell and given into the custody of the detective from London.

The wedding was, of course, postponed, for that same night the ex-Prefect was brought to London in custody. Then a strange thing happened. When charged at Bow Street he made a remarkable statement to the effect that he knew that his wife, with whom he had been on very unfriendly terms, had been murdered on that foggy night. He explained that she had confessed to him her infidelity in Brussels, and in great anger he intended to take divorce proceedings against her lover, a married man named Mitchell, a retired doctor. She had written to Mitchell telling him of her confession, whereupon the latter, while they had been on a brief visit to Brussels together, had cut the identification marks out of her clothing, determined to kill her afterwards in secret, and thus prevent proceedings. Mitchell had followed her and her husband on that foggy night, and in Howland Street, after a quarrel, she had taken off her wedding ring and thrown it away. Suddenly, as they had stopped, Mitchell had dealt the fatal blow in the fog.

The prisoner declared that, finding his wife attacked from behind, he instantly realised what had occurred. He feared to be accused of the crime, and feeling certain that he was unknown in London, had slipped away, and so escaped.

Then he had resigned his position as Prefect, and remaining in England, changing his name, and keeping his knowledge to himself, was now about to marry again.

" But how can you prove all this ? " queried the incredulous inspector when, after warning him that the statement might be used against him, he had finished taking it down.

" By this," was Monsieur Darboux's quick reply, as he drew a crumpled letter from his wallet and handed it to the police official, whose face instantly wore a look of amazement as he read it.

" This is a confession," the inspector said to the eager little group who stood beside him in the police station. " It is written by Dr. Crane Mitchell, of Sherbourne Gardens, Hampstead, to the effect that he killed young Madame Darboux in the fog in Howland Street, and that her husband is innocent. The letter explains that, fearing arrest, he is taking his own life."

And he handed it to the investigators to read.

Within an hour the police had established that Dr. Crane Mitchell had unaccountably committed suicide at his house in Hampstead on the very day that the letter had been written, six months before, and further, in a drawer in his writing-table there still lay, wrapped carefully in paper, a lady's long steel hat-pin with a black glass knob, evidently the weapon he used on that fatal night.

Thus was solved the very curious problem of " The Crooked Sou."

THE MURDERS IN THE RUE MORGUE

What song the Syrens sang or what name Achilles assumed when he hid himself among women, although puzzling questions, are not beyond *all* conjecture.—Sir Thomas Browne, *Urn-Burial*.

THE mental features discoursed of as the analytical, are, in themselves, but little susceptible of analysis. We appreciate them only in their effects. We know of them, among other things, that they are always to their possessor, when inordinately possessed, a source of the liveliest enjoyment. As the strong man exults in his physical ability, delighting in such exercises as call his muscles into action, so glories the analyst in that moral activity which *disentangles*. He derives pleasure from even the most trivial occupations bringing his talents into play. He is fond of enigmas, of conundrums, of hieroglyphics; exhibiting in his solutions of each a degree of *acumen* which appears to the ordinary apprehension preternatural. His results, brought about by the very soul and essence of method, have, in truth, the whole air of intuition. The faculty of re-solution is possibly much invigorated by mathematical study, and especially by that highest branch of it which, unjustly, and merely on account of its retrograde operations, has been called, as if *par excellence*, analysis. Yet to calculate is not in itself to analyse. A chess-player, for example, does the one without effort at the other. It follows that the game of chess, in its effects upon mental character, is greatly misunderstood. I am not now writing a treatise, but simply prefacing a somewhat peculiar narrative by observations very much at random; I will, therefore, take occasion to assert that the higher powers of the reflective intellect are more decidedly and more usefully tasked by the unostentatious game of draughts than by all the elaborate frivolity of chess. In this latter, where the pieces have different and *bizarre* motions, with various and variable values, what is only complex is mistaken (a not unusual error) for what is profound. The *attention* is here called powerfully into play.

169

If it flag for an instant, an oversight is committed, resulting in injury or defeat. The possible moves being not only manifold but involute, the chances of such oversights are multiplied; and in nine cases out of ten it is the more concentrative rather than the more acute player who conquers. In draughts, on the contrary, where the moves are *unique* and have but little variation, the probabilities of inadvertence are diminished, and the mere attention being left comparatively unemployed, what advantages are obtained by either party are obtained by superior *acumen*. To be less abstract— Let us suppose a game of draughts where the pieces are reduced to four kings, and where, of course, no oversight is to be expected. It is obvious that here the victory can be decided (the players being at all equal) only by some *recherché* movement, the result of some exertion of the intellect. Deprived of ordinary resources, the analyst throws himself into the spirit of his opponent, identifies himself therewith, and not unfrequently sees thus, at a glance, the sole methods (sometimes indeed absurdly simple ones) by which he may seduce into error or hurry into miscalculation.

Whist had long been noted for its influence upon what is termed the calculating power; and men of the highest order of intellect have been known to take an apparently unaccountable delight in it, while eschewing chess as frivolous. Beyond doubt there is nothing of a similar nature so greatly tasking the faculty of analysis. The best chess-player in Christendom *may* be little more than the best player of chess; but proficiency in whist implies capacity for success in all these more important undertakings where mind struggles with mind. When I say proficiency, I mean that perfection in the game which includes a comprehension of *all* the sources whence legitimate advantage may be derived. These are not only manifold but multiform, and lie frequently among recesses of thought altogether inaccessible to the ordinary understanding. To observe attentively is to remember distinctly; and, so far, the concentrative chess-player will do very well at whist; while the rules of Hoyle (themselves based upon the mere mechanism of the game) are sufficiently and generally comprehensible. Thus to have a retentive memory, and to proceed by " the book," are points commonly regarded as the sum total of good playing. But it is in matters beyond the limits of mere rule that the skill of

the analyst is evinced. He makes, in silence, a host of observations and inferences. So, perhaps, do his companions;
and the difference in the extent of the information obtained,
lies not so much in the validity of the inference as in the
quality of the observation. The necessary knowledge is that
of *what* to observe. Our player confines himself not at all;
nor, because the game is the object, does he reject deductions
from things external to the game. He examines the countenance of his partner, comparing it carefully with that of
each of his opponents. He considers the mode of assorting
the cards in each hand; often counting trump by trump, and
honour by honour, through the glances bestowed by their
holders upon each. He notes every variation of face as the
play progresses, gathering a fund of thought from the differences in the expression of certainty, of surprise, of triumph,
or chagrin. From the manner of gathering up a trick he
judges whether the person taking it can make another in
the suit. He recognises what is played through feint, by
the air with which it is thrown upon the table. A casual
or inadvertent word; the accidental dropping or turning
of a card, with the accompanying anxiety or carelessness in
regard to its concealment; the counting of the tricks, with
the order of their arrangement; embarrassment, hesitation,
eagerness or trepidation—all afford, to his apparently intuitive
perception, indications of the true state of affairs. The
first two or three rounds having been played, he is in full
possession of the contents of each hand, and thenceforward
puts down his cards with as absolute a precision of purpose
as if the rest of the party had turned outward the faces of
their own.

The analytical power should not be confounded with
simple ingenuity; for while the analyst is necessarily ingenious, the ingenious man is often remarkably incapable of
analysis. The consecutive or combining power, by which
ingenuity is usually manifested, and to which the phrenolo-
gists (I believe erroneously) have assigned a separate organ,
supposing it a primitive faculty, has been so frequently seen
in those whose intellect bordered otherwise upon idiocy, as to
have attracted general observation among writers on morals.
Between ingenuity and the analytic ability there exists a
difference far greater, indeed, than that between the fancy
and the imagination, but of a character very strictly anal-

ogous. It will be found, in fact, that the ingenious are always fanciful, and the *truly* imaginative never otherwise than analytic.

The narrative which follows will appear to the reader somewhat in the light of a commentary upon the propositions just advanced.

Residing in Paris during the spring and part of the summer of 18—, I there became acquainted with a Monsieur C. Auguste Dupin. This young gentleman was of an excellent—indeed of an illustrious family, but, by a variety of untoward events, had been reduced to such poverty that the energy of his character succumbed beneath it, and he ceased to bestir himself in the world, or to care for the retrieval of his fortunes. By courtesy of his creditors, there still remained in his possession a small remnant of his patrimony; and, upon the income arising from this, he managed, by means of a rigorous economy, to procure the necessaries of life, without troubling himself about its superfluities. Books, indeed, were his sole luxuries, and in Paris these are easily obtained.

Our first meeting was at an obscure library in the Rue Montmartre, where the accident of our both being in search of the same very rare and very remarkable volume, brought us into closer communion. We saw each other again and again. I was deeply interested in the little family history which he detailed to me with all that candour which a Frenchman indulges whenever mere self is the theme. I was astonished, too, at the vast extent of his reading; and, above all, I felt my soul enkindled within me by the wild fervour, and the vivid freshness of his imagination. Seeking in Paris the objects I then sought, I felt that the society of such a man would be to me a treasure beyond price; and this feeling I frankly confided to him. It was at length arranged that we should live together during my stay in the city; and as my worldly circumstances were somewhat less embarrassed than his own, I was permitted to be at the expense of renting, and furnishing in a style which suited the rather fantastic gloom of our common temper, a time-eaten and grotesque mansion, long deserted through superstitions into which we did not inquire, and tottering to its fall in a retired and desolate portion of the Faubourg St. Germain.

Had the routine of our life at this place been known to the world, we should have been regarded as madmen—although, perhaps, as madmen of a harmless nature. Our seclusion was perfect. We admitted no visitors. Indeed the locality of our retirement had been carefully kept a secret from my own former associates; and it had been many years since Dupin had ceased to know or be known in Paris. We existed within ourselves alone.

It was a freak of fancy in my friend (for what else shall I call it?) to be enamoured of the Night for her own sake; and into this *bizarrerie,* as into all his others, I quietly fell; giving myself up to his wild whims with a perfect *abandon.* The sable divinity would not herself dwell with us always; but we could counterfeit her presence. At the first dawn of the morning we closed all the massy shutters of our old building; lighted a couple of tapers which, strongly perfumed, threw out only the ghastliest and feeblest of rays. By the aid of these we then busied our souls in dreams— reading, writing, or conversing, until warned by the clock of the advent of the true Darkness. Then we sallied forth into the streets, arm in arm, continuing the topics of the day, or roaming far and wide until a late hour, seeking, amid the wild lights and shadows of the populous city, that infinity of mental excitement which quiet observation can afford.

At such times I could not help remarking and admiring (although from his rich ideality I had been prepared to expect it) a peculiar analytic ability in Dupin. He seemed, too, to take an eager delight in its exercise—if not exactly in its display—and did not hesitate to confess the pleasure thus derived. He boasted to me, with a low chuckling laugh, that most men, in respect to himself, wore windows in their bosoms, and was wont to follow up such assertions by direct and very startling proofs of his intimate knowledge of my own. His manner at these moments was frigid and abstract; his eyes were vacant in expression; while his voice, usually a rich tenor, rose into a treble which would have sounded petulantly but for the deliberateness and entire distinctness of the enunciation. Observing him in these moods, I often dwelt meditatively upon the old philosophy of the Bi-Part Soul, and amused myself with the fancy of a double Dupin —the creative and the resolvent.

Let it not be supposed, from what I have just said, that I am detailing any mystery, or penning any romance. What I have described in the Frenchman, was merely the result of an excited, or perhaps of a diseased intelligence. But of the character of his remarks at the periods in question an example will best convey the idea.

We were strolling one night down a long dirty street, in the vicinity of the Palais Royal. Being both, apparently, occupied with thought, neither of us had spoken a syllable for fifteen minutes at least. All at once Dupin broke forth with these words:

"He is a very little fellow, that's true, and would do better for the *Théâtre des Variétés.*"

"There can be no doubt of that," I replied unwittingly, and not at first observing (so much had I been absorbed in reflection) the extraordinary manner in which the speaker had chimed in with my meditations. In an instant afterwards I recollected myself, and my astonishment was profound.

"Dupin," said I, gravely, "this is beyond my comprehension. I do not hesitate to say that I am amazed, and can scarcely credit my senses. How was it possible you should know I was thinking of——?" Here I paused, to ascertain beyond a doubt whether he really knew of whom I thought.

——"of Chantilly," said he, "why do you pause? You were remarking to yourself that his diminutive figure unfitted him for tragedy."

This was precisely what had formed the subject of my reflections. Chantilly was a *quondam* cobbler of the Rue St. Denis, who, becoming stage-mad, had attempted the *rôle* of Xerxes, in Crébillon's tragedy so called, and been notoriously Pasquinaded for his pains.

"Tell me, for Heaven's sake," I exclaimed, "the method —if method there is—by which you have been enabled to fathom my soul in this matter." In fact I was even more startled than I would have been willing to express.

"It was the fruiterer," replied my friend, "who brought you to the conclusion that the mender of soles was not of sufficient height for Xerxes *et id genus omne.*"

"The fruiterer!—you astonish me—I know no fruiterer whomsoever."

"The man who ran up against you as we entered the street—it may have been fifteen minutes ago."

I now remembered that, in fact, a fruiterer, carrying upon his head a large basket of apples, had nearly thrown me down, by accident, as we passed from the Rue C—— into the thoroughfare where we stood; but what this had to do with Chantilly I could not possibly understand.

There was not a particle of *charlatanerie* about Dupin. "I will explain," he said, "and that you may comprehend all clearly, we will first retrace the course of your meditations, from the moment in which I spoke to you until that of the *rencontre* with the fruiterer in question. The larger links of the chain run thus—Chantilly, Orion, Dr. Nichols, Epicurus, Stereototomy, the street stones, the fruiterer."

There are few persons who have not, at some period of their lives, amused themselves in retracing the steps by which particular conclusions of their own minds have been attained. The occupation is often full of interest; and he who attempts it for the first time is astonished by the apparently illimitable distance and incoherence between the starting-point and the goal. What, then, must have been my amazement when I heard the Frenchman speak what he had just spoken, and when I could not help acknowledging that he had spoken the truth. He continued:

"We had been talking of horses, if I remember aright, just before leaving the Rue C——. This was the last subject we discussed. As we crossed into this street, a fruiterer with a large basket upon his head, brushing quickly past us, thrust you upon a pile of paving-stones collected at a spot where the causeway is undergoing repair. You stepped upon one of the loose fragments, slipped, slightly strained your ankle, appeared vexed or sulky, muttered a few words, turned to look at the pile, and then proceeded in silence. I was not particularly attentive to what you did; but observation has become with me, of late, a species of necessity.

"You kept your eyes upon the ground—glancing, with a petulant expression, at the holes and ruts in the pavement (so that I saw you were still thinking of the stones), until we reached the little alley called Lamartine, which has been paved, by way of experiment, with the overlapping and riveted blocks. Here your countenance brightened up, and, perceiving your lips move, I could not doubt that you murmured the word ' stereotomy,' a term very affectedly applied to this species of pavement. I knew that you could not say to yourself ' stereotomy ' without being brought to think of atomies, and thus of the theories of Epicurus; and since, when we discussed this subject not very long ago, I mentioned to you how singularly, yet with how little notice, the vague guesses of that noble Greek had met with confirmation in the late nebular cosmogony, I felt that you could not avoid casting your eyes upwards to the great *nebula* in Orion, and I certainly expected that you would do so. You did look up; and I was now assured that I had correctly followed your steps. But in that bitter *tirade* upon Chantilly, which appeared in yesterday's ' *Musée,*' the satirist, making some disgraceful allusions to the cobbler's change of name upon assuming the buskin, quoted a Latin line about which we have often conversed. I mean the line

Perdidit antiquum litera prima sonum.

I had told you that this was in reference to Orion, formerly written Urion; and, from certain pungencies connected with this explanation, I was aware that you could not have forgotten it. It was clear, therefore, that you would not fail to combine the two ideas of Orion and Chantilly. That you did combine them I saw by the character of the smile which passed over your lips. You thought of the poor cobbler's immolation. So far, you had been stooping in your gait; but now I saw you draw yourself up to your full height. I was then sure that you reflected upon the diminutive figure of Chantilly. At this point I interrupted your meditations to remark that as, in fact, he *was* a very little fellow—that Chantilly—he would do better at the *Théâtre des Variétés.*"

Not long after this, we were looking over an evening edition of the *Gazette des Tribunaux,* when the following paragraphs arrested our attention.

" EXTRAORDINARY MURDERS.—This morning, about three o'clock, the inhabitants of the Quartier St. Roch were aroused from sleep by a succession of terrific shrieks, issuing, apparently, from the fourth story of a house in the Rue Morgue, known to be in the sole occupancy of one Madame L'Espanaye, and her daughter, Mademoiselle Camille L'Espanaye.

After some delay, occasioned by a fruitless attempt to procure admission in the usual manner, the gateway was broken in with a crowbar, and eight or ten of the neighbours entered, accompanied by two *gendarmes.* By this time the cries had ceased; but, as the party rushed up the first flight of stairs, two or more rough voices, in angry contention, were distinguished, and seemed to proceed from the upper part of the house. As the second landing was reached, these sounds, also, had ceased, and everything remained perfectly quiet. The party spread themselves, and hurried from room to room. Upon arriving at a large back chamber in the fourth story (the door of which, being found locked, with the key inside, was forced open), a spectacle presented itself which struck every one present not less with horror than with astonishment.

" The apartment was in the wildest disorder—the furniture broken and thrown about in all directions. There was only one bedstead; and from this the bed had been removed, and thrown into the middle of the floor. On a chair lay a razor, besmeared with blood. On the hearth were two or three long and thick tresses of grey human hair, also dabbled in blood, and seeming to have been pulled out by the roots. Upon the floor were found four Napoleons, an ear-ring of topaz, three large silver spoons, three smaller of *métal d'Alger,* and two bags, containing nearly four thousand francs in gold. The drawers of a *bureau,* which stood in one corner, were open, and had been, apparently, rifled, although many articles still remained in them. A small iron safe was discovered under the *bed* (not under the bedstead). It was open, with the key still in the door. It had no contents beyond a few old letters, and other papers of little consequence.

" Of Madame L'Espanaye no traces were here seen; but an unusual quantity of soot being observed in the fireplace, a search was made in the chimney, and (horrible to relate!) the corpse of the daughter, head downwards, was dragged therefrom; it having been thus forced up the narrow aperture for a considerable distance. The body was quite warm. Upon examining it, many excoriations were perceived, no doubt occasioned by the violence with which it had been thrust up and disengaged. Upon the face were many severe scratches, and, upon the throat, dark bruises, and deep indentations of finger-nails, as if the deceased had been throttled to death.

"After a thorough investigation of every portion of the house, without farther discovery, the party made its way into a small paved yard in the rear of the building, where lay the corpse of the old lady, with her throat so entirely cut that, upon an attempt to raise her, the head fell off. The body, as well as the head, was fearfully mutilated—the former so much so as scarcely to retain any semblance of humanity.

"To this horrible mystery there is not as yet, we believe, the slightest clue."

The next day's paper had these additional particulars.

"*The Tragedy in the Rue Morgue.* Many individuals have been examined in relation to this most extraordinary and frightful affair" (the word "*affaire*" has not yet, in France, that levity of import which it conveys with us), "but nothing whatever has transpired to throw light upon it. We give below all the material testimony elicited.

"*Pauline Dubourg*, laundress, deposes that she has known both the deceased for three years, having washed for them during that period. The old lady and her daughter seemed on good terms—very affectionate towards each other. They were excellent pay. Could not speak in regard to their mode or means of living. Believed that Madame L. told fortunes for a living. Was reputed to have money put by. Never met any persons in the house when she called for the clothes or took them home. Was sure that they had no servant in employ. There appeared to be no furniture in any part of the building except in the fourth story.

"*Pierre Moreau*, tobacconist, deposes that he has been in the habit of selling small quantities of tobacco and snuff to Madame L'Espanaye for nearly four years. Was born in the neighbourhood, and has always resided there. The deceased and her daughter had occupied the house in which the corpses were found, for more than six years. It was formerly occupied by a jeweller, who under-let the upper rooms to various persons. The house was the property of Madame L. She became dissatisfied with the abuse of the premises by her tenant, and moved into them herself, refusing to let any portion. The old lady was childish. Witness had seen the daughter some five or six times during the six years. The two lived an exceedingly retired life—were reputed to have money. Had heard it said among the neighbours that Madame L. told fortunes—did not believe it. Had never seen any person enter the door except the old lady and her daughter, a porter once or twice, and a physician some eight or ten times.

" Many other persons, neighbours, gave evidence to the same effect. No one was spoken of as frequenting the house. It was not known whether there were any living connections of Madame L. and her daughter. The shutters of the front windows were seldom opened. Those in the rear were always closed, with the exception of the large back room, fourth story. The house was a good house—not very old.

" *Isidore Musèt, gendarme,* deposes that he was called to the house about three o'clock in the morning, and found some twenty or thirty persons at the gateway, endeavouring to gain admittance. Forced it open, at length, with a bayonet—not with a crowbar. Had but little difficulty in getting it open, on account of its being a double or folding gate, and bolted neither at bottom nor top. The shrieks were continued until the gate was forced—and then suddenly ceased. They seemed to be screams of some person (or persons) in great agony—were loud and drawn out, not short and quick. Witness led the way upstairs. Upon reaching the first landing, heard two voices in loud and angry contention—the one a gruff voice, the other much shriller—a very strange voice. Could distinguish some words of the former, which was that of a Frenchman. Was positive that it was not a woman's voice. Could distinguish the words ' *sacré* ' and ' *diable.*' The shrill voice was that of a foreigner. Could not be sure whether it was the voice of a man or of a woman. Could not make out what was said, but believed the language to be Spanish. The state of the room and of the bodies was described by this witness as we described them yesterday.

" *Henri Duval,* a neighbour, and by trade a silversmith, deposes that he was one of the party who first entered the house. Corroborates the testimony of Musèt in general. As soon as they forced an entrance, they reclosed the door, to keep out the crowd, which collected very fast, notwithstanding the lateness of the hour. The shrill voice, the witness thinks, was that of an Italian. Was certain it was not French. Could not be sure that it was a man's voice. It might have been a woman's. Was not acquainted with the Italian language. Could not distinguish the words, but was convinced by the intonation that the speaker was an Italian. Knew Madame L. and her daughter. Had conversed with both frequently. Was sure that the shrill voice was not that of either of the deceased.

"——*Odenheimer, restaurateur.* This witness volunteered his testimony. Not speaking French, was examined through an interpreter. Is a native of Amsterdam. Was passing the house at the time of the shrieks. They lasted for several minutes—probably ten. They were long and loud—very awful and distressing. Was one of those who entered the building. Corroborated the previous evidence in every respect but one. Was sure that the shrill voice was that of a man—of a Frenchman. Could not distinguish the words uttered. They were loud and quick—unequal—spoken apparently in fear as well as in anger. The voice was harsh—not so much shrill as harsh. Could not call it a shrill voice. The gruff voice said repeatedly ' *sacré*,' ' *diable*,' and once ' *mon Dieu*.'

" *Jules Mignaud*, banker, of the firm of Mignaud et Fils, Rue Deloraine. Is the elder Mignaud. Madame L'Espanaye had some property. Had opened an account with his banking house in the spring of the year —— (eight years previously). Made frequent deposits in small sums. Had checked for nothing until the third day before her death, when she took out in person the sum of 4000 francs. This sum was paid in gold, and a clerk sent home with the money.

" *Adolphe Le Bon*, clerk to Mignaud et Fils, deposes that on the day in question, about noon, he accompanied Madame L'Espanaye to her residence with the 4000 francs, put up in two bags. Upon the door being opened, Mademoiselle L. appeared and took from his hands one of the bags, while the old lady relieved him of the other. He then bowed and departed. Did not see any person in the street at the time. It is a bye-street—very lonely.

" *William Bird*, tailor, deposes that he was one of the party who entered the house. Is an Englishman. Has lived in Paris two years. Was one of the first to ascend the stairs. Heard the voices in contention. The gruff voice was that of a Frenchman. Could make out several words, but cannot now remember all. Heard distinctly 'sacré' and 'mon Dieu.' There was a sound at the moment as if of several persons struggling—a scraping and scuffling sound. The shrill voice was very loud—louder than the gruff one. Is sure that it was not the voice of an Englishman. Appeared to be that of a German. Might have been a woman's voice. Does not understand German.

" Four of the above-named witnesses, being recalled, deposed that the door of the chamber in which was found the body of Mademoiselle L. was locked on the inside when the party reached it. Everything was perfectly silent—no groans or noises of any kind. Upon forcing the door no person was seen. The windows, both of the back and front room, were down and firmly fastened from within. A door between the two rooms was closed, but not locked. The door leading from the front room into the passage was locked, with the key on the inside. A small room in the front of the house, on the fourth story, at the head of the passage, was open, the door being ajar. This room was crowded with old beds, boxes, and so forth. These were carefully removed and searched. There was not an inch of any portion of the house which was not carefully searched. Sweeps were sent up and down the chimneys. The house was a four-story one, with garrets (*mansardes*). A trap-door on the roof was nailed down very securely—did not appear to have been opened for years. The time elapsing between the hearing of the voices in contention and the breaking open of the room door, was variously stated by the witnesses. Some made it as short as three minutes—some as long as five. The door was opened with difficulty.

" *Alfonzo Carcio*, undertaker, deposes that he resides in the Rue Morgue. Is a native of Spain. Was one of the party who entered the house. Did not proceed up-stairs. Is nervous, and was apprehensive of the consequences of agitation. Heard the voices in contention. The gruff voice was that of a Frenchman. Could not distinguish what was said. The shrill voice was that of an Englishman—is sure of this. Does not understand the English language, but judges by the intonation.

" *Alberto Montani*, confectioner, deposes that he was among the first to ascend the stairs. Heard the voices in question. The gruff voice was that of a Frenchman. Distinguished several words. The speaker appeared to be expostulating. Could not make out the words of the shrill voice. Spoke quick and unevenly. Thinks it the voice of a Russian. Corroborates the general testimony. Is an Italian. Never conversed with a native of Russia.

" Several witnesses, recalled, here testified that the chimneys of all the rooms on the fourth story were too narrow to admit the passage of a human being. By ' sweeps ' were meant cylindrical sweeping-brushes, such as are employed by those who clean chimneys. These brushes were passed up and down every flue in the house. There is no back passage by which any one could have descended while the party proceeded upstairs. The body of Mademoiselle L'Espanaye was so firmly wedged in the chimney that it could not be got down until four or five of the party united their strength.

" *Paul Dumas*, physician, deposes that he was called to view the bodies about daybreak. They were both then lying on the sacking of the bedstead in the chamber where Mademoiselle L. was found. The corpse of the young lady was much bruised and excoriated. The fact that it had been thrust up the chimney would sufficiently account for these appearances. The throat was greatly chafed. There were several deep scratches just below the chin, together with a series of livid spots which were evidently the impression of fingers. The face was fearfully discoloured, and the eyeballs protruded. The tongue had been partially bitten through. A large bruise was discovered upon the pit of the stomach, produced, apparently, by the pressure of a knee. In the opinion of M. Dumas, Mademoiselle L'Espanaye had been throttled to death by some person or persons unknown. The corpse of the mother was horribly mutilated. All the bones of the right leg and arm were more or less shattered. The left *tibia* much splintered, as well as all the ribs of the left side. Whole body dreadfully bruised and discoloured. It was not possible to say how the injuries had been inflicted. A heavy club of wood, or a broad bar of iron—a chair— any large, heavy, and obtuse weapon would have produced such results, if wielded by the hands of a very powerful man. No woman could have inflicted the blows with any weapon. The head of the deceased, when seen by witness, was entirely separated from the body, and was also greatly shattered. The throat had evidently been cut with some very sharp instrument—probably with a razor.

" *Alexandre Etienne*, surgeon, was called with M. Dumas to view the bodies. Corroborated the testimony, and the opinions of M. Dumas.

" Nothing farther of importance was elicited, although several other persons were examined. A murder so mysterious, and so perplexing in all its particulars, was never before committed in Paris—if indeed a murder has been committed at all. The police are entirely at fault—an unusual occurrence in affairs of this nature. There is not, however, the shadow of a clue apparent."

The evening edition of the paper stated that the greatest excitement still continued in the Quartier St. Roch—that the premises in question had been carefully re-searched, and fresh examinations of witnesses instituted, but all to no purpose. A postscript, however, mentioned that Adolphe Le Bon had been arrested and imprisoned—although nothing appeared to criminate him, beyond the facts already detailed.

Dupin seemed singularly interested in the progress of this affair—at least so I judged from his manner, for he made no comments. It was only after the announcement that Le Bon had been imprisoned, that he asked me my opinion respecting the murders.

I could merely agree with all Paris in considering them an insoluble mystery. I saw no means by which it would be possible to trace the murderer.

" We must not judge of the means," said Dupin, " by this shell of an examination. The Parisian police, so much extolled for *acumen*, are cunning, but no more. There is no method in their proceedings, beyond the method of the moment. They make a vast parade of measures; but, not unfrequently, these are so ill adapted to the objects proposed, as to put us in mind of Monsieur Jourdain's calling for his *robe-de-chambre—pour mieux entendre la musique*. The results attained by them are not unfrequently surprising, but, for the most part, are brought about by simple diligence and activity. When these qualities are unavailing, their schemes fail. Vidocq, for example, was a good guesser, and a persevering man. But, without educated thought, he erred continually by the very intensity of his investigations. He impaired his vision by holding the object too close. He might see, perhaps, one or two points with unusual clearness, but in so doing he, necessarily, lost sight of the matter as a whole. Thus there is such a thing as being too profound. Truth is not always in a well. In fact, as regards the more important knowledge, I do believe that she is invariably superficial. The depth lies in the valleys where we seek her, and not upon the mountain-tops where she is found. The modes and sources of this kind of error are well typified in the contemplation of the heavenly bodies. To look at a star by glances—to view it in a side-long way, by turning towards it the exterior portions of the *retina* (more susceptible of feeble impressions of light than the interior), is to behold the star distinctly—is to have the best appreciation of its lustre —a lustre which grows dim just in proportion as we turn our vision *fully* upon it. A greater number of rays actually fall upon the eye in the latter case, but, in the former, there is the more refined capacity for comprehension. By undue profundity we perplex and enfeeble thought; and it is possible to make even Venus herself vanish from the firmament by a scrutiny too sustained, too concentrated, or too direct.

" As for these murders, let us enter into some examinations for ourselves, before we make up an opinion respecting them. An inquiry will afford us amusement " (I thought this an odd term, so applied, but said nothing), " and, besides, Le Bon once rendered me a service for which I am not ungrateful. We will go and see the premises with our own eyes. I know G——, the Prefect of Police, and shall have no difficulty in obtaining the necessary permission."

The permission was obtained, and we proceeded at once to the Rue Morgue. This is one of those miserable thoroughfares which intervene between the Rue Richelieu and the Rue St. Roch. It was late in the afternoon when we reached it; as this quarter is at a great distance from that in which we resided. The house was readily found; for there were still many persons gazing up at the closed shutters, with an objectless curiosity, from the opposite side of the way. It was an ordinary Parisian house, with a gateway, on one side of which was a glazed watch-box, with a sliding panel in the window, indicating a *loge de concierge*. Before going in we walked up the street, turned down an alley, and then, again turning, passed in the rear of the building—Dupin, meanwhile, examining the whole neighbourhood, as well as the house, with a minuteness of attention for which I could see no possible object.

Retracing our steps, we came again to the front of the dwelling, rang, and, having shown our credentials, were admitted by the agents in charge. We went upstairs—into the chamber where the body of Mademoiselle L'Espanaye had been found, and where both the deceased still lay. The disorders of the room had, as usual, been suffered to exist. I saw nothing beyond what had been stated in the *Gazette des Tribunaux*. Dupin scrutinised everything—not excepting the bodies of the victims. We then went into the other rooms, and into the yard; a *gendarme* accompanying us throughout. The examination occupied us until dark, when we took our departure. On our way home my companion stopped in for a moment at the office of one of the daily papers.

I have said that the whims of my friend were manifold, and that *Je les ménageais*:—for this phrase there is no English equivalent. It was his humour, now, to decline all conversation on the subject of the murder, until about noon the next day. He then asked me, suddenly, if I had observed anything *peculiar* at the scene of the atrocity.

There was something in his manner of emphasising the word "peculiar," which caused me to shudder, without knowing why.

"No, nothing *peculiar*," I said; "nothing more, at least, than we both saw stated in the paper."

"The *Gazette*," he replied, "has not entered, I fear, into the unusual horror of the thing. But dismiss the idle opinions of this print. It appears to me that this mystery is considered insoluble, for the very reason which should cause it to be regarded as easy of solution—I mean for the *outré* character of its features. The police are confounded by the seeming absence of motive—not for the murder itself—but for the atrocity of the murder. They are puzzled, too, by the seeming impossibility of reconciling the voices heard in contention with the facts that no one was discovered upstairs but the assassinated Mademoiselle L'Espanaye, and that there were no means of egress without the notice of the party ascending. The wild disorder of the room; the corpse thrust, with the head downwards, up the chimney; the frightful mutilation of the body of the old lady; these considerations, with those just mentioned, and others which I need not mention, have sufficed to paralyse the powers by putting completely at fault the boasted *acumen,* of the government agents. They have fallen into the gross but common error of confounding the unusual with the abstruse. But it is by these deviations from the plane of the ordinary, that reason feels its way, if at all, in its search for the true. In investigations such as we are now pursuing, it should not be so much asked ' what has occurred,' as ' what has occurred that has never occurred before.' In fact, the facility with which I shall arrive, or have arrived, at the solution of this mystery, is in the direct ratio of its apparent insolubility in the eyes of the police."

I stared at the speaker in mute astonishment.

" I am now awaiting," continued he, looking towards the door of our apartment—" I am now awaiting a person who, although perhaps not the perpetrator of these butcheries, must have been in some measure implicated in their perpetration. Of the worst portion of the crimes committed, it is probable that he is innocent. I hope that I am right in this supposition; for upon it I build my expectation of reading the entire riddle. I look for the man here—in this room—every moment. It is true that he may not arrive; but the probability is that he will. Should he come, it will be necessary to detain him. Here are pistols; and we both know how to use them when occasion demands their use."

I took the pistols, scarcely knowing what I did, or believing what I heard, while Dupin went on, very much as if in a soliloquy. I have already spoken of his abstract manner at such times. His discourse was addressed to myself; but his voice, although by no mean loud, had that intonation which is commonly employed in speaking to some one at a great distance. His eyes, vacant in expression, regarded only the wall.

" That the voices heard in contention," he said, " by the party upon the stairs, were not the voices of the women themselves, was fully proved by the evidence. This relieves us of all doubt upon the question whether the old lady could have first destroyed the daughter, and afterwards have committed suicide. I speak of this point chiefly for the sake of method; for the strength of Madame L'Espanaye would have been utterly unequal to the task of thrusting her daugh-

ter's corpse up the chimney as it was found; and the nature
of the wounds upon her own person entirely preclude the
idea of self-destruction. Murder, then, has been committed
by some third party; and the voices of this third party were
those heard in contention. Let me now advert—not to the
whole testimony respecting these voices—but to what was
peculiar in that testimony. Did you observe anything peculiar about it? "

I remarked that, while all the witnesses agreed in supposing the gruff voice to be that of a Frenchman, there was
much disagreement in regard to the shrill, or, as one individual termed it, the harsh voice.

" That was the evidence itself," said Dupin, " but it was
not the peculiarity of the evidence. You have observed
nothing distinctive. Yet there *was* something to be observed.
The witnesses, as you remark, agreed about the gruff voice;
they were here unanimous. But in regard to the shrill
voice, the peculiarity is—not that they disagreed—but that,
while an Italian, an Englishman, a Spaniard, a Hollander,
and a Frenchman attempted to describe it, each one spoke of
it as that *of a foreigner.* Each is sure that it was not the
voice of one of his own countrymen. Each likens it—not
to the voice of an individual of any nation with whose language he is conversant—but the converse. The Frenchman
supposes it the voice of a Spaniard, and ' might have distinguished some words *had he been acquainted with the
Spanish.*' The Dutchman maintains it to have been that of
a Frenchman; but we find it stated that ' *not understanding
French this witness was examined through an interpreter.*'
The Englishman thinks it the voice of a German, and ' *does
not understand German.*' The Spaniard ' is sure ' that it
was that of an Englishman, but ' judges by the intonation '
altogether, ' *as he has no knowledge of the English.*' The
Italian believes it the voice of a Russian, but ' *has never conversed with a native of Russia.*' A second Frenchman differs,
moreover, with the first, and is positive that the voice was
that of an Italian, but, ' *not being cognisant of that tongue,
is,* like the Spaniard, convinced by the intonation.' Now, how
strangely unusual must that voice have really been, about
which such testimony as this *could* have been elicited!—in
whose *tones,* even, denisens of the five great divisions of
Europe could recognise nothing familiar! You will say that

it might have been the voice of an Asiatic—of an African. Neither Asiatics nor Africans abound in Paris; but, without denying the inference, I will now merely call your attention to three points. The voice is termed by one witness ' harsh rather than shrill.' It is represented by two others to have been ' quick and *unequal.*' No words—no sounds resembling words—were by any witness mentioned as distinguishable.

" I know not," continued Dupin, " what impression I may have made, so far, upon your own understanding; but I do not hesitate to say that legitimate deductions even from this portion of the testimony—the portion respecting the gruff and shrill voices—are in themselves sufficient to engender a suspicion which should give direction to all farther progress in the investigation of the mystery. I said ' legitimate deductions '; but my meaning is not thus fully expressed. I designed to imply that the deductions are the *sole* proper ones, and that the suspicion arises *inevitably* from them as the single result. What the suspicion is, however, I will not say just yet. I merely wish you to bear in mind that, with myself, it was sufficiently forcible to give a definite form —a certain tendency—to my inquiries in the chamber.

" Let us now transport ourselves, in fancy, to this chamber. What shall we first seek here? The means of egress employed by the murderers. It is not too much to say that neither of us believe in præternatural events. Madame and Mademoiselle L'Espanaye were not destroyed by spirits. The doers of the deed were material, and escaped materially. Then how? Fortunately, there is but one mode of reasoning upon the point, and that mode *must* lead us to a definite decision.—Let us examine, each by each, the possible means of egress. It is clear that the assassins were in the room where Mademoiselle L'Espanaye was found, or at least in the room adjoining, when the party ascended the stairs. It is then only from these two apartments that we have to seek issues. The police have laid bare the floors, the ceilings, and the masonry of the walls, in every direction. No *secret* issues could have escaped their vigilance. But not trusting to *their* eyes, I examined with my own. There were, then, *no* secret issues. Both doors leading from the rooms into the passage were securely locked, with the keys inside. Let us turn to the chimneys. These, although of ordinary width for some

eight or ten feet above the hearths, will not admit, throughout their extent, the body of a large cat. The impossibility
of egress, by means already stated, being thus absolute, we
are reduced to the windows. Through those of the front
room no one could have escaped without notice from the
crowd in the street. The murderers *must* have passed, then,
through those of the back room. Now, brought to this conclusion in so unequivocal a manner as we are, it is not our
part, as reasoners, to reject it on account of apparent impossibilities. It is only for us to prove that these apparent
' impossibilities ' are, in reality, not such.

"There are two windows in the chamber. One of them
is unobstructed by furniture, and is wholly visible. The lower
portion of the other is hidden from view by the head of
the unwieldy bedstead which is thrust close up against it.
The former was found securely fastened from within. It
resisted the utmost force of those who endeavoured to raise
it. A large gimlet-hole had been pierced in its frame to the
left, and a very stout nail was found fitted therein, nearly
to the head. Upon examining the other window, a similar
nail was seen similarly fitted in it; and a vigorous attempt to
raise this sash, failed also. The police were now entirely
satisfied that egress had not been in these directions. And,
therefore, it was thought a matter of supererogation to withdraw the nails and open the windows.

"My own examination was somewhat more particular,
and was so for the reason I have just given—because here it
was, I knew, that all apparent impossibilities *must* be proved
to be not such in reality.

"I proceeded to think thus—*à posteriori.* The murderers
did escape from one of these windows. This being so, they
could not have re-fastened the sashes from the inside, as they
were found fastened;—the consideration which put a stop,
through its obviousness, to the scrutiny of the police in this
quarter. Yet the sashes *were* fastened. They *must,* then,
have the power of fastening themselves. There was no
escape from this conclusion. I stepped to the unobstructed
casement, withdrew the nail with some difficulty, and attempted to raise the sash. It resisted all my efforts, as I
had anticipated. A concealed spring must, I now knew,
exist; and this corroboration of my idea convinced me that
my premises, at least, were correct, however mysterious still

appeared the circumstances attending the nails. A careful search soon brought to light the hidden spring. I pressed it, and, satisfied with the discovery, forbore to upraise the sash.

"I now replaced the nail and regarded it attentively. A person passing out through this window might have re-closed it, and the spring would have caught—but the nail could not have been replaced. The conclusion was plain, and again narrowed in the field of my investigations. The assassins *must* have escaped through the other window. Sup-posing, then, the springs upon each sash to be the same, as was probable, there *must* be found a difference between the nails, or at least between the modes of their fixture. Getting upon the sacking of the bedstead, I looked over the head-board minutely at the second casement. Passing my hand down behind the board, I readily discovered and pressed the spring, which was, as I had supposed, identical in character with its neighbour. I now looked at the nail. It was as stout as the other, and apparently fitted in the same manner —driven in nearly up to the head.

"You will say that I was puzzled; but, if you think so, you must have misunderstood the nature of the inductions. To use a sporting phrase, I had not been once ' at fault.' The scent had never for an instant been lost. There was no flaw in any link of the chain. I had traced the secret to its ulti-mate result,—and that result was *the nail*. It had, I say, in every respect, the appearance of its fellow in the other win-dow; but this fact was an absolute nullity (conclusive as it might seem to be) when compared with the consideration that here, at this point, terminated the clue. 'There *must* be something wrong,' I said, ' about the nail.' I touched it; and the head, with about a quarter of an inch of the shank, came off in my fingers. The rest of the shank was in the gimlet-hole, where it had been broken off. The fracture was an old one (for its edges were incrusted with rust), and had apparently been accomplished by the blow of a hammer, which had partially imbedded, in the top of the bottom sash, the head portion of the nail. I now carefully replaced this head portion in the indentation whence I had taken it, and the resemblance to a perfect nail was complete—the fissure was invisible. Pressing the spring, I gently raised the sash for a few inches; the head went up with it, remaining firm in its bed. I closed the window, and the semblance of the whole nail was again perfect.

"The riddle, so far, was now unriddled. The assassin had escaped through the window which looked upon the bed. Dropping of its own accord upon his exit (or perhaps purposely closed), it had become fastened by the spring; and it was the retention of this spring which had been mistaken by the police for that of the nail—farther inquiry being thus considered unnecessary.

"The next question is that of the mode of descent. Upon this point I had been satisfied in my walk with you around the building. About five feet and a half from the casement in question there runs a lightning-rod. From this rod it would have been impossible for any one to reach the window itself, to say nothing of entering it. I observed, however, that the shutters of the fourth story were of the peculiar kind called by Parisian carpenters *ferrades*—a kind rarely employed at the present day, but frequently seen upon very old mansions at Lyons and Bordeaux. They are in the form of an ordinary door (a single, not a folding door), except that the upper half is latticed or worked in open trellis— thus affording an excellent hold for the hands. In the present instance these shutters are fully three feet and a half broad. When we saw them from the rear of the house, they were both about half open—that is to say, they stood off at right angles from the wall. It is probable that the police, as well as myself, examined the back of the tenement; but, if so, in looking at these *ferrades* in the line of their breadth (as they must have done), they did not perceive this great breadth itself, or, at all events, failed to take it into due consideration. In fact, having once satisfied themselves that no egress could have been made in this quarter, they would naturally bestow here a very cursory examination. It was clear to me, however, that the shutter belonging to the window at the head of the bed, would, if swung fully back to the wall, reach to within two feet of the lightning-rod. It was also evident that, by exertion of a very unusual degree of activity and courage, an entrance into the window, from the rod, might have been thus effected.—By reaching to the distance of two feet and a half (we now suppose the shutter open to its whole extent) a robber might have taken a firm grasp upon the trellis-work. Letting go, then, his hold upon

the rod, placing his feet securely against the wall, and springing boldly from it, he might have swung the shutter so
as to close it, and, if we imagine the window open at the
time, might even have swung himself into the room.

" I wish you to bear especially in mind that I have spoken
of a *very* unusual degree of activity as requisite to success
in so hazardous and so difficult a feat. It is my design to show
you, first, that the thing might possibly have been accomplished:—but, secondly and *chiefly*, I wish to impress upon
your understanding the *very extraordinary*—the almost præternatural character of that agility which could have accomplished it.

" You will say, no doubt, using the language of the law,
that ' to make out my case ' I should rather undervalue, than
insist upon a full estimation of the activity required in this
matter. This may be the practice in law, but it is not the
usage of reason. My ultimate object is only the truth. My
immediate purpose is to lead you to place in juxtaposition that
very unusual activity of which I have just spoken, with that
very peculiar shrill (or harsh) and *unequal* voice, about whose
nationality no two persons could be found to agree, and in
whose utterance no syllabification could be detected."

At these words a vague and half-formed conception of the
meaning of Dupin flitted over my mind. I seemed to be upon
the verge of comprehension, without power to comprehend
—as men, at times, find themselves upon the brink of re-
membrance, without being able in the end, to remember.
My friend went on with his discourse.

" You will see," he said, " that I have shifted the question from the mode of egress to that of ingress. It was my
design to suggest that both were effected in the same manner,
at the same point. Let us now revert to the interior of the
room. Let us survey the appearances here. The drawers of
the bureau, it is said, had been rifled, although many articles
or apparel still remained within them. The conclusion here
is absurd. It is a mere guess—a very silly one—and no
more. How are we to know that the articles found in the
drawers were not all these drawers had originally contained?
Madame L'Espanaye and her daughter lived an exceedingly
retired life—saw no company—seldom went out—had little
use for numerous changes of habiliment. Those found were
at least of as good quality as any likely to be possessed by

these ladies.   If a thief had taken any, why did he not take the best—why did he not take all?   In a word, why did he abandon four thousand francs in gold to encumber himself with a bundle of linen?   The gold *was* abandoned.   Nearly the whole sum mentioned by Monsieur Mignaud, the banker, was discovered, in bags, upon the floor.   I wish you, therefore, to discard from your thoughts the blundering idea of *motive*, engendered in the brains of the police by that portion of the evidence which speaks of money delivered at the door of the house.   Coincidences ten times as remarkable as this (the delivery of the money, and murder committed within three days upon the party receiving it), happen to all of us every hour of our lives, without attracting even momentary notice.   Coincidences, in general, are great stumbling-blocks in the way of that class of thinkers who have been educated to know nothing of the theory of probabilities—that theory to which the most glorious objects of human research are indebted for the most glorious of illustration.   In the present instance, had the gold been gone, the fact of its delivery three days before would have formed something more than a coincidence.   It would have been corroborative of this idea of motive.   But, under the real circumstances of the case, if we are to suppose gold the motive of this outrage, we must also imagine the perpetrator so vacillating an idiot as to have abandoned his gold and his motive together.

"Keeping now steadily in mind the points to which I have drawn your attention—that peculiar voice, that unusual agility, and that startling absence of motive in a murder so singularly atrocious as this—let us glance at the butchery itself.   Here is a woman strangled to death by manual strength, and thrust up a chimney, head downwards.   Ordinary assassins employ no such modes of murder as this.   Least of all, do they thus dispose of the murdered.   In the manner of thrusting the corpse up the chimney, you will admit that there was something *excessively outré*—something altogether irreconcilable with our common notions of human action, even when we suppose the actors the most depraved of men.   Think, too, how great must have been that strength which could have thrust the body *up* such an aperture so forcibly that the united vigour of several persons was found barely sufficient to drag it *down!*

" Turn, now, to other indications of the employment of a

vigour most marvellous.   On the hearth were thick tresses
—very thick tresses—of grey human hair. These had been
torn out by the roots. You are aware of the great force in
tearing thus from the head even twenty or thirty hairs together. You saw the locks in question as well as myself.
Their roots (a hideous sight!) were clotted with fragments
of the flesh of the scalp—sure token of the prodigious power
which had been exerted in uprooting perhaps half a million
of hairs at a time. The throat of the old lady was not
merely cut, but the head absolutely severed from the body:
the instrument was a mere razor. I wish you also to look at
the *brutal* ferocity of these deeds. Of the bruises upon the
body of Madame L'Espanaye I do not speak. Monsieur
Dumas, and his worthy coadjutor Monsieur Etienne, have
pronounced that they were inflicted by some obtuse instrument; and so far these gentlemen are very correct. The obtuse instrument was clearly the stone pavement in the yard,
upon which the victim had fallen from the window which
looked in upon the bed. This idea, however simple it may
now seem, escaped the police for the same reason that the
breadth of the shutters escaped them—because, by the affair
of the nails, their perceptions had been hermetically sealed
against the possibility of the windows having ever been
opened at all.

" If now, in addition to all these things, you have properly
reflected upon the odd disorder of the chamber, we have
gone so far as to combine the ideas of an agility astounding,
a strength superhuman, a ferocity brutal, a butchery without
motive, a *grotesquerie* in horror absolutely alien from humanity, and a voice foreign in tone to the ears of men of
many nations, and devoid of all distinct or intelligible syllabification. What result, then, has ensued? What impression
have I made upon your fancy? "

I felt a creeping of the flesh as Dupin asked me the question. "A madman," I said, " has done this deed—some
raving maniac, escaped from a neighbouring *Maison de
Santé*."

" In some respects," he replied, " your idea is not irrelevant. But the voices of madmen, even in their wildest parox-
ysms, are never found to tally with that peculiar voice heard
upon the stairs. Madmen are of some nation, and their
language, however incoherent in its words, has always the

coherence of syllabification. Besides, the hair of a madman is not such as I now hold in my hand. I disentangled this little tuft from the rigidly clutched fingers of Madame L'Espanaye. Tell me what you can make of it."

"Dupin!" I said, completely unnerved; "this hair is most unusual—this is no *human* hair."

"I have not asserted that it is," said he; "but, before we decide this point, I wish you to glance at the little sketch I have here traced upon this paper. It is a *fac-simile* drawing of what has been described in one portion of the testimony as 'dark bruises, and deep indentations of finger-nails,' upon the throat of Mademoiselle L'Espanaye, and in another (by Messrs. Dumas and Etienne), as a 'series of livid spots, evidently the impression of fingers.'

"You will perceive," continued my friend, spreading out the paper upon the table before us, "that this drawing gives the idea of a firm and fixed hold. There is no *slipping* apparent. Each finger has retained—possibly until the death of the victim—the fearful grasp by which it originally imbedded itself. Attempt, now, to place all your fingers, at the same time, in the respective impressions as you see them."

I made the attempt in vain.

"We are possibly not giving this matter a fair trial," he said. "The paper is spread out upon a plane surface; but the human throat is cylindrical. Here is a billet of wood, the circumference of which is about that of the throat. Wrap the drawing around it, and try the experiment again."

I did so; but the difficulty was even more obvious than before.

"This," I said, "is the mark of no human hand."

"Read now," replied Dupin, "this passage from Cuvier."

It was a minute anatomical and generally descriptive account of the large fulvous Ourang-Outang of the East Indian Islands. The gigantic stature, the prodigious strength and activity, the wild ferocity, and the imitative propensities of these mammalia are sufficiently well known to all. I understood the full horrors of the murder at once.

"The description of the digits," said I, as I made an end of reading, "is in exact accordance with this drawing. I see that no animal but an Ourang-Outang, of the species here mentioned, could have impressed the indentations as you have traced them. This tuft of tawny hair, too, is identical with that of the beast of Cuvier. But I cannot possibly comprehend the particulars of this frightful mystery. Besides, there were *two* voices heard in contention, and one of them was unquestionably the voice of a Frenchman."

"True; and you will remember an expression attributed almost unanimously, by the evidence, to this voice,—the expression, 'mon Dieu!' This, under the circumstances, has been justly characterised by one of the witnesses (Montani, the confectioner), as an expression of remonstrance or expostulation. Upon these two words, therefore, I have mainly built my hopes of a full solution of the riddle. A Frenchman was cognisant of the murder. It is possible—indeed it is far more than probable—that he was innocent of all participation in the bloody transactions which took place. The Ourang-Outang may have escaped from him. He may have traced it to the chamber; but, under the agitating circumstances which ensued, he could never have recaptured it. It is still at large. I will not pursue these guesses—for I have no right to call them more—since the shades of reflection upon which they are based are scarcely of sufficient depth to be appreciable by my own intellect, and since I could not pretend to make them intelligible to the understanding of another. We will call them guesses then, and speak of them as such. If the Frenchman in question is indeed, as I suppose, innocent of this atrocity, this advertisement, which I left last night, upon our return home, at the office of *Le Monde* (a paper devoted to the shipping interest, and much sought by sailors), will bring him to our residence."

He handed me a paper, and I read thus:

CAUGHT—*In the Bois de Boulogne, early in the morning of the —— inst.* (the morning of the murder), *a very large, tawny Ourang-Outang of the Bornese species. The owner (who is ascertained to be a sailor, belonging to a Maltese vessel) may have the animal again, upon identifying it satisfactorily and paying a few charges arising from its capture and keeping. Call at No. ——, Rue ——, Faubourg St. Germain—— au troisième.*

"How was it possible," I asked, "that you should know the man to be a sailor, and belonging to a Maltese vessel?"

"I do *not* know it," said Dupin. "I am not *sure* of it. Here, however, is a small piece of ribbon, which from its form, and from its greasy appearance, has evidently been used in tying the hair in one of those long *queues* of which sailors are so fond. Moreover, this knot is one which few besides sailors can tie, and is peculiar to the Maltese. I picked the ribbon up at the foot of the lightning-rod. It could not have belonged to either of the deceased. Now if, after all, I am wrong in my induction from this ribbon, that the Frenchman was a sailor belonging to a Maltese vessel, still I can have done no harm in saying what I did in the advertisement. If I am in error, he will merely suppose that I have been misled by some circumstance into which he will not take the trouble to inquire. But if I am right, a great point is gained. Cognisant although innocent of the murder, the Frenchman will naturally hesitate about replying to the advertisement—about demanding the Ourang-Outang. He will reason thus: ' I am innocent; I am poor; my Ourang-Outang is of great value—to one in my circumstances a fortune of itself—why should I lose it through idle apprehensions of danger? Here it is, within my grasp. It was found in the Bois de Boulogne—at a vast distance from the scene of that butchery. How can it ever be suspected that a brute beast should have done the deed? The police are at fault—they have failed to procure the slightest clue. Should they even trace the animal, it would be impossible to prove me cognisant of the murder, or to implicate me in guilt on account of that cognisance. Above all, *I am known.* The advertiser designates me as the possessor of the beast. I am not sure to what limit his knowledge may extend. Should I avoid claiming a property of so great value, which it is known that I possess, I will render the animal, at least, liable to suspicion. It is not my policy to attract attention either to myself or to the beast. I will answer the advertisement, get the Ourang-Outang, and keep it close until this matter has blown over.' "

At this moment we heard a step upon the stairs.

" Be ready," said Dupin, " with your pistols, but neither use them nor show them until at a signal from myself."

The front door of the house had been left open, and the visitor had entered, without ringing, and advanced several steps upon the staircase. Now, however, he seemed to hesitate. Presently we heard him descending. Dupin was moving quickly to the door, when we again heard him coming up. He did not turn back a second time, but stepped up with decision and rapped at the door of our chamber.

" Come in," said Dupin, in a cheerful and hearty tone.

A man entered. He was a sailor, evidently,—a tall, stout,

and muscular-looking person, with a certain dare-devil expression of countenance, not altogether unprepossessing. His face, greatly sunburnt, was more than half hidden by whisker and *mustachio*. He had with him a huge oaken cudgel, but appeared to be otherwise unarmed. He bowed awkwardly, and bade us " good evening," in French accents, which, although somewhat Neufchatelish, were still sufficiently indicative of a Parisian origin.

" Sit down, my friend," said Dupin. " I suppose you have called about the Ourang-Outang. Upon my word, I almost envy you the possession of him; a remarkably fine, and no doubt a very valuable animal. How old do you suppose him to be? "

The sailor drew a long breath, with the air of a man relieved of some intolerable burthen, and then replied, in an assured tone:

" I have no way of telling—but he can't be more than four or five years old. Have you got him here? "

" Oh no; we have no conveniences for keeping him here. He is at a livery stable in the Rue Dubourg, just by. You can get him in the morning. Of course you are prepared to identify the property? "

" To be sure I am, sir."

" I shall be sorry to part with him," said Dupin.

" I don't mean that you should be at all this trouble for nothing, sir," said the man. " Couldn't expect it. Am very willing to pay a reward for the finding of the animal —that is to say, anything in reason."

" Well," replied my friend, " that is all very fair, to be sure. Let me think!—what should I have? Oh! I will tell you. My reward shall be this. You shall give me all the information in your power about these murders in the Rue Morgue."

Dupin said the last words in a very low tone, and very quietly. Just as quietly, too, he walked toward the door, locked it, and put the key in his pocket. He then drew a pistol from his bosom and placed it, without the least flurry, upon the table.

The sailor's face flushed up as if he were struggling with suffocation. He started to his feet and grasped his cudgel; but the next moment he fell back into his seat, trembling violently, and with the countenance of death itself. He spoke not a word. I pitied him from the bottom of my heart.

"My friend," said Dupin, in a kind tone, "you are alarming yourself unnecessarily—you are indeed. We mean you no harm whatever. I pledge you the honour of a gentleman, and of a Frenchman, that we intend you no injury. I perfectly well know that you are innocent of the atrocities in the Rue Morgue. It will not do, however, to deny that you are in some measure implicated in them. From what I have already said, you must know that I have had means of information about this matter—means of which you could never have dreamed. Now the thing stands thus. You have done nothing which you could have avoided—nothing, certainly, which renders you culpable. You were not even guilty of robbery, when you might have robbed with impunity. You have nothing to conceal. You have no reason for concealment. On the other hand, you are bound by every principle of honour to confess all you know. An innocent man is now imprisoned, charged with that crime of which you can point out the perpetrator."

The sailor had recovered his presence of mind, in a great measure, while Dupin uttered these words; but his original boldness of bearing was all gone.

"So help me God!" said he, after a brief pause, "I *will* tell you all I know about this affair;—but I do not expect you to believe one half I say—I would be a fool indeed if I did. Still, I *am* innocent, and I will make a clean breast if I die for it."

What he stated was, in substance, this. He had lately made a voyage to the Indian Archipelago. A party, of which he formed one, landed at Borneo, and passed into the interior on an excursion of pleasure. Himself and a companion had captured the Ourang-Outang. This companion dying, the animal fell into his own exclusive possession. After great trouble, occasioned by the intractable ferocity of his captive during the home voyage, he at length succeeded in lodging it safely at his own residence in Paris, where, not to attract toward himself the unpleasant curiosity of his neighbours, he kept it carefully secluded, until such time as it should recover from a wound in the foot, received from a splinter on board ship. His ultimate design was to sell it.

Returning home from some sailors' frolic on the night, or rather in the morning of the murder, he found the beast occupying his own bedroom, into which it had broken from a closet adjoining, where it had been, as was thought, securely confined. Razor in hand, and fully lathered, it was sitting before a looking-glass, attempting the operation of shaving, in which it had no doubt previously watched its master through the keyhole of the closet. Terrified at the sight of so dangerous a weapon in the possession of an animal so ferocious, and so well able to use it, the man, for some moments, was at a loss what to do. He had been accustomed, however, to quiet the creature, even in its fiercest moods, by the use of a whip, and to this he now resorted. Upon sight of it, the Ourang-Outang sprang at once through the door of the chamber, down the stairs, and thence through a window, unfortunately open, into the street.

The Frenchman followed in despair; the ape, razor still in hand, occasionally stopping to look back and gesticulate at its pursuer, until the latter had nearly come up with it. It then again made off. In this manner the chase continued for a long time. The streets were profoundly quiet, as it was nearly three o'clock in the morning. In passing down an alley in the rear of the Rue Morgue, the fugitive's attention was arrested by a light gleaming from the open window of Madame L'Espanaye's chamber, in the fourth story of her house. Rushing to the building, it perceived the lightning-rod, clambered up with inconceivable agility, grasped the shutter, which was thrown fully back against the wall, and, by its means, swung itself directly upon the head-board of the bed. The whole feat did not occupy a minute. The shutter was kicked open again by the Ourang-Outang as it entered the room.

The sailor, in the meantime, was both rejoiced and perplexed. He had strong hopes of now recapturing the brute, as it could scarcely escape from the trap into which it had ventured, except by the rod, where it might be intercepted as it came down. On the other hand, there was much cause for anxiety as to what it might do in the house. This latter reflection urged the man still to follow the fugitive. A lightning-rod is ascended without difficulty, especially by a sailor; but, when he had arrived as high as the window, which lay far to his left, his career was stopped; the most that he

could accomplish was to reach over so as to obtain a glimpse
of the interior of the room. At this glimpse he nearly fell
from his hold through excess of horror. Now it was that
those hideous shrieks arose upon the night, which had startled
from slumber the inmates of the Rue Morgue. Madame
L'Espanaye and her daughter, habituated in their night
clothes, had apparently been arranging some papers in the
iron chest already mentioned, which had been wheeled into
the middle of the room. It was open, and its contents lay
beside it on the floor. The victims must have been sitting
with their backs toward the window; and, from the time
elapsing between the ingress of the beast and the screams, it
seems probable that it was not immediately perceived. The
flapping-to of the shutter would naturally have been
attributed to the wind.

As the sailor looked in, the gigantic animal had seized
Madame L'Espanaye by the hair (which was loose, as she
had been combing it), and was flourishing the razor about
her face, in imitation of the motions of a barber. The
daughter lay prostrate and motionless; she had swooned.
The screams and struggles of the old lady (during which the
hair was torn from her head) had the effect of changing the
probably pacific purposes of the Ourang-Outang into those
of wrath. With one determined sweep of its muscular arm
it nearly severed her head from her body. The sight of
blood inflamed its anger into frenzy. Gnashing its teeth,
and flashing fire from its eyes, it flew upon the body of the
girl, and imbedded its fearful talons in her throat, retaining
its grasp until she expired. Its wandering and wild glances
fell at this moment upon the head of the bed, over which the
face of its master, rigid with horror, was just discernible.
The fury of the beast, who no doubt bore still in the mind
the dreaded whip, was instantly converted into fear. Conscious of having deserved punishment, it seemed desirous of
concealing its bloody deeds, and skipped about the chamber
in an agony of nervous agitation; throwing down and breaking the furniture as it moved, and dragging the bed from
the bedstead. In conclusion, it seized first the corpse of the
daughter, and thrust it up the chimney, as it was found; then
that of the old lady, which it immediately hurled through
the window headlong.

As the ape approached the casement with its mutilated

burthen, the sailor shrank aghast to the rod, and, rather gliding than clambering down it, hurried at once home—dreading the consequences of the butchery, and gladly abandoning, in his terror, all solicitude about the fate of the Ourang-Outang. The words heard by the party upon the staircase were the Frenchman's exclamations of horror and affright, commingled with the fiendish jabberings of the brute.

I have scarcely anything to add. The Ourang-Outang must have escaped from the chamber by the rod, just before the breaking of the door. It must have closed the window as it passed through it. It was subsequently caught by the owner himself, who obtained for it a very large sum at the *Jardin des Plantes*. Le Bon was instantly released, upon our narration of the circumstances (with some comments from Dupin) at the *bureau* of the Prefect of Police. This functionary, however well disposed to my friend, could not altogether conceal his chagrin at the turn which affairs had taken, and was fain to indulge in a sarcasm or two, about the propriety of every person minding his own business.

"Let him talk," said Dupin, who had not thought it necessary to reply. "Let him discourse; it will ease his conscience. I am satisfied with having defeated him in his own castle. Nevertheless, that he failed in the solution of this mystery is by no means that matter for wonder which he supposes it; for in truth, our friend the Prefect is somewhat too cunning to be profound. In his wisdom is no *stamen*. It is all head and no body, like the pictures of the Goddess Laverna,—or, at best, all head and shoulders, like a codfish. But he is a good creature after all. I like him especially for one master stroke of cant, by which he has attained his reputation for ingenuity. I mean the way he has ' *de nier ce qui est, et d'expliquer ce qui n'est pas.*' " [1]

[1] Rousseau, *Nouvelle Heloise.*

THE MYSTERY OF MARIE ROGÊT [1]

A SEQUEL TO "THE MURDERS IN THE RUE MORGUE"

Es giebt eine Reihe idealischer Begebenheiten, die der Wirklichkeit parallel
läuft. Selten fallen sie zusammen. Menschen und Zufälle modificiren
gewöhnlich die idealische Begebenheit, so dass sie unvollkommen ercheint,
und ihre Folgen gleichfalls unvollkommen sind. So bei der Reformation ; statt des Protestantismus kam das Lutherthum hervor.

There are ideal series of events which run parallel with the real ones. They
rarely coincide. Men and circumstances generally modify the ideal
train of events, so that it seems imperfect, and its consequences are equally
imperfect. Thus with the Reformation ; instead of Protestantism came
Lutheranism.—NOVALIS. *Moral Ansichten*.

THERE are few persons, even among the calmest
thinkers, who have not occasionally been startled into a
vague yet thrilling half-credence in the supernatural, by
coincidences of so seemingly marvellous a character that, as
mere coincidences, the intellect has been unable to receive
them. Such sentiments—for the half-credences of which I
speak have never the full force of *thought*—such sentiments
are seldom thoroughly stifled unless by reference to the doc-
trine of chance, or, as it is technically termed, the Calculus

[1] Upon the original publication of *Marie Rogêt*, the foot-notes now appended
were considered unnecessary ; but the lapse of several years since the tragedy
upon which the tale is based, renders it expedient to give them, and also to
say a few words in explanation of the general design. A young girl, *Mary
Cecilia Rogers*, was murdered in the vicinity of New York ; and although her
death occasioned an intense and long-enduring excitement, the mystery attending it had remained unsolved at the period when the present paper was written
and published (November, 1842). Herein, under pretence of relating the fate
of a Parisian *grisette*, the author has followed, in minute detail, the essentials
while merely paralleling the inessential, facts of the real murder of Mary Rogers.
Thus all argument upon the fiction is applicable to the truth : and the investigation of the truth was the object.

The *Mystery of Marie Rogêt* was composed at a distance from the scene of
the atrocity, and with no other means of investigation than the newspapers
afforded. Thus much escaped the writer of which he could have availed
himself had he been upon the spot and visited the localities. It may not be
improper to record, nevertheless, that the confessions of *two* persons (one of
them the Madame Deluc of the narrative), made, at different periods, long
subsequent to the publication, confirmed, in full, not only the general conclusion, but absolutely *all* the chief hypothetical details by which that conclusion
was attained.

203

of Probabilities. Now this Calculus is, in its essence, purely mathematical; and thus we have the anomaly of the most rigidly exact in science applied to the shadow and spirituality of the most intangible in speculation.

The extraordinary details which I am now called upon to make public, will be found to form, as regards sequence of time, the primary branch of a series of scarcely intelligible *coincidences,* whose secondary or concluding branch will be recognised by all readers in the late murder of MARY CECILIA ROGERS, at New York.

When, in an article entitled, *The Murders in the Rue Morgue,* I endeavoured, about a year ago, to depict some very remarkable features in the mental character of my friend, the Chevalier C. Auguste Dupin, it did not occur to me that I should ever resume the subject. This depicting of character constituted my design; and this design was thoroughly fulfilled in the wild train of circumstances brought to instance Dupin's idiosyncrasy. I might have adduced other examples, but I should have proven no more. Late events, however, in their surprising development, have startled me into some further details, which will carry with them the air of extorted confession. Hearing what I have lately heard, it would be indeed strange should I remain silent in regard to what I both heard and saw long ago.

Upon the winding up of the tragedy involved in the deaths of Madame L'Espanaye and her daughter, the Chevalier dismissed the affair at once from his attention, and relapsed into his old habits of moody reverie. Prone, at all times, to abstraction, I readily fell in with his humour; and continuing to occupy our chambers in the Faubourg Saint Germain, we gave the Future to the winds, and slumbered tranquilly in the Present, weaving the dull world around us into dreams.

But these dreams were not altogether uninterrupted. It may readily be supposed that the part played by my friend, in the drama at the Rue Morgue, had not failed of its impression upon the fancies of the Parisian police. With its emissaries, the name of Dupin had grown into a household word. The simple character of those inductions by which he had disentangled the mystery never having been explained even to the Prefect, or to any other individual than myself, of course it is not surprising that the affair was regarded as little less than miraculous, or that the Chevalier's analytical abilities acquired for him the credit of intuition. His frankness would have led him to disabuse every inquirer of such prejudice; but his indolent humour forbade all further agitation of a topic whose interest to himself had long ceased. It thus happened that he found himself the cynosure of the political eyes; and the cases were not few in which attempt was made to engage his services at the Prefecture. One of the most remarkable instances was that of the murder of a young girl named Marie Rogêt.

This event occurred about two years after the atrocity in the Rue Morgue. Marie, whose Christian and family name will at once arrest attention from their resemblance to those of the unfortunate " cigar-girl," was the only daughter of the widow Estelle Rogêt. The father had died during the child's infancy, and from the period of his death, until within eighteen months before the assassination which forms the subject of our narrative, the mother and daughter had dwelt together in the Rue Pavée Saint Andrée [1]; Madame there keeping a *pension*, assisted by Marie. Affairs went on thus until the latter had attained her twenty-second year, when her great beauty attracted the notice of a perfumer, who occupied one of the shops in the basement of the Palais Royal, and whose custom lay chiefly among the desperate adventurers infesting that neighbourhood. Monsieur Le Blanc [2] was not unaware of the advantages to be derived from the attendance of the fair Marie in his perfumery; and his liberal proposals were accepted eagerly by the girl, although with somewhat more of hesitation by Madame.

The anticipations of the shopkeeper were realised, and his rooms soon became notorious through the charms of the sprightly *grisette*. She had been in his employ about a year, when her admirers were thrown into confusion by her sudden disappearance from the shop. Monsieur Le Blanc was unable to account for her absence, and Madame Rogêt was distracted with anxiety and terror. The public papers immediately took up the theme, and the police were upon the point of making serious investigations, when, one morning, after the lapse of a week, Marie, in good health, but with a somewhat saddened air, made her reappearance at her usual counter in the perfumery. All inquiry, except

---

[1] Nassau Street.   [2] Anderson.

that of a private character, was, of course, immediately hushed. Monsieur Le Blanc professed total ignorance, as before. Marie, with Madame, replied to all questions, that the last week had been spent at the house of a relation in the country. Thus the affair died away, and was generally forgotten; for the girl, ostensibly to relieve herself from the impertinence of curiosity, soon bade a final adieu to the perfumer, and sought the shelter of her mother's residence in the Rue Pavée Saint Andrée.

It was about five months after this return home, that her friends were alarmed by her sudden disappearance for the second time. Three days elapsed, and nothing was heard of her. On the fourth her corpse was found floating in the Seine,[1] near the shore which is opposite the Quartier of the Rue Saint Andrée, and at a point not very far distant from the secluded neighbourhood of the Barrière du Roule.[2]

The atrocity of this murder (for it was at once evident that murder had been committed), the youth and beauty of the victim, and, above all, her previous notoriety, conspired to produce intense excitement in the minds of the sensitive Parisians. I can call to mind no similar occurrence producing so general and so intense an effect. For several weeks, in the discussion of this one absorbing theme, even the momentous political topics of the day were forgotten. The Prefect made unusual exertions; and the powers of the whole Parisian police were, of course, tasked to the utmost extent.

Upon the first discovery of the corpse, it was not supposed that the murderer would be able to elude, for more than a very brief period, the inquisition which was immediately set on foot. It was not until the expiration of a week that it was deemed necessary to offer a reward; and even then this reward was limited to a thousand francs. In the meantime the investigation proceeded with vigour, if not always with judgment, and numerous individuals were examined to no purpose; while, owing to the continual absence of all clue to the mystery, the popular excitement greatly increased. At the end of the tenth day it was thought advisable to double the sum originally proposed; and, at length, the second week having elapsed without leading to any discoveries, and the prejudice which always exists

_____
[1] The Hudson.   [2] Weehawken.

in Paris against the police having given vent to itself in
several serious *émeutes,* the Prefect took it upon himself
to offer the sum of twenty thousand francs " for the conviction of the assassin," or, if more than one should prove
to have been implicated, " for the conviction of any one
of the assassins." In the proclamation setting forth this reward, a full pardon was promised to any accomplice who
should come forward in evidence against his fellow; and
to the whole was appended, wherever it appeared, the private
placard of a committee of citizens, offering ten thousand
francs, in addition to the amount proposed by the Prefecture.
The entire reward thus stood at no less than thirty thousand
francs, which will be regarded as an extraordinary sum when
we consider the humble condition of the girl, and the great
frequency, in large cities, of such atrocities as the one
described.

No one doubted now that the mystery of this murder
would be immediately brought to light. But although, in
one or two instances, arrests were made which promised
elucidation, yet nothing was elicited which could implicate
the parties suspected; and they were discharged forthwith.
Strange as it may appear, the third week from the discovery of the body had passed, and passed without any light
being thrown upon the subject, before even a rumour of
the events which had so agitated the public mind reached
the ears of Dupin and myself. Engaged in researches which
had absorbed our whole attention, it had been nearly a
month since either of us had gone abroad, or received a
visitor, or more than glanced at the leading political articles
in one of the daily papers. The first intelligence of the
murder was brought us by G——, in person. He called
upon us early in the afternoon of the thirteenth of July
18—, and remained with us until late in the night. He
had been piqued by the failure of all his endeavours to ferret
out the assassins. His reputation—so he said with a peculiarly Parisian air—was at stake. Even his honour was
concerned. The eyes of the public were upon him; and
there was really no sacrifice which he would not be willing
to make for the development of the mystery. He concluded a somewhat droll speech with a compliment upon
what he was pleased to term the *tact* of Dupin, and made
him a direct and certainly a liberal proposition, the precise

nature of which I do not feel myself at liberty to disclose, but which has no bearing upon the proper subject of my narrative.

The compliment my friend rebutted as best he could, but the proposition he accepted at once, although its advantages were altogether provisional. This point being settled, the Prefect broke forth at once into explanations of his own views, interspersing them with long comments[1] upon the evidence; of which latter we were not yet in possession. He discoursed much and, beyond doubt, learnedly; while I hazarded an occasional suggestion as the night wore drowsily away. Dupin, sitting steadily in his accustomed arm-chair, was the embodiment of respectful attention. He wore spectacles, during the whole interview; and an occasional glance beneath their green glasses sufficed to convince me that he slept not the less soundly, because silently, throughout the seven or eight leaden-footed hours which immediately preceded the departure of the Prefect.

In the morning, I procured, at the Prefecture, a full report of all the evidence elicited, and, at the various newspaper offices, a copy of every paper in which, from first to last, had been published any decisive information in regard to this sad affair. Freed from all that was positively disproved, the mass of information stood thus:

Marie Rogêt left the residence of her mother, in the Rue Pavée St. Andrée, about nine o'clock in the morning of Sunday, June the twenty-second, 18—. In going out, she gave notice to a Monsieur Jacques St. Eustache,[1] and to him only, of her intention to spend the day with an aunt, who resided in the Rue des Drômes. The Rue des Drômes is a short and narrow but populous thoroughfare, not far from the banks of the river, and at a distance of some two miles, in the most direct course possible, from the *pension* of Madame Rogêt. St. Eustache was the accepted suitor of Marie, and lodged, as well as took his meals, at the *pension*. He was to have gone for his betrothed at dusk, and to have escorted her home. In the afternoon, however, it came on to rain heavily; and, supposing that she would remain at her aunt's (as she had done under similar circumstances before), he did not think it necessary to keep his promise. As night drew on, Madame

[1] Payne.

Rogêt (who was an infirm old lady, seventy years of age) was heard to express a fear " that she should never see Marie again "; but this observation attracted little attention at the time.

On Monday it was ascertained that the girl had not been to the Rue des Drômes; and when the day elapsed without tidings of her, a tardy search was instituted at several points in the city and its environs. It was not, however, until the fourth day from the period of her disappearance that anything satisfactory was ascertained respecting her. On this day (Wednesday, the twenty-fifth of June) a Monsieur Beauvais,[1] who, with a friend, had been making inquiries for Marie near the Barrière du Roule, on the shore of the Seine which is opposite the Rue Pavée St. Andrée, was informed a corpse had just been towed ashore by some fishermen, who had found it floating in the river. Upon seeing the body, Beauvais, after some hesitation, identified it as that of the perfumery-girl. His friend recognised it more promptly.

The face was suffused with dark blood, some of which issued from the mouth. No foam was seen, as in the case of the merely drowned. There was no discoloration in the cellular tissue. About the throat were bruises and impressions of fingers. The arms were bent over on the chest, and were rigid. The right hand was clenched; the left partially open. On the left wrist were two circular excoriations, apparently the effect of ropes, or of a rope in more than one volution. A part of the right wrist, also, was much chafed, as well as the back throughout its extent, but more especially at the shoulder-blades. In bringing the body to the shore the fishermen had attached to it a rope, but none of the excoriations had been effected by this. The flesh of the neck was much swollen. There were no cuts apparent, or bruises which appeared the effect of blows. A piece of lace was found tied so tightly around the neck as to be hidden from sight; it was completely buried in the flesh, and was fastened by a knot which lay just under the left ear. This alone would have sufficed to produce death. The medical testimony spoke confidently of the virtuous character of the deceased. She had been subjected, it said, to brutal violence. The corpse was in such a condition when

[1] Crommelin.

found that there could have been no difficulty in recognition by friends.

The dress was much torn and otherwise disordered. In the outer garment, a slip, about a foot wide, had been torn upward from the bottom hem to the waist, but not torn off. It was wound three times around the waist, and secured by a sort of hitch in the back. The dress immediately beneath the frock was of fine muslin; and from this a slip eighteen inches wide had been torn entirely out—torn very evenly and with great care. It was found around her neck, fitting loosely, and secured with a hard knot. Over this muslin slip and the slip of lace the strings of a bonnet were attached, the bonnet being appended. The knot by which the strings of the bonnet were fastened was not a lady's, but a slip or sailor's knot.

After the recognition of the corpse, it was not, as usual, taken to the Morgue (this formality being superfluous), but hastily interred not far from the spot at which it was brought ashore. Through the exertions of Beauvais, the matter was industriously hushed up, as far as possible; and several days had elapsed before any public emotion resulted. A weekly paper,[1] however, at length took up the theme; the corpse was disinterred, and a re-examination instituted; but nothing was elicited beyond what has been already noted. The clothes, however, were now submitted to the mother and friends of the deceased and fully identified as those worn by the girl upon leaving home.

Meantime, the excitement increased hourly. Several individuals were arrested and discharged. St. Eustache fell especially under suspicion; and he failed, at first, to give an intelligible account of his whereabouts during the Sunday on which Marie left home. Subsequently, however, he submitted to Monsieur G——, affidavits, accounting satisfactorily for every hour of the day in question. As time passed and no discovery ensued, a thousand contradictory rumours were circulated, and journalists busied themselves in *suggestions*. Among these, the one which attracted the most notice, was the idea that Marie Rogêt still lived—that the corpse found in the Seine was that of some other unfortunate. It will be proper that I submit to the reader some passages which embody the suggestion alluded to. These

[1] The New York *Mercury*.

passages are *literal* translations from *L'Etoile*, a paper conducted, in general, with much ability.

"Mademoiselle Rogêt left her mother's house on Sunday morning, June the twenty-second, 18—, with the ostensible purpose of going to see her aunt, or some other connection in the Rue des Drômes. From that hour, nobody is proved to have seen her. There is no trace or tidings of her at all. . . . There has no person, whatever, come forward, so far, who saw her at all, on that day, after she left her mother's door. . . . Now, though we have no evidence that Marie Rogêt was in the land of the living after nine o'clock on Sunday, June the twenty-second, we have proof that, up to that hour, she was alive. On Wednesday noon, at twelve, a female body was discovered afloat on the shore of the Barrière du Roule. This was, even if we presume that Marie Rogêt was thrown into the river within three hours after she left her mother's house, only three days from the time she left her home—three days to an hour. But it is folly to suppose that the murder, if murder was committed on her body, could have been consummated soon enough to have enabled her murderers to throw the body into the river before midnight. Those who are guilty of such horrid crimes choose darkness rather than light. . . . Thus we see that if the body found in the river *was* that of Marie Rogêt, it could only have been in the water two and a half days, or three at the outside. All experience has shown that drowned bodies, or bodies thrown into the water immediately after death by violence, require from six to ten days for sufficient decomposition to take place to bring them to the top of the water. Even where a cannon is fired over a corpse, and it rises before, at least, five or six days' immersion, it sinks again, if let alone. Now, we ask what was there in this case to cause a departure from the ordinary course of nature? . . . If the body had been kept in its mangled state on shore until Tuesday night, some trace would be found on shore of the murderers. It is a doubtful point, also, whether the body would be so soon afloat, even were it thrown in after having been dead two days. And, furthermore, it is exceedingly improbable that any villains who had committed such a murder as is here supposed, would have thrown the body in without weight to sink it,

---

[1] The New York *Brother Jonathan*, edited by H. Hastings Weld, Esq.

when such a precaution could have so easily been taken."

The editor here proceeds to argue that the body must have been in water " not three days merely, but, at least, five times three days," because it was so far decomposed that Beauvais had great difficulty in recognising it.   This latter point, however, was fully disproved.   I continue the translation:

" What, then, are the facts on which M. Beauvais says that he has no doubt the body was that of Marie Rogêt? He ripped up the gown sleeve, and says he found marks which satisfied him of the identity.   The public generally supposed those marks to have consisted of some description of scars.   He rubbed the arm and found *hair* upon it—something as indefinite, we think, as can readily be imagined— as little conclusive as finding an arm in the sleeve.   M. Beauvais did not return that night, but sent word to Madame Rogêt, at seven o'clock, on Wednesday evening, that an investigation was still in progress respecting her daughter. If we allow that Madame Rogêt, from her age and grief, could not go over (which is allowing a great deal), there certainly must have been some one who would have thought it worth while to go over and attend the investigation, if they thought the body was that of Marie.   Nobody went over.   There was nothing said or heard about the matter in the Rue Pavée St. Andrée, that reached even the occupants of the same building.   M. St. Eustache, the lover and intended husband of Marie, who boarded in her mother's house, deposes that he did not hear of the discovery of the body of his intended until the next morning, when M. Beauvais came into his chamber and told him of it.   For an item of news like this, it strikes us it was very coolly received."

In this way the journal endeavoured to create the impression of an apathy on the part of the relatives of Marie, inconsistent with the supposition that these relatives believed the corpse to be hers.   Its insinuations amount to this: that Marie, with the connivance of her friends, had absented herself from the city for reasons involving a charge against her chastity; and that these friends upon the discovery of a corpse in the Seine, somewhat resembling that of the girl, had availed themselves of the opportunity to impress the public with the belief of her death.   But *L'Etoile* was again over-hasty. It was distinctly proved that no apathy, such as was imagined, existed; that the old lady was exceedingly feeble, and so agitated as to be unable to attend to any duty; that St. Eustache, so far from receiving the news coolly, was distracted with grief, and bore himself so frantically, that M. Beauvais prevailed upon a friend and relative to take charge of him, and prevent his attending the examination at the disinterment. Moreover, although it was stated by *L'Etoile*, that the corpse was re-interred at the public expense, that an advantageous offer of private sepulture was absolutely declined by the family, and that no member of the family attended the ceremonial;—although, I say, all this was asserted by *L'Etoile* in furtherance of the impression it designed to convey—yet *all* this was satisfactorily disproved. In a subsequent number of the paper, an attempt was made to throw suspicion upon Beauvais himself. The editor says:

" Now, then, a change comes over the matter. We are told that, on one occasion, while a Madame B—— was at Madame Rogêt's house, M. Beauvais, who was going out, told her that a *gendarme* was expected there, and that she, Madame B——, must not say anything to the *gendarme* until he returned, but let the matter be for him. . . . In the present posture of affairs M. Beauvais appears to have the whole matter locked up in his head. A single step cannot be taken without M. Beauvais, for go which way you will, you run against him. . . . For some reason he determined that nobody shall have anything to do with the proceedings but himself, and he has elbowed the male relatives out of the way, according to their representations, in a very singular manner. He seems to have been very much averse to permitting the relatives to see the body."

By the following fact, some colour was given to the suspicion thus thrown upon Beauvais. A visitor at his office, a few days prior to the girl's disappearance, and during the absence of its occupant, had observed a *rose* in the key-hole of the door, and the name " Marie " inscribed upon a slate which hung near at hand.

The general impression, so far as we were enabled to glean it from the newspapers, seemed to be, that Marie had been the victim of a *gang* of desperadoes—that by these she had been borne across the river, maltreated, and murdered. *Le*

Commerciel,[1] however, a print of extensive influence, was earnest in combating this popular idea. I quote a passage or two from its columns:

" We are persuaded that pursuit has hitherto been on a false scent so far as it has been directed to the Barrière du Roule. It is impossible that a person so well known to thousands as this young woman was, should have passed three blocks without someone having seen her; and any one who saw her would have remembered it, for she interested all who knew her. It was when the streets were full of people, when she went out. . . . It is impossible that she could have gone to the Barrière du Roule, or to the Rue des Drômes, without being recognised by a dozen persons; yet no one has come forward who saw her outside her mother's door, and there is no evidence except the testimony concerning her *expressed intentions,* that she did go out at all. Her gown was torn, bound round her, and tied; and by that the body was carried as a bundle. If the murder had been committed at the Barrière du Roule, there would have been no necessity for any such arrangement. The fact that the body was found floating near the Barrière is no proof as to where it was thrown into the water. . . . A piece of one of the unfortunate girl's petticoats, two feet long and one foot wide, was torn out and tied under her chin around the back of her head, probably to prevent screams. This was done by fellows who had no pocket-handkerchief."

A day or two before the Prefect called upon us, however, some important information reached the police, which seemed to overthrow, at least, the chief portion of *Le Commerciel's argument.* Two small boys, sons of a Madame Deluc, while roaming among the woods near the Barrière du Roule, chanced to penetrate a close thicket, within which were three or four large stones, forming a kind of seat with a back and footstool. On the upper stone lay a white petticoat; on the second, a silk scarf. A parasol, gloves, and a pocket-handkerchief were also here found. The handkerchief bore the name " Marie Roget." Fragments of dress were discovered on the brambles around. The earth was trampled, the bushes were broken, and there was every evidence of a struggle. Between the thicket and the river, the fences were found taken down, and the ground bore

[1] New York *Journal of Commerce.*

evidence of some heavy burthen having been dragged along it.

A weekly paper, *Le Soleil*,[1] had the following comments upon this discovery—comments which merely echoed the sentiment of the whole Parisian press:

" The things had all evidently been there at least three or four weeks; they were all mildewed down hard with the action of the rain, and stuck together from mildew. The grass had grown around and over some of them. The silk on the parasol was strong, but the threads of it were run together within. The upper part, where it had been doubled and folded, was all mildewed and rotten, and tore on its being opened. . . . The pieces of her frock torn out by the bushes were about three inches wide and six inches long. One part was the hem of the frock, and it had been mended; the other piece was part of the skirt, not the hem. They looked like strips torn off, and were on the thorn bush, about a foot from the ground. . . . There can be no doubt, therefore, that the spot of this appalling outrage has been discovered."

Consequent upon this discovery, new evidence appeared. Madame Deluc testified that she keeps a roadside inn not far from the bank of the river, opposite the Barrière du Roule. The neighbourhood is secluded—particularly so. It is the usual Sunday resort of blackguards from the city, who cross the river in boats. About three o'clock, in the afternoon of the Sunday in question, a young girl arrived at the inn accompanied by a young man of dark complexion. The two remained here for some time. On their departure, they took the road to some thick woods in the vicinity. Madame Deluc's attention was called to the dress worn by the girl, on account of its resemblance to one worn by a deceased relative. A scarf was particularly noticed. Soon after the departure of the couple, a gang of miscreants made their appearance, behaved boisterously, ate and drank without making payment, followed in the route of the young man and girl, returned to the inn about dusk, and re-crossed the river, as if in great haste.

It was soon after dark, upon this same evening, that Madame Deluc, as well as her eldest son, heard the screams of a female in the vicinity of the inn. The screams were

[1] Philadelphia *Saturday Evening Post*, edited by C. I. Peterson, Esq.

violent but brief. Madame D. recognised not only the scarf which was found in the thicket, but the dress which was discovered upon the corpse. An omnibus driver, Valence,[1] now also testified that he saw Marie Rogêt cross a ferry on the Seine, on the Sunday in question, in company with a young man of dark complexion. He, Valence, knew Marie, and could not be mistaken in her identity. The articles found in the thicket were fully identified by the relatives of Marie.

The items of evidence and information thus collected by myself, from the newspapers, at the suggestion of Dupin, embraced only one more point—but this was a point of seemingly vast consequence. It appears that, immediately after the discovery of the clothes as above described, the lifeless or nearly lifeless body of St. Eustache, Marie's be-trothed, was found in the vicinity of what all now sup-posed the scene of the outrage. A phial labelled "laudanum," and emptied, was found near him. His breath gave evidence of the poison. He died without speaking. Upon his person was found a letter, briefly stating his love for Marie, with his design of self-destruction.

"I need scarcely tell you," said Dupin, as he finished the perusal of my notes, "that this is a far more intricate case than that of the Rue Morgue; from which it differs in one important respect. This is an *ordinary*, although an atro-cious, instance of crime. There is nothing peculiarly *outré* about it. You will observe that, for this reason, the mystery has been considered easy, when, for this reason, it should have been considered difficult of solution. Thus, at first, it was thought unnecessary to offer a reward. The myr-midons of G—— were able at once to comprehend how and why such an atrocity *might have been committed*. They could picture to their imaginations a mode—many modes,—and a motive—many motives; and because it was not im-possible that either of these numerous modes and motives *could* have been the actual one, they have taken it for granted that one of them *must*. But the ease with which these variable fancies were entertained, and the very plausi-bility which each assumed, should have been understood as indicative rather of the difficulties than of the facilities which must attend elucidation. I have therefore observed that it

[1] Adam.

is by prominences above the plane of the ordinary, that reason feels her way, if at all, in her search for the true, and that the proper question in cases such as this is not so much ' what has occurred? ' as ' what has occurred that has never occurred before? ' In the investigations at the house of Madame L'Espanaye,[1] the agents of G—— were discouraged and confounded by that very *unusualness* which, to a properly regulated intellect, would have afforded the surest omen of success; while this same intellect might have been plunged in despair at the ordinary character of all that met the eye in the case of the perfumery-girl, and yet told of nothing but easy triumph to the functionaries of the Prefecture.

" In the case of Madame L'Espanaye and her daughter, there was, even at the beginning of our investigation, no doubt that murder had been committed. The idea of suicide was excluded at once. Here, too, we are freed, at the commencement, from all supposition of self-murder. The body found at the Barrière du Roule was found under such circumstances as to leave us no room for embarrassment upon this important point. But it has been suggested that the corpse discovered is not that of the Marie Rogêt for the conviction of whose assassin, or assassins, the reward is offered, and respecting whom, solely, our agreement has been arranged with the Prefect. We both know this gentleman well. It will not do to trust him too far. If, dating our inquiries from the body found, and then tracing a murderer, we yet discover this body to be that of some other individual than Marie; or if, starting from the living Marie, we find her, yet find her unassassinated—in either case we lose our labour; since it is Monsieur G—— with whom we have to deal. For our own purpose, therefore, if not for the purpose of justice, it is indispensable that our first step should be the determination of the identity of the corpse with the Marie Rogêt who is missing.

" With the public the arguments of *L'Etoile* have had weight; and that the journal itself is convinced of their importance would appear from the manner in which it commences one of its essays upon the subject—' Several of the morning papers of the day,' it says, ' speak of the *conclusive* article in Monday's *Etoile*.' To me, this article ap-

[1] See *Murders in the Rue Morgue*.

pears conclusive of little beyond the zeal of its inditer. We should bear in mind that, in general, it is the object of our newspapers rather to create a sensation—to make a point—than to further the cause of truth. The latter end is only pursued when it seems coincident with the former. The print which merely falls in with ordinary opinion (however well founded this opinion may be) earns for itself no credit with the mob. The mass of the people regard as profound only him who suggests *pungent contradictions* of the general idea. In ratiocination, not less than in literature, it is the *epigram* which is the most immediately and the most universally appreciated. In both, it is of the lowest order of merit.

" What I mean to say is, that it is the mingled epigram and melodrame of the idea, that Marie Rogêt still lives, rather than any true plausibility in this idea, which have suggested it to *L'Etoile*, and secured it a favourable reception with the public. Let us examine the heads of this journal's argument; endeavouring to avoid the incoherence with which it is originally set forth.

" The first aim of the writer is to show, from the brevity of the interval between Marie's disappearance and the finding of the floating corpse, that this corpse cannot be that of Marie. The reduction of this interval to its smallest possible dimension, becomes thus, at once, an object with the reasoner. In the rash pursuit of this object, he rushes into mere assumption at the outset. ' It is folly to suppose,' he says, ' that the murder, if murder was committed on her body, could have been consummated soon enough to have enabled her murderers to throw the body into the river before midnight.' We demand at once, and very naturally, *why*? Why is it folly to suppose that the murder was committed *within five minutes* after the girl's quitting her mother's house? Why is it folly to suppose that the murder was committed at any given period of the day? There have been assassinations at all hours. But, had the murder taken place at any moment between nine o'clock in the morning of Sunday and a quarter before midnight, there would still have been time enough ' to throw the body into the river before midnight.' This assumption, then, amounts precisely to this—that the murder was not committed on Sunday at all—and, if we allow *L'Etoile* to assume this, we may permit it any liberties whatever. The paragraph beginning 'It is folly to suppose that the murder,' etc., however it appears as printed in *L'Etoile,* may be imagined to have existed actually *thus* in the brain of the inditer: 'It is folly to suppose that the murder, if murder was committed on the body, could have been committed soon enough to have enabled her murderers to throw the body into the river before midnight; it is folly, we say, to suppose all this, and to suppose at the same time (as we are resolved to suppose), that the body was *not* thrown in until *after* midnight'— a sentence sufficiently inconsequential in itself, but not so utterly preposterous as the one printed.

"Were it my purpose," continued Dupin, "merely to *make out a case* against this passage of *L'Etoile's* argument, I might safely leave it where it is. It is not, however, with *L'Etoile* that we have to do, but with the truth. The sentence in question has but one meaning, as it stands; and this meaning I have fairly stated; but it is material that we go behind the mere words for an idea which these words have obviously intended, and failed to convey. It was the design of the journalists to say that at whatever period of the day or night of Sunday this murder was committed, it was improbable that the assassins would have ventured to bear the corpse to the river before midnight. And herein lies, really, the assumption of which I complain. It is assumed that the murder was committed at such a position, and under such circumstances, that *the bearing it* to the river became necessary. Now, the assassination might have taken place upon the river's brink, or on the river itself; and, thus, the throwing the corpse in the water might have been resorted to at any period of the day or night, as the most obvious and most immediate mode of disposal. You will understand that I suggest nothing here as probable, or as coincident with my own opinion. My design, so far, has no reference to the *facts* of the case. I wish merely to caution you against the whole tone of *L'Etoile's* suggestion, by calling your attention to its *ex-parte* character at the outset.

"Having prescribed thus a limit to suit its own preconceived notions; having assumed that, if this were the body of Marie, it could have been in the water but a very brief time, the journal goes on to say:

"'All experience has shown that drowned bodies, or

bodies thrown into the water immediately after death by violence, require from six to ten days for sufficient decomposition to take place to bring them to the top of the water. Even when a cannon is fired over a corpse, and it rises before at least five or six days' immersion, it sinks again if let alone.'

" These assertions have been tacitly received by every paper in Paris, with the exception of *Le Moniteur*.[1] This latter print endeavours to combat that portion of the paragraph which has reference to ' drowned bodies ' only, by citing some five or six instances in which the bodies of individuals known to be drowned were found floating after the lapse of less time than is insisted upon by *L'Etoile*. But there is something excessively unphilosophical in the attempt, on the part of *Le Moniteur,* to rebut the general assertion of *L'Etoile,* by a citation of particular instances militating that assertion. Had it been possible to adduce fifty instead of five examples of bodies found floating at the end of two or three days, these fifty examples could still have been properly regarded only as exceptions to *L'Etoile's* rule, until such time as the rule itself should be confuted. Admitting the rule (and this *Le Moniteur* does not deny, insisting merely upon its exceptions), the argument of *L'Etoile* is suffered to remain in full force; for this argument does not pretend to involve more than a question of the *probability* of the body having risen to the surface in less than three days; and this probability will be in favour of *L'Etoile's* position until the instances so childishly adduced shall be sufficient in number to establish an antagonistical rule.

" You will see at once that all argument upon this head should be urged, if at all, against the rule itself; and for this end we must examine the *rationale* of the rule. Now the human body, in general, is neither much lighter nor much heavier than the water of the Seine; that is to say, the specific gravity of the human body, in its natural condition, is about equal to the bulk of fresh water which it displaces. The bodies of fat and fleshy persons, with small bones, and of women generally, are lighter than those of the lean and large-boned, and of men; and the specific gravity of the water of a river is somewhat influenced by the presence of the tide from the sea. But, leaving this

[1] The New York *Commercial Advertiser*, edited by Col. Stone.

tide out of the question, it may be said that *very* few
human bodies will sink at all, even in fresh water, *of their
own accord*. Almost any one, falling into a river, will be
enabled to float, if he suffer the specific gravity of the water
fairly to be adduced in comparison with his own—that is
to say, if he suffer his whole person to be immersed, with as
little exception as possible. The proper position for one
who cannot swim, is the upright position of the walker on
land, with the head thrown fully back, and immersed; the
mouth and nostrils alone remaining above the surface. Thus
circumstanced, we shall find that we float without difficulty
and without exertion. It is evident, however, that the
gravities of the body, and of the bulk of water displaced,
are very nicely balanced, and that a trifle will cause either
to preponderate. An arm, for instance, uplifted from the
water, and thus deprived of its support, is an additional
weight sufficient to immerse the whole head, while the accidental aid of the smallest piece of timber will enable us to
elevate the head so as to look about. Now, in the struggles
of one unused to swimming, the arms are invariably thrown
upward, while an attempt is made to keep the head in its
usual perpendicular position. The result is the immersion
of the mouth and nostrils, and the inception, during efforts
to breathe while beneath the surface, of water into the lungs.
Much is also received into the stomach, and the whole body
becomes heavier by the difference between the weight of the
air originally distending these cavities, and that of the fluid
which now fills them. This difference is sufficient to cause
the body to sink, as a general rule; but is insufficient in the
cases of individuals with small bones and an abnormal quantity of flaccid or fatty matter. Such individuals float even
after drowning.

"The corpse, being supposed at the bottom of the river,
will there remain until, by some means, its specific gravity
again becomes less than that of the bulk of water which it
displaces. This effect is brought about by decomposition,
or otherwise. The result of decomposition is the generation
of gas, distending the cellular tissues and all the cavities, and
giving the *puffed* appearance which is so horrible. When
this distension has so far progressed that the bulk of the
corpse is materially increased without a corresponding increase of *mass* or weight, its specific gravity becomes less

than that of the water displaced, and it forthwith makes its appearance at the surface. But decomposition is modified by innumerable circumstances—is hastened or retarded by innumerable agencies; for example, by the heat or cold of the season, by the mineral impregnation or purity of the water, by its depth or shallowness, by its currency or stagnation, by the temperament of the body, by its infection or freedom from disease before death. Thus it is evident that we can assign no period, with anything like accuracy, at which the corpse shall rise through decomposition. Under certain conditions this result would be brought about within an hour, under others it might not take place at all. There are chemical infusions by which the animal frame can be preserved *for ever* from corruption; the bichloride of mercury is one. But, apart from decomposition, there may be, and very usually is, a generation of gas within the stomach, from the acetous fermentation of vegetable matter (or within other cavities from other causes), sufficient to induce a distension which will bring the body to the surface. The effect produced by the firing of a cannon is that of simple vibration. This may either loosen the corpse from the soft mud or ooze in which it is embedded, thus permitting it to rise when other agencies have already prepared it for so doing: or it may overcome the tenacity of some putrescent portions of the cellular tissues, allowing the cavities to distend under the influence of the gas.

"Having thus before us the whole philosophy of this subject, we can easily test by it the assertions of *L'Etoile*. 'All experience shows,' says this paper, 'that drowned bodies, or bodies thrown into the water immediately after death by violence, require from six to ten days for sufficient decomposition to take place to bring them to the top of the water. Even when a cannon is fired over a corpse, and it rises before at least five or six days' immersion, it sinks again if let alone.'

"The whole of this paragraph must now appear a tissue of inconsequence and incoherence. All experience does *not* show that 'drowned bodies' *require* from six to ten days for sufficient decomposition to take place to bring them to the surface. Both science and experience show that the period of their rising is, and necessarily must be, indeterminate. If, moreover, a body has risen to the surface through firing of cannon, it will *not* 'sink again if let alone,' until decomposition has so far progressed as to permit the escape of the generated gas.   But I wish to call your attention to the distinction which is made between 'drowned bodies,' and 'bodies thrown into water immediately after death by violence.'   Although the writer admits the distinction, he yet includes them all in the same category.   I have shown how it is that the body of a drowning man becomes specifically heavier than its bulk of water, and that he would not sink at all, except for the struggle by which he elevates his arms above the surface, and his gasps for breath while beneath the surface—gasps which supply by water the place of the original air in the lungs.   But these struggles and these gasps would not occur in the body 'thrown into the water immediately after death by violence.'   Thus, in the latter instance, *the body, as a general rule, would not sink at all*—a fact of which *L'Etoile* is evidently ignorant.   When decomposition had proceeded to a very great extent—when the flesh had in a great measure left the bones—then, indeed, but not *till* then, should we lose sight of the corpse.

"And now what are we to make of the argument, that the body found could not be that of Marie Rogêt, because, three days only having elapsed, this body was found floating?   If drowned, being a woman, she might never have sunk; or, having sunk, might have reappeared in twenty-four hours or less.   But no one supposes her to have been drowned; and, dying before being thrown into the river, she might have been found floating at any period afterward whatever.

"'But,' says *L'Etoile*, 'if the body had been kept in its mangled state on shore until Tuesday night, some trace would be found on shore of the murderers.'   Here it is at first difficult to perceive the intention of the reasoner.   He means to anticipate what he imagines would be an objection to his theory—viz.: that the body was kept on shore two days, suffering rapid decomposition—*more* rapid than if immersed in water.   He supposes that, had this been the case, it *might* have appeared at the surface on the Wednesday, and thinks that *only* under such circumstances it could have so appeared.   He is accordingly in haste to show that it *was not* kept on shore; for, if so, 'some trace would be found on shore of the murderers.'   I presume you smile at the *sequitur*. You cannot be made to see how the mere *dura-tion* of the corpse on the shore could operate to *multiply traces* of the assassins. Nor can I.

" ' And furthermore it is exceedingly improbable,' continues our journal, ' that any villains who had committed such a murder as is here supposed, would have thrown the body in without weight to sink it, when such a precaution could have so easily been taken.' Observe, here, the laughable confusion of thought! No one—not even *L'Etoile*— disputes the murder committed *on the body found*. The marks of violence are too obvious. It is our reasoner's object merely to show that this body is not Marie's. He wishes to prove that *Marie* is not assassinated—not that the corpse was not. Yet his observation proves only the latter point. Here is a corpse without weight attached. Murderers, casting it in, would not have failed to attach a weight. Therefore it was not thrown in by murderers. This is all which is proved, if anything is. The question of identity is not even approached, and *L'Etoile* has been at great pains merely to gainsay now what it has admitted only a moment before. ' We are perfectly convinced,' it says, ' that the body found was that of a murdered female.'

" Nor is this the sole instance, even in this division of his subject, where our reasoner unwittingly reasons against himself. His evident object, I have already said, is to reduce, as much as possible, the interval between Marie's disappearance and the finding of the corpse. Yet we find him *urging* the point that no person saw the girl from the moment of her leaving her mother's house. ' We have no evidence,' he says, ' that Marie Rogêt was in the land of the living after nine o'clock on Sunday, June the twenty-second.' As his argument is obviously an *ex-parte* one, he should, at least, have left this matter out of sight; for had any one been known to see Marie, say on Monday, or on Tuesday, the interval in question would have been much reduced, and, by his own ratiocination, the probability much diminished of the corpse being that of the *grisette*. It is, nevertheless, amusing to observe that *L'Etoile* insists upon its point in the full belief of its furthering its general argument.

" Re-peruse now that portion of this argument which has reference to the identification of the corpse by Beauvais. In regard to the *hair* upon the arm, *L'Etoile* has been obviously disingenuous.   M. Beauvais, not being an idiot, could never have urged in identification of the corpse, simply *hair upon its arm*.   No arm is *without* hair.   The *generality* of the expression of *L'Etoile* is a mere perversion of the witness' phraseology.   He must have spoken of some *peculiarity* in this hair.   It must have been a peculiarity of colour, of quantity, of length, or of situation.

" ' Her foot,' says the journal, ' was small—so are thousands of feet.   Her garter is no proof whatever—nor is her shoe—for shoes and garters are sold in packages.   The same may be said of the flowers in her hat.   One thing upon which M. Beauvais strongly insists is, that the clasp on the garter found had been set back to take it in.   This amounts to nothing; for most women find it proper to take a pair of garters home and fit them to the size of the limbs they are to encircle, rather than to try them in the store where they purchase.'   Here it is difficult to suppose the reasoner in earnest.   Had M. Beauvais, in his search for the body of Marie, discovered a corpse corresponding in general size and appearance to the missing girl, he would have been warranted (without reference to the question of habiliment at all) in forming an opinion that his search had been successful.   If, in addition to the point of general size and contour, he had found upon the arm a peculiar hairy appearance which he had observed upon the living Marie, his opinion might have been justly strengthened; and the increase of positiveness might well have been in the ratio of the peculiarity, or unusualness of the hairy mark.   If the feet of Marie being small, those of the corpse were also small, the increase of probability that the body was that of Marie would not be an increase in a ratio merely arithmetical, but in one highly geometrical, or accumulative.   Add to all this shoes such as she had been known to wear upon the day of her disappearance, and, although these shoes may be ' sold in packages,' you so far augment the probability as to verge upon the certain. What, of itself, would be no evidence of identity, becomes, through its corroborative position, proof most sure.   Give us then, flowers in the hat corresponding to those worn by the missing girl, and we seek for nothing further.   If only *one* flower, we seek for nothing further—what then if two or three, or more?   Each successive one is multiple evidence —proof not *added* to proof, but *multiplied* by hundreds or thousands. Let us now discover, upon the deceased, garters such as the living used, and it is almost folly to proceed. But these garters are found to be tightened, by the setting back of a clasp, in just such a manner as her own had been tightened by Marie shortly previous to her leaving home. It is now madness or hypocrisy to doubt. What *L'Etoile* says in respect to this abbreviation of the garters being an unusual occurrence, shows nothing beyond its own pertinacity in error. The elastic nature of the clasp-garter is self-demonstration of the *unusualness* of the abbreviation. What is made to adjust itself, must of necessity require foreign adjustment but rarely. It must have been by an accident, in its strictest sense, that these garters of Marie needed the tightening described. They alone would have amply established her identity. But it is not that the corpse was found to have the garters of the missing girl, or found to have her shoes, or her bonnet, or the flowers of her bonnet, or her feet, or a peculiar mark upon the arm, or her general size and appearance—it is that the corpse had each, and *all collectively*. Could it be proved that the editor of *L'Etoile really* entertained a doubt, under the circumstances, there would be no need, in his case, of a commission *de lunatico inquirendo*. He has thought it sagacious to echo the small talk of the lawyers, who, for the most part, content themselves with echoing the rectangular precepts of the courts. I would here observe that very much of what is rejected as evidence by a court is the best of evidence to the intellect. For the court, guided itself by the general principles of evidence—the recognised and *booked* principles— is averse from swerving at particular instances. And this steadfast adherence to principle, with rigorous disregard of the conflicting exception, is a sure mode of attaining the *maximum* of attainable truth, in any long sequence of time. The practice, *en masse,* is therefore philosophical; but it is not the less certain that it engenders vast individual error.[1]

"In respect to the insinuations levelled at Beauvais, you

[1] " A theory based on the qualities of an object, will prevent its being unfolded according to its objects ; and he who arranges topics in reference to their causes, will cease to value them according to their results. Thus the jurisprudence of every nation will show that, when law becomes a science and a system, it ceases to be justice. The errors into which a blind devotion to *principles* of classification has led the common law, will be seen by observing how often the legislature has been obliged to come forward to restore the equity its scheme had lost."—*Landor*.

will be willing to dismiss them in a breath. You have already
fathomed the true character of this good gentleman. He is
a *busy-body*, with much of romance and little of wit. Any
one so constituted will readily so conduct himself, upon
occasion of *real* excitement, as to render himself liable to
suspicion on the part of the over-acute, or the ill-disposed.
M. Beauvais (as it appears from your notes) had some personal interviews with the editor of *L'Etoile*, and offended
him by venturing an opinion that the corpse, notwithstanding the theory of the editor, was, in sober fact, that of Marie.
' He persists,' says the paper, ' in asserting the corpse to be
that of Marie, but cannot give a circumstance, in addition
to those which we have commented upon, to make others
believe.' Now, without re-adverting to the fact that stronger
evidence ' to make others believe,' could *never* have been
adduced, it may be remarked that a man may very well be
understood to believe, in a case of this kind, without the
ability to advance a single reason for the belief of a second
party. Nothing is more vague than impressions of individual identity. Each man recognises his neighbour, yet
there are few instances in which any one is prepared *to give
a reason* for his recognition. The editor of *L'Etoile* had no
right to be offended at M. Beauvais' unreasoning belief.

" The suspicious circumstances which invest him, will be
found to tally much better with my hypothesis of *romantic
busy-bodyism*, than with the reasoner's suggestion of guilt.
Once adopting the more charitable interpretation, we shall
find no difficulty in comprehending the rose in the key-hole;
the ' Marie ' upon the slate; the ' elbowing the male relatives out of the way '; the ' aversion to permitting them to
see the body '; the caution given to Madame B——, that
she must hold no conversation with the *gendarme* until his
(Beauvais') return; and, lastly, his apparent determination,
' that nobody should have anything to do with the proceedings except himself.' It seems to me unquestionable that
Beauvais was a suitor of Marie's; that she coquetted with
him; and that he was ambitious of being thought to enjoy
her fullest intimacy and confidence. I shall say nothing
more upon this point; and, as the evidence fully rebuts the
assertion of *L'Etoile*, touching the matter of *apathy* on the
part of the mother and other relatives—an apathy inconsistent with the supposition of their believing the corpse to

be that of the perfumery-girl—we shall now proceed as if the question of *identity* were settled to our perfect satisfaction."

" And what," I here demanded, " do you think of the opinions of *Le Commerciel*? "

" That, in spirit, they are far more worthy of attention than any which have been promulgated upon the subject. The deductions from the premises are philosophical and acute; but the premises, in two instances, at least, are founded in imperfect observation. *Le Commerciel* wishes to intimate that Marie was seized by some gang of low ruffians not far from her mother's door. ' It is impossible,' it urges, ' that a person so well known to thousands as this young woman was, should have passed three blocks without some one having seen her.' This is the idea of a man long resident in Paris—a public man—and one whose walks to and fro in the city have been mostly limited to the vicinity of the public offices. He is aware that he seldom passes so far as a dozen blocks from his own *bureau*, without being recognised and accosted. And, knowing the extent of his personal acquaintance with others, and of others with him, he compares his notoriety with that of the perfumery-girl, finds no great difference between them, and reaches at once the conclusion that she, in her walks, would be equally liable to recognition with himself in his. This could only be the case were her walks of the same unvarying methodical character, and within the same *species* of limited region as are his own. He passes to and fro, at regular intervals, within a confined periphery, abounding in individuals who are led to observation of his person through interest in the kindred nature of his occupation with their own. But the walks of Marie, may, in general, be supposed discursive. In this particular instance, it will be understood as most probable that she proceeded upon a route of more than average diversity, from her accustomed ones. The parallel which we imagine to have existed in the mind of *Le Commerciel* would only be sustained in the event of the two individuals traversing the whole city. In this case, granting the personal acquaintances to be equal, the chances would be also equal that an equal number of personal rencontres would be made. For my own part, I should hold it not only as possible, but as far more than probable, that Marie might have proceeded,

at any given period, by any one of the many routes between
her own residence and that of her aunt, without meeting a
single individual whom she knew, or by whom she was
known.   In viewing this question in its full and proper
light, we must hold steadily in mind the great disPropor-
tion between the personal acquaintances of even the most
noted individual in Paris, and the entire population of Paris
itself.

"But whatever force there may still appear to be in the
suggestion of *Le Commerciel*, will be much diminished when
we take into consideration *the hour* at which the girl went
abroad.   'It was when the streets were full of people,' says
Le Commerciel, 'that she went out.'   But not so.   It was at
nine o'clock in the morning.   Now at nine o'clock of every
morning in the week, *with the exception of Sunday*, the
streets in the city are, it is true, thronged with people.   At
nine on Sunday, the populace are chiefly within doors *preparing for church*.   No observing person can have failed to
notice the peculiarly deserted air of the town, from about
eight until ten on the morning of every Sabbath.   Between
ten and eleven the streets are thronged, but not at so early
a period as that designated.

"There is another point at which there seems a deficiency
of *observation* on the part of *Le Commerciel*.   'A piece,'
it says, 'of one of the unfortunate girl's petticoats, two
feet long, and one foot wide, was torn out and tied under
her chin, and around the back of her head, probably to
prevent screams.   This was done by fellows who had no
pocket-handkerchief.'   Whether this idea is or is not well
founded, we will endeavour to see hereafter; but by ' fellows
who have no pocket-handkerchiefs,' the editor intends the
lowest class of ruffians.   These, however, are the very description of people who will always be found to have handkerchiefs even when destitute of shirts.   You must have
had occasion to observe how absolutely indispensable, of late
years, to the thorough blackguard, has become the pocket-
handkerchief."

"And what are we to think," I asked, "of the article in
Le Soleil? "

"That it is a vast pity its inditer was not born a parrot—
in which case he would have been the most illustrious parrot
of his race.   He has merely repeated the individual items of

the already published opinion; collecting them, with a laudable industry, from this paper and from that. 'The things had all *evidently* been there,' he says, ' at least three or four weeks, and there can be *no doubt* that the spot of this appalling outrage has been discovered.' The facts here restated by *Le Soleil* are very far indeed from removing my own doubts upon this subject, and we will examine them more particularly hereafter in connection with another division of the theme.

" At present we must occupy ourselves with other investigations. You cannot fail to have remarked the extreme laxity of the examination of the corpse. To be sure, the question of identity was readily determined, or should have been; but there were other points to be ascertained. Had the body been in any respect *despoiled*? Had the deceased any articles of jewellery about her person upon leaving home? if so, had she any when found? These are important questions utterly untouched by the evidence; and there are others of equal moment, which have met with no attention. We must endeavour to satisfy ourselves by personal inquiry. The case of St. Eustache must be re-examined. I have no suspicion of this person; but let us proceed methodically. We will ascertain beyond a doubt the validity of the *affidavits* in regard to his whereabouts on the Sunday. Affidavits of this character are readily made matter of mystification. Should there be nothing wrong here, however, we will dismiss St. Eustache from our investigations. His suicide, however corroborative of suspicion, were there found to be deceit in the affidavits, is, without such deceit, in no respect an unaccountable circumstance, or one which need cause us to deflect from the line of ordinary analysis.

" In that which I now propose, we will discard the interior points of this tragedy, and concentrate our attention upon its outskirts. Not the least usual error in investigations such as this is the limiting of inquiry to the immediate, with total disregard of the collateral or circumstantial events. It is the malpractice of the courts to confine evidence and discussion to the bounds of apparent relevancy. Yet experience has shown, and a true philosophy will always show, that a vast, perhaps the larger, portion of truth arises from the seemingly irrelevant. It is through the spirit of this principle, if not precisely through its letter, that modern science has resolved to *calculate upon the unforeseen.* But perhaps you do not comprehend me. The history of human knowledge has so uninterruptedly shown that to collateral, or incidental, or accidental events we are indebted for the most numerous and most valuable discoveries, that it has at length become necessary, in prospective view of improvement, to make not only large, but the largest, allowances for inventions that shall arise by chance, and quite out of the range of ordinary expectation. It is no longer philosophical to base upon what has been a vision of what is to be. *Accident* is admitted as a portion of the substructure. We make chance a matter of absolute calculation. We subject the unlooked-for and unimagined to the mathematical *formulæ* of the schools.

" I repeat that it is more than fact that the *larger* portion of all truth has sprung from the collateral; and it is but in accordance with the spirit of the principle involved in this fact that I would divert inquiry, in the present case, from the trodden and hitherto unfruitful ground of the event itself to the contemporary circumstances which surround it. While you ascertain the validity of the affidavits, I will examine the newspapers more generally than you have as yet done. So far, we have only reconnoitred the field of investigation; but it will be strange, indeed, if a comprehensive survey, such as I propose, of the public prints will not afford us some minute points which shall establish a *direction* for inquiry."

In pursuance of Dupin's suggestion, I made scrupulous examination of the affair of the affidavits. The result was a firm conviction of their validity, and of the consequent innocence of St. Eustache. In the meantime my friend occupied himself, with what seemed to me a minuteness altogether objectless, in a scrutiny of the various newspaper files. At the end of a week he placed before me the following extracts:

" About three years and a half ago, a disturbance very similar to the present was caused by the disappearance of this same Marie Rogêt from the *parfumerie* of Monsieur Le Blanc, in the Palais Royal. At the end of a week, however, she re-appeared at her customary *comptoir*, as well as ever, with the exception of a slight paleness not altogether usual. It was given out by Monsieur Le Blanc and her mother that she had merely been on a visit to some friend in the country; and the affair was speedily hushed up. We presume that the present absence is a freak of the same nature, and that, at the expiration of a week or, perhaps, of a month, we shall have her among us again."—*Evening Paper*, Monday, June 23.[1]

" An evening journal of yesterday refers to a former mysterious disappearance of Mademoiselle Rogêt. It is well known that, during the week of her absence from Le Blanc's *parfumerie*, she was in the company of a young naval officer much noted for his debaucheries. A quarrel, it is supposed, providentially led to her return home. We have the name of the Lothario in question, who is at present stationed in Paris, but for obvious reasons forbear to make it public."—*La Mercure*, Tuesday morning, June 24.[2]

" An outrage of the most atrocious character was perpetrated near this city the day before yesterday. A gentleman, with his wife and daughter, engaged about dusk, the services of six young men, who were idly rowing a boat to and fro near the banks of the Seine, to convey him across the river. Upon reaching the opposite shore the three passengers stepped out, and had proceeded so far as to be beyond the view of the boat, when the daughter discovered that she had left in it her parasol. She returned for it, was seized by the gang, carried out into the stream, gagged, brutally treated, and finally taken to the shore at a point not far from that at which she had originally entered the boat with her parents. The villains have escaped for the time, but the police are upon their trail, and some of them will soon be taken."—*Morning Paper*, June 25.[3]

" We have received one or two communications, the object of which is to fasten the crime of the late atrocity upon Mennais;[4] but as this gentleman has been fully exonerated by a legal inquiry, and as the arguments of our several correspondents appear to be more zealous than profound, we do not think it advisable to make them public."—*Morning Paper*, June 28.[5]

" We have received several forcibly written communi-

---

[1] New York *Express*.   [2] New York *Herald*.   [3] New York *Courier and Inquirer*.

[4] Mennais was one of the parties originally suspected and arrested, but discharged through total lack of evidence.

[5] New York *Courier and Inquirer*.

cations, apparently from various sources, and which go far to render it a matter of certainty that the unfortunate Marie Rogêt has become a victim of one of the numerous bands of blackguards which infest the vicinity of the city upon Sunday. Our own opinion is decidedly in favour of this supposition. We shall endeavour to make room for some of these arguments hereafter."—*Evening Paper*—Tuesday June 31.[1]

" On Monday, one of the bargemen connected with the revenue service saw an empty boat floating down the Seine. Sails were lying in the bottom of the boat. The bargeman towed it under the barge office. The next morning it was taken from thence without the knowledge of any of the officers. The rudder is now at the barge office."—*La Diligence*, Thursday, June 26.[2]

Upon reading these various extracts, they not only seemed to me irrelevant, but I could perceive no mode in which any one of them could be brought to bear upon the matter in hand. I waited for some explanation from Dupin.

" It is not my present design," he said, " to *dwell* upon the first and second of these extracts. I have copied them chiefly to show you the extreme remissness of the police, who, as far as I can understand from the Prefect, have not troubled themselves, in any respect, with an examination of the naval officer alluded to. Yet it is mere folly to say that between the first and second disappearance of Marie there is no *supposable* connection. Let us admit the first elopement to have resulted in a quarrel between the lovers, and the return home of the betrayed. We are now prepared to view a second *elopement* (if we *know* that an elopement has again taken place) as indicating a renewal of the betrayer's advances, rather than as the result of new proposals by a second individual—we are prepared to regard it as a 'making up' of the old *amour*, rather than as the commencement of a new one. The chances are ten to one, that he who had once eloped with Marie would again propose an elopement, rather than that she to whom proposals of elopement had been made by one individual, should have them made to her by another. And here let me call your attention to the fact, that the time elapsing between the first ascertained and the second supposed elopement is a few months more than the general period of the cruises of our men-of-war. Had the lover been interrupted in his first villainy by the necessity of departure to sea, and had he seized the first moment of his return to renew the base designs not yet altogether accomplished—or not yet altogether accomplished *by him*? Of all these things we know nothing.

"You will say, however, that, in the second instance, there was *no* elopement as imagined. Certainly not—but are we prepared to say that there was not the frustrated design? Beyond St. Eustache, and perhaps Beauvais, we find no recognised, no open, no honourable suitors of Marie. Of none other is there anything said. Who, then, is the secret lover, of whom the relatives (*at least most of them*) know nothing, but whom Marie meets upon the morning of Sunday, and who is so deeply in her confidence, that she hesitates not to remain with him until the shades of the evening descend, amid the solitary groves of the Barrière du Roule? Who is that secret lover, I ask, of whom, at least, *most* of the relatives know nothing? And what means the singular prophecy of Madame Rogêt on the morning of Marie's departure—'I fear that I shall never see Marie again.'

"But if we cannot imagine Madame Rogêt privy to the design of elopement, may we not at least suppose this design entertained by the girl? Upon quitting home, she gave it to be understood that she was about to visit her aunt in the Rue des Drômes, and St. Eustache was requested to call for her at dark. Now, at first glance, this fact strongly militates against my suggestion;—but let us reflect. That she *did* meet some companion, and proceed with him across the river, reaching the Barrière du Roule at so late an hour as three o'clock in the afternoon, is known. But in consenting so to accompany this individual (*for whatever purpose—to her mother known or unknown*), she must have thought of her expressed intention when leaving home, and of the surprise and suspicion aroused in the bosom of her affianced suitor, St. Eustache, when, calling for her, at the hour appointed, in the Rue des Drômes, he should find that she had not been there, and when, moreover, upon returning to the *pension* with this alarming intelligence, he should become aware of her continued absence from home. She must have thought of these things, I say. She must have foreseen the chagrin of St. Eustache, the suspicion of all. She could not have thought of returning to brave this suspicion; but the suspicion becomes a point of trivial importance to her, if we suppose her *not* intending to return.

"We may imagine her thinking thus—'I am to meet a certain person for the purpose of elopement, or for certain other purposes known only to myself. It is necessary that there be no chance of interruption—there must be a sufficient time given us to elude pursuit—I will give it to be understood that I shall visit and spend the day with my aunt at the Rue des Drômes—I will tell St. Eustache not to call for me until dark—in this way, my absence from home for the longest possible period, without causing suspicion or anxiety, will be accounted for, and I shall gain more time than in any other manner. If I bid St. Eustache call for me at dark, he will be sure not to call before; but if I wholly neglect to bid him call, my time for escape will be diminished, since it will be expected that I return the earlier, and my absence will the sooner excite anxiety. Now, if it were my design to return *at all*—if I had in contemplation merely a stroll with the individual in question—it would not be my policy to bid St. Eustache call; for, calling, he will be *sure* to ascertain that I have played him false—a fact of which I might keep him for ever in ignorance, by leaving home without notifying him of my intention, by returning before dark, and by then stating that I had been to visit my aunt in the Rue des Drômes. But, as it is my design *never* to return—or not for some weeks—or not until certain concealments are effected—the gaining of time is the only point about which I need give myself any concern.'

"You have observed, in your notes, that the most general opinion in relation to this sad affair is, and was from the first, that the girl had been the victim of a *gang* of blackguards. Now, the popular opinion, under certain conditions, is not to be disregarded. When arising of itself—when manifesting itself in a strictly spontaneous manner—we should look upon it as analogous with that *intuition* which is the idiosyncrasy of the individual man of genius. In ninety-nine cases from the hundred I would abide by its decision. But it is important that we find no palpable traces of *suggestion*. The opinion must be rigorously *the public's own*; and the distinction is often exceedingly difficult to perceive

and to maintain.   In the present instance, it appears to me
that this 'public opinion,' in respect to *a gang*, has been
superinduced by the collateral event which is detailed in
the third of my extracts.   All Paris is excited by the discovered corpse of Marie, a girl young, beautiful, and
notorious.   This corpse is found, bearing marks of violence,
and floating in the river.   But it is now made known that,
at the very period, or about the very period, in which it is
supposed that the girl was assassinated, an outrage similar
in nature to that endured by the deceased, although less
in extent, was perpetrated, by a gang of young ruffians,
upon the person of a second young female.   It is wonderful
that the one known atrocity should influence the popular
judgment in regard to the other unknown?   This judgment
awaited direction, and the known outrage seemed so oppor-
tunely to afford it!   Marie, too, was found in the river;
and upon this very river was this known outrage committed?
The connection of the two events had about it so much of
the palpable, that the true wonder would have been a
failure of the populace to appreciate and to seize it.   But,
in fact, the one atrocity, known to be so committed, is, if
anything, evidence that the other, committed at a time nearly
coincident, was *not* so committed.   It would have been a
miracle indeed, if, while a gang of ruffians were perpetrating,
at a given locality, a most unheard-of wrong, there should
have been another similar gang, in a similar locality, in the
same city, under the same circumstances, with the same
means and appliances, engaged in a wrong of precisely the
same aspect, at precisely the same period of time!   Yet in
what, if not in this marvellous train of coincidence, does
the accidentally *suggested* opinion of the populace call upon
us to believe?

  " Before proceeding further, let us consider the supposed
scene of the assassination, in the thicket at the Barrière du
Roule.   This thicket, although dense, was in the close
vicinity of a public road.   Within were three or four large
stones forming a kind of seat with a back and a footstool.
On the upper stone was discovered a white petticoat; on
the second, a silk scarf.   A parasol, gloves, and a pocket-
handkerchief were also here found.   The handkerchief bore
the name 'Marie Rogêt.'   Fragments of dress were seen on
the branches around.   The earth was trampled, the bushes

were broken, and there was every evidence of a violent struggle.

"Notwithstanding the acclamation with which the discovery of this thicket was received by the Press, and the unanimity with which it was supposed to indicate the precise scene of the outrage, it must be admitted that there was some very good reason for doubt. That it *was* the scene, I may or I may not believe—but there was excellent reason for doubt. Had the *true* scene been, as *Le Commerciel* suggested, in the neighbourhood of the Rue Pavée St. Andrée, the perpetrators of the crime, supposing them still resident in Paris, would naturally have been stricken with terror at the public attention thus acutely directed into the proper channel; and, in certain classes of minds, there would have arisen, at once, a sense of the necessity of some exertion to redivert the attention. And thus, the thicket of the Barrière du Roule having been already suspected, the idea of placing the articles where they were found, might have been naturally entertained. There is no real evidence, although *Le Soleil* so supposes, that the articles discovered had been more than a few days in the thicket; while there is much circumstantial proof that they could not have remained there, without attracting attention, during the twenty days elapsing between the fatal Sunday and the afternoon upon which they were found by the boys. 'They were all *mildewed* down hard,' says *Le Soleil*, adopting the opinions of its predecessors, 'with the action of the rain and stuck together from *mildew*. The grass had grown around and over some of them. The silk of the parasol was strong, but the threads of it were run together within. The upper part, where it had been doubled and folded, was all *mildewed* and rotten, and tore on being opened.' In respect to the grass having 'grown around and over some of them,' it is obvious that the fact could only have been ascertained from the words, and thus from the recollections, of two small boys; for these boys removed the articles and took them home before they had been seen by a third party. But the grass will grow, especially in warm and damp weather (such as was that of the period of the murder), as much as two or three inches in a single day. A parasol lying upon a newly turfed ground, might, in a single week, be entirely concealed from sight by the upspringing grass.

And touching that *mildew* upon which the editor of *Le Soleil* so pertinaciously insists, that he employs the word no less than three times in the brief paragraph just quoted, is he really unaware of the nature of this *mildew*? Is he to be told that it is one of many classes of *fungus*, of which the most ordinary feature is its upspringing and decadence within twenty-four hours?

" Thus we see, at a glance, that what has been most triumphantly adduced in support of the idea that the articles had been ' for at least three or four weeks ' in the thicket, is most absurdly null as regards any evidence of that fact. On the other hand, it is exceedingly difficult to believe that these articles could have remained in the thicket specified for a longer period than a single week— for a longer period than from one Sunday to the next. Those who know anything of the vicinity of Paris, know the extreme difficulty of finding *seclusion*, unless at a great distance from its suburbs. Such a thing as an unexplored or even an unfrequently visited recess, amid its woods or groves, is not for a moment to be imagined. Let any one who, being at heart a lover of nature, is yet chained by duty to the dust and heat of this great metropolis—let any such one attempt, even during the week-days, to slake his thirst for solitude amid the scenes of natural loveliness which immediately surround us. At every second step, he will find the growing charm dispelled by the voice and personal intrusion of some ruffian or party of carousing blackguards. He will seek privacy amid the densest foliage all in vain. Here are the very nooks where the unwashed most abound —here are the temples most desecrate. With sickness of the heart the wanderer will flee back to the polluted Paris as to a less odious because less incongruous sink of pollution. But if the vicinity of the city is so beset during the working days of the week, how much more so on the Sabbath! It is now especially that, released from the claims of labour, or deprived of the customary opportunities of crime, the town blackguard seeks the precincts of the town, not through love of the rural, which in his heart he despises, but by way of escape from the restraints and conventionalities of society. He desires less the fresh air and the green trees, than the utter *licence* of the country. Here at the roadside inn, or beneath the foliage of the woods, he indulges, unchecked by any eye except those of his boon companions, in all the mad excess of a counterfeit hilarity—the joint offspring of liberty and of rum.   I say nothing more than what must be obvious to every dispassionate observer, when I repeat that the circumstance of the articles in question having remained undiscovered, for a longer period than from one Sunday to another, in *any* thicket in the immediate neighbourhood of Paris, is to be looked upon as little less than miraculous.

"But there are not wanting other grounds for the suspicion that the articles were placed in the thicket with the view of diverting attention from the real scene of the outrage.   And, first, let me direct your notice to the *date* of the discovery of the articles.   Collate this with the date of the fifth extract made by myself from the newspapers. You will find that the discovery followed, almost immediately, the urgent communications sent to the evening paper. These communications, although various, and apparently from various sources, tended all to the same point—viz., the directing of attention to *a gang* as the perpetrators of the outrage, and to the neighbourhood of the Barrière du Roule as its scene.   Now, here, of course, the situation is not that, in consequence of these communications, or of the public attention by them directed, the articles were found by the boys; but the suspicion might and may well have been, that the articles were not *before* found by the boys, for the reason that the articles had not before been in the thicket; having been deposited there only at so late a period as at the date, or shortly prior to the date of the communications, by the guilty authors of these communications themselves.

"This thicket was a singular—an exceedingly singular one.   It was unusually dense.   Within its naturally walled enclosure were three extraordinary stones, *forming a seat with a back and a footstool.*   And this thicket, so full of art, was in the immediate vicinity, *within a few rods,* of the dwelling of Madame Deluc, whose boys were in the habit of closely examining the shrubberies about them in search of the bark of the sassafras.   Would it be a rash wager— a wager of one thousand to one—that a *day* never passed over the heads of these boys without finding at least one of them ensconced in the umbrageous hall, and enthroned upon its natural throne?   Those who would hesitate at

such a wager, have either never been boys themselves, or
have forgotten the boyish nature. I repeat—it is exceedingly hard to comprehend how the articles could have
remained in this thicket undiscovered, for a longer period
than one or two days; and that thus there is good ground
for suspicion, in spite of the dogmatic ignorance of *Le Soleil*,
that they were, at a comparatively late date, deposited where
found.

" But there are still other and stronger reasons for believing them so deposited, than any which I have as yet
urged. And, now, let me beg your notice to the highly
artificial arrangement of the articles. On the *upper* stone
lay a white petticoat; on the *second*, a silk scarf; scattered
around, were a parasol, gloves, and a pocket-handkerchief
bearing the name ' Marie Rogêt.' Here is just such an
arrangement as would *naturally* be made by a not-over-acute
person wishing to dispose the articles *naturally*. But it is
by no means a *really* natural arrangement. I should rather
have looked to see the things *all* lying on the ground and
trampled under foot. In the narrow limits of that bower,
it would have been scarcely possible that the petticoat and
scarf should have retained a position upon the stones, when
subjected to the brushing to and fro of many struggling
persons. ' There was evidence,' it is said, ' of a struggle;
and the earth was trampled, the bushes were broken,'—but
the petticoat and the scarf are found deposited as if upon
shelves. ' The pieces of the frock torn out by the bushes
were about three inches wide and six inches long. One
part was the hem of the frock, and it had been mended.
They *looked like strips torn off.*' Here, inadvertently, *Le
Soleil* has employed an exceedingly suspicious phrase. The
pieces, as described, do indeed ' look like strips torn off ';
but purposely and by hand. It is one of the rarest of
accidents that a piece is ' torn off,' from any garment such
as is now in question, by the agency *of a thorn*. From the
very nature of such fabrics, a thorn or nail becoming tangled
in them, tears them rectangularly—divides them into two
longitudinal rents, at right angles with each other, and
meeting at an apex where the thorn enters—but it is scarcely
possible to conceive the piece ' torn off.' I never so knew
it, nor did you. To tear a piece *off* from such fabric, two
distinct forces, in different directions, will be, in almost

every case, required. If there be two edges to the fabric—
if, for example, it be a pocket-handkerchief, and it is desired
to tear from it a slip, then, and then only, will the one
force serve the purpose. But in the present case the question
is of a dress, presenting but one edge. To tear a piece from
the interior, where no edge is present, could only be effected
by a miracle through the agency of thorns, and no *one* thorn
could accomplish it. But, even where an edge is presented,
two thorns will be necessary, operating, the one in two
distinct directions, and the other in one. And this in the
supposition that the edge is unhemmed. If hemmed, the
matter is nearly out of the question. We thus see the
numerous and great obstacles in the way of pieces being
' torn off ' through the simple agency of ' thorns '; yet we
are required to believe not only that one piece but that
many have been so torn. ' And one part,' too, ' *was the
hem of the frock* '! Another piece was ' *part of the skirt,
not the hem,* '—that is to say, was torn completely out,
through the agency of thorns, from the unedged interior
of the dress! These, I say, are things which one may well
be pardoned for disbelieving; yet, taken collectedly, they
form, perhaps, less of reasonable ground for suspicion, than
the one startling circumstance of the articles having been
left in this thicket at all, by any *murderers* who had enough
precaution to think of removing the corpse. You will not
have apprehended me rightly, however, if you suppose it
my design to *deny* this thicket as the scene of the outrage.
There might have been a wrong *here*, or, more possibly, an
accident at Madame Deluc's. But, in fact, this is a point
of minor importance. We are not engaged in an attempt
to discover the scene, but to produce the perpetrators of
the murder. What I have adduced, notwithstanding the
minuteness with which I have adduced it, has been with
the view, first, to show the folly of the positive and headlong assertions of *Le Soleil*, but secondly and chiefly, to
bring you, by the most natural route, to a further contemplation of the doubt whether this assassination has, or has
not, been the work of *a gang.*

   " We will resume this question by mere allusion to the
revolting details of the surgeon examined at the inquest.
It is only necessary to say that his published *inferences*,
in regard to the number of the ruffians, have been properly

ridiculed as unjust and totally baseless, by all the reputable anatomists of Paris. Not that the matter *might not* have been as inferred, but that there was no ground for the inference:—was there not much for another?

"Let us reflect now upon ' the traces of a struggle '; and let me ask what these traces have been supposed to demonstrate. A gang. But do they not rather demonstrate the absence of a gang? What *struggle* could have taken place —what struggle so violent and so enduring as to have left its ' traces ' in all directions—between a weak and defenceless girl and the *gang* of ruffians imagined? The silent grasp of a few rough arms and all would have been over. The victim must have been absolutely passive at their will. You will here bear in mind that the arguments used against the thicket as the scene, are applicable, in chief part, only against it as the scene of an outrage committed by *more than a single individual*. If we imagine but *one* violator, we can conceive, and thus only conceive, the struggle of so violent and so obstinate a nature as to have left the ' traces ' apparent.

"And again. I have already mentioned the suspicion to be excited by the fact that the articles in question were suffered to remain *at all* in the thicket where discovered. It seems almost impossible that these evidences of guilt should have been accidentally left where found. There was sufficient presence of mind (it is supposed) to remove the corpse; and yet a more positive evidence than the corpse itself (whose features might have been obliterated by decay), is allowed to lie conspicuously in the scene of the outrage —I allude to the handkerchief with the *name* of the deceased. If this was accident, it was not the accident *of a gang*. We can imagine it only the accident of an individual. Let us see. An individual has committed the murder. He is alone with the ghost of the departed. He is appalled by what lies motionless before him. The fury of his passion is over, and there is abundant room in his heart for the natural awe of the deed. His is none of that confidence which the presence of numbers inevitably inspires. He is *alone* with the dead. He trembles and is bewildered. Yet there is a necessity for disposing of the corpse. He bears it to the river, and leaves behind him the other evidences of his guilt; for it is difficult, if not impossible, to carry all the burthen at once, and it will be easy to return for what is left. But in his toilsome journey to the water his fears redouble within him. The sounds of life encompass his path. A dozen times he hears or fancies he hears the step of an observer. Even the very lights from the city bewilder him. Yet, in time, and by long and frequent pauses of deep agony, he reaches the river's brink, and disposes of his ghastly charge—perhaps through the medium of a boat. But *now* what treasure does the world hold— what threat of vengeance could it hold out—which would have power to urge the return of that lonely murderer over that toilsome and perilous path, to the thicket and its blood-chilling recollections? He returns *not*, let the consequences be what they may. He *could* not return if he would. His sole thought is immediate escape. He turns his back *for ever* upon those dreadful shrubberies, and flees as from the wrath to come.

"But how with a gang? Their number would have inspired them with confidence; if, indeed, confidence is ever wanting in the breast of the arrant blackguard; and of arrant blackguards alone are the supposed *gangs* ever constituted. Their number, I say, would have prevented the bewildering and unreasoning terror which I have imagined to paralyse the single man. Could we suppose an oversight in one, or two, or three, this oversight would have been remedied by a fourth. They would have left nothing behind them; for their number would have enabled them to carry *all* at once. There would have been no need of *return*.

"Consider now the circumstance that, in the outer garment of the corpse when found, 'a slip, about a foot wide, had been torn upward from the bottom hem to the waist, wound three times round the waist, and secured by a sort of hitch in the back.' This was done with the obvious design of affording *a handle* by which to carry the body. But would any *number* of men have dreamed of resorting to such an expedient? To three or four, the limbs of the corpse would have afforded not only a sufficient, but the best possible, hold. The device is that of a single individual; and this brings us to the fact that 'between the thicket and the river the rails of the fences were found taken down, and the ground bore evident traces of some heavy burden

having been dragged along it!' But would a *number* of
men have put themselves to the superfluous trouble of taking
down a fence, for the purpose of dragging through it a
corpse which they might have *lifted over* any fence in an
instant? Would a *number* of men have so *dragged* a corpse
at all as to have left evident *traces* of the dragging?

"And here we must refer to an observation of *Le Commerciel*; an observation upon which I have already, in some
measure, commented. 'A piece,' says this journal, 'of one
of the unfortunate girl's petticoats was torn out and tied
under her chin, and around the back of her head, probably
to prevent screams. This was done by fellows who had no
pocket-handkerchiefs.'

"I have before suggested that a genuine blackguard is
never *without* a pocket-handkerchief. But it is not to this
fact that I now specially advert. That it was not through
want of a handkerchief for the purpose imagined by *Le Commerciel*, that this bandage was employed, is rendered apparent by the handkerchief left in the thicket; and that
the object was not 'to prevent screams' appears, also, from
the bandage having been employed in preference to what
would so much better have answered the purpose. But the
language of the evidence speaks of the strip in question as
'found around the neck, fitting loosely, and secured with a
hard knot.' These words are sufficiently vague, but differ
materially from those of *Le Commerciel*. The slip was
eighteen inches wide, and therefore, although of muslin,
would form a strong band when folded or rumpled longitudinally. And thus rumpled it was discovered. My inference is this. The solitary murderer, having borne the
corpse for some distance (whether from the thicket or elsewhere) by means of the bandage *hitched* around its middle,
found the weight, in this mode of procedure, too much for
his strength. He resolved to drag the burthen—the evidence
goes to show that it *was* dragged. With this object in view,
it became necessary to attach something like a rope to one
of the extremities. It could be best attached about the
neck, where the head would prevent its slipping off. And
now the murderer bethought him, unquestionably, of the
bandage about the loins. He would have used this, but for
its volution about the corpse, the *hitch* which embarrassed
it, and the reflection that it had not been 'torn off' from

the garment. It was easier to tear a new slip from the petticoat. He tore it, made it fast about the neck, and so *dragged* his victim to the brink of the river. That this 'bandage,' only attainable with trouble and delay, and but imperfectly answering its purpose—that this bandage was employed *at all*, demonstrates that the necessity for its employment sprang from circumstances arising at a period when the handkerchief was no longer attainable—that is to say, arising, as we have imagined, after quitting the thicket (if the thicket it was), and on the road between the thicket and the river.

"But the evidence, you will say, of Madame Deluc (!) points especially to the presence of *a gang* in the vicinity of the thicket, at or about the epoch of the murder. This I grant. I doubt if there were not a *dozen* gangs, such as described by Madame Deluc, in and about the vicinity of the Barrière du Roule at *or about* the period of this tragedy. But the gang which has drawn upon itself the pointed animadversion, although the somewhat tardy and very suspicious evidence of Madame Deluc, is the *only* gang which is represented by that honest and scrupulous old lady as having eaten her cakes, and swallowed her brandy, without putting themselves to the trouble of making her payment. *Et hinc illæ iræ?*

"But what *is* the precise evidence of Madame Deluc? 'A gang of miscreants made their appearance, behaved boisterously, ate and drank without making payment, followed in the route of the young man and the girl, returned to the inn *about dusk*, and re-crossed the river as if in great haste.'

"Now, this 'great haste' very possibly seemed *greater* haste in the eyes of Madame Deluc, since she dwelt lingeringly and lamentingly upon her violated cakes and ale,—cakes and ale for which she might still have entertained a faint hope of compensation. Why, otherwise, since it was *about dusk*, should she make a point of the *haste*? It is no cause for wonder, surely, that a gang of blackguards should make *haste* to get home when a wide river is to be crossed in small boats, when storm impends, and when night *approaches*.

"I say *approaches*; for the night had *not yet arrived*. It was only *about dusk* that the indecent haste of these 'miscreants' offended the sober eyes of Madame Deluc. But we are told that it was upon this evening that Madame Deluc, as well as her eldest son, 'heard the screams of a female in the vicinity of the inn.' And in what words does Madame Deluc designate the period of the evening at which these screams were heard? 'It was *soon after dark*,' she says. But 'soon *after* dark' is at least *dark*; and '*about dusk*' is as certainly daylight. Thus it is abundantly clear that the gang quitted the Barrière du Roule *prior* to the screams overheard (?) by Madame Deluc. And although, in all the many reports of the evidence, the relative expressions in question are distinctly and invariably employed just as I have employed them in this conversation with yourself, no notice whatever of the gross discrepancy has, as yet, been taken by any of the public journals, or by any of the myrmidons of police.

"I shall add but one to the arguments against a *gang*; but this *one* has, to my own understanding at least, a weight altogether irresistible. Under the circumstances of large reward offered, and full pardon to any king's evidence, it is not to be imagined, for a moment, that some member of *a gang* of low ruffians, or of any body of men, would not long ago have betrayed his accomplices. Each one of a gang, so placed, is not so much greedy of reward, or anxious for escape, as *fearful of betrayal*. He betrays eagerly and early that *he may not himself be betrayed*. That the secret has not been divulged is the very best of proof that it is, in fact, a secret. The horrors of this dark deed are known only to *one*, or two, living human beings, and to God.

"Let us sum up now the meagre yet certain fruits of our long analysis. We have attained the idea either of a fatal accident under the roof of Madame Deluc, or of a murder perpetrated in the thicket at the Barrière du Roule, by a lover, or at least by an intimate and secret associate of the deceased. The associate is of swarthy complexion. This complexion, the 'hitch' in the bandage, and the 'sailor's knot' with which the bonnet-ribbon is tied, point to a seaman. His companionship with the deceased—a gay but not abject young girl—designates him as above the grade of the common sailor. Here the well-written and urgent communications to the journals are much in the way of corroboration. The circumstance of the first elopement, as mentioned by *Le Mercurie*, tends to blend the idea of this seaman with that of the ' naval officer ' who is first known to have led the unfortunate into crime.

" And here, most fitly, comes the consideration of the continued absence of him of the dark complexion. Let me pause to observe that the complexion of this man is dark and swarthy; it was no common swarthiness which constituted the *sole* point of resemblance, both as regards Valence and Madame Deluc. But why is this man absent? Was he murdered by the gang? If so, why are there only *traces* of the assassinated girl? The scene of the outrages will naturally be supposed identical. And where is his corpse? The assassins would most probably have disposed of both in the same way. But it may be said that this man lives, and is deterred from making himself known through dread of being charged with the murder. This consideration might be supposed to operate upon him now—at this late period— since it has been given in evidence that he was seen with Marie, but it would have had no force at the period of the deed. The first impulse of an innocent man would have been to announce the outrage, and to aid in identifying the ruffians. This *policy* would have suggested. He had been seen with the girl. He had crossed the river with her in an open ferry-boat. The denouncing of the assassins would have appeared, even to an idiot, the surest and sole means of relieving himself from suspicion. We cannot suppose him, on the night of the fatal Sunday, both innocent himself and incognisant of an outrage committed. Yet only under such circumstances is it possible to imagine that he would have failed, if alive, in the denouncement of the assassins.

" And what means are ours of attaining the truth? We shall find these means of multiplying and gathering distinctness as we proceed. Let us sift to the bottom this affair of the first elopement. Let us know the full history of ' the officer,' with his present circumstances, and his whereabouts at the precise period of the murder. Let us carefully compare with each other the various communications sent to the evening paper, in which the object was to inculpate a *gang*. This done, let us compare these communications, both as regards style and MS., with those sent to the morning paper, at a previous period, and insisting so vehemently upon the guilt of Mennais. And, all this done, let us again compare these various communications with the known MSS. of the officer. Let us endeavour to ascertain, by repeated questionings of Madame Deluc and her boys, as well as of the omnibus-driver, Valence, something more of the personal appearance and bearing of the 'man of dark complexion.' Queries, skilfully directed, will not fail to elicit, from some of these parties, information on this particular point (or upon others)—information which the parties themselves may not even be aware of possessing. And let us now trace *the boat* picked up by the bargeman on the morning of Monday the twenty-third of June, and which was removed from the barge-office, without the cognisance of the officer in attendance, and *without the rudder,* at some period prior the discovery of the corpse. With a proper caution and perseverance we shall infallibly trace this boat; for not only can the bargeman who picked it up identify it, but the *rudder is at hand.* The rudder *of a sail boat* would not have been abandoned without inquiry, by one altogether at ease in heart. And here let me pause to insinuate a question. There was no *advertisement* of the picking up of this boat. It was silently taken to the barge-office, and as silently removed. But its owner or employer —how *happened* he, at so early a period on Tuesday morning, to be informed, without the agency of advertisement, of the locality of the boat taken up on Monday, unless we imagine some connection with the *navy*—some personal permanent connection leading to cognisance of its minute interests—its petty local news?

" In speaking of the lonely assassin dragging his burden to the shore, I have already suggested the probability of his availing himself *of a boat.* Now we are to understand that Marie Rogêt *was* precipitated from a boat. This would naturally have been the case. The corpse could not have been trusted to the shallow waters of the shore. The peculiar marks on the back and shoulders of the victim tell of the bottom ribs of a boat. That the body was found without weight is also corroborative of the idea. If thrown from the shore a weight would have been attached. We can only account for its absence by supposing the murderer to have neglected the precaution of supplying himself with it before pushing off. In the act of consigning the corpse to the water he would unquestionably have noticed his oversight; but then no remedy would have been at hand. Any risk would have been preferred to a return to that accursed shore. Having rid himself of his ghastly charge, the murderer would have hastened to the city. There, at some obscure wharf, he would have leaped on land. But the boat, would he have secured it? He would have been in too great haste for such things as securing a boat. Moreover, in fastening it to the wharf, he would have felt as if securing evidence against himself. His natural thought would have been to cast from him, as far as possible, all that held connection with his crime. He would not only have fled from the wharf, but he would not have permitted *the boat* to remain. Assuredly he would have cast it adrift. Let us pursue our fancies.—In the morning, the wretch is stricken with unutterable horror at finding that the boat has been picked up and detained at a locality which he is in the daily habit of frequenting—at a locality, perhaps, which his duty compels him to frequent. The next night, *without daring to ask for the rudder,* he removes it. Now *where* is that rudderless boat? Let it be one of our first purposes to discover. With the first glimpse we obtain of it, the dawn of our success shall begin. This boat shall guide us, with a rapidity which will surprise even ourselves, to him who employed it in the midnight of the fatal Sabbath. Corroboration will rise upon corroboration, and the murderer will be traced."

[For reasons which we shall not specify, but which to many readers will appear obvious, we have taken the liberty of here omitting, from the MSS. placed in our hands, such portion as details the *following up* of the apparently slight clue obtained by Dupin. We feel it advisable only to state, in brief, that the result desired was brought to pass; and that the Prefect fulfilled punctually, although with reluctance, the terms of his compact with the Chevalier. Mr. Poe's article concludes with the following words.—*Eds.*[1]]

It will be understood that I speak of coincidences and *no more.* What I have said above upon this topic must suffice. In my own heart there dwells no faith in præter-nature. That Nature and its God are two, no man who thinks will deny. That the latter, creating the former, can, at will, control or modify it, is also unquestionable. I say " at will "; for the question is of will, and not, as the insanity of logic

[1] Of *Snowden's Lady's Companion.*

has assumed, of power. It is not that the Deity *cannot* modify his laws, but that we insult him in imagining a possible necessity for modification. In their origin these laws were fashioned to embrace *all* contingencies which *could* lie in the Future. With God all is *Now*.

I repeat, then, that I speak of these things only as of coincidences. And further: in what I relate it will be seen that between the fate of the unhappy Mary Cecilia Rogers, so far as that fate is known, and the fate of one Marie Rogêt up to a certain epoch in her history, there has existed a parallel in the contemplation of whose wonderful exactitude the reason becomes embarrassed. I say all this will be seen. But let it not for a moment be supposed that, in proceeding with the sad narrative of Marie from the epoch just mentioned, and in tracing to its *dénouement* the mystery which enshrouded her, it is my covert design to hint at an extension of the parallel, or even to suggest that the measures adopted in Paris for the discovery of the assassin of a grisette, or measures founded in any similar ratiocination, would produce any similar result.

For, in respect to the latter branch of the supposition, it should be considered that the most trifling variation in the facts of the two cases might give rise to the most important miscalculations, by diverting thoroughly the two courses of events; very much as, in arithmetic, an error which, in its own individuality, may be inappreciable, produces at length, by dint of multiplication at all points of the process, a result enormously at variance with truth. And, in regard to the former branch, we must not fail to hold in view that the very Calculus of Probabilities to which I have referred, forbids all idea of the extension of the parallel,—forbids it with a positiveness strong and decided just in proportion as this parallel has been already long-drawn and exact. This is one of those anomalous propositions which, seemingly, appealing to thought altogether apart from the mathematical, is yet one which only the mathematician can fully entertain. Nothing, for example, is more difficult than to convince the merely general reader that the fact of sixes having been thrown twice in succession by a player at dice, is sufficient cause for betting the largest odds that sixes will not be thrown in the third attempt. A suggestion to this effect is usually rejected by the intellect at once. It does not appear that the two throws which have been completed, and which lie now absolutely in the Past, can have influence upon the throw which exists only in the Future. The chance for throwing sixes seems to be precisely as it was at any ordinary time—that is to say, subject only to the influence of the various other throws which may be made by the dice. And this is a reflection which appears so exceedingly obvious that attempts to controvert it are received more frequently with a derisive smile than with anything like respectful attention. The error here involved—a gross error redolent of mischief—I cannot pretend to expose within the limits assigned me at present; and with the philosophical it needs no exposure. It may be sufficient here to say that it forms one of an infinite series of mistakes which arise in the path of Reason through her propensity for seeking truth *in detail*.

THE PURLOINED LETTER

Nil sapientiae odiosius acumine nimio.—SENECA.

AT Paris, just after dark one gusty evening in the autumn of 18—, I was enjoying the twofold luxury of meditation and a meerschaum, in company with my friend C. Auguste Dupin, in his little back library, or book-closet, *au troisième*, *No*. 33, *Rue Dunôt, Faubourg St. Germain*. For one hour at least we had maintained a profound silence ; while each, to any casual observer, might have seemed intently and exclusively occupied with the curling eddies of smoke that oppressed the atmosphere of the chamber. For myself, however, I was mentally discussing certain topics which had formed matter for conversation between us at an earlier period of the evening ; I mean the affair of the Rue Morgue, and the mystery attending the murder of Marie Rogêt. I looked upon it, therefore, as something of a coincidence, when the door of our apartment was thrown open and admitted our old acquaintance, Monsieur G——, the Prefect of the Parisian police.

We gave him a hearty welcome ; for there was nearly half as much of the entertaining as of the contemptible about the man, and we had not seen him for several years. We had been sitting in the dark, and Dupin now arose for the purpose of lighting a lamp, but sat down again, without doing so, upon G.'s saying that he had called to consult us, or rather to ask the opinion of my friend, about some official business which had occasioned a great deal of trouble.

" If it is any point requiring reflection," observed Dupin, as he forebore to enkindle the wick, " we shall examine it to better purpose in the dark."

" That is another of your odd notions," said the Prefect, who had a fashion of calling everything " odd " that was beyond his comprehension, and thus lived amid an absolute legion of " oddities."

" Very true," said Dupin, as he supplied his visitor with a pipe, and rolled towards him a comfortable chair.

" And what is the difficulty now ? " I asked. " Nothing more in the assassination way, I hope ? "

" Oh, no ; nothing of that nature. The fact is, the business is *very* simple indeed, and I make no doubt that we can manage it sufficiently well ourselves : but then I thought Dupin would like to hear the details of it, because it is so excessively *odd*."

" Simple and odd," said Dupin.

" Why, yes ; and not exactly that, either. The fact is, we have all been a good deal puzzled because the affair *is* so simple, and yet baffles us altogether."

" Perhaps it is the very simplicity of the thing which puts you at fault," said my friend.

" What nonsense you *do* talk ! " replied the Prefect, laughing heartily.

" Perhaps the mystery is a little *too* plain," said Dupin.

" Oh, good heavens ! who ever heard of such an idea ? "

" A little *too* self-evident."

" Ha ! ha ! ha !—ha ! ha ! ha !—ho ! ho ! ho ! " roared our visitor, profoundly amused, " oh, Dupin, you will be the death of me yet ! "

" And what, after all, *is* the matter on hand ? " I asked.

" Why, I will tell you," replied the Prefect, as he gave a long, steady, and contemplative puff, and settled himself in his chair. " I will tell you in a few words ; but, before I begin, let me caution you that this is an affair demanding the greatest secrecy, and that I should most probably lose the position I now hold, were it known that I confided it to any one."

" Proceed," said I.

" Or not," said Dupin.

" Well, then ; I have received personal information, from a very high quarter, that a certain document of the last importance has been purloined from the royal apartments. The individual who purloined it is known ; this beyond a doubt ; he was seen to take it. It is known, also, that it still remains in his possession."

" How is this known ? " asked Dupin.

" It is clearly inferred," replied the Prefect, " from the nature of the document, and from the non-appearance of certain results which would at once arise from its passing *out* of the robber's possession ;—that is to say, from his employing it as he must design in the end to employ it."

" Be a little more explicit," I said.

" Well, I may venture so far as to say that the paper gives its holder a certain power in a certain quarter where such power is immensely valuable." The Prefect was fond of the cant of diplomacy.

" Still I do not quite understand," said Dupin.

" No ? Well ; the disclosure of the document to a third person, who shall be nameless, would bring in question the honour of a personage of most exalted station ; and this fact gives the holder of the document an ascendancy over the illustrious personage whose honour and peace are so jeopardised."

" But this ascendancy," I interposed, " would depend upon the robber's knowledge of the loser's knowledge of the robber. Who would dare——"

" The thief," said G., " is the Minister D——, who dares all things, those unbecoming as well as those becoming a man. The method of the theft was not less ingenious than bold. The document in question—a letter, to be frank—had been received by the personage robbed while alone in the royal *boudoir*. During its perusal she was suddenly interrupted by the entrance of the other exalted personage from whom especially it was her wish to conceal it. After a hurried and vain endeavour to thrust it in a drawer, she was forced to place it, open as it was, upon a table. The address, however, was uppermost, and, the contents thus unexposed, the letter escaped notice. At this juncture enters the Minister D——. His lynx eye immediately perceives the paper, recognises the handwriting of the address, observes the confusion of the personage addressed, and fathoms her secret. After some business transactions, hurried through in his ordinary manner, he produces a letter somewhat similar to the one in question, opens it, pretends to read it, and then places it in close juxtaposition to the other. Again he converses, for some fifteen minutes, upon the public affairs. At length, in taking leave, he takes also from the table the letter to which he had no claim. Its rightful owner saw, but, of course, dared not call attention to the act, in the presence of the third personage who stood at her elbow.

The Minister decamped ; leaving his own letter—one of no importance—upon the table."

" Here, then," said Dupin to me, " you have precisely what you demand to make the ascendancy complete—the robber's knowledge of the loser's knowledge of the robber."

" Yes," replied the Prefect ; " and the power thus attained has, for some months past, been wielded, for political purposes, to a very dangerous extent. The personage robbed is more thoroughly convinced, every day, of the necessity of reclaiming her letter. But this, of course, cannot be done openly. In fine, driven to despair, she has committed the matter to me."

" Than whom," said Dupin, amid a perfect whirlwind of smoke, " no more sagacious agent could, I suppose, be desired, or even imagined."

" You flatter me," replied the Prefect ; " but it is possible that some such opinion may have been entertained."

" It is clear," said I, " as you observe, that the letter is still in possession of the Minister ; since it is this possession, and not any employment of the letter, which bestows the power. With the employment the power departs."

" True," said G. ; " and upon this conviction I proceeded. My first care was to make thorough search of the Minister's hotel ; and here my chief embarrassment lay in the necessity of searching without his knowledge. Beyond all things, I have been warned of the danger which would result from giving him reason to suspect our design."

" But," said I, " you are quite *au fait* in these investigations. The Parisian police have done this thing often before."

" Oh yes ; and for this reason I did not despair. The habits of the Minister gave me, too, a great advantage. He is frequently absent from home all night. His servants are by no means numerous. They sleep at a distance from their master's apartment, and, being chiefly Neapolitans, are readily made drunk. I have keys, as you know, with which I can open any chamber or cabinet in Paris. For three months a night has not passed, during the greater part of which I have not been engaged, personally, in ransacking the D—— Hotel. My honour is interested, and, to mention a great secret, the reward is enormous. So I did not abandon the search until I had become fully satisfied that the thief is a more astute man than myself. I fancy that I have investigated every nook and corner of the premises in which it is possible that the paper can be concealed."

" But is it not possible," I suggested, " that although the letter may be in possession of the Minister, as it unquestionably is, he may have concealed it elsewhere than upon his own premises ? "

" This is barely possible," said Dupin. " The present peculiar condition of affairs at court, and especially of those intrigues in which D—— is known to be involved, would render the instant availability of the document—its susceptibility of being produced at a moment's notice— a point of nearly equal importance with its possession."

" Its susceptibility of being produced ? " said I.

" That is to say, of being *destroyed*," said Dupin.

" True," I observed ; " the paper is clearly then upon the premises. As for its being upon the person of the Minister, we may consider that as out of the question."

" Entirely," said the Prefect. " He has been twice waylaid, as if by footpads, and his person rigorously searched under my own inspection."

" You might have spared yourself this trouble," said Dupin. " D——, I presume, is not altogether a fool, and, if not, must have anticipated these waylayings, as a matter of course."

" Not *altogether* a fool," said G., " but then he's a poet, which I take to be only one remove from a fool."

" True," said Dupin, after a long and thoughtful whiff from his meerschaum, " although I have been guilty of certain doggerel myself."

" Suppose you detail," said I, " the particulars of your search."

" Why, the fact is, we took our time, and we searched *everywhere*. I have had long experience in these affairs. I took the entire building, room by room ; devoting the nights of a whole week to each. We examined, first, the furniture of each apartment. We opened every possible drawer ; and I presume you know that, to a properly trained police agent, such a thing as a *secret* drawer is impossible. Any man is a dolt who permits a ' secret ' drawer to escape him in a search of this kind. The thing is *so* plain. There is a certain amount of bulk—of space—

to be accounted for in every cabinet. Then we have accurate rules. The fiftieth part of a line could not escape us. After the cabinets we took the chairs. The cushions we probed with the fine long needles you have seen me employ. From the tables we removed the tops."

" Why so ? "

" Sometimes the top of a table, or other similarly arranged piece of furniture, is removed by the person wishing to conceal an article ; then the leg is excavated, the article deposited within the cavity, and the top replaced. The bottoms and tops of bedposts are employed in the same way."

" But could not the cavity be detected by sounding ? " I asked.

" By no means, if, when the article is deposited, a sufficient wadding of cotton be placed around it. Besides, in our case, we were obliged to proceed without noise."

" But you could not have removed—you could not have taken to pieces *all* articles of furniture in which it would have been possible to make a deposit in the manner you mention. A letter may be compressed into a thin spiral roll, not differing much in shape or bulk from a large knitting-needle, and in this form it might be inserted into the rung of a chair, for example. You did not take to pieces all the chairs ? "

" Certainly not ; but we did better—we examined the rungs of every chair in the hotel, and, indeed, the jointings of every description of furniture, by the aid of a most powerful microscope. Had there been any traces of recent disturbance we should not have failed to detect it instantly. A single grain of gimlet-dust, for example, would have been as obvious as an apple. Any disorder in the glueing—any unusual gaping in the joints would have sufficed to insure detection."

" I presume you looked to the mirrors, between the boards and the plates, and you probed the beds and the bed-clothes, as well as the curtains and carpets."

" That of course ; and when we had absolutely completed every particle of the furniture in this way, then we examined the house itself. We divided its entire surface into compartments, which we numbered, so that none might be missed ; then we scrutinised each individual square inch

throughout the premises, including the two houses immediately adjoining, with the microscope, as before."

" The two houses adjoining ! " I exclaimed ; " you must
have had a great deal of trouble."

" We had ; but the reward offered is prodigious."

" You include the *grounds* about the houses ? "

" All the grounds are paved with brick. They gave us
comparatively little trouble. We examined the moss
between the bricks, and found it undisturbed."

" You looked among D——'s papers, of course, and into
the books of the library ? "

" Certainly ; we opened every package and parcel ; we
not only opened every book, but we turned over every leaf
in each volume, not contenting ourselves with a mere shake,
according to the fashion of some of our police officers.
We also measured the thickness of every book-*cover*, with
the most accurate admeasurement, and applied to each the
most jealous scrutiny of the microscope. Had any of the
bindings been recently meddled with, it would have been
utterly impossible that the fact should have escaped
observation. Some five or six volumes, just from the hands
of the binder, we carefully probed, longitudinally, with the
needles."

" You explored the floors beneath the carpets ? "

" Beyond doubt. We removed every carpet, and examined the boards with the microscope."

" And the paper on the walls ? "

" Yes."

" You looked into the cellars ? "

" We did."

" Then," I said, " you have been making a miscalculation,
and the letter is *not* upon the premises, as you suppose."

" I fear you are right there," said the Prefect. " And now,
Dupin, what would you advise me to do ? "

" To make a thorough research of the premises."

" That is absolutely needless," replied G——. " I am
not more sure that I breathe than I am that the letter is
not at the Hotel."

" I have no better advice to give you," said Dupin.
"You have, of course, an accurate description of the letter ? "

" Oh yes ! "—And here the Prefect, producing a memoran-
dum-book, proceeded to read aloud a minute account of the

internal, and especially of the external, appearance of the missing document. Soon after finishing the perusal of this description, he took his departure, more entirely depressed in spirits than I had ever known the good gentleman before.

In about a month afterwards he paid us another visit, and found us occupied very nearly as before. He took a pipe and a chair and entered into some ordinary conversation. At length I said,—

" Well, but G——, what of the purloined letter ? I presume you have at last made up your mind that there is no such thing as overreaching the Minister ? "

" Confound him, say I—yes ; I made the re-examination, however, as Dupin suggested—but it was all labour lost, as I knew it would be."

" How much was the reward offered, did you say ? " asked Dupin.

" Why, a very great deal—a *very* liberal reward—I don't like to say how much, precisely ; but one thing I *will* say, that I wouldn't mind giving my individual cheque for fifty thousand francs to any one who could obtain me that letter. The fact is, it is becoming of more and more importance every day ; and the reward has been lately doubled. If it were trebled, however, I could do no more than I have done."

" Why, yes," said Dupin, drawlingly, between the whiffs of his meerschaum, " I really—think, G——, you have not exerted yourself—to the utmost in this matter. You might —do a little more, I think, eh ? "

" How ?—in what way ? "

" Why—puff, puff—you might—puff, puff—employ counsel in the matter, eh ?—puff, puff, puff. Do you remember the story they tell of Abernethy ? "

" No ; hang Abernethy ! "

" To be sure ! hang him and welcome. But, once upon a time, a certain rich miser conceived the design of sponging upon this Abernethy for a medical opinion. Getting up, for this purpose, an ordinary conversation in a private company, he insinuated his case to the physician, as that of an imaginary individual.

" ' We will suppose,' said the miser, ' that his symptoms are such and such ; now, doctor, what would *you* have directed him to take ? '

"'Take!' said Abernethy, 'why, take *advice*, to be sure.'"

"But," said the Prefect, a little discomposed, "*I* am *perfectly* willing to take advice, and to pay for it. I would *really* give fifty thousand francs to any one who would aid me in the matter."

"In that case," replied Dupin, opening a drawer, and producing a cheque-book, "you may as well fill me up a cheque for the amount mentioned. When you have signed it, I will hand you the letter."

I was astounded. The Prefect appeared absolutely thunderstricken. For some minutes he remained speechless and motionless, looking incredulously at my friend with open mouth, and eyes that seemed starting from their sockets; then, apparently recovering himself in some measure, he seized a pen, and after several pauses and vacant stares, finally filled up and signed a cheque for fifty thousand francs, and handed it across the table to Dupin. The latter examined it carefully and deposited it in his pocket-book; then, unlocking an *escritoire*, took thence a letter and gave it to the Prefect. This functionary grasped it in a perfect agony of joy, opened it with a trembling hand, cast a rapid glance at its contents, and then, scrambling and struggling to the door, rushed at length unceremoniously from the room and from the house, without having uttered a syllable since Dupin had requested him to fill up the cheque.

When he had gone, my friend entered into some explanations.

"The Parisian police," he said, "are exceedingly able in their way. They are persevering, ingenious, cunning, and thoroughly versed in the knowledge which their duties seem chiefly to demand. Thus, when G—— detailed to us his mode of searching the premises at the Hotel D——, I felt entire confidence in his having made a satisfactory investigation—so far as his labours extended."

"So far as his labours extended?" said I.

"Yes," said Dupin. "The measures adopted were not only the best of their kind, but carried out to absolute perfection. Had the letter been deposited within the range of their search, these fellows would, beyond a question, have found it."

I merely laughed—but he seemed quite serious in all that he said.

" The measures, then," he continued, " were good in their kind, and well executed ; their defect lay in their being inapplicable to the case, and to the man. A certain set of highly ingenious resources are, with the Prefect, a sort of Procrustean bed, to which he forcibly adapts his designs. But he perpetually errs by being too deep or too shallow, for the matter in hand ; and many a schoolboy is a better reasoner than he. I knew one about eight years of age, whose success at guessing in the game of ' even and odd ' attracted universal admiration. This game is simple, and is played with marbles. One player holds in his hand a number of these toys, and demands of another whether that number is even or odd. If the guess is right, the guesser wins one ; if wrong, he loses one. The boy to whom I allude won all the marbles of the school. Of course he had some principle of guessing ; and this lay in mere observation and admeasurement of the astuteness of his opponents. For example, an arrant simpleton is his opponent, and, holding up his closed hand, asks, ' are they even or odd ? ' Our schoolboy replies, ' odd,' and loses ; but upon the second trial he wins, for he then says to himself, ' the simpleton had them even upon the first trial, and his amount of cunning is just sufficient to make him have them odd upon the second ; I will therefore guess odd ; '—he guesses odd, and wins. Now, with a simpleton a degree above the first, he would have reasoned thus : ' This fellow finds that in the first instance I guessed odd, and, in the second, he will propose to himself, upon the first impulse, a simple variation from even to odd, as did the first simpleton ; but then a second thought will suggest that this is too simple a variation, and finally he will decide upon putting it even as before. I will therefore guess even ; '—he guesses even, and wins. Now this mode of reasoning in the schoolboy, whom his fellows termed ' lucky,'—what, in its last analysis, is it ? "

" It is merely," I said, " an identification of the reasoner's intellect with that of his opponent."

" It is," said Dupin ; " and, upon inquiring of the boy by what means he effected the *thorough* identification in which his success consisted, I received answer as follows : ' When I wish to find out how wise, or how stupid, or how good, or how wicked is any one, or what are his thoughts at the moment, I fashion the expression of my face, as accurately as possible, in accordance with the expression of his, and then wait to see what thoughts or sentiments arise in my mind or heart, as if to match or correspond with the expression.' This response of the schoolboy lies at the bottom of all the spurious profundity which has been attributed to Rochefoucault, to La Bruyère, to Machiavelli, and to Campanella."

" And the identification," I said, " of the reasoner's intellect with that of his opponent, depends, if I understand you aright, upon the accuracy with which the opponent's intellect is admeasured."

" For its practical value it depends upon this," replied Dupin ; " and the Prefect and his cohort fail so frequently, first, by default of this identification, and secondly, by ill-admeasurement, or rather through non-admeasurement, of the intellect with which they are engaged. They consider only their *own* ideas of ingenuity ; and, in searching for anything hidden, advert only to the modes in which *they* would have hidden it. They are right in this much—that their own ingenuity is a faithful representative of that of *the mass* ; but when the cunning of the individual felon is diverse in character from their own, the felon foils them, of course. This always happens when it is above their own, and very usually when it is below. They have no variation of principle in their investigations ; at best, when urged by some unusual emergency—by some extraordinary reward—they extend or exaggerate their old modes of *practice*, without touching their principles. What, for example, in this case of D——, has been done to vary the principle of action ? What is all this boring, and probing, and sounding, and scrutinising with the microscope, and dividing the surface of the building into registered square inches—what is it all but an exaggeration *of the application* of the one principle or set of principles of search, which are based upon the one set of notions regarding human ingenuity, to which the Prefect, in the long routine of his duty, has been accustomed ? Do you not see he has taken it for granted that *all* men proceed to conceal a letter,—not exactly in a gimlet-hole bored in a chair-leg—but, at least, in *some* out-of-the-way hole or corner suggested by the same tenor of thought which would urge a man to secrete a letter in a gimlet-hole bored in a chair-leg? And do you not see also, that such *recherchés* nooks for concealment are adapted only for ordinary occasions, and would be adopted only by ordinary intellects; for, in all cases of concealment, a disposal of the article concealed—a disposal of it in this *recherché* manner, —is, in the very first instance, presumable and presumed; and thus its discovery depends, not at all upon the acumen, but altogether upon the mere care, patience, and determination of the seekers; and where the case is of importance— or, what amounts to the same thing in the policial eyes, when the reward is of magnitude,—the qualities in question have *never* been known to fail. You will now understand what I meant in suggesting that, had the purloined letter been hidden anywhere within the limits of the Prefect's examination—in other words, had the principle of its concealment been comprehended within the principles of the Prefect—its discovery would have been a matter altogether beyond question. This functionary, however, has been thoroughly mystified; and the remote source of his defeat lies in the supposition that the Minister is a fool, because he has acquired renown as a poet. All fools are poets; this the Prefect *feels*; and he is merely guilty of a *non distributio medii* in thence inferring that all poets are fools."

"But is this really the poet?" I asked. "There are two brothers, I know; and both have attained reputation in letters. The Minister I believe has written learnedly on the Differential Calculus. He is a mathematician, and no poet."

"You are mistaken; I know him well; he is both. As poet *and* mathematician, he would reason well; as mere mathematician, he could not have reasoned at all, and thus would have been at the mercy of the Prefect."

"You surprise me," I said, "by these opinions, which have been contradicted by the voice of the world. You do not mean to set at naught the well-digested idea of centuries. The mathematical reason has long been regarded as *the* reason *par excellence*."

"' *Il y a à parier*,'" replied Dupin, quoting from Chamfort, "' *que toute idée publique, toute convention reçue, est une sottise, car elle a convenue au plus grand nombre.*' The mathematicians, I grant you, have done their best to promulgate

the popular error to which you allude, and which is none
the less an error for its promulgation as truth.   With an art
worthy a better cause, for example, they have insinuated
the term 'analysis' into application to algebra.   The
French are the originators of this particular deception ; but
if a term is of any importance—if words derive any value
from applicability—then 'analysis' conveys 'algebra'
about as much as, in Latin, '*ambitus*' implies 'ambition,'
'*religio*' 'religion,' or '*homines honesti*' a set of *honourable*
men."

" You have a quarrel on hand, I see," said I, " with some
of the algebraists of Paris ; but proceed."

" I dispute the availability, and thus the value, of that
reason which is cultivated in any especial form other than
the abstractly logical.   I dispute, in particular, the reason
educed by mathematical study.   The mathematics are the
science of form and quantity ; mathematical reasoning is
merely logic applied to observation upon form and quantity.   The great error lies in supposing that even the truths
of what is called *pure* algebra are abstract or general truths.
And this error is so egregious that I am confounded at the
universality with which it has been received.   Mathematical
axioms are *not* axioms of general truth.   What is true of
relation—of form and quantity—is often grossly false in
regard to morals, for example.   In this latter science it is
very usually *un*true that the aggregated parts are equal to
the whole.   In chemistry also the axiom fails.   In the consideration of motive it fails ; for two motives, each of a
given value, have not, necessarily, a value when united,
equal to the sum of their values apart.   There are numerous
other mathematical truths which are only truths within
the limits of *relation*.   But the mathematician argues, from
his *finite truths*, through habit, as if they were of an absolutely
general applicability—as the world indeed imagines them
to be.   Bryant, in his very learned *Mythology*, mentions
an analogous source of error, when he says that ' although
the Pagan fables are not believed, yet we forget ourselves
continually, and make inferences from them as existing
realities.'   With the algebraists, however, who are Pagans
themselves, the ' Pagan fables ' *are* believed, and the inferences are made, not so much through lapse of memory,
as through an unaccountable addling of the brains.   In

short, I never yet encountered the mere mathematician who could be trusted out of equal roots, or one who did not clandestinely hold it as a point of his faith that $x^2 + px$ was absolutely and unconditionally equal to q. Say to one of these gentlemen, by way of experiment if you please, that you believe occasions may occur where $x^2 + px$ is *not* altogether equal to q, and, having made him understand what you mean, get out of his reach as speedily as convenient, for, beyond doubt, he will endeavour to knock you down.

" I mean to say," continued Dupin, while I merely laughed at his last observations, " that if the Minister had been no more than a mathematician, the Prefect would have been under no necessity of giving me this cheque. I knew him, however, as both mathematician and poet, and my measures were adapted to his capacity, with reference to the circumstances by which he was surrounded. I knew him as a courtier, too, and as a bold *intriguant*. Such a man, I considered, could not fail to be aware of the ordinary policial modes of action. He could not have failed to anticipate—and events have proved that he did not fail to anticipate—the waylayings to which he was subjected. He must have foreseen, I reflected, the secret investigations of his premises. His frequent absences from home at night, which were hailed by the Prefect as certain aids to his success, I regarded only as *ruses*, to afford opportunity for thorough search to the police, and thus the sooner to impress them with the conviction to which G——, in fact, did finally arrive—the conviction that the letter was not upon the premises. I felt, also, that the whole train of thought, which I was at some pains in detailing to you just now, concerning the invariable principle of policial action in searches for articles concealed—I felt that this whole train of thought would necessarily pass through the mind of the Minister. It would imperatively lead him to despise all the ordinary *nooks* of concealment. *He* could not, I reflected, be so weak as not to see that the most intricate and remote recess of his hotel would be as open as his commonest closets to the eyes, to the probes, to the gimlets, and to the microscopes of the Prefect. I saw, in fine, that he would be driven, as a matter of course, to *simplicity*, if not deliberately induced to it as a matter of choice. You will remember, perhaps, how desperately the Prefect laughed when I suggested, upon our first interview, that it was just possible this mystery troubled him so much on account of its being so *very* self-evident."

" Yes," said I, " I remember his merriment well. I really thought he would have fallen into convulsions."

" The material world," continued Dupin, " abounds with very strict analogies to the immaterial ; and thus some colour of truth has been given to the rhetorical dogma, that metaphor, or simile, may be made to strengthen an argument, as well as to embellish a description. The principle of the *vis inertiæ*, for example, seems to be identical in physics and metaphysics. It is not more true in the former, that a large body is with more difficulty set in motion than a smaller one, and that its subsequent *momentum* is commensurate with this difficulty, than it is, in the latter, that intellects of the vaster capacity, while more forcible, more constant, and more eventful in their movements than those of inferior grade, are yet the less readily moved, and more embarrassed and full of hesitation in the first few steps of their progress. Again : have you ever noticed which of the street signs, over the shop-doors, are the most attractive of attention ? "

" I have never given the matter a thought," I said.

" There is a game of puzzles," he resumed, " which is played upon a map. One party playing requires another to find a given word—the name of town, river, state or empire—any word, in short, upon the motley and perplexed surface of the chart. A novice in the game generally seeks to embarrass his opponents by giving them the most minutely lettered names ; but the adept selects such words as stretch, in large characters, from one end of the chart to the other. These, like the over-largely lettered signs and placards of the street, escape observation by dint of being excessively obvious ; and here the physical oversight is precisely analogous with the moral inapprehension by which the intellect suffers to pass unnoticed those considerations which are too obtrusively and too palpably self-evident. But this is a point, it appears, somewhat above or beneath the understanding of the Prefect. He never once thought it probable, or possible, that the Minister had deposited the letter immediately beneath the nose of the whole world, by way of best preventing any portion of that world from perceiving it.

" But the more I reflected upon the daring, dashing, and discriminating ingenuity of D—— ; upon the fact that the document must always have been *at hand*, if he intended to use it to good purpose ; and upon the decisive evidence, obtained by the Prefect, that it was not hidden within the limits of that dignitary's ordinary search—the more satisfied I became that, to conceal this letter, the Minister had re-sorted to the comprehensive and sagacious expedient of not attempting to conceal it at all.

" Full of these ideas, I prepared myself with a pair of green spectacles, and called one fine morning, quite by accident, at the Ministerial hotel. I found D—— at home, yawning, lounging, and dawdling, as usual, and pretending to be in the last extremity of *ennui*. He is, perhaps, the most really energetic human being now alive—but that is only when nobody sees him.

" To be even with him, I complained of my weak eyes, and lamented the necessity of the spectacles, under cover of which I cautiously and thoroughly surveyed the whole apartment, while seemingly intent only upon the conversation of my host.

" I paid especial attention to a large writing-table near which he sat, and upon which lay confusedly, some miscellaneous letters and other papers, with one or two musical instruments and a few books. Here, however, after a long and very deliberate scrutiny, I saw nothing to excite particular suspicion.

" At length my eyes, in going the circuit of the room, fell upon a trumpery filigree card-rack of pasteboard, that hung dangling by a dirty blue ribbon, from a little brass knob just beneath the middle of the mantel-piece. In this rack, which had three or four compartments, were five or six visiting cards and a solitary letter. This last was much soiled and crumpled. It was torn nearly in two, across the middle—as if a design, in the first instance, to tear it entirely up as worthless, had been altered, or stayed, in the second. It had a large black seal, bearing the D—— cipher *very* conspicuously, and was addressed, in a diminutive female hand, to D——, the minister, himself. It was thrust carelessly, and even, as it seemed, contemptuously, into one of the uppermost divisions of the rack.

" No sooner had I glanced at this letter, than I concluded it to be that of which I was in search. To be sure, it was, to all appearance, radically different from the one of which the Prefect had read us so minute a description. Here the seal was large and black, with the D—— cipher ; there it was small and red, with the ducal arms of the S—— family. Here, the address, to the Minister, was diminutive and feminine ; there the superscription, to a certain royal personage, was markedly bold and decided ; the size alone formed a point of correspondence. But, then, the *radicalness* of these differences, which was excessive ; the dirt ; the soiled and torn condition of the paper, so inconsistent with the *true* methodical habits of D——, and so suggestive of a design to delude the beholder into an idea of the worthlessness of the document ; these things, together with the hyperobtrusive situation of this document, full in the view of every visitor, and thus exactly in accordance with the conclusions to which I had previously arrived ; these things, I say, were strongly corroborative of suspicion, in one who came with the intention to suspect.

" I protracted my visit as long as possible, and, while I maintained a most animated discussion with the Minister, upon a topic which I knew well had never failed to interest and excite him, I kept my attention really riveted upon the letter. In this examination, I committed to memory its external appearance and arrangement in the rack ; and also fell, at length, upon a discovery which set at rest whatever trivial doubt I might have entertained. In scrutinising the edges of the paper, I observed them to be more *chafed* than seemed necessary. They presented the *broken* appearance which is manifested when a stiff paper, having been once folded and pressed with a folder, is refolded in a reversed direction, in the same creases or edges which had formed the original fold. This discovery was sufficient. It was clear to me that the letter had been turned, as a glove, inside out, redirected, and resealed. I bade the Minister good morning, and took my departure at once, leaving a gold snuff-box upon the table.

" The next morning I called for the snuff-box, when we resumed, quite eagerly, the conversation of the preceding

day.   While thus engaged, however, a loud report, as if of
a pistol, was heard immediately beneath the windows of the
hotel, and was succeeded by a series of fearful screams, and
the shoutings of a terrified mob.   D—— rushed to a casement, threw it open, and looked out.   In the meantime, I
stepped to the card-rack, took the letter, put it in my
pocket, and replaced it by a *fac-simile* (so far as regards
externals), which I had carefully prepared at my lodgings—
imitating the D—— cipher, very readily, by means of a seal
formed of bread.

" The disturbance in the street had been occasioned by
the frantic behaviour of a man with a musket.   He had
fired it among a crowd of women and children.   It proved,
however, to have been without ball, and the fellow was
suffered to go his way as a lunatic or a drunkard.   When he
had gone, D—— came from the window, whither I had
followed him immediately upon securing the object in view.
Soon afterwards I bade him farewell.   The pretended
lunatic was a man in my own pay."

" But what purpose had you," I asked, " in replacing the
letter by a *fac-simile* ?   Would it not have been better, at the
first visit, to have seized it openly, and departed ? "

" D—— " replied Dupin, " is a desperate man, and a
man of nerve.   His hotel, too, is not without attendants
devoted to his interests.   Had I made the wild attempt you
suggest, I might never have left the Ministerial presence
alive.   The good people of Paris might have heard of me no
more.   But I had an object apart from these considerations.
You know my political prepossessions.   In this matter, I act
as a partisan of the lady concerned.   For eighteen months
the Minister has had her in his power.   She has now him in
hers—since, being unaware that the letter is not in his
possession, he will proceed with his exactions as if it was.
Thus will he inevitably commit himself, at once, to his
political destruction.   His downfall, too, will not be more
precipitate than awkward.   It is all very well to talk about
the *facilis descensus Averni* ; but in all kinds of climbing, as
Catalani said of singing, it is far more easy to get up than to
come down.   In the present instance I have no sympathy—at
least no pity—for him who descends.   He is that *monstrum
horrendum*, an unprincipled man of genius.   I confess, however, that I should like very well to know the precise

character of his thoughts, when, being defied by her whom the Prefect terms ' a certain personage,' he is reduced to opening the letter which I left for him in the card-rack."

" How ? did you put anything particular in it ? "

" Why—it did not seem altogether right to leave the interior blank—that would have been insulting. D——, at Vienna once, did me an evil turn, which I told him, quite good-humouredly, that I should remember. So, as I knew he would feel some curiosity in regard to the identity of the person who had outwitted him, I thought it a pity not to give him a clue. He is well acquainted with my MS., and I just copied into the middle of the blank sheet the words—

—— Un dessein si funeste,
S'il n'est digne d'Atrée, est digne de Thyeste.

They are to be found in Crébillon's ' Atrée.' "

11
MARK TWAIN
The Stolen White Elephant

THE STOLEN WHITE ELEPHANT

I

THE following curious history was related to me by a chance railway acquaintance. He was a gentleman more than seventy years of age, and his thoroughly good and gentle face and earnest and sincere manner imprinted the unmistakable stamp of truth upon every statement which fell from his lips. He said :

You know in what reverence the royal white elephant of Siam is held by the people of that country. You know it is sacred to kings, only kings may possess it, and that it is indeed in a measure even superior to kings, since it receives not merely honour but worship. Very well ; five years ago, when the troubles concerning the frontier line arose between Great Britain and Siam, it was presently manifest that Siam had been in the wrong. Therefore every reparation was quickly made, and the British representative stated that he was satisfied and the past should be forgotten. This greatly relieved the King of Siam, and partly as a token of gratitude, but partly also, perhaps, to wipe out any little remaining vestige of unpleasantness which England might feel toward him, he wished to send the Queen a present—the sole sure way of propitiating an enemy, according to Oriental ideas. This present ought not only to be a royal one, but transcendently royal. Wherefore, what offering could be so meet as that of a white elephant ? My position in the Indian Civil Service was such that I was deemed peculiarly worthy the honour of conveying the present to Her Majesty. A ship was fitted out for me and my servants and the officers and attendants of the elephant, and in due time I arrived in New York harbour and placed my royal charge in admirable quarters in Jersey City. It was necessary to remain awhile in order to recruit the animals' health before resuming the voyage.

All went well during a fortnight—then my calamities began. The white elephant was stolen! I was called up at dead of night and informed of this fearful misfortune. For some moments I was beside myself with terror and anxiety; I was helpless. Then I grew calmer and collected my faculties. I soon saw my course—for indeed there was but the one course for an intelligent man to pursue. Late as it was, I flew to New York and got a policeman to conduct me to the headquarters of the detective force. Fortunately I arrived in time, though the chief of the force, the celebrated Inspector Blunt, was just on the point of leaving for his home. He was a man of middle size and compact frame, and when he was thinking deeply he had a way of knitting his brows and tapping his forehead reflectively with his finger, which impressed you at once with the conviction that you stood in the presence of a person of no common order. The very sight of him gave me confidence and made me hopeful. I stated my errand. It did not flurry him in the least; it had no more visible effect upon his iron self-possession than if I had told him somebody had stolen my dog. He motioned me to a seat, and said calmly:

"Allow me to think a moment, please."

So saying, he sat down at his office table and leaned his head upon his hand. Several clerks were at work at the other end of the room; the scratching of their pens was all the sound I heard during the next six or seven minutes. Meantime the Inspector sat there buried in thought. Finally he raised his head, and there was that in the firm lines of his face which showed me that his brain had done its work and his plan was made. Said he—and his voice was low and impressive:

"This is no ordinary case. Every step must be warily taken; each step must be made sure before the next is ventured. And secrecy must be observed—secrecy profound and absolute. Speak to no one about the matter, not even the reporters. I will take care of *them*; I will see that they get only what it may suit my ends to let them know." He touched a bell; a youth appeared. "Alaric, tell the reporters to remain for the present." The boy retired. "Now let us proceed to business—and systematically. Nothing can be accomplished in this trade of mine without strict and minute method."

He took a pen and some paper. "Now—name of the elephant ?"

"Hassan Ben Ali Ben Selim Abdallah Mohammed Moisé Alhammal Jamsetjejeebhoy Dhuleep Sultan Ebu Bhudpoor."

"Very well. Given name ?"

"Jumbo."

"Very well. Place of birth ?"

"The capital city of Siam."

"Parents living ?"

"No—dead."

"Had they any other issue besides this one ?"

"None—he was an only child."

"Very well. These matters are sufficient under that head. Now please describe the elephant, and leave out no particular, however insignificant—that is, insignificant from *your* point of view. To men in my profession there *are* no insignificant particulars ; they do not exist."

I described ; he wrote. When I was done, he said : "Now listen. If I have made any mistakes, correct me." He read as follows :

> "Height, 19 feet ; length, from apex of forehead to insertion of tail, 26 feet ; length of trunk, 16 feet ; length of tail, 6 feet ; total length, including trunk and tail, 48 feet ; length of tusks, 9½ feet ; ears in keeping with these dimensions ; footprint resembles the mark when one up-ends a barrel in the snow ; colour of the elephant, a dull white ; has a hole the size of a plate in each ear for the insertion of jewellery, and possesses the habit in a remarkable degree of squirting water upon spectators and of maltreating with his trunk not only such persons as he is acquainted with, but even entire strangers ; limps slightly with his right hind leg, and has a small scar in his left armpit caused by a former boil ; had on, when stolen, a castle containing seats for fifteen persons, and a gold-cloth saddle-blanket the size of an ordinary carpet."

There were no mistakes. The Inspector touched the bell, handed the description to Alaric, and said :

"Have fifty thousand copies of this printed at once and mailed to every detective office and pawnbroker's shop on the continent." Alaric retired. "There—so far, so good. Next, I must have a photograph of the property."

I gave him one. He examined it critically, and said :

"It must do, since we can do no better ; but he has his trunk curled up and tucked into his mouth. That is unfortunate, and is calculated to mislead, for of course he does not usually have it in that position." He touched his bell.

"Alaric, have fifty thousand copies of this photograph made, the first thing in the morning, and mail them with the descriptive circulars."

Alaric retired to execute his orders. The Inspector said :

"It will be necessary to offer a reward, of course. Now as to the amount ?"

"What sum would you suggest ?"

"To *begin* with, I should say—well, twenty-five thousand dollars. It is an intricate and difficult business ; there are a thousand avenues of escape and opportunities of concealment. These thieves have friends and pals everywhere——"

"Bless me, do you know who they are ?"

The wary face, practised in concealing the thoughts and feelings within, gave me no token, nor yet the replying words, so quietly uttered :

"Never mind about that. I may, and I may not. We generally gather a pretty shrewd inkling of who our man is by the manner of his work and the size of the game he goes after. We are not dealing with a pickpocket or a hall thief, now, make up your mind to that. This property was not 'lifted' by a novice. But, as I way saying, considering the amount of travel which will have to be done, and the diligence with which the thieves will cover up their traces as they move along, twenty-five thousand may be too small a sum to offer, yet I think it worth while to start with that."

So we determined upon that figure, as a beginning. Then this man, whom nothing escaped which could by any possibility be made to serve as a clue, said :

"There are cases in detective history to show that criminals have been detected through peculiarities in their appetites. Now, what does this elephant eat, and how much ?"

"Well, as to *what* he eats—he will eat *anything*. He will eat a man, he will eat a Bible—he will eat anything *between* a man and a Bible."

"Good—very good indeed, but too general. Details are necessary—details are the only valuable things in our trade.

Very well—as to men. At one meal—or, if you prefer, during one day—how many men will he eat, if fresh ?"

"He would not care whether they were fresh or not ; at a single meal he would eat five ordinary men."

"Very good ; five men ; we will put that down. What nationalities would he prefer ?"

"He is indifferent about nationalities. He prefers acquaintances, but is not prejudiced against strangers."

"Very good. Now as to Bibles. How many Bibles would he eat at a meal ?"

"He would eat an entire edition."

"It is hardly succinct enough. Do you mean the ordinary octavo, or the family illustrated ?"

"I think he would be indifferent to illustrations ; that is, I think he would not value illustrations above simple letterpress."

"No, you do not get my idea. I refer to bulk. The ordinary octavo Bible weighs about two pounds and a half while the great quarto with the illustrations weighs ten or twelve. How many Doré Bibles would he eat at a meal ?"

"If you knew this elephant, you would not ask. He would take what they had."

"Well, put it in dollars and cents, then. We must get at it somehow. The Doré costs a hundred dollars a copy, Russia leather, bevelled."

"He would require about fifty thousand dollars' worth— say an edition of five hundred copies."

"Now, that is more exact. I will put that down. Very well ; he likes men and Bibles ; so far, so good. What else will he eat ? I want particulars."

"He will leave Bibles to eat bricks, he will leave bricks to eat bottles, he will leave bottles to eat clothing, he will leave clothing to eat cats, he will leave cats to eat oysters, he will leave oysters to eat ham, he will leave ham to eat sugar, he will leave sugar to eat pie, he will leave pie to eat potatoes, he will leave potatoes to eat bran, he will leave bran to eat hay, he will leave hay to eat oats, he will leave oats to eat rice, for he was mainly raised on it. There is nothing whatever that he will not eat but European butter, and he would eat that if he could taste it."

"Very good. General quantity at a meal—say about——"

"Well, anywhere from a quarter to half a ton."

"And he drinks——"

"Everything that is fluid. Milk, water, whisky, molasses, castor oil, camphene, carbolic acid—it is no use to go into particulars ; whatever fluid occurs to you set it down. He will drink anything that is fluid, except European coffee."

"Very good. As to quantity ?"

"Put it down five to fifteen barrels—his thirst varies ; his other appetites do not."

"These things are unusual. They ought to furnish quite good clues toward tracing him."

He touched the bell.

"Alaric, summon Captain Burns."

Burns appeared. Inspector Blunt unfolded the whole matter to him, detail by detail. Then he said in the clear, decisive tones of a man whose plans are clearly defined in his head, and who is accustomed to command :

"Captain Burns, detail Detectives Jones, Davis, Halsey, Bates and Hackett to shadow the elephant."

"Yes, sir."

"Detail Detectives Moses, Dakin, Murphy, Rogers, Tupper, Higgins and Bartholomew to shadow the thieves."

"Yes, sir."

"Place a strong guard—a guard of thirty picked men, with a relief of thirty—over the place from whence the elephant was stolen, to keep strict watch there night and day, and allow none to approach—except reporters—without written authority from me."

"Yes, sir."

"Place detectives in plain clothes in the railway, steamship, and ferry depots, and upon all roadways leading out of Jersey City, with orders to search all suspicious persons."

"Yes, sir."

"Furnish all these men with photograph and accompanying description of the elephant, and instruct them to search all trains and outgoing ferry-boats and other vessels."

"Yes, sir."

"If the elephant should be found, let him be seized, and the information forwarded to me by telegraph."

"Yes, sir."

"Let me be informed at once if any clues should be found— footprints of the animal, or anything of that kind."

"Yes, sir."

"Get an order commanding the harbour police to patrol the frontages vigilantly."

"Yes, sir."

"Despatch detectives in plain clothes over all the railways, north as far as Canada, west as far as Ohio, south as far as Washington."

"Yes, sir."

"Place experts in all the telegraph offices to listen to all messages ; and let them require that all cipher despatches be interpreted to them."

"Yes, sir."

"Let all these things be done with the utmost secrecy — mind, the most impenetrable secrecy."

"Yes, sir."

"Report to me promptly at the usual hour."

"Yes, sir."

"Go !"

"Yes, sir."

He was gone.

Inspector Blunt was silent and thoughtful a moment, while the fire in his eye cooled down and faded out. Then he turned to me and said in a placid voice :

"I am not given to boasting, it is not my habit ; but— we shall find the elephant."

I shook him warmly by the hand and thanked him ; and I *felt* my thanks, too. The more I had seen of the man the more I liked him, and the more I admired and marvelled over the mysterious wonders of his profession. Then we parted for the night, and I went home with a far happier heart than I had carried with me to his office.

II

Next morning it was all in the newspapers, in the minutest detail. It even had additions—consisting of Detective This, Detective That, and Detective The Other's "Theory" as to how the robbery was done, who the robbers were, and whither they had flown with their booty. There were eleven of these theories, and they covered all the possibilities ; and this single fact shows what independent thinkers detectives are. No two theories were alike, or even much resembled each

other, save in one striking particular, and in that one all the
eleven theories were absolutely agreed. That was, that
although the rear of my building was torn out and the only
door remained locked, the elephant had not been removed
through the rent, but by some other (undiscovered) outlet.
All agreed that the robbers had made that rent only to mislead
the detectives. That never would have occurred to me or
to any other layman, perhaps, but it had not deceived the
detectives for a moment. Thus, what I had supposed was the
only thing that had no mystery about it was in fact the very
thing I had gone furthest astray in. The eleven theories all
named the supposed robbers, but no two named the same
robbers ; the total number of suspected persons was thirty-
seven. The various newspaper accounts all closed with the
most important opinion of all—that of Chief-Inspector Blunt.
A portion of this statement read as follows :

> "The chief knows who the two principals are, namely,
> 'Brick' Duffy and 'Red' McFadden. Ten days before the
> robbery was achieved he was already aware that it was to
> be attempted, and had quietly proceeded to shadow these
> two noted villains ; but unfortunately on the night in
> question their track was lost, and before it could be found
> again the bird was flown—that is, the elephant.
> "Duffy and McFadden are the boldest scoundrels in the
> profession ; the chief has reason for believing that they
> are the men who stole the stove out of the detective
> headquarters on a bitter night last winter—in consequence
> of which the chief and every detective were in the hands
> of the physicians before morning, some with frozen feet,
> others with frozen fingers, ears, and other members."

When I read the first half of that I was more astonished
than ever at the wonderful sagacity of this strange man.
He not only saw everything in the present with a clear eye,
but even the future could not be hidden from him. I was
soon at his office, and said I could not help wishing he had
had those men arrested, and so prevented the trouble, and
loss ; but his reply was simple and unanswerable :
"It is not our province to prevent crime, but to punish
it. We cannot punish it until it is committed."
I remarked that the secrecy with which we had begun had
been marred by the newspapers ; not only all our facts but

all our plans and purposes had been revealed ; even all the suspected persons had been named ; these would doubtless disguise themselves now, or go into hiding.

"Let them. They will find that when I am ready for them, my hand will descend upon them, in their secret places, as unerringly as the hand of fate. As to the newspapers, we *must* keep in with them. Fame, reputation, constant public mention—these are the detective's bread and butter. He must publish his facts, else he will be supposed to have none ; he must publish his theory, for nothing is so strange or striking as a detective's theory, or brings him so much wondering respect ; we must publish our plans, for these the journals insist upon having, and we could not deny them without offending. We must constantly show the public what we are doing, or they will believe we are doing nothing. It is much pleasanter to have a newspaper say : 'Inspector Blunt's ingenious and extraordinary theory is as follows,' than to have it say some harsh thing, or, worse still, some sarcastic one."

"I see the force of what you say. But I noticed that in one part of your remarks in the papers this morning, you refused to reveal your opinion upon a certain minor point."

"Yes, we always do that ; it has a good effect. Besides, I had not formed any opinion on that point, anyway."

I deposited a considerable sum of money with the Inspector, to meet current expenses, and sat down to wait for news. We were expecting the telegrams to begin to arrive at any moment now. Meantime I re-read the newspapers and also our descriptive circular, and observed that our $25,000 reward seemed to be offered only to detectives. I said I thought it ought to be offered to anybody who would catch the elephant. The Inspector said :

"It is the detectives who will find the elephant, hence the reward will go to the right place. If other people found the animal, it would only be by watching the detectives and taking advantage of clues and indications stolen from them, and that would entitle the detectives to the reward, after all. The proper office of a reward is to stimulate the men who deliver up their time and their trained sagacities to this sort of work, and not to confer benefits upon chance citizens who stumble upon a capture without having earned the benefits by their own merits and labours."

This was reasonable enough, certainly. Now the telegraphic machine in the corner began to click, and the following despatch was the result :

> *Flower Station, N.Y. : 7.30 a.m.*
> *Have got a clue. Found a succession of deep tracks across a farm near here. Followed them two miles east without result ; think elephant went west. Shall now shadow him in that direction.*
> *Darley, Detective.*

"Darley's one of the best men on the force," said the Inspector. "We shall hear from him again before long."

Telegram No. 2 came.

> *Barker's, N.J. : 7.40 a.m.*
> *Just arrived. Glass factory broken open here during night and eight hundred bottles taken. Only water in large quantity near here is five miles distant. Shall strike for there. Elephant will be thirsty. Bottles were empty.*
>
> *Baker, Detective.*

"That promises well, too," said the Inspector. "I told you the creature's appetites would not be bad clues."

Telegram No. 3.

> *Taylorville, L.I. : 8.15 a.m.*
> *A haystack near here disappeared during night. Probably eaten. Have got a clue, and am off.*
>
> *Hubbard, Detective.*

"How he does move around!" said the Inspector. "I knew we had a difficult job on hand, but we shall catch him yet."

> *Flower Station, N.Y. : 9 a.m.*
> *Shadowed the tracks three miles westward. Large, deep, and ragged. Have just met a farmer who says they are not elephant tracks. Says they are holes where he dug up saplings for shade-trees when ground was frozen last winter. Give me orders how to proceed.*
>
> *Darley, Detective.*

"Aha! a confederate of the thieves! The thing grows warm," said the Inspector.

He dictated the following telegram to Darley :

*Arrest the man and force him to name his pals. Continue to
follow the tracks—to the Pacific, if necessary.*

Chief Blunt.

Next telegram :

Coney Point, Pa. : 8.45 a.m.
*Gas office broken open here during night and three months' unpaid
gas bills taken. Have got a clue and am away.*

Murphy, Detective.

"Heavens !" said the inspector, "would he eat gas bills ?"
"Through ignorance—yes ; but they cannot support life.
At least, unassisted."
Now came this exciting telegram :

Ironville, N.Y. : 9.30 a.m.
*Just arrived. This village in consternation. Elephant passed
through here at five this morning. Some say he went east, some say
west, some north, some south—but all say they did not wait to notice
particularly. He killed a horse ; have secured a piece of it for a
clue. Killed it with his trunk ; from style of blow, think he struck
it left-handed. From position in which horse lies, think elephant
travelled northward along line of Berkley railway. Has four and a
half hours' start ; but I move on his track at once.*

Hawes, Detective.

I uttered exclamations of joy. The Inspector was as self-
contained as a graven image. He calmly touched his bell.
"Alaric, send Captain Burns here."
Burns appeared.
"How many men are ready for instant orders ?"
"Ninety-six, sir."
"Send them north at once. Let them concentrate along
the line of the Berkley road north of Ironville."
"Yes, sir."
"Let them conduct their movements with the utmost
secrecy. As fast as others are at liberty, hold them for orders."
"Yes, sir."
"Go !"
"Yes, sir."
Presently came another telegram.

Sage Corners, N.Y. : 10.30.

Just arrived. Elephant passed through here at 8.15. All escaped from the town but a policeman. Apparently elephant did not strike at policeman, but at the lamp-post. Got both. I have secured a portion of the policeman as clue.

Stumm, Detective.

"So the elephant has turned westward," said the Inspector. "However, he will not escape, for my men are scattered all over that region."

The next telegram said :

Glover's, 11.15.

Just arrived. Village deserted, except sick and aged. Elephant passed through three-quarters of an hour ago. The anti-temperance mass meeting was in session ; he put his trunk in at a window and washed it out with water from cistern. Some swallowed it—since dead ; several drowned. Detectives Cross and O'Shaughnessy were passing through town, but going south—so missed elephant. Whole region for many miles around in terror—people flying from their homes. Wherever they turn they meet elephant, and many are killed.

Brant, Detective.

I could have shed tears, this havoc so distressed me. But the Inspector only said :

"You see—we are closing in on him. He feels our presence ; he has turned eastward again."

Yet further troublous news was in store for us. The telegraph brought this :

Hoganport, 12.19

Just arrived. Elephant passed through half an hour ago, creating wildest fright and excitement. Elephant raged around streets ; two plumbers going by, killed one—other escaped. Regret general.

O'Flaherty, Detective.

"Now he is right in the midst of my men," said the Inspector. "Nothing can save him."

A succession of telegrams came from detectives who were scattered through New Jersey and Pennsylvania, and who were following clues consisting of ravaged barns, factories, and Sunday-school libraries, with high hopes—hopes amounting to certainties, indeed. The Inspector said :

"I wish I could communicate with them and order them

north, but that is impossible. A detective only visits a telegraph office to send his report; then he is off again, and you
don't know where to put your hand on him."

Now came this despatch:

Bridgeport, Ct.: 12.15.

*Barnum offers rate of $4,000 a year for exclusive privilege of
using elephant as travelling advertising medium from now till detectives find him. Wants to paste circus-posters on him. Desires
immediate answer.*

Boggs, Detective.

"That is perfectly absurd!" I exclaimed.

"Of course it is," said the Inspector. "Evidently Mr.
Barnum, who thinks he is so sharp, does not know me—but
I know him."

Then he dictated this answer to the despatch:

Mr. Barnum's offer declined. Make it $7,000 or nothing.

Chief Blunt.

"There. We shall not have to wait long for an answer,
Mr. Barnum is not at home; he is in the telegraph office—
it is his way when he has business on hand. Inside of
three——"

Done.—P. T. Barnum.

So interrupted the clicking telegraphic instrument. Before
I could make a comment upon this extraordinary episode, the
following despatch carried my thoughts into another and
very distressing channel:

Bolivia, N.Y.: 12.50.

*Elephant arrived here from the south and passed through toward
the forest at 11.50, dispersing a funeral on the way, and diminishing
the mourners by two. Citizens fired some small cannon-balls into
him, and then fled. Detective Burke and I arrived ten minutes later,
from the north, but mistook some excavations for footprints, and so
lost a good deal of time; but at last we struck the right trail and
followed it to the woods. We then got down on our hands and knees
and continued to keep a sharp eye on the track, and so shadowed it
into the brush. Burke was in advance. Unfortunately the animal
had stopped to rest; therefore, Burke having his head down, intent
upon the track, butted up against the elephant's hind legs before he*

was aware of his vicinity. Burke instantly rose to his feet, seized the tail, and exclaimed joyfully : "I claim the re——" but got no further, for a single blow of the huge trunk laid the brave fellow's fragments low in death. I fled rearward, and the elephant turned and shadowed me to the edge of the wood, making tremendous speed, and I should inevitably have been lost, but that the remains of the funeral providentially intervened again, and diverted his attention. I have just learned that nothing of that funeral is now left ; but this is no loss, for there is an abundance of material for another. Meantime the elephant has disappeared again.

Mulrooney, Detective.

We heard no news except from the diligent and confident detectives scattered about New Jersey, Pennsylvania, Delaware and Virginia—who were all following fresh and encouraging clues—until shortly after 2 p.m., when this telegram came :

Baxter Centre, 2.15.

Elephant been here, plastered over with circus-bills, and broke up a revival, striking down and damaging many who were on the point of entering upon a better life. Citizens penned him up, and established a guard. When Detective Brown and I arrived, some time after, we entered enclosure and proceeded to identify elephant by photograph and description. All marks tallied exactly except one, which we could not see—the boil-scar under armpit. To make sure, Brown crept under to look, and was immediately brained— that is, head crushed and destroyed, though nothing issued from debris. All fled ; so did elephant, striking right and left with much effect. Has escaped, but left bold blood-track from cannon-wounds. Rediscovery certain. He broke southward through a dense forest.

Brent, Detective.

That was the last telegram. At nightfall a fog shut down which was so dense that objects but three feet away could not be discerned. This lasted all night. The ferry boats and even the omnibuses had to stop running.

III

Next morning the papers were as full of detective theories as before ; they had all our tragic facts in detail also, and a great many more which they had received from their telegraphic correspondents. Column after column was occupied, a third of its way down, with glaring head-lines, which it made my heart sick to read. Their general tone was like this :

"The White Elephant at Large ! He moves upon his Fatal March ! Whole Villages Deserted by their Fright-stricken Occupants ! Pale Terror goes before Him, Death and Devastation follow after ! After these, the Detectives. Barns Destroyed, Factories Gutted, Harvests Devoured, Public Assemblages Dispersed, accompanied by Scenes of Carnage Impossible to Describe ! Theories of Thirty-four of the Most Distinguished Detectives on the Force ! Theory of Chief Blunt !

"There !" said Inspector Blunt, almost betrayed into excitement, "this is magnificent ! This is the greatest windfall that any detective organization ever had. The fame of it will travel to the ends of the earth, and endure to the end of time, and my name with it."

But there was no joy for me. I felt as if I had committed all those red crimes, and that the elephant was only my irresponsible agent. And how the list had grown ! In one place he had "interfered with an election and killed five repeaters." He had followed this act with the destruction of two poor fellows, named O'Donohue and McFlannigan, who had "found a refuge in the home of the oppressed of all lands only the day before, and were in the act of exercising for the first time the noble right of American citizens at the polls, when stricken down by the relentless hand of the Scourge of Siam." In another, he had "found a crazy sensation-preacher preparing his next season's heroic attacks on the dance, the theatre, and other things which can't strike back, and had stepped on him." And in still another place he had "killed a lightning-rod agent." And so the list went on, growing redder and redder, and more and more heart-breaking. Sixty persons had been killed, and two hundred and forty wounded. All the accounts bore just testimony to the activity and devotion of the detectives, and all closed with the remark that "three hundred thousand citizens and four detectives saw the dread creature, and two of the latter he destroyed."

I dreaded to hear the telegraphic instrument begin to

click again. By-and-by the messages began to pour in, but I was happily disappointed in their nature. It was soon apparent that all trace of the elephant was lost. The fog had enabled him to search out a good hiding-place unobserved. Telegrams from the most absurdly distant points reported that a dim vast mass had been glimpsed there through the fog at such and such an hour, and was "undoubtedly the elephant." This dim vast mass had been glimpsed in New Haven, in New Jersey, in Pennsylvania, in interior New York, in Brooklyn, and even in the city of New York itself! But in all cases the dim vast mass had vanished quickly and left no trace. Every detective of the large force scattered over this huge extent of country sent his hourly report and each and every one of them had a clue, and was shadowing something, and was hot upon the heels of it.

But the day passed without other result.

The next day the same.

The next just the same.

The newspaper reports began to grow monotonous with facts that amounted to nothing, clues which led to nothing, and theories which had nearly exhausted the elements which surprise and delight and dazzle.

By advice of the inspector, I doubled the reward.

Four more dull days followed. Then came a bitter blow to the poor, hard-working detectives—the journalists declined to print their theories, and coldly said, "Give us a rest."

Two weeks after the elephant's disappearance I raised the reward to $75,000 by the Inspector's advice. It was a great sum, but I felt that I would rather sacrifice my whole private fortune than lose my credit with my Government. Now that the detectives were in adversity, the newspapers turned upon them, and began to fling the most stinging sarcasms at them. This gave the minstrels an idea, and they dressed themselves as detectives and hunted the elephant on the stage in the most extravagant way. The caricaturists made pictures of detectives scanning the country with spy-glasses, while the elephant, at their backs, stole apples out of their pockets. And they made all sorts of ridiculous pictures of the detective badge—you have seen that badge printed in gold on the back of detective novels, no doubt—it is a wide-staring eye, with the legend, "WE NEVER SLEEP." When detectives called for a drink, the would-be facetious barkeeper resurrected an obsolete form of expression, and said, "Will you have an eye-opener ?" All the air was thick with sarcasms.

But there was one man who moved calm, untouched, unaffected through it all. It was that heart of oak, the Chief Inspector. His brave eye never drooped, his serene confidence never wavered. He always said—

"Let them rail on ; he laughs best who laughs last."

My admiration for the man grew into a species of worship. I was at his side always. His office had become an unpleasant place to me, and now became daily more and more so. Yet if he could endure it I meant to do so also ; at least, as long as I could. So I came regularly, and stayed—the only outsider who seemed to be capable of it. Everybody wondered how I could ; and often it seemed to me that I must desert, but at such times I looked into that calm and apparently unconscious face, and held my ground.

About three weeks after the elephant's disappearance I was about to say, one morning, that I should *have* to strike my colours and retire, when the great detective arrested the thought by proposing one more superb and masterly move.

This was to compromise with the robbers. The fertility of this man's invention exceeded anything I have ever seen, and I have had a wide intercourse with the world's finest minds. He said he was confident he could compromise for $100,000 and recover the elephant. I said I believed I could scrape the amount together ; but what would become of the poor detectives who had worked so faithfully ? He said :

"In compromises they always get half."

This removed my only objection. So the Inspector wrote two notes, in this form :

Dear Madam,
Your husband can make a large sum of money (and be entirely protected from the law) by making an immediate appointment with me.

Chief Blunt.

He sent one of these by his confidential messenger to the "reputed wife" of Brick Duffy, and the other to the reputed wife of Red McFadden.

Within the hour these offensive answers came :

Ye Owld fool : brick McDuffys bin ded 2 yere.

Bridget Mahoney.

Chief Bat,
Red McFadden is hung and in heving 18 month. Any Ass but a detective knose that.

Mary O' Hooligan.

"I had long suspected these facts," said the Inspector; "this testimony proves the unerring accuracy of my instinct."

The moment one resource failed him he was ready with another. He immediately wrote an advertisement for the morning papers, and I kept a copy of it—

"A.—xwblv. 242 N. Tjnd—fz328wmlg. Ozpo,—; 2 m. ! ogw. Mum."

He said that if the thief was alive this would bring him to the usual rendezvous. He further explained that the usual rendezvous was a place where all business affairs between detectives and criminals were conducted. This meeting would take place at twelve the next night.

We could do nothing till then, and I lost no time in getting out of the office, and was grateful indeed for the privilege.

At eleven the next night I brought $100,000 in banknotes and put them into the chief's hands, and shortly afterward he took his leave, with the brave old undimmed confidence in his eye. An almost intolerable hour dragged to a close : then I heard his welcome tread, and rose gasping and tottered to meet him. How his fine eyes flamed with triumph ! He said—

"We've compromised ! The jokers will sing a different tune to-morrow ! Follow me !"

He took a lighted candle and strode down into the vast vaulted basement where sixty detectives always slept, and where a score were now playing cards to while the time. I followed close after him. He walked swiftly down to the dim remote end of the place, and just as I succumbed to the pangs of suffocation and was swooning away he stumbled and fell over the outlying members of a mighty object, and I heard him exclaim as he went down :

"Our noble profession is vindicated. Here is your elephant !"

I was carried to the office above and restored with carbolic acid. The whole detective force swarmed in, and such another season of triumphant rejoicing ensured as I had never witnessed before. The reporters were called, baskets of champagne were opened, toasts were drunk, the handshakings and congratulations were continuous and enthusiastic. Naturally the chief was the hero of the hour, and his happiness was so complete and had been so patiently and worthily and bravely won that it made me happy to see it, though I stood there a homeless beggar, my priceless charge dead, and my position in my country's service lost to me through what would always seem my fatally careless execution of a great trust. Many an eloquent eye testified its deep admiration for the chief, and many a detective's voice murmured, "Look at him—just the king of the profession—only give him a clue, it's all he wants, and there ain't anything hid that he can't find." The dividing of the $50,000 made great pleasure ; when it was finished the chief made a little speech while he put his share in his pocket, in which he said, "Enjoy it, boys, for you've earned it ; and more than that—you've earned for the detective profession undying fame."

A telegram arrived, which read :

Monroe, Mich. : 10 *p.m.*
First time I've struck a telegraph office in over three weeks. Have followed those footprints, horseback, through the woods, a thousand miles to here, and they get stronger and bigger and fresher every day. Don't worry—inside of another week I'll have the elephant. This is dead sure.

Darley, Detective.

The chief ordered three cheers for "Darley, one of the finest minds on the force," and then commanded that he be telegraphed to come home and receive his share of the reward.

So ended that mavellous episode of the stolen elephant. The newspapers were pleasant with praises once more, the next day, with one contemptible exception. This sheet said :

"Great is the detective ! He may be a little slow in
finding a little thing like a mislaid elephant—he may hunt
him all day and sleep with his rotting carcase all night for
three weeks, but he will find him at last—if he can get the
man who mislaid him to show him the place !"

Poor Hassan was lost to me for ever. The cannon-shots had wounded him fatally. He had crept to that unfriendly place in the fog; and there, surrounded by his enemies and in constant danger of detection, he had wasted away with hunger and suffering till death gave him peace.

The compromise cost me $100,000; my detective expenses were $42,000 more; I never applied for a place again under my Government; I am a ruined man and a wanderer in the earth—but my admiration for that man, whom I believe to be the greatest detective the world has ever produced, remains undimmed to this day, and will so remain unto the end.

THE SUNNINGDALE MURDER

THERE was a certain assistant commissioner of police at Scotland Yard who used to get very annoyed with Inspector Rater. Usually, commissioners are angry when their subordinates talk too much; this particular official was sore with the Orator because he talked too little.

Colonel Levington, the assistant commissioner in question, had a house in Sunningdale which gave him, so to speak, an especial interest in the Aliford Gray case, and although commissioners of police may make all sorts of statutory declarations and take all manner of solemn oaths and live theoretically in fear of the Official Secrets Act, they are human, like everybody else, and Colonel Levington had a wife and family who regarded him as an oracle, and gave him credit for the fate that overtook every picturesque villain who figured in the popular newspapers. And he had neighbours who respected him and would drop in to coffee and for the enlargement of their experience. In truth, Colonel Levington knew nothing whatever about criminal investigation : he was an administrator who dealt largely with estimates and statistics. If he had been called upon to arrest a man he would not have known exactly where to start first. This, however, is by the way, and it is not denied that the Orator, as he was cynically nicknamed, was a very trying man.

Mrs. Aliford Gray was a pretty widow of thirty-four, slim and dark, rather pale, with fine grey eyes, in which ever lurked the shadow of tragedy (according to her few intimate friends). Fernley Cottage, where she lived, was off the main road, a small bungalow which was the property of Mr. Leicester Vanne. Though it was small, it was very

beautifully appointed, and stood in about two acres of
ground. She kept two servants, a middle-aged woman and
her daughter who lived at Sunninghill, ten minutes' walk
from the cottage. They did not sleep on the premises, and
Mrs. Gray had not the slightest objection to spending the
night alone.

Her closest friend was this same Mr. Leicester Vanne,
a wealthy young man who had a flat in Park Lane, and
against whom there was not the slightest breath of scandal.
He had one weakness, and it was through this that Inspector
Rater had first made his acquaintance. . . .

The Orator called at the flat one evening, and found a
very pensive man walking up and down his study, his hands
thrust into his pockets ; and the lady who was the indirect
cause of his distress was standing by the window, her lips
twitching with an amusement she could not conceal.

"I'm terribly sorry about this business, Inspector," said
Leicester Vanne, ruefully. "But this fellow used the most
terrible language in the presence of Mrs. Gray, and I'm
afraid I made a fool of myself."

"You nearly made a corpse of him," said the Orator
soberly.

Vanne and Mrs. Gray had been walking late that
afternoon from Kensington through the park. There were
few people about, and they had been followed by a man
who had at first whined humbly for alms, and, when these
were refused, had grown abusive, deceived probably by
Leicester Vanne's slight frame. He was, however, a trained
athlete, and when the man's language had grown just a
little too lurid, he turned on him, picked him up bodily,
and threw him over the bridge into the Serpentine. With
great difficulty, owing to the bad light, the tramp had been
rescued ; with greater difficulty he had been brought to
life by artificial resuscitation, and had been rushed to the
hospital. Hence the Orator's visit.

"Really, Dicky, you're too terrible."

She was laughing softly, and something of that very
softness and the look in her eyes told the Orator a great
deal that was interesting, if not useful to him a week later.

"What is going to happen, Inspector?"

Vanne was anxious, irritably nervous.

"Of course, I oughtn't to have thrown the blighter into the water. The comic thing was that he knew me—in fact he called me by name. It was when he said that I was going to get murdered one of these days that I lost my—well, I got rattled. Shall I be charged or something?"

The Orator was non-committal; he wanted Dick Vanne's version of the affair, and he pretty well knew, before the story was half through, that no police action would follow. The beggar was well known both to the London and to the country police. He had an unsavoury reputation, and a string of convictions that stretched from Truro to Aberdeen.

"The best thing you can do, Mr. Vanne, is to send somebody down to see this bird at the hospital and fix it with him. I'm not telling you this as a police officer or as a legal adviser—but a few pounds might make a lot of difference."

Which was almost an oration for the Orator.

"A bad egg, is he?" said Vanne interested.

"Came out of Dartmoor last week."

The Orator happened to look round a second later. Mrs. Gray, who had been standing by the window, was now sitting, her face averted, looking through the window as though she saw something which interested her. He had a feeling that the pose was unnatural and strained, and wondered whether she was laughing at her friend and did not wish him to see her merriment.

He went back to Scotland Yard and had almost forgotten there were such people as Mrs. Aliford Gray and Mr. Dicky Leicester Vanne by the time he reached that interesting institution. A few days later, the loquacious superintendent gave him a few particulars about this friendship. The "super" was a constant visitor to the assistant commissioner's house in Sunningdale.

"She's a great friend of Vanne's. Rather a pretty woman, don't you think? . . . No, there's nothing of that kind in it—just friendship."

"I said nothing," said the Orator curtly.

"I knew what you were thinking," said the superintendent. "But they say that man's temper is terrible; and I should say he's a bit jealous, too. The people down in Sunningdale can't understand why he doesn't marry her."

"Queer thing about the people in Sunningdale," said the Orator, who had no love for the assistant commissioner, "is the number of things they don't understand."

It was half-past four on the following Sunday morning, and the Orator, who had many curious habits, had just got up after nine hours of solid sleep and had made himself a cup of tea, when his telephone bell rang. He glanced at the instrument coldly, for he had a number of reports to write, and worked best in the cold hours of the dawn. The bell shrilled again; he took up the instrument, and immediately recognized the voice of the assistant commissioner. The colonel's voice was tremulous with excitement.

"I've been trying to get . . ." The word was unintelligible, but the Orator guessed he meant the chief constable. "Will you come down right away? I've asked the Yard to pick you up; the photographers and finger-print people are coming down."

"What's wrong?" asked Rater, quickly.

There was a little pause.

". . . Mrs. Gray . . . awfully pretty woman who lives here . . . murdered !"

The Orator opened his mouth wide but did not speak.

"Murdered?" he said at last. "Have you any idea——"

"No, she's been murdered. . . . My God ! It's awful ! One of the prettiest women I've ever seen. Extraordinarily nice woman . . . perfectly ghastly ! Murdered, you understand, Rater ?"

"Yes, I understand," said Rater, calmly. "It's very interesting."

He hung up the receiver, drank his tea, and was waiting on the sidewalk when the police car swung round the corner and slowed.

"Don't stop," snapped the Orator, as he stepped on to the running-board and into the seat by the driver's side. "Are there any details?"

None of the officers in the car had heard particulars; indeed, none knew of the identity of the murdered woman.

The Orator pulled his coat collar about his ears and let himself go to sleep. The morning air always had that effect upon him.

He woke as the car stopped before the little cottage. A light was burning in the hall; the door was wide open. On the crazy pavement that led from the road to the doorway he saw a policeman, and in the hall itself, Colonel Levington talking to a man whom he recognized as an inspector of county police.

"All right, Rater. The Berkshire police have called us in."

"Called me in or you in, sir?" asked Rater, unpleasantly; for this assistant commissioner had nothing whatever to do with the Criminal Investigation Department.

"You, of course, my good chap," said the other, irritably. "I'm here merely as a—um—witness. Not that I witnessed anything," he said hastily, "but naturally, they came and dragged me out of bed."

"Where is the body?" asked Mr. Rater.

To his surprise, the colonel shook his head.

"There is no body; it's been taken away. I hope you stepped carefully as you came up the pavement; there were blood-marks there. This is where the crime was committed."

He pushed open the door of the pretty little drawing-room. The lights were full on, and Rater stepped in and took a glance round. There were signs of confusion here: a small table had been overturned, a bowl was smashed on the floor, there were two overturned chairs. These he saw immediately, and then his eyes fell to the cream-coloured carpet and the big blood-stain.

"Perhaps I'd better tell you what happened," said the chief commissioner.

"Now, sir."

The Orator was suddenly bland, and when he was bland he was most offensive.

"I'm afraid you've got to be just a common or garden citizen. If I'm in charge I'm in charge ; if I'm not I'm not."

The colonel was slightly ruffled, but he was a good soldier.

"Of course, my dear chap. I'll wait in the garden."

"Wait anywhere you like, sir," said the Orator, and turned to the Berkshire inspector.

The story was a very simple one. A police-constable going the rounds at half-past three in the morning had noticed that the hall lamp was alight. He went up the garden path, pushed the door, and found it was open. It was then that he saw a pool of blood on the door-step. He called out, but there was no answer, and knowing that Mrs. Gray lived alone, he waited no longer, but walked into the hall, saw the smears of blood on the distempered walls of the passage, and passed through the doorway of the drawing-room.

The lights were burning, and he saw just what the Orator had seen—that and no more : the signs of struggle.

Rater called in the two men who had accompanied him from Scotland Yard and pointed to the polished surface of a brass fender.

"There's a finger-print—get that. When daylight comes I'll have a more thorough search."

There were the ashes of a fire in the grate, and on the hearth a charred piece of paper. He picked it up carefully. In a woman's writing he read :

"Tried to kill me . . . defended myself . . ."

The erratic character of the writing might stand for pain or fear, certainly for some abnormal condition of mind.

He put the scrap aside, and, going out, made a tour of the house. It was getting light now, and he made as careful an inspection as he had made of the inside. He saw the blood on the flagstones, and proof positive that a bleeding body had been dragged into the roadway. Here the trail was lost.

"Had she a car?"

She had a little two-seater. They found the doors of the garage closed, and the machine intact.

"Well?" Colonel Levington could be a silent spectator no longer. "It is pretty clear, isn't it? She had a quarrel with somebody, they killed her and took her away——"

"Are these the women?" interrupted the Orator.

He saw two figures crossing the road. He had sent for the two servants, not expecting that they would throw any light upon the matter. Leading the elder woman—the cook—into the dining-room, he put the conventional questions to her. Colonel Levington came uninvited. Evidently the woman had been told what had happened, for she was white and shaking.

"Has anyone been here during the night?"

"Only Mr. Vanne, sir."

The Orator scowled at her. It was a trick of his when he was surprised.

"Mr. Leicester Vanne?"

She nodded.

"What time was he here?"

"He was here when I left, sir. A friend of mine saw his car going up the London road about twelve. It's not for me to say anything I oughtn't to say, sir," she went on, speaking with hysterical rapidity. "I don't want to swear anybody's life away, but they had a terrible quarrel."

"Who?"

"Madam and Mr. Vanne, sir. He was shouting at the top of his voice. I heard him say 'I insist upon an explanation,' and I heard madam begging him not to speak so loud."

"And you listened at the door—yes?" said the Orator.

The woman changed colour.

"Well, sir, I did. I won't lie about it. I heard the missus say: "I can't marry you and I won't marry you. I refuse to tell you why, Dicky. If you loved me '—or something of the sort—'you wouldn't be so unreasonable.'"

"And then?" said the Orator, jotting down in his notebook the gist of the conversation the cook had overheard.

"Then I heard him say: 'I'd rather kill you than lose

you.' I'm perfectly sure he said that. I could go into the witness-box and take my Bible oath on it, though he's a nice gentleman when he's quiet, and I don't want to get him into trouble."

"Was there any noise when you left ?"

The woman shook her head.

They were talking in quite a conversational tone when she said good night through the closed door. Her daughter had left an hour before the row started.

"Well, what do you make of that?" asked Colonel Levington, eagerly. "It seems to me the most obvious thing in the world. This fellow must have stayed on, there was another quarrel . . ."

"She had been to bed," said the Orator, coldly ; "and the man who committed the murder didn't come in at the front door, he came in at the back. If you go round, you'll find the jemmy-marks on the door and the lock smashed."

The colonel was silent.

"Of course I know Mr. Leicester Vanne ; in fact I've met him," he said at last. "A man of violent temper. It seems to me that that is the direction where your investigations should—er—be directed."

"That thought even occurred to me," said the Orator, coldly.

It was half-past seven when he reached the mansion block in Park Lane where Mr. Leicester Vanne had his flat. From judicious inquiries he learned that Mr. Vanne parked his car in a lock-up garage nearby. At eight o'clock he returned, to find the cleaners were busy in the vestibule, and after a while he saw the porter, who would give him little information, having only come on duty at seven.

The flat was on the first floor and it was Vanne who opened the door to him. He recognized the Orator instantly, and stiffened.

"Good morning, Inspector." His voice was cold and steady, but the detective saw that that calmness of his required an especial effort. "Come in."

He opened the door wider with a suggestion of reluctance. Rater noticed that under his silk dressing-gown he was dressed. His face looked tired ; he was unshaven ; he had the appearance of a man who had spent a sleepless night.

Vanne led the way to the small study, and closed the door behind the detective.

"Well, what is it, Mr. Rater ?"

The Orator did not answer ; his eyes were fixed on the other's.

"In the matter of Mrs. Gray, deceased," he said.

He saw the man start.

"Deceased ? Dead ?" A look of incredulity was on his face. "What do you mean ?"

With characteristic briefness, the Orator told the story of the night, and as he proceeded he saw the look of anxiety fade from the man's face. At the end Vanne was laughing hysterically.

"How absurd ! I thought——" He checked himself. "Do you think Mrs. Gray is dead ?"

The Orator did not answer.

"Good God ! You don't imagine that I—that is too absurd."

"I don't imagine anything," said the Orator. "I work on facts. There are blood-stains in that parlour at Sunning-dale ; there are blood-stains on the pavement outside the door, and signs of a body being dragged to the road." He paused. "And there are blood-stains in your car, Mr. Vanne."

Leicester Vanne was master of himself now. His face was a little paler as he realized the gravity of his position.

"Of course, you've seen the car. How stupid of me !" he said, and drew a long breath.

"Well ?" asked the Orator.

Vanne shrugged his shoulders.

"I've nothing to say. I don't know where Mrs. Gray is ; I can give you no information whatever."

Mr. Rater pursed his lips thoughtfully and stared past the man out of the window.

"Blood in your car," he mused. "Were you dressed last night—evening dress ?"

Vanne nodded slowly.

"I'd like to see that suit of yours, and particularly the shirt."

Leicester Vanne's eyes did not falter under the keen scrutiny of the other.

"I spilt some coffee on the front of my shirt, and I've burnt it," he said. "The coat and trousers were old: I also put them into the furnace this morning before anybody was up. I tell you this because the night porter will probably tell you the same thing—he saw me going down to the basement with the parcel."

"Blood-stains, of course," said the Orator, absently. "You were with Mrs. Gray last night, there was a quarrel of some kind, and——"

Vanne made a gesture of despair.

"I'm always quarrelling with somebody," he said, dejectedly. "My temper is foul! But after this . . ."

"Where is Mrs. Gray?" asked the Orator.

The man turned on him.

"I tell you I don't know. I haven't seen Mrs. Gray since last night. If you think I murdered her, arrest me."

He was shaking with fury.

"Talking about not losing your temper——" began the Orator, and Vanne laughed hysterically.

"I know I'm a fool. I'm very sorry, Inspector. I can tell you nothing more about Mrs. Gray. What a fool I've been! What an utterly hopeless idiot!"

"Yes," said the inspector, as he turned to the door. "I'll be seeing you later, Mr. Vanne."

That morning he made a few quick inquiries, and at each point was satisfied.

At noon that day there was a conference at headquarters, from which Colonel Levington was tactfully excluded. At one o'clock came a wire from a doctor in Devonshire which put the Orator on to a new trail, and simultaneously the report from a certain cottage hospital near Horsham that supplied the last clue. That afternoon he called again on Vanne. The young man was dressed, and was evidently expecting him.

"I'm not going to give you any trouble. I'll just get my hat——"

"No, I'm not arresting you, if that's what you mean. I'm only asking for information," said the Orator. "Exactly where did you leave the body?"

He was facing Vanne squarely. There was no fencing with the question.

"Exactly where did you leave the body?" asked the Orator again.

Vanne's face was as white as death.

"Five miles on the other side of Horsham—I didn't leave it——"

"It left you," said Rater grimly. "It's in Langwell Cottage Hospital, with a superficial wound in the right arm . . . curious how those wounds bleed."

Vanne stared at him open-mouthed.

"Alive?" he whispered.

The Orator nodded.

"Suffers from fits—I found that in the records of Scotland Yard, and confirmed it with the prison doctor. I thought it might be something like that. These people don't die so easily. But they look deader than any live people ought to look."

He took a telegram from his pocket and opened it.

"Henry Walter Wassingheim is the gentleman's name : he was convicted in the name of ' Smith,' which is un-original. I'm going down to Horsham to see that body," he said. "I expect it's all sober and lively by now. If Mrs. Gray had told me all about Henry Walter I could have given her all the evidence she wanted for her divorce. I don't know what's going to happen to you, Mr. Vanne, but I'd like you to do me a favour. Do you mind seeing Colonel Levington and telling him all about it ? He's naturally long-winded. I'm naturally ungifted for telling stories."

.   .   .   .   .

"I first met Mrs. Gray," said Vanne, not to Colonel Levington, but to the commissioner mostly concerned, "about five years ago. We met at the house of a mutual

friend, and I don't disguise the fact that I fell immediately
in love with her. In spite of my bad temper, she was an
angel to me in all respects but one. She would never marry
me. I thought she was a widow, and could see no reason
why we should not be married. I did not know—nobody
knew—that her husband was serving a sentence of ten years
for a crime so hideous that she would not risk the publicity
which a divorce would bring to her. They had been married
secretly; nobody knew of the horrible life she had led with
him. She was on the point of telling me, because she had
heard he was about to be released, when unexpectedly on
Saturday night he turned up at the house. He was drunk,
more like a beast than a man. Somehow he had got to hear
of her friendship with me, and put a wrong construction
upon it, partly because he is incapable of understanding
any friendship that is clean and wholesome. He tried to
strangle her, and in defence she struck at him with a stiletto
paper-knife that I had given to her, and he dropped, bleeding
profusely. I know now that he was in a fit. She thought
she had killed him, and hastily wrote a letter to me, intending
to commit suicide. Writing, she grew a little calmer, and,
burning the letter, called me up on the 'phone and told me
what had happened. I drove to Sunningdale, and, first
bringing her back to the flat, I returned to the cottage.
My intention was to take the body to the seaside and leave
it on the shore. Of course I made all sorts of blunders;
leaving the hall lights burning and the door open was a
terrible mistake if I intended covering up my tracks. I got
into the car, and drove through Horsham, but on the other
side, at the top of the hill, I developed engine trouble and
stopped my car for a quarter of an hour. It must have been
then that he recovered consciousness and crawled out of the
tonneau. I did not miss him for ten minutes, and then, coming
back, looked everywhere for him without success. Mrs.
Gray was, of course, at my flat. She is now in Bournemouth.
I was in terror when the inspector called, for fear he should
make a search. It was for that reason, to give her time,
that I told him I had burnt my clothes, which wasn't true.
How did you know, Inspector?"

Mr. Rater made a gesture of self-disparagement.

"The thumb-print on the fender was easy to identify at Scotland Yard. After that, the case worked itself out. Besides, this husband fellow had a statement in his pocket that he intended killing his unfaithful wife—I had a copy of that . . .'

He stopped, and shook his head.

"I'm talking too much," he said.

THE MIND-READERS

"THERE is no police force in the world that can counter the intelligent law-breaker," wrote that remarkable man Len Witlon, in an article he once contributed to the American Press, "providing he lays his plans carefully and skilfully and carries them through without deviation."

Len Witlon knew five languages perfectly, and had friends and sometimes confederates in at least a dozen European prisons. He himself had certainly been under detention, but had never been dishonoured by a conviction.

You met him at the American bar of Claridge's in Paris, or dining at Armonvillier; occasionally he took a cure at Vichy or Baden-Baden—there were certain mud baths in Czecho-Slovakia that he visited regularly. He was a vain and brilliant man, very jealous of his reputation for gallantry.

"To be successful in robbery one must be something of a psychologist. It is not sufficient to know where material danger is to be found : one must be able to read the mind of one's opponent. That is the art of generalship : success comes when the operator combines with his powers of organization a loyal and unswerving loyalty to his comrades."

Inspector O. Rater read this interesting article so often that he could almost quote it word for word. He had cut out the article soon after its publication, had pasted it in an exercise book against the day when Len would commence operations in England.

"Tell that friend of yours," said the Orator, to a familiar of the great man, "that if he ever puts his nose inside of London he won't be giving interviews for fourteen years."

One day Len took up the challenge. . . .

A policeman came through Burford Square at a leisurely pace, moving towards the corner of Canford Street. He had arranged with the constable patrolling the next beat to meet him there at eleven and finish the interrupted story of a

311

brother-in-law's shortcomings, and the problem of the wire and three children who had been left unsupported by the aforesaid brother-in-law's hasty departure for Canada.

He came to the rendezvous at almost the same moment as his mate appeared. And the serial was continued:

". . . 'Well,' I says to my sister, 'you've only got yourself to blame. . . .' "

He stopped dead.

The scream came from one of the dark houses of the square, and not very far away.

" Murder . . . murder ! "

The two police officers were already running. . . . On the doorstep of No. 95 a girl was standing. They saw the white of her nightgown in the dim light of a street lamp.

" Help . . . please ! Oh, thank God you've come ! "

She retreated before them through the open door into the dark hall.

" I heard him scream . . . and the struggle . . . and I tried to get into his room . . ."

She had been feeling for the switch, and she found it. A big glass lantern suspended from the high ceiling glowed with a golden light.

"What is it, miss ? Which room ? "

Her trembling fingers pointed to the stairway.

She was very pretty, though as white was chalk, the officer observed.

" Put a coat on the lady, Harry "—he indicated a little alcove where hats and coats were hanging. " Now, miss, you'll have to show us the room."

She shook her head ; her eyes were wide with horror.

" No, no, no ! I can't. . . . It is the first landing—the room overlooking the square——"

The two uniformed men raced up the stairs ; as they reached the square landing, a light came on, probably controlled from the hall below, for there was a push-button switch on the wall of the landing and nobody could have touched that. Facing them was a polished mahogany door with an ornamental gilt and enamelled door knob.

P.C. Simpson (he of the wronged sister) turned the handle. The door was locked from the inside. He shook the handle vigorously and called out :

" Open this door ! "

A futile invitation, and laughable in any other state of affairs. More futile, since when he turned the knob the door opened.

It was a large room, running the whole width of the house. Light came from a crystal chandelier. P.C. Simpson saw a big gilt and mahogany writing-table; behind that was a carved marble fireplace, and on the white hearth an electric fire glowed redly. Until they passed round the table, they did not see the quiet figure that lay, face upwards. It was in evening dress; one hand gripped the edge of the marble curb that surrounded the fireplace; the other was half raised, as though to ward off a blow.

" He's dead—shot . . . look ! "

Simpson's companion pointed to the patch of blood above the heart.

P.C. Simpson stared down at his first murder, all too aware of the tremendous importance to him and to his career; he had a confused memory of instructions he had received as to what a policeman should do in such circumstances.

" Don't let nobody come in," he said huskily, and gaped round the room. A long window was open—he stepped out on to a balcony, flashing his electric lamp along the rails.

A rope was knotted to the balcony rail and trailing down— as he saw by the rays of his lamp—to the front steps. It had not been there when they had come in or they must have knocked against it.

" He's got away since we came in, Harry. Come down with me ! "

They flew down the stairs into the silent square; they did not see the girl; she must have gone to her room.

The front door was closed. P.C. Simpson jerked at it with confidence, but this door did not open. He twisted the handle and pulled again, but it was a very heavy door, steel-lined, and did not budge.

" It's been double-locked on the inside," he said, truthfully. " That girl must have done it, Harry. Go and see her and get the key."

Harry tried the nearest door; that was locked, and the second door was locked, but the door leading into the back of the house was open. It took him down to a kitchen, and his electric lamp showed him yet another door wide open. He guessed it was the garage, the big gates leading to the mews were swinging idly in the breeze.

He went back to his companion.

"You wait here," said P.C. Simpson, flew down the stairs, and in a few seconds was in the mews.

With shaking hand he dragged his police whistle from his pocket, and sent out a shrill warning, circumnavigated the house in time to see three policemen running, and ahead of them a stolid, tall figure.

Inspector Rater had business of his own in the neighbourhood that night, but had surrendered all other interest at the alarm. Breathlessly the police-constable told his story as he half ran, half walked back to the mews.

"All right, all right," said the Orator, impatiently. "One of you fellows stand in front of the door and don't move."

He followed Simpson into the house, up to the ground floor. Harry the policeman stood rigidly to attention at the foot of the stairs.

"Where's the lady? Have you seen her?"

Harry had not seen her or heard her. He ventured the suggestion that she must be "in a faint," for he was a family man, and knew the effects of such events upon the weak frame of womanhood.

The Orator was half-way up the stairs, and missed the plausible explanation.

"That's the room, sir."

Inspector Rater turned the handle and pushed.

"Locked," he said and, stooping, squinted through the keyhole.

He could see that the door to the balcony was open, and asked a question.

"I left it like that, sir. There was a rope tied to the rails of the balcony. The man who done it must have got out that way, sir——"

"Lend your shoulders to the door," said the Orator.

Two strong men pushed together—and again. The lock broke with a snap, the door flew open. . . .

"Where's your body?"

P.C. Simpson stared: where the dead man had lain there was no dead man. The room was entirely empty.

The Orator looked at the policemen, at the floor and then at the window; and then his mind instantly moved to the house of the Marquis Parello, which was on the opposite side of the square. He thought of the Marquis Perello naturally for two reasons : the first was that Len Witlon was in town, and the second that in the Marquis's house, in a safe, and not a very safe safe, were four packets of cut emeralds that had arrived in London a few days before. They were in transit to an illustrious person in Italy who had a passion for emeralds, and had been purchased in the Argentine at great cost. The Marquis had notified the police, and Mr. O. Rater had thought it desirable to station a uniformed constable before and behind the house. He knew the names of those constables, and, leaning over the balcony, he addressed the small gathering of police officers on the pavement below.

" Is Walton here ? "

" Yes, sir," said a voice.

" And Martin ? "

" Yes, sir," said another voice.

" Then," asked the Orator gently, " why the hell *are* you here ? "

He was very hurt, because he knew just how quickly Len Witlon worked. He did not wait for the door to be opened, but slid down the rope on to the steps, and five minutes later was knocking at the door of the Marquis Perello's house. He knocked for a very long time. The marquis and his wife were at the theatre. The three maidservants were locked in a room upstairs. The armed valet who kept guard over the safe was found bludgeoned in the drawing-room, and the safe was open.

" He worked four-handed," said the Orator philosophically.

Len Witlon invariably worked four-handed, so the Orator had made no great discovery. And after a job was done the four would separate and leave England by various routes. There is, for example, a steamer that goes from Dundee to Holland, and yet another that sails from Plymouth to one of the French ports—Len never made the mistake of following the beaten track. His methods were unique : nobody but Len would have taken a furnished house in Burford Square and staged an elaborate murder mystery in order to bring all the police in the neighbourhood running to that one particular spot and leave unguarded the place he wished to burgle.

A search of the house revealed nothing of value except— in the fireplace of the dining-room were a number of burnt papers, and a little slip printed in red which was only half-burnt. It had apparently to do with passengers and guides and the difficulties of Customs.   He put the little slip in his pocket very carefully and sent forth widespread enquiries.   The only clue he had—and that came to him the next morning— was from a constable of the City police who, standing at the junction of Queen Victoria Street and Cannon Street, had seen a car in which was a woman.   He was not even certain it was a woman, but she had that appearance, for her head and the upper part of her body were enclosed in a frock.   She was, in point of fact, at the moment he saw her, engaged in slipping on a dress.

Cannon Street Station drew blank ; no woman had arrived in a car at that hour.   She had obviously gone east of Cannon Street.

The Orator was something of a psychologist himself.   He knew Witlon's methods, and knew that that gallant gentleman would first assure himself that his beautiful lady confederate was safe.   He interviewed P.C. Simpson, a crest-fallen and resentful man, from whom his first murder had been ruthlessly snatched.

" Yes, sir, she talked with a sort of foreign accent."

" I want you to remember every word she said, Simpson," said the Orator gently.

P.C. Simpson thought very hard, trying to coax, by a vigorous massage of his head, the half-forgotten facts of the conversation.

" I can't remember anything she said, sir.   The only thing that struck me as curious was that while she was a-moaning and a-groaning she had her eye on her wrist-watch.   I saw her look twice."

" The time was about eleven, I think ? "

The constable thought it was a little later.

" To me," said the Orator, " it is as clear as daylight."

When P.C. Simpson had gone, the Orator took from an envelope the little half-burned slip of printed paper that had been found in the grate of the dining-room, and reconstructed it. . . .

Early one morning, somewhere in the Bay of Biscay, a British destroyer came up over the horizon behind the slow-moving steamship *Emil* and signalled the captain to stop. The *Emil* was a small ship that carried a large number of pleasure-seeking passengers to the Moroccan ports and Madeira.   She had left London at midnight on the night of

A few days after his arrival Mr. Rater received a scented letter. It was written by a lady who signed herself "One who Knows," and it ran :

If you wish to know where the rest of the Parello emeralds are to be found, I can tell you. I want you to promise me that I shall not be arrested, but knowing that a police officer cannot make any such promises, I cannot ask you to put that into writing. I will come to Scotland Yard at 8 o'clock on Saturday evening. Will you be in your room ?

The Orator read and re-read the communication. Where women were concerned he believed in miracles. And yet he was satisfied in his mind that behind the letter was the inspiration of Mr. Witlon. For a long, long time he stood by his window looking on to the Embankment, staring at the river, and thinking himself into the mind of his enemy.

There was at the Yard at this time a most unpopular Assistant Commissioner, who did not like the Orator. Major Dawlton had had his police training in India. He was an incurable theorist, and had a weakness for interfering with his executive. He summoned the Orator into his office.

"Come, come, Mr. Rater," he said, a little pompously. "This won't do at all. Here are emeralds of an enormous value stolen under the eyes of the police, after you had been specifically instructed to protect their owner! Have you seen this morning's newspapers ? "

"I can't read "—said the Orator wearily, and waited long enough for the Assistant Commissioner to get apoplectic before he concluded—" newspapers when I have got work on hand."

"It is a scandal, Mr. Rater. Really, I am ashamed to meet my friends at the club. They are constantly asking me why we don't get detectives in from outside. And I think it would be an excellent scheme."

"You don't want detectives, you want mind-readers to deal with Witlon," said the Orator again.

"Stuff and nonsense ! " said Major Dawlton.

It was a very peaceful Saturday afternoon at Scotland Yard. The day was warm and the double windows that shut out the noises of the Thames Embankment were wide open. Sunshine bathed the deserted wharves and warehouses that form so fine a skyline on the southern bank, and laid on the river a sheet of fretted gold.

The tramway-cars were more or less empty, the promenade given over to leisurely sight-seeing folk who had brought their children for a stroll.

Inspector Rater took off his pince-nez with a sigh, folded the minute he had been reading and returned it to its envelope. He gazed pensively through the open window. A tug drawing a string of barges was moving slowly upstream. Timber barges stacked high with planks of yellow pine. On the Embankment a few loungers leaned over the parapet.

He turned his head as the door opened and Major Dawlton came in. Without a word he handed the letter to his superior. The Major fixed his eyeglass, read and sneered.

" That, I suppose, is the art of criminal detection," he said, with heavy irony—the Orator was very unpopular at that moment. " Half the good work at Scotland Yard is done by informers. I should like to see this woman when she comes."

" If she comes," said the Orator softly.

" You think it is a hoax? I don't agree. It is probably some jealous confederate who has been badly treated. These scraps of information have come to the Yard every day since I have been here."

" They have come every day I've been here," said the Orator, " and that's seventeen years."

The Major snorted under this implication of his in-experience.

" She won't come, but he will,"

" Witlon? Rubbish! He's in France. That sort of scoundrel is not going to put his nose into this country, and if he did we've sufficient evidence to convict him of simple larceny. I'll be here at eight o'clock this evening."

" Make it a quarter to," suggested the Orator, venom in in his eye.

.   .   .   .   .   .

Major Dawlton, sitting in the office chair, yawned.

" She's sold you," he said.

" I told you not to come," said Mr. Rater.

He stood with his back to the wall, glooming down at the

Assistant Commissioner thoughtfully. The Major looked at his watch.

" I'll give her another quarter of an hour——"

" Whee-e-smack ! "

Something whizzed past him ; he felt the disturbance of air, and turning his startled head, saw the glass of a framed photograph splinter disastrously.

There was no sound of a shot—no report.

He was on his feet in an instant and ran to the window.

Something struck the sill on which his hand rested, ripped a jagged wound in the stone and brought down the plaster from the ceiling.

" I'd keep away from that window," said the Orator gently. " They tell me he's a wonderful rifle shot, but I thought he'd operate from the Council building. The barge was certainly a brilliant idea."

Major Dawlton's face was white as death.

" Shooting ! " he gasped. " At me ! "

"At me," said the Orator pensively. " I hope those fellows have located him. I should think they would."

As he spoke he saw two motor-launches filled with men shoot out from the cover of the parapet ; they were making for the barge.

" That's all right," said the Orator. " Now we've got something to charge him with."

" They were shooting at me ! " squeaked the Major.

" I told you not to come," said Mr. Rater, but the joy in his eyes belied his tone of sympathy.

.   .   .   .   .   .

" The general idea was a good one," said the Orator to the Chief Commissioner, " Witlon knew my weakness for fresh air, and he must have made a reconnaissance and seen how easy it was to look into my room with the window open. Oh, yes, I knew he was in England—one of my men picked him up when he landed at Southampton from Havre."

The Chief Commissioner's stern gaze was fixed on the Orator.

" But you didn't dream he'd be shooting into your room, or you wouldn't have allowed the Major to come ? " he said.

The Orator did not answer immediately. Then he sighed.

" I suppose I wouldn't," he said.

14
MRS HENRY WOOD
Abel Crew

ABEL CREW

I

WE were at our other and chief home, Dyke Manor:
and Tod and I were there for the short Easter holidays,
which were shorter in those days than they are in these.

It was Easter Tuesday. The Squire had gone riding over
to old Jacobson's with Tod. I, having nothing else to do,
got the mater to come with me for a practice on the church
organ; and we were taking the round home again through
the village, Church Dykely.

Easter was very late that year. It was getting towards the
end of April: and to judge by the weather, it might have been
the end of May, the days were so warm and glorious.

In passing the gate of George Reed's cottage, Mrs.
Todhetley stopped.

"How are the babies, Hester?"

Hester Reed, sunning her white cap and clean cotton gown
in the garden, the three elder children around, watering the
beds with a doll's watering-pot, and a baby hiding its face on
her shoulder, dropped a curtsy as she answered:

"They be but poorly, ma'am, thank you. Look up,
Susy," turning the baby's face upwards to show it; and a pale
mite of a face it was, with sleepy eyes. "For a day or two past
they've not seemed the thing; and they be both cross."

"I should think their teeth are troubling them, Hester."

"Maybe, ma'am. I shouldn't wonder. Hetty, she seems
worse than Susy. She's a-lying there in the basket indoors.
Would you please spare a minute to step in and look at her,
ma'am?"

Mrs. Todhetley opened the gate. "I may as well go in and
see, Johnny," she said to me in an undertone; "I fear both the
children are rather sickly."

The other baby, "Hetty", lay in the kitchen in a clothes-
basket. It had just the same sort of puny white face as its

325

sister. These two were twins, and about a year old. When they were born, Church Dykely went on finely at Hester Reed, asking her if she would not have had enough with one new child but she must go and set up two.

"It does seem very poorly," remarked Mrs. Todhetley, stooping over the young mortal (which was not cross just now, but very still and quiet), and letting it clasp its little fist round one of her fingers. "No doubt it is the teeth. If the children do not get better soon, I think, were I you, Hester, I should speak to Mr. Duffham."

The advice seemed to strike Hester Reed all of a heap. "Speak to Dr. Duffham!" she exclaimed. "Why, ma'am, they must both be a good deal worse than they be afore we does that. I'll give 'em a dose o' mild physic apiece. I dare say that'll bring 'em round."

"I should think it would not hurt them," assented Mrs. Todhetley. "They both seem feverish; this one especially. I hear you have had Cathy over," she went on, passing to another subject.

"Sure enough us have," said Mrs. Reed. "She come over yesterday was a week and stayed till Friday night."

"And what is she doing now?"

"Well, ma'am, Cathy's keeping herself; and that's something. She has got a place at Tewkesbury to serve in some shop; is quite in clover there, by all accounts. Two good gownds she brought over to her back; and she's pretty nigh as lighthearted as she was afore she went off to enter on her first troubles."

"Hannah told me she was not looking well."

"She have had a nasty attack of—what was it?—neuralgy, I think she called it, and been obliged to go to a doctor," answered Hester Reed. "That's why they gave her the holiday. She was very well while she was here."

I had stood at the door, talking to the little ones with their watering-pot. As the mater was taking her final word with Mrs. Reed, I went on to open the gate for her, when some woman whisked round the corner from Piefinch Lane and in at the gate.

"Thank ye, sir," said she to me: as if I had been holding it open for her especial benefit.

It was Ann Dovey, the blacksmith's wife down Piefinch Cut: a smart young woman, fond of fine gowns and caps.

Mrs. Todhetley came away, and Ann Dovey went in. And
this is what passed at Reed's—as it leaked out to the world
afterwards.

The baby in the basket began to cry, and Ann Dovey lifted
it out and took it on her lap. She understood all about
children, having been the eldest of a numerous flock at home,
and was no doubt all the fonder of them because she had none
of her own. Mrs. Dovey was, moreover, a great gossip, liking
to have as many fingers in her neighbours' pies as she could
conveniently get in.

"And now what's amiss with these two twins ?" asked she
in confidential tones, bending her face forward till it nearly
touched Mrs. Reed's, who had sat down opposite to her with
the other baby. "Sarah Tanken, passing our shop just now,
telled me they warn't the thing at all, so I thought I'd run
round."

"Sarah Tanken looked in while I was a-washing up after
dinner, and saw 'em both," assented Mrs. Reed. "Hetty's the
worst of the two ; more peeky like."

"Which *is* Hetty ?" demanded Ann Dovey ; who, with all
her neighbourly visits, had not learnt to distinguish the two
apart.

"The one that you be a-nursing."

"Did the mistress of the Manor look at 'em ?"

"Yes ; and she thinks I'd better give 'em both some mild
physic. Leastways, I said a dose might bring 'em round,"
added Hester Reed, correcting herself, "and she said it might."

"It's the very thing for 'em, Hester Reed," pronounced
Mrs. Dovey decisively. "There's nothing like a dose of
physic for little ones ; it often stops a bout of illness. You
give it to the two and don't lose no time. Grey powder's
best."

"I've not got any grey powder by me," said Mrs. Reed.
"It crossed my mind to try 'em with one o' them pills I had
from Abel Crew."

"What pills be they ?"

"I had 'em from him for myself the beginning o' the year,
when I was getting the headache so much. They're as mild
as mild can be ; but they did me good. The box is upstairs."

"How do you know they'd be the right pills to give to
babies ?" sensibly questioned Mrs. Dovey.

"Oh, they be right enough for that ! When little Georgy

was poorly two or three weeks back, I ran out to Abel Crew, chancing to see him go by the gate, and asked whether one of his pills would do the child harm. He said no, it would do him good."

"And did it get him round?"

"I never gave it. Georgy seemed to be so much pearter afore night came, that I thought I'd wait till the morrow. He's a rare bad one to take physic, he is. You may cover a powder in treacle that thick, Ann Dovey, but the boy scents it out somehow, and can't be got to touch it. His father always has to make him ; I can't. He got well that time without the pill."

"Well, I should try the pills on the little twins," advised Ann Dovey. "I'm sure they want something o' the sort. Look at this one ! Lying like a lamb in my arms, staring up at me with its poor eyes, and never moving. You may always know when a child's ill by its quietness. Nothing ailing 'em, they worry the life out of you."

"Both of them were cross enough this morning," remarked Hester Reed, "and for that reason I know they be worse now. I'll try the pill to-night."

Now, whether it was that Ann Dovey had any especial love for presiding at the ceremony of administering pills to children, or whether she only looked in again incidentally in passing, certain it was that in the evening she was for the second time at George Reed's cottage. Mrs. Reed had put the three elder ones to bed ; or, as she expressed it, "got 'em out o' the way" ; and was undressing the twins by firelight, when Ann Dovey tripped into the kitchen. George Reed was at work in the front garden, digging ; though it was getting almost too dark to see where he inserted the spade.

"Have ye give 'em their physic yet?" was Mrs. Dovey's salutation.

"No ; but I'm a-going to," answered Hester Reed. "You be just come in time to hold 'em for me, Ann Dovey, while I go upstairs for the box."

Ann Dovey received the pair of babies, and sat down in the low chair. Taking the candle, Mrs. Reed ran up to the room where the elder children slept. The house was better furnished than cottages generally are, and the rooms were of a fairly good size. Opposite the bed stood a high deal press with a flat top to it, which Mrs. Reed made a shelf of for keeping things that must be out of the children's reach. Stepping on a chair, she put her hand out for the box of pills, which stood in its usual place near the corner, and went downstairs with it.

It was an ordinary pasteboard pill-box, containing a few pills—six or seven, perhaps. Mrs. Dovey, curious in all matters, lifted the lid and sniffed at the pills. Hester Reed was getting the moist sugar they were to be administered in.

"What did you have these here pills for?" questioned Ann Dovey, as Mrs. Reed came back with the sugar. "They bain't over big."

"For headache and pain in the side. I asked old Abel Crew if he could give me something for it, and he gave me these pills."

Mrs. Reed was moistening a teaspoonful of the sugar as she spoke with warm water. Taking out one of the pills she proceeded to crush it into small bits, and then mixed it with the sugar. It formed a sort of paste. Dose the first.

"That ain't moist enough, Hester Reed," pronounced Mrs. Dovey critically.

"No? I'll put a drop more warm water."

The water was added, and one of the children was fed with the delectable compound—Hetty. Mrs. Dovey spoke again.

"Is it all for her? Won't a whole pill be too much for one, d'ye think?"

"Not a bit. When I asked old Abel whether one pill would be too much for Georgy, he said no—two wouldn't hurt him. I tell ye, Ann Dovey, the pills be as mild as milk."

Hetty took in the whole dose by degrees. Susy had a similar one made ready, and swallowed it in her turn. Then the two babies were conveyed upstairs and put to bed side by side in their mother's room.

Mrs. Dovey, the ceremony being over, took her departure. George Reed came in to his early supper, and soon afterwards he and his wife went up to bed. Men who have to be up at five in the morning must go to rest betimes. The fire and candle were put out, the doors locked, and the cottage was steeped in quietness at a time when in larger houses the evening was not much more than beginning.

How long she slept, Mrs. Reed could not tell. Whether it might be the first part of the night, early or late, or whether morning might be close upon the dawn, she knew not; but she was startled out of her sleep by the cries of the babies. Awful cries, they seemed, coming from children so young; and there could be no mistaking that each was in terrible agony.

"Why, it's convulsions!" exclaimed George Reed, when he had lighted a candle. "Both of them, too!"

Going downstairs as he was, he hastily lighted the kitchen fire and put a kettle of water on. Then, dressing himself, he ran out for Mr. Duffham. The doctor came in soon after George Reed had got back again.

Duffham was accustomed to scenes, and he entered on one now. Mrs. Reed, in a state of distress, had put the babies in blankets and brought them down to the kitchen fire; the three elder children, aroused by the cries, had come down too, and were standing about in their night-clothes, crying with fright. One of the babies was dead—Hetty. She had just expired in her father's arms. The other was dying.

"What on earth have you been giving to these children?" exclaimed Duffham, after taking a good look at the two.

"Oh, sir, what is it, please?" sobbed Mrs. Reed, in her terror. "Convulsions?"

"Convulsions—no," said the doctor, in a fume. "It is something else, as I believe—poison."

At which she set up a shriek that might have been heard out of doors.

Well, Hetty was dead, I say; and Duffham could not do anything to save the other. It died whilst he stood there. Duffham repeated his conjecture as to poison; and Mrs. Reed, all topsy-turvy though she was, three-parts bereft of her senses, resented the implication almost angrily.

"Poison!" cried she. "How can you think of such a thing, sir!"

"I tell you that to the best of my belief these children have both died from some irritant poison," asserted Duffham, coolly imperative. "I ask what you have been giving them?"

"They have not been well this three or four days past," replied she, wandering from the point; not evasively, but in her mind's bewilderment. "It must have been their teeth, sir; I thought they were cutting 'em with fever."

"Did you give them any physic?"

"Yes, sir. A pill apiece when I put 'em to bed."

"Ah!" said Mr. Duffham. "What pill was it?"

"One of Abel Crew's."

This answer surprised him. Allowing that his suspicion of poison was correct, he assumed that these pills must have contained it; and he had never had cause to suppose that Abel Crew's pills were otherwise than innocent.

Mrs. Reed, her voice broken by sobs, explained further in answer to his questions, telling him how she had procured these pills from Abel Crew some time before, and had given one of the said pills to each of the babies. Duffham stood against the dresser, taking it all in with a solemn face, his cane held up to his chin.

"Let me see this box of pills, Mrs. Reed."

She went upstairs to get it. A tidy woman in her ways, she had put the box in its place again on the top of the press. Duffham took off the lid and examined the pills.

"Do you happen to have a bit of sealing-wax in the house, Reed?" he asked presently.

George Reed, who had stood like a man bewildered, looking first on one, then on the other of his dead little ones, answered that he had not. But the eldest child, Annie, spoke up, saying that there was a piece in her little work-box; Cathy had given it her last week when she was at home.

It was produced—part of a small stick of fancy wax, green and gold. Duffham wrapped the pill-box up in the back of a letter that he took from his pocket, and sealed it with a seal that hung to his watch-chain. He put the parcel into the hand of George Reed.

"Take care of it," he said. "This will be wanted."

"There could not have been poison in them pills, sir," burst out Mrs. Reed, her distress increasing at the possibility that he might be right. "If there had been, they'd ha' poisoned me. One night I took three of 'em."

Duffham did not answer. He was nodding his head in answer to his own thoughts.

"And who ever heard of Abel Crew mixing up poison in his pills?" went on Mrs. Reed. "If you please, sir, I don't think he could do it."

"Well, that part of it puzzles me—how he came to do it," acknowledged Duffham. "I like old Abel, and shall be sorry if it is proved that his pills have done the mischief."

Mrs. Reed shook her head. She had more faith than that in Abel Crew.

Ever so many years before—for it was in the time of Sir Peter Chavasse—there appeared one day a wanderer at Church Dykely. It was hot weather, and he seemed to think nothing of camping out in the fields by night, under the summer stars. Who he was, or what he was, or why he had come, or why he stayed, nobody knew. He was evidently not a tramp, or a gipsy, or a travelling tinker—quite superior to it all ; a slender, young, and silent man, with a pale and gentle face.

At one corner of the common, spreading itself between the village and Chavasse Grange, there stood a covered wooden shed, formerly used to impound stray cattle, but left to itself since the square space for the new pound had been railed round. By and by it was found that the wanderer had taken to this shed to sleep in. Next, his name leaked out—"Abel Crew".

He lived how he could, and as simply as a hermit. Buying a penny loaf at the baker's, and making his dinner of it with a handful of sorrel plucked from the fields, and a drink from the rivulet that ran through the wilderness outside the Chavasse grounds. His days were spent in examining roots and wild herbs, now and then in digging one up ; and his nights chiefly in studying the stars. Sir Peter struck up a sort of speaking acquaintanceship with him, and, it was said, was surprised at his stock of knowledge and the extent of his travels ; for he knew personally many foreign places where even Sir Peter himself had never been. That may have caused Sir Peter—who was lord of the manor and of the common included—to tolerate in him what it was supposed he would not in others. Anyway, when Abel Crew began to dig the ground about his shed, and plant roots and herbs in it, Sir Peter let him do it and never interfered. It was quite the opposite ; for Sir Peter would sometimes stand to watch him at his work, talking the while.

In the course of time there was quite an extensive garden round the shed—comparatively speaking, you know, for we do not expect to see a shed garden as large as that of a mansion. It was fenced in with a hedge and wooden palings, all the work of Abel Crew's hands. Sir Peter was dead then ; but Lady Chavasse, guardian to the young heir, Sir Geoffrey, extended to him the same favour that her husband had, and, if she did not absolutely sanction what he was doing, she at any rate did not oppose it. Abel Crew filled his garden with rare and choice and useful field herbs, the valuable properties of which

he alone understood; and of ordinary sweet flowers, such as
bees love to suck. He set up beehives and sold the honey;
he distilled lavender and bergamot for perfumes; he converted his herbs and roots into medicines, which he supplied
to the poor people around, charging so small a price for them
that it could scarcely more than cover the cost of making,
and not charging at all the very poor. At the end of about
ten years from his first appearance he took down the old shed
and built up a more convenient cottage in its place, doing it
all with his own pair of hands. And the years went on and
on, and Abel Crew and his cottage, and his herbs, and his
flowers, and his bees, and his medicines were just as much of an
institution in the parish as was the Grange itself.

He and I became good friends. I liked him. You have
heard how I take likes and dislikes to faces, and I rarely saw a
face that I liked as I liked Abel Crew's. Not for its beauty,
though it really was beautiful, with its perfect shape and
delicately carved features; but for its unmistakable look of
goodness and its innate refinement; perhaps also for the deep,
far-seeing, and often *sad* expression that sat in the earnest eyes.
He was old now—sixty, I dare say; tall, slender, and very
upright still; his white hair brushed back from his forehead
and worn rather long. What his original condition of life
might have been did not transpire; he never talked of it.
More than once I had seen him reading Latin books; and
though he fell into the diction of the country people around
when talking with them, he changed his tones and language
when conversing with his betters. A character, no doubt
he was, but a man to be respected; a man of religion, too—
attending church regularly twice on a Sunday, wet or dry, and
carrying his religion into the little things of everyday life.

His style of dress was old-fashioned and peculiar. So far
as I saw, it never varied. A stout coat, waistcoat, and breeches
every day all of one colour—drab; with leathern gaiters
buttoned nearly to the knee. On Sundays he wore a suit of
black silk velvet, and a frilled shirt of fine cambric. His
breeches were tied at the knee with black ribbon, in which
was a plain, glistening steel buckle; buckles to match shone
in his shoes. His stockings were black, and in the winter he
wore black-cloth gaiters. In short, on Sundays Abel Crew
looked like a fine old-fashioned English gentleman, and would
have been taken for one. The woman who got up his linen

declared he was more particular over his shirt-frills than Sir Peter himself.

Strangers in the place would sometimes ask what he was. The answer was not easy to give. He was a botanist and herbalist, and made pills and mixtures, and perfumes, and sold honey, and had built his cottage and planted out his garden, and lived alone, cooking his food and waiting on himself; doing all, in fact, with his own hands, and was very modest always. On the other side, he had travelled in his youth, he understood paintings, studied the stars, read his store of Latin and classical books, and now and then bought more, and was as good a doctor as Duffham himself. Some people said a better one. Certain it was that more than once when legitimate medical nostrums had failed—calomel and blisters and bleeding—Abel Crew's simple decoctions and leaves had worked a cure. Look at young Mrs. Sterling at the Court. When that first baby of hers came to town—and a fine squalling young brat he was, with a mouth like a crocodile's !—gatherings arose in her chest or somewhere, one after another; it was said the agony was awful. Duffham's skill seemed to have gone a-blackberrying, the other doctor's also, for neither of the two could do anything for her, and the Court thought she would have died of it. Upon that, some relation of old Sterling's was summoned from London—a great physician in a great practice. He came in answer, and was liberal with his advice, telling them to try this and to try the other. But it did no good; and she only grew worse. When they were all in despair, seeing her increasing weakness and the prolonged pain, the woman who nursed her spoke of old Abel Crew; she had known him cure in these cases when the doctor could not; and the poor young lady, willing to catch at a straw, told them to send for Abel Crew. Abel Crew took a prepared plaster of herbs with him, green leaves of some sort, and applied it. That night the patient slept more easily than she had for weeks, and in a short time was well again.

But, skilful though he seemed to be in the science of herbs as remedies for sickness and sores, Abel Crew never obtruded himself upon the ailing, or took money for his advice, or willingly interfered with the province of Duffham; he never would do it unless compelled in the interests of humanity. The patients he chiefly treated were the poor, those who could not have paid Duffham a coin worth thinking about.

Duffham knew this. And, instead of being jealous of him, as some medical men might have been, or ridiculing him for a quack, Duffham liked and respected old Abel Crew. He was simple in his habits still : living chiefly upon bread and butter, with radishes or mustard and cress for a relish, cooking vegetables for his dinner, but rarely meat : and his drink was tea or spring water.

So that Abel Crew was rather a notable character amongst us ; and when it was known abroad that two of his pills had caused the death of Mrs. Reed's twins, there arose no end of a commotion.

It chanced that the same night this occurred, just about the time in fact that the unfortunate infants were taking down the pills under the superintendence of their mother and the blacksmith's wife, Abel Crew met with an accident ; though it was curious enough that it should be so. In taking a pan of boiling herbs off the fire, he let one of the handles slip out of his fingers ; it sent the pan down on that side, spilled a lot of the stuff, and scalded his left foot on the instep. Therefore he was about the last person to hear of the calamity ; for his door was not open as usual the following morning, and no one knocked to tell him of it.

Duffham was the first. Passing by on his morning rounds, the doctor heard the comments of the people, and it arrested him. It was so unusual a thing for Abel Crew not to be about, and for his door to be closed, that some of them had been arriving at a sensible conclusion—Abel Crew, knowing the mischief his pills had done, was shutting himself up within the house, unable to face his neighbours.

"Rubbish !" said Duffham. And he strode up the garden-path, knocked at the door with his cane, and entered. Abel had dressed, but was lying down on the bed again to rest his lame foot.

Duffham would have asked to look at it, but that he knew Abel Crew was as good at burns and scalds as he himself was. It had been doctored at once, and was now wrapped up in a handkerchief.

"The fire is nearly out of it," said Abel, "but it must have rest ; by to-night I shall be able to dress it with my healing-salve. I am much obliged to you for coming in, sir : though in truth I don't know how you could have heard of the accident."

"Ah, news flies!" said Duffham evasively, knowing that he had not heard of the foot, or the neighbours either, and had come in for something altogether different. "What is this about the pills?"

"About the pills?" repeated Abel Crew, who had got up out of respect, and was putting on his coat. "What pills, sir?"

The doctor told him what had happened. Hester Reed had given one of his pills to each of her babies, and both had died of it. Abel Crew listened quietly; his face and his eyes fixed on Duffham.

"The children cannot have died of the pills," said he, speaking as gently as you please. "Something else must have killed them."

"According to Hester Reed's account, nothing can have done it but the pills," said Duffham. "The children had only taken their ordinary food throughout the day, and very little of that. George Reed came running to me in the night, but it was too late; one was dead before I got there. There could be no mistaking the children's symptoms—that both were poisoned."

"This is very strange," exclaimed Abel, looking troubled. "By what kind of poison?"

"Arsenic, I think. I——"

But here they were interrupted. Dovey, the blacksmith, hearing of the calamity, together with the fact that it was his wife who had assisted in administering the suspected doses, deemed it his duty to look into the affair a little, and to resent it. He had left his forge and a bar of iron red-hot in it, and come tearing along in his leather apron, his shirt-sleeves stripped up to the elbow, and his arms grimy. A dark-eyed, good-natured little man in general was Dovey, but exploding with rage at the present moment.

"Now then, Abel Crew, what do you mean by selling pills to poison people?" demanded he, pushing back the door with a bang, and stepping in fiercely. Duffham, foreseeing there was going to be a contest, and having no time to waste, took his departure.

"I have not sold pills to poison people," replied Abel.

"Look here," said Dovey, folding his black arms, "be you going to eat them pills, or be you not? Come!"

"What do you mean, Dovey?"

"What do I mean! Ain't my meaning plain? Do you own to having selled a box of pills to Hester Reed last winter? —be you thinking to eat that there fact, and deny of it? Come, Abel Crew!"

"I remember it well," readily spoke up Abel. "Mrs. Reed came here one day, complaining that her head ached continually, and her side often had a dull pain in it, and asked me to give her something. I did so; I gave her a box of pills. It was early in January, I think. I know there was ice on the ground."

"Then do you own to them pills?" returned Dovey more quietly, his fierceness subdued by Abel's civility. "It were you that furnished 'em?"

"I furnished the box of pills I speak of, that Hester Reed had from me in the winter. There's no mistake about that."

"And made 'em too?"

"Yes, and made them."

"Well, I'm glad to hear you say that; and now don't you go for to eat your words later, Abel Crew. Our Ann, my wife, helped to give them there two pills to the children; and I'm not a-going to let her get into trouble over it. You've confessed to the pills, and I'm a witness."

"My pills did not kill the children, Dovey," said Abel in a pleasant tone, resting his lame foot upon an opposite chair.

"Not kill 'em?"

"No, that they did not. I've not made pills all these years to poison children at last."

"But what done it if the pills didn't?"

"How can I say? 'Twasn't my pills."

"Dr. Duffham says it was the pills. And he——"

"Dr. Duffham says it was?"

"Reed told me that the doctor asked outright, all in a flurry, what his wife had gave the babies, and she said she had gave 'em nothing but them there two pills of Abel Crew's. Duffham said the pills must have had poison in 'em, and he asked for the box; and Hester Reed, she give him the box, and he sealed it up afore their eyes with his own seal."

Abel nodded. He knew that any suspected medicine must in such a case be sealed up.

"And now that I've got that there word from ye, I'll say good-day to ye, neighbour, for I've left my forge to itself,

and some red-hot iron in it.   And I hope with all my heart
and mind"—the blacksmith turned round from the door to
say more kindly, his good-nature cropping up again—"that
it'll turn out it *warn't* the pills, but some'at else : our Ann
won't have no cause to be in a fright then."   Which was as
much as to say that Ann Dovey was frightened, you observe.

That same afternoon, going past the common, I saw Abel
Crew in his garden, sitting against the cottage wall in the sun,
his foot resting on a block of wood.

"How did it all happen, Abel ?" I asked, turning in at the
gate.   "Did you give Mrs. Reed the wrong pills ?"

"No, sir," he answered, "I gave her the right pills ; the
pills I make expressly for such complaints as hers.   But if I
had, in one sense, given her the wrong, they could not have
brought about any ill effect such as this, for my pills are all
innocent of poison."

"I should say it could not have been the pills that did the
mischief after all, then."

"You might swear it as well, Master Johnny, with perfect
safety.   What killed the poor children I don't pretend to
know, but my pills never did.   I tried to get down as far as
Reed's to inquire particulars, and found I could not walk.
It was a bit of ill-luck, disabling myself just at this time."

"Shall you have to appear at the inquest to-morrow ?"

He lifted his head quickly at the question—as though it
surprised him, perhaps not having cast his thoughts that
way.

"Is there to be an inquest, Master Johnny ?"

"I heard so from old Jones.   He has gone over to see the
coroner."

"Well, I wish the investigation was all over and done with,"
said he.   "It makes me uneasy, though I know I am innocent."

Looking at him sitting there in the sun, at his beautiful
face with its truthful eyes and its silver hair, it was next to
impossible to believe he could be the author of the two
children's death.   Only—the best of us are liable to mistakes,
and sometimes make them.   I said as much.

"*I* made none, Master Johnny," was his answer.   "When
my pills come to be analysed—as of course they must be—
they will be found wholesome and innocent."

The inquest did not take place till the Friday. Old Jones had fixed it for the Thursday, but the coroner put it off to the next day. And by the time Friday morning dawned opinion had veered round, and was strongly in favour of Abel Crew. All the parish had been to see him; and his protestations, that he had never in his life put any kind of poison into his medicines, made a great impression. The pills could not have been in fault, said everybody. Dr. Duffham might have sealed them up as a matter of precaution, but the mischief would not be found there.

In the middle of Church Dykely, next door to Perkins the butcher's, stood the Silver Bear Inn, a better sort of public-house, kept by Henry Rimmer. It was there that the inquest was held. Henry Rimmer himself and Perkins the butcher were two of the jurymen. Dobbs the blacksmith was another. They all dressed themselves in their Sunday-going clothes to attend it. It was called for two in the afternoon; and soon after that hour the county coroner (who had dashed up to the Silver Bear in a fast gig, his clerk driving) and the jury trooped down to George Reed's cottage and took a look at the two pale little faces lying there side by side. Then they went back again, and the proceedings began.

Of course as many spectators went crowding into the room as it would hold. Three or four chairs were there (besides those occupied by the jury at the table), and a bench stood against the wall. The bench was speedily fought for and filled; but Henry Rimmer's brother, constituting himself master of the ceremonies, reserved the chairs for what he called the "big people", meaning those of importance in the place. The Squire was bowed into one; and to my surprise I had another. Why, I could not imagine, unless it was that they remembered I was the owner of George Reed's cottage. But I did not like to sit down when so many older persons were standing, and I would not take the chair.

Some little time was occupied with preliminaries before what might be called the actual inquest set in. First of all, the coroner flew into a passion because Abel Crew had not put in an appearance, asking old Jones if he supposed that was the way justice must be administered in England, and that he ought to have had Crew present. Old Jones, who was in a regular fluster with it all, and his legs more gouty than ever, told the coroner, calling him "his worship", that he had understood Crew meant to be present. Upon which the coroner sharply answered that "understanding" went for nothing, and Jones should know his business better.

However, in walked Abel Crew in the midst of the contest. His delayed arrival was caused by his difficulty in getting his damaged foot there ; which had been accomplished by the help of a stick and somebody's arm. Abel had dressed himself in his black velvet suit ; and as he took off his hat on entering and bowed respectfully to the coroner, I declare he could not be taken for anything but a courtly gentleman of the old school. Nobody offered him a chair. I wished I had not given up mine ; he should have had it.

Evidence was first tendered of the death of the children, and of the terrible pain they had died in. Duffham and a medical man, who was a stranger and had helped at the post-mortem, testified to arsenic being the cause of death. The next question was, how had it been administered ? A rumour arose in the room that the pills had been analysed ; but the result had not transpired. Everyone could see a small paper parcel standing on the table before the coroner, and knew by its shape that it must contain the pill-box.

Hester Reed was called. She said (giving her evidence very quietly, just a sob and a sigh every now and then alone betraying what she felt) that she was the wife of George Reed. Her two little ones—twins, aged eleven and a half months— had been ailing for a day or two, seemed feverish, would not eat their food, were very cross at times and unnaturally still at others, and she came to the conclusion that their teeth must be plaguing them, and thought she would give them some mild physic. Mrs. Todhetley, the Squire's lady at Dyke Manor, had called in on the Tuesday afternoon, and agreed with her that some mild physic——

"Confine your statement to what is evidence," interrupted the coroner sternly.

Hester Reed, looking scared at the check, and perhaps not knowing what was evidence and what not, went on the best way she could. She and Ann Dovey—who had been neigh-bourly enough to look in and help her—had given the children a pill apiece in the evening after they were undressed, mashing the pill up in a little sugar and warm water. She then put them to bed upstairs and went to bed herself not long after. In the night she and her husband were awoke by the babies' screams, and they thought it must be convulsions. Her husband lighted the fire and ran for Dr. Duffham ; but one had died before the doctor could get there, and the other died close upon it.

"What food had you given them during the day ?" asked the coroner.

"Very little indeed, sir. They wouldn't take it."

"What did the little that they did take consist of ?"

"It were soaked bread, sir, with milk and some sprinkled sugar. I tried them with some potato mashed up in a spoonful o' broth at mid-day—we'd had a bit o' biled neck o' mutton for dinner—but they both turned from it."

"Then all they took that day was bread soaked in milk and sweetened with sugar ?"

"Yes, it were, sir. But the bread was soaked in warm water and the milk and sugar was put in afterwards. 'Twas but the veriest morsel they'd take, poor little dears !"

"Was the bread—and the milk—and the sugar, the same that the rest of your household used ?"

"In course it were, sir. My other children ate plenty of it. *Their* appetites didn't fail 'em."

"Where did you get the warm water from that you say you soaked the bread in ?"

"Out o' the tea-kettle, sir. The water was the same that I biled for our tea morning and night."

"The deceased children, then, had absolutely no food given to them apart from what you had yourselves ?"

"Not a scrap, sir. Not a drop."

"Except the pills ?"

"Excepting them, in course, sir. None o' the rest of us wanted physic."

"Where did you procure these pills ?"

She went into the history of the pills. Giving the full account of them, as already related.

"By your own showing, witness, it must be three months, or thereabouts, since you had that box from Abel Crew, spoke the coroner. "How do you know that the two pills you administered to the deceased children came from the same box ?"

Hester Reed's eyes opened wide. She looked as surprised as though she had been asked whether she had procured the two pills from the moon.

"Yes, yes," interposed one of the jury, "how do you know it was the same box?"

"Why, gentlemen, I had no other box of pills at all, save that," she said, when her speech came to her. "We've had no physic but that in the cottage since winter, nor for ever so long afore. I'll swear it was the same box, sirs; there can't be no mistake about it."

"Did you leave it about in the way of people," resumed the coroner, "so that it might be handled by anybody who might come into your cottage?"

"No, sir," she answered earnestly. "I never kept the pill-box but in one place, and that was on the top of the high press upstairs out of harm's way. I put it there the first night Abel Crew gave it me, and when I wanted to get a pill or two out for my own taking, I used to step on a chair—for it's too high for me to reach without—and help myself. The box have never been took from the place at all, sir, till Tuesday night, when I brought it downstairs with me. When I've wanted to dust the press-top, I've just lifted the pill-box with one hand and passed the duster along under it with the other, as I stood on the chair. It's the same box, sir; I'll swear to that much; and it's the same pills."

Strong testimony. The coroner paused a moment. "You swear that, you say? You are quite sure?"

"Sir, I am sure and positive. The box was never took from its place since Abel Crew gave it me, till I reached up for it on Tuesday evening and carried it downstairs."

"You had been in the habit of taking these pills yourself, you say?"

"I took two three or four times when I first had 'em, sir; once I took three; but since then I've felt better and not wanted any."

"Did you feel any inconvenience from them? Any pain?"

"Not a bit, sir. As I said to Ann Dovey that night, when she asked whether they was fit pills to give the children, they seemed as mild as milk."

"Should you know the box again, witness?"

"Law yes, sir, what should hinder me?" returned Hester Reed, inwardly marvelling at what seemed so superfluous a question.

The coroner undid the paper and handed the box to her.

She was standing close to him, on the other side his clerk, who sat writing down the evidence. "Is this the box?" he asked. "Look at it well."

Mrs. Reed did as she was bid : turned it about and looked "well". "Yes, sir, it is the same box," said she. "That is, I am nearly sure of it."

"What do you mean by *nearly* sure?" quickly asked the coroner, catching at the word. "Have you any doubt?"

"Not no moral doubt at all, sir. Only them pill-boxes is all so like one another. Yes, sir, I'm sure it is the same box."

"Open it, and look at the pills. Are they, in your judgment, the same?"

"Just the same, sir," she answered, after taking off the lid. "One might a'most know 'em anywhere. Only——"

"Only what?" demanded the coroner, as she paused.

"Well, sir, I fancied I had rather more left—six or seven say. There's only five here."

The coroner made no answer to that. He took the box from her and put on the lid. We soon learnt that two had been taken out for the purpose of being analysed.

For who should loom into the room at that juncture but Pettipher, the druggist from Piefinch Cut. He had been analysing the pills in a hasty way in obedience to orders received half an hour ago, and came to give the result. The pills contained arsenic, he said ; not enough to kill a grown person, he thought, but enough to kill a child. As Pettipher was only a small man (in a business point of view) and sold groceries as well as drugs, and spectacles and ear-trumpets, some of us did not think much of his opinion, and fancied the pills should have been analysed by Duffham. That was just like old Jones : giving work to the wrong man.

George Reed was questioned, but could tell nothing, except that he had never touched either box or pills. While Ann Dovey was being called, and the coroner had his head bent over his clerk's notes, speaking to him in an undertone, Abel Crew suddenly asked to be allowed to look at the pills. The coroner, without lifting his head, just pushed the box down on the green cloth, and one of the jury handed it over his shoulder to Abel Crew.

"This is not the box I gave Mrs. Reed," said Abel, in a clear, firm tone, after diving into it with his eyes and nose. "Nor are these the pills."

Up went the coroner's head with a start.   He had supposed the request to see the box came from a juryman.   It might have been irregular for Abel Crew to be allowed so much ; but as it arose partly through the coroner's own fault he was too wise to make a commotion over it.

"What is that you say ?" he asked, stretching out his hand for the box as eagerly as though it had contained gold.

"That this box and these pills are not the same that I furnished to Mrs. Reed, sir," replied Abel, advancing and placing the box in the coroner's hand.   "They are not indeed."

"Not the same pills and box !" exclaimed the coroner. "Why, man, you have heard the evidence of the witness, Hester Reed ; you may see for yourself that she spoke nothing but truth.   Don't talk nonsense here."

"But they are *not* the same, sir," respectfully persisted Abel.   "I know my own pills, and I know my own boxes : these are neither the one nor the other."

"Now that won't do ; you must take us all for fools !" exploded the coroner, who was a man of quick temper. "Just you stand back and be quiet."

"Never a pill-box went out from my hands, sir, but it had my little private mark upon it," urged Abel.   "That box does not bear the mark."

"What is the mark, pray ?" asked the coroner.

"Four little dots of ink inside the rim of the lid, sir ; and four similar dots inside the box near the edge.   They are so faint that a casual observer might not notice them ; but they are always there.   Of all the pill-boxes now in my house, sir—and I suppose there may be two or three dozen of them— you will not find one but has the mark."

Some whispering had been going on in different parts of the room ; but this silenced it.   You might have heard a pin drop.   The words seemed to make an impression on the coroner : they and Abel Crew were both so earnest.

"You assert also that the pills are not yours," spoke the coroner, who was known to be fond of desultory conversations while holding his inquests.   "What proof have you of that ?"

"No proof ; that is, no proof that I can advance, that would satisfy the eye or ear.   But I am certain, by the look of them, that those were never my pills."

All this took the jury aback ; the coroner also.   It had

seemed to some of them an odd thing that Hester Reed should
have swallowed two or three of the pills at once without their
entailing an ache or a pain, and that one each had poisoned the
babies. Perkins the butcher observed to the coroner that the
box must have been changed since Mrs. Reed helped herself
from it. Upon which the coroner, after pulling at his whiskers
for a moment as if in thought, called out for Mrs. Reed to
return.

But when she did so, and was further questioned, she only
kept to what she had said before, strenuously denying that
the box *could* have been changed. It had never been touched
by any hands but her own while it stood in its place on the
press, and had never been removed from it at all until she took
it downstairs on the past Tuesday night.

"Is the room where this press stands your own sleeping-
room?" asked the coroner.

"No, sir. It's the other room, where my three children
sleep."

"Could these children get to the box?"

"Dear no, sir! 'Twould be quite impossible."

"Had anyone an opportunity of handling the box when
you took it down on Tuesday night?" went on the coroner
after a pause.

"Only Mrs. Dovey, sir. Nobody else was there."

"Did she touch it?"

"She laid hold of it to look at the pills."

"Did you leave her *alone* with it?"

"No, sir. Leastways—yes, I did for a minute or so, while
I went into the back'us to get the sugar and a saucer and spoon."

"Had she the box in her hands when you returned?"

"Yes, sir, I think she had. I think she was still smelling
at the pills. I know the poor little innocents was lying one
on one knee and one on t'other, all flat, and her two hands was
lifted with the box in 'em."

"It was after that that you took the pills out of it to give
the children?"

"Yes, sir; directly after. But Ann Dovey wouldn't do
nothing wrong to the pills, sir."

"That will do," said the coroner in his curt way. "Call Ann
Dovey."

Ann Dovey walked forward with a face as red as her new
bonnet-strings. She had heard the whole colloquy: some-

thing seemed, too, to have put her out. Possessing scant veneration for coroners at the best of times, and none for the jury at present assembled, she did not feel disposed to keep down her temper.

The few first questions asked her, however, afforded no opportunity for resentment, for they were put quietly, and tended only to extract confirmation of Mrs. Reed's evidence as to fetching the pill-box from upstairs and administering the pills. Then the coroner cleared his throat.

"Did you see the last witness, Hester Reed, go into the back kitchen for a spoon and saucer?"

"I saw her go and fetch 'em from somewhere," replied Ann Dovey, who felt instinctively the ball was beginning, and gave the reins to her temper accordingly.

"Did you take charge of the pill-box while she was gone?"

"I had it in my hand, if you mean that."

"Did anybody come into the kitchen during that interval?"

"No, they didn't," was the tart response.

"You were alone, except for the two infants?"

"I were. What of it?"

"Now, witness, did you do anything with that box? Did you, for instance, exchange it for another?" ·

"I think you ought to be ashamed o' yourselves, all on you, to sit and ask a body such a thing!" exploded Mrs. Dovey, growing every moment more resentful at being questioned. "If I had knowed the bother that was to spring up, I'd have chucked the box, pills and all, into the fire first. I wish I had!"

"Was the box that you handed to Hester Reed on her return the same box she left with you? Were the pills the same pills?"

"Why, where d'ye think I could have got another box from?" shrieked Ann Dovey. "D'you suppose, sir, I carry boxes and pills about with me? I bain't so fond o' physic as all that comes to."

"Dovey takes pills on occasion for that giddiness of his; I've seen him take 'em; mayhap you'd picked up a box of his," spoke Dobbs the blacksmith mildly.

That was adding fuel to fire. Two of a trade don't agree. Dovey and Dobbs were both blacksmiths: the one in Church Dykely, the other in Piefinch Cut, not much more, so to say, than a stone's-throw from each other. The men were good friends enough ; but their respective ladies were apt to regard jealously all work taken to the rival establishment. Any other of the jurymen might have made the remark with comparative impunity ; not so Dobbs. And, besides the turn the inquiry seemed to be taking, Mrs. Dovey had not been easy about it in her mind from the first ; proof of which was furnished by the call, already mentioned, made by her husband on Abel Crew.

"Dovey takes pills on occasion, do he !" she shrilly retorted. "And what do you take, Bill Dobbs? Pints o' beer when you can get 'em. Who lamed Poole's white horse the t'other day a-shoeing him ?"

"Silence !" sternly interrupted the coroner. While Dobbs, conscious of the self-importance imparted to him by the post he was now filling, and of the necessity of maintaining the dignity of demeanour which he was apt to put on with his best clothes, bore the aspersion with equanimity and a stolid face.

"Attend to me, witness, and confine yourself to replying to the questions I put to you," continued the coroner. "Did you take with you any pills or pill-box of your own when you went to Mrs. Reed's that evening ?"

"No, I *didn't*," returned Ann Dovey, the emphasis culminating in a sob : and why she should have set on to shiver and shake was more than the jury could understand.

"Do you wear pockets ?"

"What if I do ?" she said, after a momentary pause. But her lips grew white, and I thought she was trying to brave it out.

"Had you a pocket on that evening ?"

"Heaven be good to me !" I heard her mutter under her breath. And if ever I saw a woman look frightened nearly to death, Ann Dovey looked it then.

"Had you a pocket on that evening, witness ?" repeated the coroner sharply.

"Y—es."

"What articles were in it ? Do you recollect ?"

"It were a key or two," came the answer at length, her very teeth chattering and all the impudence suddenly gone out of her. "And my thimble, sir ;—and some coppers ; and a part of a nutmeg ;—and—and I don't remember nothing else, sir."

"No box of pills ? You are sure you had not that ?"

"Haven't I said so, sir ?" she rejoined, bursting into a flood of tears. For which, and for the sudden agitation, nobody could see any reason : and perhaps it was only that which made the coroner harp upon the same string.   Her demeanour had become suspicious.

"You had no poison of any kind in your pocket, then ?"

But he asked the question in jest more than earnest.   For when she went into hysterics instead of replying, he let her go.   He was used to seeing witnesses scared when brought before him.

The verdict was not arrived at that day.   When other witnesses had been examined, the coroner addressed the jury. Ten of them listened deferentially, and were quite prepared to return a verdict of Manslaughter against Abel Crew ; seemed red-hot to do it, in fact.   But two of them dissented. They were not satisfied, they said ;   and they held out for adjourning the inquest to see if any more light could be thrown upon the affair.   As they evidently had the room with them, the coroner yielded, and adjourned the inquest in a temper.

And then it was discovered that the name was not Crew but Carew.   Abel himself corrected the coroner.   Upon that, the coroner sharply demanded why he had lived under a false name.

"Nay, sir," replied Abel, as dignified as you please, "I have had no intention of doing so.   When I first came to this neighbourhood I gave my name correctly—Carew :   but the people at once converted it into Crew by their mode of pronunciation."

"At any rate, you must have sanctioned it."

"Tacitly I have done so.   What did it signify ?   When I have had occasion to write my name—but that has been very rare—I have written it Carew.   Old Sir Peter Chavasse knew it was Carew, and used to call me so ; as did Sir Geoffrey. Indeed, sir, I have had no reason to conceal my name."

"That's enough," said the coroner, cutting him short. "Stand back, Abel Carew.   The proceedings are adjourned to this day week."

II

Things are done in remote country places that would not be done in towns.   Whether the law is understood by us, or whether it is not, it often happens that it is very much exceeded, or otherwise not acted upon.   Those who have to exercise it sometimes show themselves as ignorant of it as if they had lived all their lives in the wilds of America.

Old Jones the constable was one of these. When not checked by his masters, the magistrates, he would do most outrageous things—speaking of the law and of common sense. And he did one in reference to Abel Crew. I still say Crew. Though it had come out that his name was Carew, we should be sure to call him Crew to the end.

The inquest might have been concluded at its first sitting, but for the two who stood out against the rest of the jury. Perkins the butcher and Dobbs the blacksmith. Truth to say, these two had plenty of intelligence—which could not be said of all the rest. Ten of the jury pronounced the case to be as clear as daylight : the infants had been poisoned by Abel Crew's pills : and the coroner seemed to agree with them—he hated trouble. But Dobbs and Perkins held out. They were not satisfied, they said ; the pills furnished by Abel Crew might not have been the pills that were taken by the children ; moreover, they considered that the pills should be "more officially" analysed. Pettipher the druggist was all very well in his small way, but hardly up, in their opinion, to pronouncing upon pills when a man's life or liberty was at stake. They pressed for an adjournment, that the pills might be examined by some competent authority. The coroner, as good as telling them they were fools to their faces, had adjourned the inquest in suppressed passion to that day week.

"And I've got to take care of you, Abel Crew," said old Jones, floundering up on his gouty legs to Abel as the jury and crowd dispersed. "You've got to come along o' me."

"To come where ?" asked Abel, who was hobbling towards home on his scalded foot, by the help of his stick and the arm of Gibbon the gamekeeper.

"To the lock-up," said old Jones.

"To the lock-up !" echoed Abel Crew.

"In course," returned old Jones. "Where else but the lock-up ? Did you think it was to the pound ?"

Abel Crew, lifting his hand that held his stick to brush a speck of dirt off his handsome velvet coat, turned to the constable ; his refined face, a little paler than usual, gazing inquiringly at old Jones's, his silver hair glistening in the setting sun.

"I don't understand you, Mr. Jones," he said calmly.
"You cannot mean to lock me up ?"

"Well, I never !" cried old Jones, who had a knack of
considering every suspected person guilty, and treating them
accordingly. "You have a cheek, you have, Abel Crew !
'Not going to take me to the lock-up, Mr. Jones,' says you !
Where would you be took to ?"

"But there's no necessity for it," said Abel. "I shall not
run away.   I shall be in my house if I'm wanted again."

"I dare say you would !" said old Jones ironically. "You
might or you mightn't, you know. You be as good as
committed for the killing and slaying o' them there two twins,
and it's my business to see as you *don't* make your escape
aforehand, Abel Crew."

Quite a company of us, sauntering out of the inquest-
room, were listening by this time. I gave old Jones a bit
of my mind.

"He is not yet committed, Jones, therefore you have no
right to take him or to lock him up."

"You don't know nothing about it, Mr. Ludlow. I do.
The crowner gave me a hint, and I'm acting on it.   'Don't you
go and let that man escape,' says his worship to me ; 'it'll be
at your peril if you do.'   'I'll see to him, your worship,' says
I.   And I be a-doing of it."

But it was hardly likely that the coroner meant Abel
Crew to be confined in that precious lock-up for a whole
week.   One night there was bad enough.   At least, I did not
think he meant it ; but the crowd, to judge by their comments,
seemed divided on the point.

"The shortest way to settle the question will be to ask the
coroner, old Jones," said I, turning back to the Silver Bear.
"Come along."

"You'd be clever to catch him, Master Johnny," roared
out old Jones after me.   "His worship jumped into his gig ;
it was a-waiting for him when he come out ; and his clerk
druv him off at a slapping pace."

It was true.   The coroner was gone ; and old Jones had
it all his own way ; for, you see, none of us liked to interfere
with the edict of an official gentleman who held sway in the
county and sat on dead people.   Abel Crew accepted the
alternative meekly.

"Anyway, you must allow me to go home first to lock my

house up, and to see to one or two other little matters," said
he.

"Not unless you goes under my own eyes," retorted old
Jones. "You might be for destroying your stock o' pills for
fear they should bear evidence again' you, Abel Crew."

"My pills are, of all things, what I would not destroy,"
said Abel. "They would bear testimony for me, instead of
against me, for they are harmless."

So Abel Crew hobbled to his cottage on the common,
attended by old Jones and a tail of followers. Arrived there,
he attended the first thing to his scalded foot, dressing it
with some of his own ointment. Then he secured some bread
and butter, not knowing what the accommodation at the lock-
up might be in the shape of eatables, and changed his handsome
quaint suit of clothes for those he wore every day. After
that, he was escorted back to the lock-up.

Now, the lock-up was in Piefinch Cut, nearly opposite to
Dovey the blacksmith's. The Squire remembered the time
when the lock-up stood alone; when Piefinch Cut had no
more houses in it than Piefinch Lane now has; but since then
Piefinch Cut had been built upon and inhabited, houses
touching even the sacred walls of the lock-up. A tape-and-
cotton and sweetstuff shop supported it on one side, and a
small pork-butcher's on the other. Pettipher's drug shop,
should anybody be curious on the point, was next to the tape-
and-cotton mart.

To see Abel Crew arriving in the custody of old Jones the
constable, the excited stragglers after them, astonished Piefinch Cut not a little. Figg the pawnbroker—who was originally from Alcester—considered himself learned in the law.
Anyway, he was a great talker, and liked to give his opinion
upon every topic that might turn up. His shop joined
Dovey's forge, and when we arrived there Figg was outside,
holding forth to Dovey, who had his shirt-sleeves rolled up
above his elbows as usual, his leather apron on. Mrs. Dovey
stood listening behind, in the smart gown and red-ribboned
bonnet she had worn at the inquest.

"Why—what on earth!—have they been and gone and
took up Crew?" cried Figg in surprise.

"It is an awful shame of old Jones," I broke in, speaking
more to Dovey than Figg, for Figg was no favourite of mine.
"A whole week of the lock-up! Only think of it, Dovey!"

"But have they brought it in again' him, Master Johnny?" cried Dovey, unfolding his grimy arms to touch his paper cap to me as he spoke.

"*No*; that's what they have not done. The inquest is adjourned for a week; and I don't believe old Jones has a right to take him at all. Not legally, you know."

"That's just what her brought word," said Dovey, with a nod in the direction of his wife. " 'Well, how be it turned, Ann?' says I to her when her come back—for I'd a sight o' work in to-day and couldn't go myself. 'Oh, it haven't turned no ways yet, Jack,' says her; 'it be put off to next week.' There he goes—right in !"

This last remark applied to Abel Crew. After fumbling in his pocket for the two big keys, tied together with string, and then fumbling at the latch, old Jones succeeded in opening the door. Not being much used, the lock was apt to grow rusty. Then he stood back, and with a flourish of hands motioned Abel in. He made no resistance.

"They must know for certain as 'twere his pills what done it," struck in Mrs. Dovey.

"No, they don't," said I. "What's more, I do not think it was his pills. Abel Crew says he never put poison in his pills yet, and I believe him."

"Well, and no more it don't stand to reason as he would, Mr. Ludlow," said Figg, a man whose self-complaisance was not to be put down by any amount of discouragement. "I were just a-saying so to Dovey—— Why have old Jones took him up?" went on Figg to Gibbon the gamekeeper, who came striding by.

"Jones says he has the coroner's orders for it," answered Gibbon.

"Look here, I know a bit about law, and I know a man oughtn't to be shut up till some charge is brought again' him," contended Figg. "Crew's pills is suspected, but he have not been charged yet."

"Anyway, it's what Jones has gone and done," said Gibbon. "Perhaps he is right. And a week's not much; it'll soon pass. But as to any pills of Abel Crew's having killed them children, it's just preposterous to think of it."

"What d'ye suppose did kill 'em, then, Richard Gibbon?" demanded Ann Dovey, a hot flush on her face, her tone full of resentment.

"That's just what has to be found out," returned Gibbon, passing on his way.

"If it hadn't been for Dobbs and Butcher Perkins holding out again' it, Crew 'ud ha' been brought in guilty safe enough," said Ann Dovey. And the tone was again so excited, so bitterly resentful against Dobbs and Perkins, that I could not help looking at her in wonder. It sounded just as though the non-committal of Abel were a wrong inflicted upon herself.

"No, he would not have been brought in guilty," I answered her; "he would have been committed for trial; but that's a different thing. If the matter could be sifted to the bottom, I know it would be found that the mischief did not lie with Abel Crew's pills. There, Mrs. Dovey!"

She was looking at me out of the corners of her eyes— for all the world as if she were afraid of me, or of what I said. I could not make her out.

"Why should you wish so particularly to bring it home to Crew?" I pointedly asked her; and Figg turned round to look at her, as if seconding the question.

"Me want particular to bring it home to Crew!" she retorted, her voice rising with temper; or perhaps with fear, for she trembled like an aspen leaf. "I don't want to bring it home particular to him, Mr. Ludlow. It were his pills, though, all the same, that did it."

And with that she whisked through the forge to her kitchen.

.   .   .   .   .

On the morning following I got old Jones to let me into the lock-up. The place consisted of two rooms opening into one another, and a small square space, no bigger than a closet, at the end of the passage, where they kept the pen and ink. For that small space had a window in it, looking on to the fields at the back; the two rooms had only skylights in the roof. In the inner room a narrow iron bedstead stood against the wall, a mattress and blanket on it. Abel was sitting on that when we went in.

"You must have been lively here last night, Abel!"

"Yes, very, sir," answered he, with a half-smile. "I did not really mind it; I am used to being alone. I could have done with fewer rats, though."

"Oh, are there rats here ?"

"Lots of them, Master Johnny. I don't like rats. They came upon my face, and all about me."

"Why does old Jones not set traps for them ? He considers this place to be under his special protection."

"There are too many for any trap to catch," answered Abel.

Old Jones had gone off to the desk in the closet, having placed some bread-and-butter and milk on the shelf for Abel. His errand there was to enter the cost of the bread in the account-book, to be settled for later. A prisoner in the lock-up was commonly treated to bread and water : old Jones had graciously allowed this one to pay for some butter and milk out of his own pocket.

"I don't want to treat 'em harsher nor I be obliged, Master Ludlow," he said to me when coming in, in reference to the butter and the milk he was carrying. "Abel Crew have been known as a decent man ever since he come among us : and if he chooses to pay for the butter and the milk, there ain't no law against his having 'em. 'Tain't as if he was a burglar."

"No, he is not a burglar," I answered. "And you must mind that you do not get into the wrong box about him. There's neither law nor justice in locking him up, Jones, before he is charged."

"If I had never locked up nobody till they was charged, I should ha' been in the wrong box many a time afore now," said old Jones doggedly. "Look at that there man last Christmas ; what I caught prowling in the grounds at Parrifer Hall, with a whole set of housebreaking things concealed in his pockets ! After I'd took him, and lodged him in here safe, it was found that he was one o' the worst characters in the county, only let out o' Worcester gaol two days before. Suppose I'd not took him, Master Johnny ? Where 'ud the spoons at Parrifer Hall ha' been ?"

"That was a different case altogether."

"*I* know what I'm about," returned Jones. "The coroner, he just give me a nod or two, looking at Crew as he give it. I knew what it meant, sir : a nod's as good as a wink to a blind horse."

Anyway, Jones had him here in the lock-up ; and had gone off to enter the loaf in the account-book ; and I was sitting on the bench opposite Abel.

"It is a wicked shame of them to have put you here, Abel."

"It is not legal—as I believe," he answered. "And I am sure it is not just, sir. I swear those pills and that box produced at the inquest were none of mine. They never went out of my hands. Old Jones thinks he is doing right to secure me, I suppose, and he is civil over it; so I must not grumble. He brought me some water to wash in this morning, and a comb."

"But there's no *sense* in it. You would not attempt to escape; you would wait for the reassembling of the inquest."

"Escape!" he exclaimed. "I should be the first to remain for it. I am more anxious than anyone to have the matter investigated. Truth to say, Master Johnny, my curiosity is excited. Hester Reed is so persistent in regard to their being the pills and box that I gave her; and as she is a truthful, honest woman, one can't see where the mistake lies. There must be a mystery in it somewhere."

"Suppose you are committed to take your trial? And found guilty?"

"That I shall be committed, I look upon as certain," he answered. "As to being found guilty—if I am, I must bear it. God knows my innocence, and I shall hope that in time He will bring it to light."

"All the same, Abel, they ought not to put you in here."

"That's true, sir."

"And then there will be the lying in prison until the assizes—two or three good months to come! Don't go and die of it, Abel."

"No, I shall not do that," he answered, smiling a little. "The consciousness of innocence will keep me up."

I sat looking at him. What light could get in through the dusty skylight fell on his silver hair, which fell back from his pale face. He held his head down in thought, only raising it to answer me. Some movement in the closet betokened old Jones's speedy approach, and I hastened to assure Abel that all sensible people would not doubt his innocence.

"No one need doubt it, Master Johnny," he answered firmly, his eye kindling. "I never had a grain of arsenic in my house; I have never had any other poison. There are herbs from which poison may be distilled, but I have never gathered them. When it comes to people needing poison—

and there are some diseases of the human frame that it may be good for—they should go to a qualified medical man, not to a herbalist. No. I have never, never had poison or poisonous herbs within my dwelling ; therefore (putting other reasons aside) it is *impossible* that those pills can have been my pills. God hears me say it, and knows that it is true."

Old Jones, balancing the keys in his hand, was standing within the room, listening. Abel Crew was so respectable and courteous a prisoner, compared with those he generally had in the lock-up, burglars, tipsy men, and the like, returning him a "thank you" instead of an oath, that he had already begun to regard him with some favour, and the assertion seemed to make an impression on him.

"Look here," said he. "Whose pills could they have been, if they warn't yours ?"

"I cannot imagine," returned Abel Carew. "I am as curious about it as anyone else—Master Ludlow here knows I am. I dare say it will come out some time. They *could not* have been made up by me."

"What was that you told the coroner about your pill-boxes being marked ?" asked old Jones.

"And so they are marked ; all of them. The pill-box I saw there——"

"I mean the stock o' boxes you've got at home. Be they all marked ?"

"Every one of them. When I have in a fresh lot of pill-boxes the first thing I do, on bringing them home, is to mark them."

"Then look here. You just trust me with the key of your place, and tell me where the boxes are to be found, and I'll go and secure 'em, and lay 'em afore the coroner. If they be all found marked, it'll tell in your favour."

The advice sounded good, and Abel Crew handed over his key. Jones looked solemn as he and I went away together.

"It's an odd thing, though, Master Johnny, ain't it, how the pison could ha' got into them there pills," said he slowly, as he put the big key into the lock of the outer door.

And we had an audience round us before the words were well spoken. To see the lock-up made fast when there was a prisoner within it was always a coveted recreation in Piefinch Cut. Several individuals had come running up ; not to speak of children from the gutters. Dovey stood gazing in front of his forge ; Figg, who liked to be lounging about outside when he had no customers transacting delicate negotiations within, backed against his shop-window, and stared in concert with Dovey.   Jones, flourishing the formidable keys, crossed over to them.

"How do he feel to-day ?" asked Figg, nodding towards the lock-up.

"He don't feel no worse appariently than he do other days," replied old Jones.   "It be a regular odd thing, it be."

"What be odd ?" asked Dovey.

"How the pison could ha' got into them there pills.   Crew says he has never had no pison in his place o' no kind, herbs nor else."

"And I would pledge my word that it is the truth," I put in.

"Well, and so I think it is," said Dovey.   "Last night George Reed was in here a-talking. He says he one day come across Abel Crew looking for herbs in the copse behind the Grange.   Crew was picking and choosing : some herbs he'd leave alone, and some he dug up.   Reed spied out a fine-looking plant, and called to him.   Up comes Crew, trowel in hand, bends down to take a look, and then gives his head a shake.   'That won't do for me,' says he ; 'that plant has poisonous properties,' says he ; 'and I never meddles with them that has,' says he.   George Reed told us that much in this here forge last night.   Him and his wife have a'most had words about it."

"Had words about what ?" asked old Jones.

"Why, about them pills.   Reed tells her that if it is the pills what poisoned the young ones, she have made some mull o' the box Abel give her and got it changed.   But he don't believe as 'twere the pills at all.   And Hester Reed, she sticks to it that she never made no mull o' the box, and that the pills is the same."

At this juncture, happening to turn my head, I saw Mrs. Dovey at the door at the back of the forge, her face screwed round the doorpost, listening : and there was a great fear on it.   Seeing me looking at her, she disappeared like a shot, and quietly closed the door.   A thought flashed across me.

"That woman knows more about it than she will say ! And it is frightening her.   What can the mystery be ?"

The children were buried on the Sunday afternoon, all the parish flocking to the funeral; and the next morning Abel Crew was released. Whether old Jones had become doubtful as to the legality of what he had done, or whether he received a mandate from the coroner by the early post, no one knew. Certain it was that before nine o'clock old Jones held the lock-up doors open, and Abel Crew walked out. It was thought that someone must have written privately to the coroner—which was more than likely. Old Jones was down in the mouth all day, as if he had had an official blowing-up.

Abel and his stick went home. The rest and his own doctoring had very nearly cured the instep. On the Saturday old Jones had made a descent upon the cottage and cleared it of the pill-boxes. Jones found that every box had Abel's private mark upon it.

"Well, this is a curious start, Crew!" exclaimed Mr. Duffham, meeting him as he was turning in at his gate. "Now in the lock-up, and now out of it! It may be old Jones's notion of law, but it is not mine. How have you enjoyed it?"

"It would not have been so bad but for the rats, sir," replied Abel. "I could see a few stars shining through the skylight."

The days went on to the Thursday, and it was now the evening before the adjourned inquest. Tod and I, in consideration of the popular ferment, had taken the Squire at a favourable moment and extracted from him another week's holiday. Opinions were divided: some believed in Crew, others in the poisoned pills. As to Crew himself, he was out in his garden as usual, attending to his bees, and his herbs and flowers, and quietly awaiting the good or the ill luck that Fate might have in store for him.

It was Thursday evening, I say; and I was taking tea with Duffham. Having looked in upon him, when rushing about the place, he asked me to stay. The conversation turned upon the all-engrossing topic; and I chanced to mention that the behaviour of Ann Dovey puzzled me. Upon that, Duffham said that it was puzzling him. He had been called in to her the previous day, and found her in a regular fever, eyes anxious, breath hysterical, face hectic. Since the day of the inquest she had been more or less in this state, and the blacksmith told Duffham he could not make out what had come to her. "Them pills have drove her mad, sir," were Dovey's words; "she can't get 'em off her mind."

The last cup of tea was poured out, and Duffham was shaking round the old black pot to see if he could squeeze out any more, when we received an interruption. Dovey came bursting in upon us straight from his forge, his black hair ruffled, his small dark face hot with flurry. It was a singular tale he had come to tell. His wife had been making a confession to him. Driven pretty nearly out of her mind by the weight of a secret, she could hold it no longer.

To begin at the beginning. Dovey's house swarmed with blackbeetles. Dovey himself did not mind them, but Mrs. Dovey did; and no wonder, when she could not step out of bed in the night without putting her foot on one. But, if Dovey did not dislike blackbeetles, there was another thing he did dislike—hated in fact; and that was the stuff called beetle-powder, which professed to kill them. Mrs. Dovey would have scattered some on the floor every night, but Dovey would not allow it. He forbid her to bring a grain of it into the house : it was nothing but poison, he said, and might chance to kill themselves as well as the beetles. Ann Dovey had her way in most matters, for Dovey was easy, as men and husbands go; but when once he put his veto on a thing, she knew she might as well try to turn the house round as turn him.

Now what did Ann Dovey do? On that very Easter Tuesday, as it chanced, as soon as dusk had set in, off she went to Dame Chad's general shop in Church Dykely, where the beetle-powder was sold, and bought a packet of it. It seemed to her that of the choice between two evils—to put up with the horrible black insects, or to disobey Dovey, the latter was the more agreeable. She could easily shake some of the powder down lightly of a night; the beetles would eat it up before morning, and Dovey would never know of it. Accordingly, paying for the powder—a square packet done up in blue paper, on which was labelled "Poison" in as large letters as the printer could get into the space—she thrust it into the depths of her gown-pocket—it was her holiday gown—and set off home again. Calling in at George Reed's cottage on her way, she there assisted, as it also chanced, in administering the pills to the unfortunate children. And perhaps her motive for calling in was not so much from a love of presiding at physic-giving, as that she might be able, when she got home, to say "at Reed's", if her husband asked her where she had been. It fell out as she thought. No sooner had she put foot inside the forge than Dovey began, "Where'st been, Ann?" and she told him at Reed's, helping with the sick little ones. Dovey's work was over for the night; he wanted his supper; and she had no opportunity of using the beetle-powder. It was left untouched in the pocket of her gown. The following morning came the astounding news of the children's death; and in the excitement caused by that, Mrs. Dovey lost sight of the powder. Perhaps she thought that the general stir might cause Dovey to be more wakeful than usual, and that she might as well let the powder be for a short time. It was safe where it was, in her hung-up gown. Dovey never meddled with her pockets : on or off, they were no concern of his.

But on the Friday morning, when putting on this same holiday gown to attend the inquest to which she had been summoned, what was her horror to find the packet burst and her pocket filled with the loose powder. Mrs. Dovey had no greater love for beetle-powder in itself than she had for beetles, and visibly shuddered. She could not empty it out; there it had to remain; for Dovey, excited by his wife's having to give evidence, was in and out of her room like a dog in a fair; and she went off perforce with the stuff in her pocket. And when, during her examination, the questions took the turn they did take, and the coroner asked her whether she had had any poison in her pocket that night at George Reed's, this, with the consciousness of what had been that night in her pocket, of what was in her pocket at that very moment, then present, nearly frightened her into fits. From that hour Ann Dovey had lived in a state of terror. It was not that she believed any of the beetle-powder *could* have got inside the ill-fated young ones (though she did not feel quite easy on the point), as that she feared the accusation might be shifted off Crew's shoulders and on to hers. On this Thursday evening she could hold out no longer, and disclosed all to Dovey.

Dovey burst upon us in a heat. He was as straightforward a man as ever lived, of an intensely honest nature, and could no more have kept it in, now that he knew it, than he could have given up all righteous dealing together. His chief concern was to tell the truth, and to restore peace to his wife. He went through the narrative to Duffham without stopping, and seemed not in the least to care for my being present.

"It ain't *possible*, sir, there ain't a moral *possibility* that any o' that there dratted powder could have come anigh the babies," wound up Dovey. "I should be thankful, sir, if you'd come down and quieten her a bit; her be in a fine way."

What with surprise, and what with the man's rapid speech, Duffham had not taken in one half of the tale. He had simply sat behind the teapot and stared.

"My good fellow, I don't understand," he said. "A pocketful of poison! What on earth made her take poison to George Reed's?"

So Dovey went over the heads of the story again.

"'Twas in her pocket, sir, our Ann's, it's true; but the chances are that at that time the paper hadn't burst. None of it *couldn't* ha' got to them there two young ones."

To see the blacksmith's earnestness was good. His face was as eager, his tone as imploring, as though he were pleading for his life.

"And it 'ud be a work of charity, sir, if you'd just step down and see her. I'd pay handsome for the visit, sir; anything you please to charge. She's like one going right out of her mind."

"I'll come," said Duffham, who had his curiosity upon the point.

And the blacksmith set off on the run home again.

"Well, this is a curious thing!" exclaimed Duffham, when he had gone.

"Could the beetle-powder have poisoned the children?" I asked.

"I don't know, Johnny. It is an odd tale altogether. We will go down and inquire into it."

Which of course implied that he expected me to go with him. Nothing loth was I; more eager than he.

Finishing what was left of the tea and bread-and-butter, we went on to Piefinch Cut. Ann Dovey was alone, except for her husband and mother. She flung herself on the sofa when she saw us—the blacksmith's house was comfortably off for furniture—and began to scream.

"Now just you stop that, Ann Dovey," said Duffham,

who was always short with hysterics. "I want to come to the bottom of this business; you can't tell it me while you scream. What in the world possessed you to go about with your pocket full of poison?"

She had her share of sense, and knew Duffham was not one to be trifled with; so she told the tale as well as she could for sobbing.

"Have you mentioned this out of doors?" was the first question Duffham asked when it was over.

"No," interposed Dovey. "I told 'er afore I come to you not to be soft enough for that. Not a soul have heard it, sir, but me and her"—pointing to the old mother—"and you and Master Johnny. We don't want all the parish swarming about us like so many hornets."

"Good," said Duffham. "But it is rather a serious thing, I fear. Uncertain, at any rate."

"Be it, sir?" returned Ann, raising her heavy eyes questioningly. "Do you think so?"

"Why, you see, the mischief must have lain between that beetle-powder and Crew's pills. As Crew is so careful a man, I don't think it could have been the pills; and that's the truth."

"But how could the beetle-powder have got anigh the children out of my pocket, sir?" she asked, her eyes wild. "I never put my hand into my pocket while I sat there; I never did."

"You can't be sure of that," returned Duffham. "We may put our hands into our pockets fifty times a day without remembering it."

"D'you suppose, sir, I should take out some o' that there beetle-powder and cram it down the poor innocents' throats?" she demanded, on the verge of further screaming.

"Where is the powder?" questioned Duffham.

The powder was where it had been all along: in the gown-pocket. Want of opportunity, through fear of Dovey's eyes, or dread of touching the stuff, had kept her from meddling with it. When she took the gown off, the night of the inquest, she hung it up on the accustomed hook, and there it was still. The old mother went to the bedroom and brought it forward, handling it gingerly: a very smart print gown with bright flowers upon it.

Duffham looked round, saw a tin pie-dish, and turned the

pocket inside out into it. A speckled sort of powder, brown and white. He plunged his fingers into it fearlessly, felt it, and smelt it. The blue paper it had been sold in lay amidst it, cracked all across. Duffham took it up.

"Poison !" read out he aloud, gazing at the large letters through his spectacles. "How came you to let it break open in your pocket, Ann Dovey ?"

"I didn't let it ; it braked of itself," she sobbed. "If you saw the blackbeedles we gets here of a night, sir, you'd be fit to dance a hornpipe, you would. The floor be covered with 'em."

"If the ceiling was covered with 'em too, I wouldn't have that there dangerous stuff brought into the place—and so I've telled ye often," roared Dovey.

"It's frightful uncomfortable, is blackbeedles ; mother knows it," said his wife in a subdued voice—for Dovey in great things was master. "I thought if I just sprinkled a bit on't down, it 'ud take 'em away, and couldn't hurt nobody."

"And you went off on the sly that there Tuesday night and bought it," he retorted ; "and come back and telled me you had been to Reed's helping to physic the babies."

"And so I had been there, helping to physic 'em."

"Did you go straight to Reed's from the shop—with this powder ?" asked Duffham.

"It was right at the bottom o' my pocket : I put it there as soon as Dame Chad had served me with it," sobbed Ann Dovey. "And I can be upon my Bible oath, Dr. Duffham, that I never touched it after ; and I don't believe it had then burst. A-coming hasty out of Reed's back-gate, for I were in a hurry to get home, the pocket swung again' the post, and I think the blue paper must ha' burst then. I never knowed it had burst, for I'd never thought no more about the beedles till I put on the gownd to go up to the inquest. Master Johnny, you be a-staring at me fearful, but I'm telling nothing but the naked truth."

She did seem to be telling the truth. And as to my "staring at her fearful", that was just her imagination. I was listening to the talk from the elbow of the wooden chair on which I had perched myself. Duffham recommended Dovey to put the tin dish and its contents away safely, so that it did not get near any food, but not to destroy the stuff just yet. He talked a bit with Ann, left her a composing draught, and came away.

"I don't see that the powder could have had anything to do with the children's death," I said to him as we went along.

"Neither do I, Johnny."

"Shall you have to declare this at the inquest to-morrow, Mr. Duffham ?"

"I am sure I don't know," he answered, looking up at the sky through his spectacles, just as a perplexed owl might do. "It might only serve to complicate matters ; and I don't think it's possible it could have been the powder. On the other hand, if it be proved not to have been the pills, we have only this poisonous powder to fall back upon. It is a strange affair altogether, take it in all its bearings."

I did not answer. The evening star was beginning to show itself in the sky.

"I must feel my way in this, Johnny ; be guided by circumstances," he resumed, when we halted at the stile that led across the fields to the Manor. "We must watch the turn matters take to-morrow at the inquest. Of course if I find it necessary to declare it, I shall declare it. Meanwhile, lad, you had better not mention it to anyone."

"All right, Mr. Duffham. Good evening."

The jury went straggling into the Silver Bear by twos and threes. Up dashed the coroner's gig, as before, he and his clerk seated side by side. All the parish had collected about the doors, and were trying to push into the inquest-room.

Gliding quietly in, before the proceedings were opened, came Abel Crew in his quaint velvet suit, his silver hair gleaming in the sunlight, his pale face calm as marble. The coroner ordered him to sit on a certain chair, and whispered to old Jones. Upon which the constable turned his gouty legs round, marched up, and stood guard over Crew, just as though Abel were his prisoner.

"Do you see that, sir ?" I whispered to Duffham.

"Yes, lad, and understand it. Crew's pills have been analysed—officially this time, as the jury put it—and found to contain arsenic. Pettipher was right. The pills killed the children."

Well, you might have knocked me down with a feather. I had been fully trusting in Crew's innocence.

About the first witness called, and sworn, was the professional man from a distance who had analysed the pills. He said that they contained arsenic. Not in sufficient quantity to hurt a grown-up person; more than sufficient to kill a little child. The coroner drew in his lips.

"I thought it must be so," he said, apparently for the benefit of the jury. "Am I to understand that these were improper pills to send out—pills that no medical man would be likely to send?"

"Not improper at all, sir," replied the witness. "A medical man would prescribe them for certain cases. Not for children; to an infant one would be what it has been here—destruction."

I felt a nudge at my elbow, and turned to see the Squire's hot face close to mine.

"Johnny, don't you ever stand up for that Crew again. He ought to be hanged."

But the coroner, after a bit, seemed puzzled; or, rather, doubtful; led to be so, perhaps, by a question put by one of the jury. It was Perkins the butcher.

"If these pills were furnished by Abel Crew for Hester Reed, a growed woman, and she went and gave one of her own accord to the two babies, ought Crew to be held responsible for that?"

Upon which there ensued some cavilling. Some of the jury holding that he was *not* responsible; others that he was. The coroner reminded them of what Hester Reed had stated in her evidence—that she had asked Crew's opinion about the suitability of the pills for children, and he had told her they were suitable.

Hester Reed was called. As the throng parted to make way for her to advance, I saw Ann Dovey seated at the back of the room, looking more dead than alive. Dovey stood by her, having made himself spruce for the occasion. Ann would have gone off a mile in some opposite direction, but old Jones's orders to all witnesses of the former day to appear again had been peremptory. They had been wanted before, he told them, and might be wanted again.

"You need not look such a scarecrow with fright," I whispered in Ann Dovey's ear, making my way to her side to reassure her, the woman was so evidently miserable. "It was the pills that did the mischief, after all—didn't you hear? Nothing need come out about your pocket and the powder."

"Master Johnny, I'm just about skeered out o' my life, I am. Fit to go and drown myself."

"Nonsense ! It will be all right as far as you are concerned."

"I said it was Crew's pills all along, I did ; it couldn't have been anything else, sir. All the same, I wish I was dead."

As good try to console a post, seemingly, as Ann Dovey. I went back to my standing-place between the Squire and Duffham. Hester Reed was being questioned then.

"Yes, sir, it were some weeks ago. My little boy was ailing, and I ran out o' the house to Abel Crew, seeing the old gentleman go past the gate, and asked whether I might give him one of them there same pills, or whether it would hurt the child. Crew said I might give it freely ; he said two even wouldn't hurt him."

"And did you give the pill ?" asked the coroner.

"No, sir. He's a rare bad one to give physic to, Gregory is, and I let him get well without it."

"How old is he ?"

"Turned of three, sir."

"You are absolutely certain, Mrs. Reed, that these pills from which you took out two to give the deceased children were the very selfsame pills you had from Abel Crew ?"

"I be sure and certain of it, sir. Nobody never put a finger upon the box but me. It stood all the while in the corner o' the press-shelf in the children's bedroom. Twice a week when I got upon a chair to dust the shelf I see it there. There was nobody in the house but me, except the little ones. My husband don't concern himself with the places and things."

Circumstantial evidence could not well go farther. Mrs. Reed was dismissed, and the coroner told Abel Crew to come near the table. He did as he was bid, and stood there upright and manly, a gentle look on his face.

"You have heard the evidence, Abel Crew," said the coroner. "The pills have been analysed and found to contain a certain portion of arsenic—a great deal more than enough to kill a child. What have you to say to it ?"

"Only this, sir ; only what I said before : that the pills analysed were not my pills. The pills I gave to Mrs. Reed contained neither arsenic nor any other poison."

"It is showing great obstinacy on your part to repeat that," returned the coroner impatiently. "Mrs. Reed swears that the pills were the same pills ; and she evidently speaks the truth."

"I am sure she thinks she speaks it," replied Abel gently. "Nevertheless, sir, I assure you she is mistaken. In some way the pills must have been changed whilst in her possession, box and all."

"Why, man, in what manner do you suppose they could have been changed?"

"I don't know, sir. All I do know is that the pills and the box produced here last week were not, either of them, the pills and the box she had from me. Never a box went out from me, sir, but had my private mark on it—the mark I spoke of. Jones, the constable, searched my place whilst I was detained in the lock-up, and took away all the pill-boxes out of it. Let him testify whether he found one without the mark."

At this juncture a whole cargo of pill-boxes were shot out of a bag on the table by old Jones, some empty, some filled with pills. The coroner and jury began to examine them, and found the mark on all, lids and boxes.

"And if you'd be so good as to cause the pills to be analysed, sir, they would be found perfectly free from poison," resumed Abel. "They are made from herbs that possess healing properties, not irritant; a poisonous herb, whether poisonous in itself, or one from which poison may be extracted, I never plucked. Believe me, sir, for I am telling the truth; the truth before Heaven."

The coroner said nothing for a minute or two: I think the words impressed him. He began lifting the lid again from one or two of the boxes.

"What are these pills for? All for the same disorder?"

"They were made up for different disorders, sir."

"And pray, how do you distinguish them?"

"I cannot distinguish them now. They have been mixed. Even if returned to me I could not use them. I have a piece of furniture at home, sir, that I call my pill-case. It has various drawers in it, each drawer being labelled with the sort of pills kept in it: camomile, dandelion, and so on. Mr. Jones must be able to corroborate this."

Old Jones nodded. He had never seen nothing neater nor more exact in all his life than the keeping o' them there pills. He, Mr. Jones, had tumbled the drawerfuls indiscriminately into his bag, and so mixed them.

"And they will be so much loss to me," quietly observed Abel. "It does not matter."

"Were you brought up to the medical profession?" cried the coroner—and some of us thought he put the question in irony.

"No, sir," replied Abel, taking it seriously. "I have learnt the healing art, as supplied by herbs and roots, and I know their value. Herbs will cure sometimes where the regular doctor fails. I have myself cured cases with them that the surgeons could not cure: cases that but for me, under God, might never have been cured in this world. I make no boast of it; anyone else might do as much who had made herbs a study as I have."

"Are you making a fortune by it?" went on the coroner. Abel shook his head.

"I have a small income of my own, sir, and it is enough for my simple wants. What little money I make by my medicines, and honey, and that—it is not much—I find uses for in other ways. I indulge in a new book now and then; and there are many poor people around who need a bit of help sometimes."

"You 'read' the stars, I am told, Abel Crew. What do you read in them?"

"The same that I read, sir, in all other of Nature's works: God's wonderful hand. His wisdom, His power, His providence."

Perhaps the coroner thought to bring Abel to ridicule in his replies; if so, it was a mistake, for he seemed to be getting the worst of it himself. At any rate, he quitted the subject abruptly, brushed his energy up, and began talking to the jury.

The drift of the conversation was, so far as the room could hear it, that Crew's pills, and only Crew's, could have been the authors of the mischief to the two deceased children, whose bodies they were sitting upon, and that Crew must be committed to take his trial for manslaughter. "Hester Reed's evidence," he continued, "is so clear and positive, that it quite puts aside any suspicion of the box of pills having been changed——"

"The box had not my mark upon it, sir," respectfully spoke Abel Crew, his tone anxious.

"Don't interrupt me," rebuked the coroner sharply. "As to the box not having what he calls his private mark upon it," he added to the jury, "that in my opinion tells little. Because a man has put a mark on fifty pill-boxes, he is not obliged to have put it on the fifty-first. An unintentional omission is readily made. It appears to me——"

"Am I in time? Is it all over? Is Abel Crew found guilty?"

This unceremonious interruption to the official speech came from a woman's voice. The door of the room was thrown open with a fling, considerably discomposing those who had their backs against it and were taken unawares, and they were pushed right and left by the struggles of someone to get to the front. The coroner looked daggers; old Jones lifted his staff; but the intruder forced her way forward with resolute equanimity. Cathy Reed—Cathy, in her Sunday-going gown and pink bonnet.

"How dare you?" cried the coroner. "What do you mean by this? Who are you?"

"I have come rushing over from Tewkesbury to clear Abel Crew," returned Cathy, recovering her breath after the fight. "The pills that killed the children were my pills."

The commotion this avowal caused in the room was beyond describing. The coroner stared; the jury all turned to look at the speaker, the crowd trod upon one another.

"And sorry to my heart I am that it should have been so," went on Cathy. "I loved those two dear little ones as if they were my own, and I'd rather my pills had killed myself. Just look at that, please, Mr. Coroner."

The ease with which Cathy spoke to the official gentleman, the coolness with which she put down a pill-box on the green cloth before him, took the room by surprise.

"What is this?" questioned the coroner curtly, picking up the box.

"Perhaps you'll ask Mr. Crew whether he knows it, sir, before I say what it is," returned Cathy.

The coroner had opened it. It contained seven pills; just the size of the other pills, and looking exactly like them. On the lid and on the box was the private mark spoken of by Abel Crew.

"That is my box, sir; and these—I am certain of it—are my pills," spoke Abel earnestly, bending over the shoulder of the first juryman to look into the box. "The box and the pills that I gave to Mrs. Reed."

"And so they are, Abel Crew," rejoined Cathy emphatically.

"The week before last, which I was spending at home at father's, I changed the one pill-box for the other, inadvertent, you see"—with a nod to the coroner—"and took the wrong box away with me. And I wish both boxes had been in the sea before I'd done it."

Cathy was ordered to give her account more clearly, and did so. She had been suffering from illness, accompanied by neuralgia, and a doctor at Tewkesbury had prescribed some pills for it, one to be taken occasionally. The chemist who made them up told her they contained arsenic. He was about to write the directions on the box when Cathy, who was in a hurry, snatched it from him, saying she could not wait for that bother, flung down the money and departed. This box of pills she had brought with her on her visit to her father's, lest she should find occasion to take one; and she had put it on the shelf of the press, side by side with the other pill-box, to be out of the way of the children. Upon leaving, she took up the wrong box inadvertently : carrying away Abel Crew's pills, leaving her own. There lay the explanation of the mystery of the fatal mistake. Mrs. Reed had not known that Cathy had any pills with her, the girl, who was just as light-headed as ever, not having chanced to mention it , and Cathy had the grace to dust the room herself whilst she was there.

"When father and his wife sent me word about the death of the two little twins, and that it was some pills of Abel Crew's that had done it, I never once thought o' my pills," added Cathy. "They didn't as much as come into my head. But late last night I got lent to me last Saturday's *Worcester Herald*, and there I read the inquest, and what Crew had said about the marks he put on his pill-boxes, and mother's evidence about never having shifted the pill-box from its place on the press. 'Sure and I couldn't have changed the boxes', thought I to myself; and upstairs I ran in a fright to look at the box I had brought away. Yes, there it was—Abel Crew's box with the marks on it; and I knew then that I had left my own pills at home here, and that they had killed the babies. As soon as I could get away this morning—which was not as soon as I wanted to—I started to come over. And that's the history—and the blessed truth."

Of course it was the truth. Abel's beautiful face had a glow upon it. "I knew I should be cleared in God's good time," he breathed. The Squire pounced upon him and shook both his hands as if he would never let them go again. Duffham held out his.

So that was the end of the story. Cathy was reprimanded by the coroner for her carelessness, and burst into tears in his face.

"And thee come off home wi' thee, and see me chuck that there powder into the fire ; and don't go making a spectacle o' th'self again," cried Dovey sharply in his wife's ear. "Thee just let me catch thee bringing in more o' the dratted stuff, that's all !"

"I shall never look at a blackbeetle again, Jack, without shivering," she answered—going in for a slight instalment of shivering there and then. "It might ha' come to hanging. Leastways, that's what I've been dreaming of."

15
ALAN K. RUSSELL
The Authors

THE AUTHORS

Eight authors have contributed the fourteen stories in *The Book of the Sleuth*. These contributors range from famous figures, giants of crime and detection writing, to authors whose work has received little attention in recent years. Biographical sketches of all are provide in this section, to introduce the contributors to you.

J. J. Bell was a journalist and author who wrote a wide range of stories, from crime and humour to romance. His short stories appear in several anthologies, but his only crime fiction book is *Till the Clock Stops* (1917).

One of the leading Scottish humourists in the early part of this century, Bell created a number of characters, the best-known being 'Wee MacGregor'.

John Joy Bell was born in 1871 and died in 1934 aged 63 years.

William Wilkie Collins' *The Woman In White* and *The Moonstone* are regarded as two of the cornerstones of crime fiction.

London-born, Collins was twenty-seven years old when, in 1851, he met Charles Dickens. The two writers became close friends, often collaborated and both became leading popular novelists of their time. Dickens was but one of the many friends Collins had among popular nineteenth-century writers.

The Woman In White was published in serial form in 1859, before appearing as a book the following year. In 1868 came his masterpiece, *The Moonstone*, which would be described by T. S. Eliot as 'the first, the longest, and the best of modern detective novels'. *The Moonstone's* main character, Sergeant Cuff, is one of the novel's first and most distinguished detectives. Both *The Woman In White* and *The Moonstone* have been filmed.

Collins, in fact, wrote on many subjects, especially for Dickens' periodicals, to which he contributed both articles and short stories. But several of Collins' lesser known books do involve mystery, suspense and crime; *After Dark* (1856), *The Queen of Hearts* (1859), in which *The Biter Bit* was first published, *No Name* (1862), *Armadale* (1866), *Alicia Warlock* (1875), *Hide and Seek* (1854) and *The Law and the Lady* (1875).

In 1873-4 Wilkie Collins undertook a lecture tour of the United States. He died at the age of sixty-five on 23 September 1889.

Sir Arthur Conan Doyle created the greatest detective in literature, Sherlock Holmes, when he was twenty-eight years old.

Born in Edinburgh on 22 May 1859, Arthur Conan Doyle wrote and sold his first story while still an impecunious medical student at university and thus began his illustrious career as an author − a master storyteller − and historian.

Conan Doyle's first Sherlock Holmes' story *A Study in Scarlet* appeared in 1887 and *The Sign of Four* followed in 1890, but the short stories − and Conan Doyle's great success − made their appearance in the monthly magazine, *The Strand*. The stories were the sensation of the day. The two that appear in this volume, *The Adventures of The Three Students* and *The Adventure of Priory School*, were first published in *The Strand* in 1904 and, with others, make up *The Return of Sherlock Holmes*.

The Sherlock Holmes books are:

> Novels:
> *A Study in Scarlet* (1887)
> *The Sign of Four* (1890)
> *The Hound of the Baskervilles* (1902)
> *The Valley of Fear* (1915)
>
> Short Stories:
> *The Adventures of Sherlock Holmes* (1892)
> *The Memoirs of Sherlock Holmes* (1894)
> *The Return of Sherlock Holmes* (1905)
> *His Last Bow* (1917)
> *The Case-book of Sherlock Holmes* (1927)

There have been innumerable films and plays featuring the now immortal Holmes. Such is the continuing interest in this character that enthusiasts still gather to pore over the literature to understand the most minute aspects of Sherlock Holmes' life and background.

Doyle wrote other crime fiction, and books by him which are either entirely or partially about crime include:

> *The Captain of the Polestar*
> *Danger!*
> *The Doings of Raffles Haw*
> *The Mystery of Cloombar*
> *Round the Fire Mysteries*

In addition, Doyle wrote a number of splendid historical novels, adventure novels, featuring Professor Challenger, and also works of history.

Conan Doyle died in Sussex in July 1930.

William Le Queux was born in London. He was a journalist whose overseas travels became linked with suggestions of work for the Secret Service.

After being Foreign Editor of the London *Globe,* he was for a number of years a freelance journalist before becoming Balkan Correspondent for the London *Daily Mail* during the war there in 1912 and 1913, which presaged the First World War.

Reported to have started writing about the Secret Service so as to finance his intelligence work, he became the London Chargé D'Affairs of the republic of San Marino.

His many spy stories and novels set patterns that were to be followed by other writers and anticipated many themes that Eric Ambler would later develop. His then futuristic novels about the invasion of Britain – *The Great War in England in 1897* (published in 1894) and *The Invasion of 1910* (published in 1905) – were sensations. Indeed, *The Invasion of 1910* is credited with forecasting World War I.

Le Queux wrote just over 200 books, many of which are now regarded as being somewhat melodramatic.

The two stories in this volume are taken from *The Crime Club: A Record of Secret Investigations into some Amazing Crimes, Mostly Withheld from the Public,* and published in 1927. Other outstanding crime fiction by him includes *The Count's Chauffeur* and *Mysteries of a Great City.*

Born on 2 July 1864, Le Queux died at the age of sixty-three on 13 October 1927.

Although aged only forty at the time of his death on 7 October 1849, Edgar Allan Poe is regarded by many as the leading American writer of the nineteenth century. He invented the detective story and has been hailed as 'the father of the genre'.

Born in Boston on 19 January 1809, Poe led an unsettled life with moments of genius in a downward spiral which left him drunk and dying in a Baltimore gutter. There is still debate as to whether or not he was an alcoholic, took drugs, and what may have occurred during a number of unrecorded periods of his life.

Poe wrote little enough, and only a few of his stories were crime fiction, for most had occult, bizarre and macabre themes.

The three masterpieces included in this book were written in a very short timespan and feature C. Auguste Dupin, the first fictional detective of importance. The modern detective story effectively begins with *The Murders of the Rue Morgue,* which was published in 1841 and has been described as 'the single most important story in the history of the genre'. *The Mystery of Marie Rogêt* was published in 1842 and *The Purloined Letter* in 1844.

Five other stories of crime and suspense by Poe are:

> *The Narrative of Arthur Gordon Pym of Nantucket*
> *William Wilson*
> *The Gold Bug*
> *The Black Cat*
> *Thou Art the Man*

Mark Twain is regarded as one of the greatest American authors and humourists, and has a string of first-rate books to his name, among them *The Adventures of Tom Sawyer, The Prince and the Pauper, The Adventures of Huckleberry Finn* and *A Connecticut Yankee in King Arthur's Court*.

Among his writings are several excursions into the realms of crime and detection although the theme is overlaid by the humorous intent of the author.

The Stolen White Elephant, a parody and now included in this volume, was first published in 1882. Other stories of crime by Mark Twain include *A Double-Barrelled Detective Story* and *The Tragedy of Pudd'nhead Wilson* plus several episodes about Tom Sawyer.

Edgar Wallace, dubbed 'The King of Thrillers', is one of the all time most popular thriller writers. It has been estimated that in Britain in the 1920s and 1930s one in every four books read was written by him.

Edgar Wallace's first and most famous novel was *The Four Just Men,* published when he was thirty years old. It created a sensation upon publication and established Wallace as a popular writer, one who would write prolifically for nearly three decades. *The Four Just Men* is still in print, as are other adventures of the Four, like *The Council of Justice*.

In all, Wallace produced nearly 200 books, and is reputed to have once dictated an entire novel during a single weekend. Certainly he worked at a hectic pace. For collectors, a bibliography of first editions has been published by Charles Kiddle, and there is an Edgar Wallace Society of enthusiasts to research and exchange information about his writings.

In addition to *The Four Just Men,* Wallace created a number of characters who featured in several books, such as Sanders, the Commissioner maintaining law and order in British Imperial Africa (in a sequence of eleven books commencing with *Sanders of the River*). Other Wallace characters include a CID detective called 'Sure Foot' Smith, James Mortlake of US Intelligence, The Sooper,

The Ringer, The Twister, The Squealer, and Mr. J. G. Reeder and Oliver Rater. In this volume are two stories featuring Rater, a detective from Scotland Yard. First published in the monthly magazine *Pall Mall,* both were included in the compilation of Wallace's short stories, *The Orator.*

Edgar Wallace was born in Greenwich, England on 1 April 1875 and died on 10 February 1932 in Hollywood where he had been working on the script for the film *King Kong.*

Mrs. Henry Wood, author of *Abel Crew,* was a best-selling novelist during the Victorian period.

Mrs. Wood wrote nearly forty novels and many short stories which were gathered into books, such as the Johnny Ludlow stories, making a total of nearly one hundred volumes. Her most famous novel is the immensely successful *East Lynne* (1861) although all her work was popularly received and was even known to outsell some of Dickens' work.

Married when she was twenty-two years old, she followed the custom in early nineteenth century England of writing under her married name. Had she been writing at a later time, or today, her writing would probably have been published under her maiden name, Ellen Price, or as Ellen Wood.

Mrs. Henry Wood died on 10 February 1887, aged sixty-three.